RISE OF THE

WOLF

Book 3 in *The Forest Lord* series

By Steven A. McKay

Also by Steven A. McKay –

Wolf's Head

The Wolf and the Raven

Knight of the Cross

For my wife Yvonne,
and everything we've been through together.

Love you.

Acknowledgements

As always, lots of people have been a great help to me in writing this novel. Kathryn Warner, author and historian, provided me with invaluable information on King Edward II's movements in 1323. Her fantastic blog also provided much interesting information on the much-maligned king's character. He wasn't all bad despite what you may have read.

Archery expert Chris Verwijmeren, as always, proved invaluable when it came to both my cover design and technical details. The sections about fletching were made easier to write thanks to his help. I am greatly indebted to him for his time and patience.

My beta-readers gave much useful feedback when I was in the early stages of editing, so big thanks to them: Bill Moore, Bernadette McDade and Robin Carter.

Again, I have to thank the team at Amazon's KDP for their continued support and also the staff at Audible and ACX.

You, my readers, are the people that have most helped these books enjoy the success they have though, so cheers to everyone who's bought the books, left a review, joined in with me on Facebook or Twitter or at my website and generally been so kind and supportive to a humble lad from Scotland.

Now, sit back, and enjoy Rise of the Wolf.

Prologue

The two girls smiled at one another as they pushed their way through the sparse late-winter foliage and caught sight of the snares they'd set the day before. One of the traps had managed to catch a hare in mid-hop and its little brown body hung, dead and ready for the pot.

"Well done," Matilda said, clapping her younger friend on the back. "That was one of your snares – you set it at just the right height and now," she glanced down at her own empty hands, "we have at least something to contribute to dinner tonight."

They moved forward to collect their prize but, as they reached it, a man pushed his way through the trees from the right, startling them with his sudden appearance and his size. Although he was a tall man, he wore light green and brown foresters garb which had allowed him to remain undetected by the two villagers.

"I think we've found our hunters, lads."

As the man spoke, a satisfied smirk appearing on his lips, more men revealed themselves from amongst the branches and bushes of Barnsdale Forest.

Matilda mentally kicked herself – she'd lived with her husband, Robin Hood, and his men within this very greenwood not so long ago and had learned much in that time. "I should have seen them hiding there," she muttered to her companion.

Marjorie was Robin's younger sister, a thin girl of fifteen, and her face twisted in fear at the prospect of arrest at the foresters' hands. "What will they do with us?"

"Well, now, that'll be for the warden to decide," the tall man shrugged, overhearing her wavering voice. "But you only seem to have caught one tired-looking old hare. Probably just be a fine."

Marjorie relaxed a little at that; her family had money enough thanks to her infamous brother's exploits. She'd been worried about losing a hand or even worse.

The man stepped in close, inspecting the two girls. "Or perhaps we could come to some other arrangement and we'll just forget this ever happened?"

As he raised a hand to touch Matilda's face the young woman suddenly lashed out, ramming the point of her knee into the forester's groin, and giving him a shove so hard that he fell, gasping, onto the damp ground.

Marjorie cowered, mouth open, eyes wide as her sister-in-law produced a wicked looking knife from somewhere inside her tunic and held it defensively in front of herself, daring the other lawmen to come for her.

"Any of you touch me or the girl here and I'll rip your bollocks off! Wouldn't be the first time I've done that."

The downed forester pushed himself onto one knee, blowing hard, face scarlet with fury. "You bitch, there was no call for that. I'll make sure the warden deals with the pair of you harshly. Take them lads."

His comrades didn't seem in any rush to challenge the confident girl with the blade whose stance suggested knowledge of fighting techniques so he pulled himself up with a growl and drew his own weapon. "Fine, I'll deal with her myself you cowards."

"He's got a sword, Matilda."

"I can see that, don't worry. I've beaten Little John and Will Scarlet; I can take this whoreson too, no problem." Her words were spoken calmly, designed to soothe the younger girl, but Matilda's darting eyes betrayed her nervousness. She'd never beaten either of those famous outlaws, not really, but these foresters didn't know that.

One of the other men slowly circled his way around to stand a little way off to the side, looking intently at the girls before recognition flared in his eyes and he raised a hand just as his leader was about to strike.

"Wait."

"Wait?" The big forester hesitated, glaring irritably at his mate. "Wait for what? It's two girls in God's name, I'm

2

sure I can handle them even if you lot want to stand there gaping like landed trout."

"That's Robin Hood's wife. I've seen her before."

"So?"

There was silence as the implications of harming or arresting these two girls from nearby Wakefield hit the tall lawman and he stepped back, thoughtfully, sword still raised but obviously not intending to use it any time soon.

The forester that had recognised Matilda shook his head. "If we were to bring in Hood or one of his gang, aye, we'd be well rewarded. But I fear the only thanks we'll get for arresting these two is a sword in the guts from the wolf's head."

The leader stood, hesitating, angry at being made to look like a craven but sharing his comrade's respect – and fear – of the notorious outlaw who always repaid those who crossed him or his friends with brutal, deadly violence.

"All right," he grunted, sheathing his sword and waving the girls away. "You can go but –" He smirked and reached out to grab the hare from the little wire noose "– we're having this."

Matilda nodded and grabbed Marjorie's arm, hauling her backwards into the bushes, happy enough to let the man have that one small victory. A single hare wasn't much of a price to pay for their freedom after all.

When they were hidden by the foliage they broke into a run.

Matilda's eyes sparkled, the excitement and joy at surviving the unexpected encounter coursing through her veins like fire.

Marjorie's face, though, was streaked with tears of humiliation.

CHAPTER ONE

"He's got me Will... gutted me like a fish. I'm done for..." Little John fell to the ground clutching his midriff, bearded face twisted in pain as he looked up in despair at his companion. "Avenge me..."

Will Scarlet cried out, racing over to his giant friend's side, weapon held aloft, ready to fend off any more blows.

Their attacker laughed and the outlaws shrank back, begging for mercy, their faces twisted in fear.

"Arthur! What are those two doing with you?" Matilda Hood strode into the neatly-tended garden with its bright daffodils and snowdrops and scooped up her smiling infant. The boy waved the tiny wooden sword gleefully, almost hitting his mother in the face. "That's enough of that game," she scolded John and Will who shrugged innocently and grinned at the baby when Matilda turned away. "Robin, will you tell these two? I don't want Arthur growing up to be a fighter."

Her young husband wandered over to his two friends, smiling and tugging gently on his nine month-old son's chubby cheek as he passed. "Aye, all right, I will."

Matilda carried their son back into the Fletcher's house where she still lived with her parents. In a perfect world she and Robin would have had a nice house of their own to live in but with her husband being an outlaw that was an impossible dream.

"Come on, let's go to the inn for a couple of ales," John suggested, seeing the troubled look on his nineteen year-old leader's face and wondering at its cause.

Will agreed readily but Robin glanced towards the door his wife had just disappeared through, provoking an amused grunt from Scarlet. "You need to ask the wife for permission to go down to the inn, lad? I wonder what the men would think of that."

Robin laughed along with his friends, cursing them, and, with a sheepish wave to Matilda who had appeared at the window with a knowing look, the three of them made their way along the road towards the local ale-house.

"Three ales, please, Alex," Will shouted to the fat, purple-nosed inn-keep, who waved merrily in response and moved to fill the wooden mugs as ordered.

The room was cold and dim, the early afternoon sunlight not really penetrating the windows which were half-shuttered to keep out some of the chill spring breeze. The outlaws pulled their thick cloaks up around their necks and sat in silence until Alex had placed their drinks on the rickety table and, after accepting a coin in payment from Robin, disappeared discreetly into the kitchen.

"What's on your mind, lad?" Little John asked Robin, drying the froth from his beard with a grimy sleeve.

The young wolf's head lifted his own ale and took a drink, shrugging as he did so. "I'm just worried we've had things too easy recently, and it probably won't last."

"It makes a nice change, having Gisbourne out of the way and the sheriff's men not making much of an effort to catch us," John nodded. "I know what you mean though."

"Aye," Will agreed. "Some of the lads seem to have forgotten the fact we're still outlaws and fair game for anyone that might decide to stick a knife in our guts. And that includes you." He pointed a thick, grubby finger at his leader with an earnest frown. "Playing happy families with Matilda and the little one."

"I know!" Robin raised a placatory hand as he took another sip from his mug. "I'm as bad as any of them. It's been an easy life the past few months since I beat Gisbourne but we all know someone's going to come hunting us sooner or later. We have to be ready for it."

Little John smiled, his open face almost childlike despite his great bushy beard. "What do you suggest? That we gather the men and go back to living in the forest? I'm not sure if they'll take too kindly to that idea."

Some of the outlaw band maintained their camp deep in the Barnsdale greenwood, where the communal funds were stored, but most of the men had taken to spending their time in whatever town or village held most attraction for them. Little John had gone back to Holderness where his family lived, only coming today to visit his two friends, Will and Robin, who spent days at a time here in Wakefield with their own kin.

The bounty hunter, Sir Guy of Gisbourne, who had come to Yorkshire on the king's orders specifically to hunt down Robin and his outlaws, had been mutilated and almost killed in one-on-one combat with the young wolf's head the previous year. Without his single-minded leadership and the onset of another hard winter, the sense of danger that hung over the outlaws for so long had dissipated, as had the iron discipline that had kept them alive up until now.

It had been a wonderful period for Robin, who'd been able to spend the days and nights with Matilda, watching his little baby son grow. He offered a silent prayer of thanks to God and the Magdalene for his good fortune before returning John's smile.

"No, I don't want to go back to living in Barnsdale until we need to."

"Good lad!" the giant boomed, raising his own mug to his lips. "I'll drink to that!"

"Aye, me too," Will Scarlet nodded. "Although you really need to do more combat training, Robin – you're starting to get a paunch."

"And jowls," John laughed. "You're spending too much time in bed with your wife and drinking ale" –

Suddenly the front door burst open and one of the local men rushed in from the bright sunshine outside, squinting as his eyes adjusted to the gloomy interior. Finally, he spotted Robin and the other two outlaws.

"Come quick, one of your lads is getting a hiding from the fuller!"

Cursing, drinks forgotten, the three friends leapt up and hurried after the man.

It didn't take long for them to hear the commotion just a few streets away. A voice was raised in anger, while a small crowd of villagers had gathered to watch the entertainment and were laughing and shouting encouragement to the stocky little fuller who was grappling with a thin youngster with a bloody nose.

"It's Gareth," John growled.

"Pissed no doubt," Will replied. "Again."

They pushed their way through the small crowd of onlookers until they were able to pull the fighting men apart. John held the fuller but the man was so enraged and filled with battle-fever that he kept swinging his fists, almost catching Robin before his giant friend hurled the small man onto the ground and held him there with a hand around his throat until he finally calmed down.

The skinny outlaw, Gareth, was also furious, but too dazed to even attempt fighting off Will who shoved him back and, with a menacing stare, ordered him to be silent. Gareth knew better than to cross Scarlet, so he stood, swaying slightly, glaring at the fuller who had bloodied his nose.

"What the hell's going on here?" Robin demanded, his eyes moving from the fuller to Gareth and back again.

"That little bastard was calling my wife an ugly old cow," the fuller, Hugh, spat and struggled to his feet as John moved back to let him rise. "Drunk again he is – in the middle of the day, when honest people should be out earning a living!"

Robin winced at the barb, hearing a small ripple of muttered agreement at the fuller's words from the gathered villagers.

"Are you saying we're not fucking honest?" the volatile Will Scarlet moved towards Hugh threateningly, but the little man was so angry he didn't back down.

"Aye, I am!" the fuller retorted, pushing his chest out and waving a fist at the outlaws. "We're all out working to earn our keep, while you lot saunter around the village like

4

lords, throwing coin about like it was nothing. You've outstayed your welcome here!"

Robin grabbed Scarlet, holding him back to prevent him from really hurting Hugh as the onlookers crowded in on them.

Although the villagers weren't openly hostile, it was clear they were ready to support the fuller, despite everything Robin and the other outlaws had done for Wakefield over the past two years. It was galling, but the wolf's head had learned not to take things like this too personally.

Life was hard and people had short memories, especially when they saw others apparently having an easier time of it than themselves.

"Outstayed our welcome, you little prick?" Will shouted at the fuller, before rounding on the other locals. "You lot must have forgotten what we did for you during the winters. The food we gave you when your bellies were shrinking!"

Robin grasped Gareth by the arm and hauled him away, gesturing for Little John to bring Will before any more trouble could develop, although Scarlet's angry words had mollified the crowd somewhat. Even the fuller had given up his rant and now stood, grumbling and shaking his head as the outlaws headed back towards the alehouse.

"What's the matter with you, boy?" Robin demanded of Gareth as they reached the low building and made their way back inside, seating themselves at the table they'd left not so long ago.

"I'll have an ale!" Gareth shouted across to Alexander, but Robin waved a hand at the inn-keep, telling him not to bother.

"No you won't, you've had more than enough."

Despite his intoxication, Gareth knew it would be a mistake to argue with his young leader, angry and flanked as he was by his two loyal lieutenants.

"We've got an easy life here in Wakefield," Robin said. "But your drinking's causing ill-feeling amongst the villagers. What the hell's wrong with you?"

Until recently Gareth had barely touched strong drink. He'd been a tiny, malnourished child who had been outlawed and chased from his home in Wrangbrook for stealing food for his sickly mother when he was barely into his teens. Despite that, he had become a valued member of the outlaw band, even saving Friar Tuck from drowning a few months previously.

Since then though, it seemed, the seventeen year-old had taken more and more to drinking and, like many men, he was an unpleasant companion when inebriated.

"It was that shit he got from the barber in Penyston," Will said. "The grain drink the man made himself from some foreign recipe. Ever since the lad tasted it he's been a drunk."

Gareth looked balefully at them but held his peace as his friends spoke about him as if he wasn't there.

John shook his head sadly. "It's true. He got a taste for it and he's not been the same since."

Robin was in no mood to listen to excuses for their companion's behaviour, not when it jeopardised his own fine life here in Wakefield with Matilda and Arthur.

"I don't care what's wrong with him, he'd better get a fucking grip of himself soon or he's going back to live in the camp in the forest. We can't have the people turning against us."

John shrugged his massive shoulders. "Maybe we *should* all head back into Barnsdale..."

Will snorted angrily and Robin gazed despondently into his mug.

Aye, he'd enjoyed the last few months with his family, living practically a normal life, but Will Scarlet had also been able to spend the time with his little daughter Beth, while John had greatly enjoyed his days in Holderness with his wife Amber and son John who he'd hardly seen in the years since he'd been outlawed for accidentally killing a man who was raping his own daughter.

6

Heading back into the greenwood was going to be hard on all of them and Robin vowed to hold off on their return for as long as possible.

Again, the front door was thrown open, sunlight flooding the dim interior of the ale-house and Will groaned as he placed his wooden mug back on the table with a thump. "For fuck sake, what now?"

As before, the newcomer gazed around the room, his eyes unused to the dim interior, and Robin shouted across, recognising the burly figure of Patrick Prudhomme, the village headman. "You're looking for us, no doubt. What's the matter?"

"Robin!" Prudhomme hurried over to their table breathlessly, his eyes wide. "You lads better gather your things. Gisbourne's here."

CHAPTER TWO

"There they are – get 'em!"

"Shit." Robin turned at the shout and spotted at least half-a-dozen foresters coming towards them. John, Will and Gareth had followed him at a run to his house where he collected his weapons and said a hasty goodbye to his family, hand lingering tenderly on Arthur's chubby cheek, savouring the moment. Now, the four outlaws headed for the trees on the outskirts of the village with the lawmen hurtling along behind, shouting for them to stop in the name of the king.

"Split up," Robin ordered. "It'll make it harder for them to follow us. We'll meet back at the camp."

Without a word the others broke left and right, the foresters cursing at their backs, wondering which of them to follow. For some reason all of them chose to stay on Robin's trail; he could hear them barging through the undergrowth although, to be fair, they seemed to be better woodsmen than most of the oafs that came hunting the wolf's head.

The young man was supremely fit, but his strength lay mostly in his upper body – the shoulders and arms that he used to deadly effect with his longbow. There was a good chance at least one of his pursuers would be a faster runner than him and he never liked the idea of an enemy at his back.

He had his bow in his hand and, fiddling inside the pouch at his waist, produced the string which he placed over the end of the weapon. Hoping he had enough time, he came to a stop and stepped across the bow, using his limbs to bend the massive weapon enough to slip the other end of the string into place.

His suspicions had been correct; one of the chasing foresters was right behind him, indeed, would have been close enough to plunge the tip of his sword into Robin's back before much longer if the outlaw had continued on his previous course.

With practised ease he pulled an arrow from his belt, nocked it to the string, took aim, and let fly. The missile took the unfortunate lawman hard in the chest, throwing him backwards and killing him instantly.

Without waiting to find out how the other foresters took the death of their companion, Robin turned and, moving off at a different angle this time, plunged back into the forest as silently as possible.

It seemed to work. There were cries of dismay and anger from behind but, mercifully, they didn't seem to be coming any closer. After a while the wolf's head relaxed and slowed his pace, breathing heavily as the effects of the chase and his unwanted but necessary kill wore off.

He hoped the others had managed to evade capture. He also wondered where Sir Guy of Gisbourne was; there had been no sign of the Raven amongst the lawmen that had come after them.

As he pushed through the branches dark thoughts assailed him but, before he realised it, he had reached the outlaws' camp. Home, for now.

He hadn't noticed the soft footsteps that shadowed his own. Nor did he see, a little while later, the watching forester that headed back the way he'd just come after tracking the wolf's head.

Back, towards Wakefield, and Gisbourne.

* * *

"So you're leaving us after all, Tuck, and going back to that bastard prior?"

The portly friar nodded his tonsured head, a look of regret on his normally cheery face. "Aye, Allan," he replied. "Once the weather gets a bit better I'll make the journey down to Lewes and return the holy relic to de Martini."

Allan-a-Dale spat on the hard grass of their camp which was flattened by weeks of heavy footprints and little sunlight. The outlaws all knew about Prior John de Monte Martini, the man who had threatened to sell Robin's wife Matilda to a brothel he owned in Nottingham and been rewarded for his threat with a broken nose from the brawny young archer.

Robin had been forced to join the outlaw gang to evade the prior's justice after that. Then Tuck had come along, escorting a wagon full of de Martini's money which the outlaws had stolen, although Tuck had soundly beaten Adam Bell, the leader of the outlaws at that time.

Rather than returning to the prior empty handed, knowing his fate would be an unpleasant one, the friar had remained in Barnsdale with the outlaws.

That had all happened two years earlier though, and, when Tuck realised Robin had come into possession of a hugely expensive relic stolen years earlier from Prior de Martini the big friar knew he held the key to a pardon in his hand. Freedom again. A normal life, without the threat of death around every tree stump or innocently babbling stream.

"The relic isn't ours though," Allan said, poking a stick into the camp-fire, making the flames leap and dance a little higher in the cool spring air. "It might have belonged to de Martini once, a long time ago, but it seems like you can't just take it back to him. Robin borrowed it in good faith from Father de Nottingham in Brandesburton. He promised to return it to him months ago."

Tuck remained silent, knowing the minstrel's words were true. Their young leader had asked to borrow the relic from St Mary's in order to revive Tuck after he'd been shot by Sir Guy of Gisbourne and almost drowned. Father de Nottingham had let the wolf's head take the holy relic, fully expecting it would be returned at some point.

It had done its job – Tuck had come to after days in an unnatural deep sleep, but when he saw it, the friar realised it wasn't the thumb of St Peter as the priest at St Mary's thought. It was actually strands of hair from Christ's own beard, held securely in an exquisitely decorated little box only Tuck – who had learned the secret years ago when he had bought the thing in a French village – had been able to unlock.

"It was good of the priest to let Robin take it," Tuck agreed. "But it belongs to Prior de Martini, no matter what anyone thinks of the man." He shrugged. "I'll go to Brandesburton and explain things. Leave Father de Nottingham some money to pay for his troubles..."

His voice trailed off and his bright blue eyes remained fixed on the fire in front of them. In truth, Tuck couldn't stand the wealthy de Martini who abused his position to gather wealth in most un-Christian ways. But the friar was getting on – he was forty-five years old as far as he knew – and although it was spring now, the thought of spending another winter in the greenwood, which wasn't anything like as green once the frost and snow descended upon it, wasn't a pleasant one.

He loved these outlaws like brothers, or even sons in some cases, but he knew he couldn't live out the remainder of his days here. He had found his true purpose in life: to spread the word of God. It was a task he couldn't perform very well while stuck in a forest in Yorkshire.

"Yes," he sighed, "I'll take the relic back to Prior de Martini. The thing's worth an obscene amount of gold so he'll be overjoyed to have it in his hands at last. Although he's a nasty piece of work, I'm sure he'll appreciate what I've done for him and the church will take me back into its service." His eyes flicked up and he gazed at Allan earnestly. "You know I really did enjoy life as a friar, as boring as it probably seems to you."

Allan waved the suggestion away. "Men come in different shapes and sizes. We all have our own tastes and ideas of what's good and bad. If you enjoyed that life, who am I to judge you? And, if you want to go back to that..." He returned the clergyman's gaze, "I'll be sad to see you go, my friend. But you have to follow the path you believe God's laid out for you. So, for what it's worth" – he lifted his gittern from the ground beside him and strummed a bright chord with a smile – "you have my blessing."

"On your feet you lot!"

It was a sign of their recent easy life – their lack of immediate danger and the resulting relaxed attitude to posting lookouts – that three men had managed to burst into the outlaws' camp without anyone raising the alarm.

Now, Gareth, Will and Little John moved hurriedly amongst them, extorting the men who had remained here with Tuck and Allan to prepare for a possible attack.

"Gisbourne's on his feet again," John told them. "He came to Wakefield with his men looking for us."

"Lucky for you lot he didn't start by looking here first," Will groused. "No guards watching for approaching danger? You've all gone soft. Gisbourne would have torn through you like an arrow through dog shit."

"We're not the only ones that've gone soft," Tuck retorted, taking in Will's breathless state with a raised eyebrow. "You can hardly get the words out you're so winded after the short run. Didn't you say you'd only come from Wakefield? Or were you visiting a friend in some other village? In Scotland perhaps?"

"Fuck off, Tuck," Scarlet grinned, watching as the men strapped on weapons and hastily took up positions in the trees overhead, longbows strung and ready to shoot. "Just get off your fat arse and help us move the camp before that whoreson Gisbourne appears. He's not going to be in a good mood after Robin took half his face off at Dalton."

"Like he was ever in a good mood," Allan shouted over his shoulder while gathering his own arrows and stringing his longbow.

"Aye, well, trust me," Scarlet replied. "If you thought he was dangerous before, he'll be even worse now. Being mutilated tends to make people angry! Just ask John – the midwife pulled him out of his ma face-first and the giant's never forgiven her for giving him a face like a mastiff doing a shit."

"Where is Robin anyway?" Tuck wondered as the men laughed at Will's insult, concern creasing his face as he used his quarterstaff to lever himself onto his feet.

Little John waved a meaty hand. "He'll be along soon – we had a head start on the foresters. Robin's safe enough." He grimaced at the smirking Will. "Any more of that shit though, Scarlet, and you'll be the one with the deformed face."

Their leader did appear just then, his glance taking in the rest of the men, seeing his two grinning lieutenants and the now-sober Gareth, before he nodded in relief. "Everyone's here then, good."

"Were you followed?" Stephen, the former Hospitaller sergeant-at-arms asked, sword already drawn as he watched the trees for signs of movement.

Robin sat down, helping himself to a mug and filling it from the barrel beside the campfire.

"Nah. One of them was like a hare, would have easily overtaken me, but I took him down. The rest gave up after that."

Will let out a small sigh and dropped onto the log beside his young leader, gesturing for Robin to hand him one of the other empty mugs so he could wet his own throat.

John made his way to his pallet and lay down, stretching his great frame and yawning like some beast of the forest. "We should really move camp," he muttered, gazing up at the branches overhead.

Will drained his mug and wiped his mouth with a grubby sleeve before replying. "We'll be fine. Gisbourne wasn't even with those men, they were just foresters. And, if one of them's been taken out they'll have no stomach to come looking for us. They're not stupid."

Robin mulled it over for a while. He glanced up, noting the position of the sun which was mostly hidden by dark grey clouds and knew it would be dark in a couple of hours anyway. "Will's right, we can leave and find a new base in the morning." The men gave soft cheers – moving camp was always a time-consuming, irritating chore and they were glad to put it off, even for just a few hours – but Robin held up a hand, gazing around at them. "Be on guard though, just in case."

* * *

When the forester that had followed Robin to the outlaw camp returned to Wakefield he went directly to Sir Guy. The Raven was indeed in the village, as were two dozen of his men – not foresters but proper, hard soldiers.

"Did Hood see you?"

"No, my lord," the man shook his head, keeping his eyes down respectfully under the bounty hunter's sharp look. "I watched them for a bit, but they were relaxed. Must have thought they'd got away all right."

"They would have too, if it wasn't for your tracking skills. Well done man. Here." Gisbourne tossed a coin to the forester who caught it with a surprised grin.

"I couldn't just let the wolf's head get away, not after he shot my friend –"

"Indeed." Gisbourne turned away, the conversation at an end, and waved his men in close. "This man will lead us to the outlaws' camp. Once we're close, I will have the foresters fire a volley of arrows and then you men will rush them. You all carry shields and wear good armour. Some of you may die – these criminals we go to find are skilled longbowmen, after all. Attack swiftly and without mercy, though, and the element of surprise should carry us through." He spun around again, gesturing for the forester to lead the way.

They moved as silently as possible but, as they approached the camp the outlaws could be heard laughing and talking amongst themselves and Gisbourne smiled. The forester was right – the wolf's heads thought they were safe and it would be their downfall. At last.

The bounty hunter halted his men before they got too close, fearing sentries would spot their approach. He signalled to the five foresters that remained in his company and watched as they readied their longbows. The sun was setting by now and the outlaws' camp-fire cast a tell-tale orange glow that gave the archers something to aim for. He looked around at his swordsmen, making sure they were ready to move, then, exhaling a deep breath, swung his hand down in an arc.

The snapping of bowstrings being released seemed to echo all around the forest before there were thuds and sounds of panic from the camp-site ahead.

"Charge!"

Gisbourne wasn't entirely certain how many outlaws they faced but he knew his men outnumbered them. Confident of victory, he led his men into the clearing to begin the killing.

He was disappointed to see none of his foresters' arrows had hit their targets but it wasn't surprising since they'd been firing blind. The missiles had served their purpose, scattering the wolf's head and his lackeys and throwing them into disarray, ready for Sir Guy's swordsmen to bring death to them.

It seemed he would, finally, rid the world of the craven bastard that had taken his eye and half his nose when they had last met, blade-on-blade, outside Dalton months earlier.

The outlaws hadn't survived so long by being indisciplined or incompetent though. Gisbourne held back, knowing he couldn't fight as well as he had before the loss of his eye.

But he could see well enough, as the man people ironically called Little John took out two of the Raven's soldiers with a quarterstaff that was almost a tree trunk.

His vision was clear enough to watch, in brutal detail, as the Hospitaller that had joined the outlaws swung his blade into the neck of a second of his men while a raging berserker that must be Will Scarlet tore the guts out of another and carried on his savage assault without even pausing for breath.

And the king's bounty hunter watched in a black fury as Robin Hood himself parried a thrust before sweeping his assailant's legs from under him and hammered the tip of his sword between a gap in the man's armour.

All around it was the same story. The outlaws had been alert and on their guard and Gisbourne's men were dying as a result.

"Fall back." Gisbourne's voice came out as little more than a grunt and he had to try again before his soldiers heard him. "Fall back!"

The men were only too happy to follow the order, retreating warily, thankfully, as the outlaws let them go, back into the trees with half their number dead or dying on the floor of the outlaws' camp-site.

"You win this day, Hood," Sir Guy growled, his words somehow carrying over the panting and mewling sounds that accompanied the end of such a bloody battle. "But I'm back on my feet and I'll not rest until I see you swinging from those gallows outside Nottingham. You and all your men."

Hood's men jeered and called insults, laughing at Gisbourne for retreating like a coward but, in truth, the Raven was glad to escape with his life – and all his body-parts – intact.

Clearly an open assault wasn't going to work. He should have known. He realised that now, as they finally left the outlaws' mocking laughter in the distance. Lawmen had come and gone over the years but not one of them had managed to destroy this particular band of wolf's heads by simply attacking them – even with superior numbers.

The greenwood was *their* territory.

Clearly a new tactic was needed if Gisbourne was to have his revenge.

* * *

"Get your stuff, and get the fuck off my ship you whinging bastard, before I have the crew throw you over the side."

The burly captain stood up from the table where he had been trying to study maps for his next journey to Norway, although he knew much of his time would be spent in Iceland and the thought of the freezing waters of the North was making him irritable. He was in no mood for this man's endless complaining.

"Nothing's ever enough for you is it, Groves? When you joined us I thought you'd be an asset to the crew with your experience, but all you've done is cause splits between the men and I'll have no more of it. Now, go."

Matt Groves twisted his lip in the scowl the captain had grown to detest and shrugged. "Fine. I never came to Hull to be a damn fisherman anyway. I'll find a ship sailing to Portugal or Flanders. At least it'll be warm and won't stink of fish."

The first mate and another stocky crewman came in then, wondering what the shouting was about.

"Show Matt here out, lads," the captain ordered them. "He's going to Portugal."

The first mate grinned. He couldn't stand the surly Groves who was continually undermining his authority with the men. "With pleasure, captain."

A short time later Matt stood on the dock, surrounded by the noise and bustle of sailors and merchants readying their cargoes for the next money-making trip. After he had betrayed Robin and the other young outlaw from Wakefield, Much, to Sir Guy of Gisbourne, Groves had headed east with a pocket full of silver and plans to make a new life as a sailor, which was a job he'd done long ago in his youth.

This was the third vessel he'd been forced to leave. His time living in Barnsdale as an outlaw, where he could do almost whatever he liked, had made it impossible for him to bow to authority or accept the rigid order on board a ship. His constant questioning and refusal to carry out menial tasks made him an unpleasant companion.

He hadn't been popular when he was part of the outlaw gang either, but at least there he could take himself off to a village for the night, or visit a brothel to work out his aggression. Aboard a ship the crew had no way to escape the man's relentless grumbling, and, although he never admitted to being an outlaw, it was obvious he was a very dangerous man, making his presence on the lonely sea an altogether unsettling and unpleasant one.

He growled and spat a thick gob of phlegm onto the dock in frustration. The reward Gisbourne had given him to turn Judas on Robin and Much was long gone and he was sick of these base-born fishermen treating him like he was a nobody.

He wouldn't bother looking for that ship to Portugal or Flanders, after all. No... he had a better idea...

CHAPTER THREE

"Calm down, girl! Anger might seem like a good motivator but when it comes to a fight, it's much better to be calm." Matilda shrugged, feeling slightly foolish as she lectured the girl in front of her. She was no killing machine, but she had trained with Robin and the outlaws so, when Marjorie asked her to pass on her knowledge she had reluctantly agreed. "When people are angry they don't think things through; they just act, regardless of the consequences. The best swordsmen – or women – hold their emotions in check." She flicked her lightweight wooden practice sword out and was pleased when her pupil saw it coming and managed to parry, breathlessly.

Marjorie had always been a weak, sickly girl, despite her older brother Robin's impressive physique. She'd suffered terribly in the famine of 1315, her then seven year-old body wasting away despite her parents' best efforts to find food for the family. Robin, eleven at the time, had just enough weight on him to survive the worst of the hunger pangs but Marjorie's twin sister, Rebekah, had died.

She'd always remember her sister, and how she looked when she'd succumbed to the dreadful hunger: skin and bones, even though her empty stomach was bloated and round as if she'd eaten like a queen for weeks. It was a cruel way for a little girl to die.

Marjorie had survived – just – but, despite all the wholesome food her mother and father had prepared for her over the years, she'd never managed to put much meat on her bones. Even now, when Robin was a famous outlaw and a wealthy man who brought lots of fruit and vegetables, meat and eggs for his family to feast on, his sister remained thin, bordering on being malnourished.

"Block!" Matilda aimed a thrust at Marjorie, who appeared lost in thought, but the girl managed to twist away from the practice-sword and aim a blow of her own, which was easily batted aside although Matilda smiled encouragingly.

After the foresters had almost arrested them for trapping that hare, Marjorie had been ashamed of her fear. Ashamed of how useless she'd been, leaving her sister-in-law to protect her while she stood passively, waiting for the men do whatever they would.

Then, when news had come of Sir Guy of Gisbourne's return to action and Robin had left to go back to the forest again Marjorie had been irritated by the reaction of the people of Wakefield. The majority of them, even the men – and Matilda too! – had grown fearful at the prospect of the brutal bounty-hunter's soldiers coming back into their comfortable lives.

Marjorie could understand her big brother being wary of Gisbourne and going out of his way to avoid the man but – Christ above – the villagers needed to stand up for themselves. Why were they all content to be pushed around?

Eventually she realised the people accepted their treatment because they were weak. Not as physically weak as she was, no – the blacksmith, for example, was a bear of a man, by God and he liked to tell folk off if they got in his way. But he was no soldier; had no military training even though he'd been called up to the armies of the local lord over the years and had even seen what could loosely be termed 'action'.

He'd never faced an enemy sword on sword, or watched his own arrow pierce the body of an on-rushing foe.

Even if he had, Marjorie knew, he'd still be scared of the black-armoured king's man that people called the Raven.

Yet what could she do? She was only an abnormally skinny fifteen-year-old. She'd never, no matter how she tried, be able to draw a hunting bow never mind one of the giant warbows Robin or Little John used.

Similar thoughts had assailed her for years, even before Robin had become an outlaw. Her frail body had always angered her, but she'd never believed she could do anything to overcome the weakness.

Then the foresters had terrified and humiliated her, and Robin had left again, leaving them all to look after themselves, and Marjorie had decided enough was enough. She couldn't count on anyone to look after her – not her parents, not the burly blacksmith, not even her charismatic wolf's head brother.

Matilda came at her again and, as before, Marjorie managed to twist to the side with a strangled cry, just evading the blow although the effort left her gasping and she could feel a pain in her side that was growing worse with every passing moment.

She'd had enough of being the village weakling; the girl the adults looked down upon from sad, pitying eyes when they passed. She wanted to be like Robin. Of course, she wasn't stupid – she knew she'd never be the muscle-bound bear of a man her brother was, but she desperately wanted to toughen herself up. To learn how to wield a sword, or perhaps a crossbow since a bow would always be beyond her. *Anything* that she could use to defend herself and those she loved from the likes of Gisbourne and that filthy bailiff who had wanted to rape Matilda two years ago.

Marjorie had never been told the full story about what had happened when Adam Gurdon had arrested Matilda, but she'd listened to the gossip and had formed a rough idea in her head which she suspected was pretty accurate.

She was impressed by what the people said Matilda had done to defend herself. Marjorie, at fifteen, had not been with a young man yet but many of the girls her age or even younger were already married and gossiped freely about it, so she had a good idea what a hard, blood-engorged spindle looked like. Knowing Matilda had managed to bite almost right through Adam Gurdon's manhood told her all she needed to know about her brother's wife: she was the perfect teacher.

So, here they were.

Matilda had, at first, refused outright to train Marjorie. Not only was the girl thin and sickly, but Matilda doubted her own ability to teach anyone the ways of combat. Besides, they had more than enough to occupy their time, since she herself assisted her father in crafting arrows and Marjorie helped her own mother around the house.

But the girl had been persistent and eventually Matilda acquiesced. She didn't think the training would last for long before her student grew tired and fed-up and they could go back to normal life.

"Ha!" Marjorie, who had seemed exhausted just a moment before, suddenly jumped forward, ramming the point of her own little practice sword into Matilda's ribs.

"Ow, you little bastard!"

Marjorie grinned and raised her sword defensively as her sister-in-law grasped her bruised side and glared balefully at her.

"You told me to thrust rather than swing the sword," the girl shrugged innocently. "I'm just following your orders."

Matilda gritted her teeth and suppressed a smile. Will Scaflock had shown her how to fight with a sword and he'd based much of his technique – so he said – on the old Roman way of combat. They'd used short-swords rather than the unwieldy long-swords that men favoured nowadays and those smaller bladed weapons were ideal for women, Will had said.

One of the things he'd taught her was how to thrust with the short-sword, directly at an opponent, before stepping quickly back into a defensive stance. Most people didn't expect it, since the common long-sword – never mind the axe or two-handed bastard sword – was too slow for such a manoeuvre. It simply wasn't done.

That was why Matilda had shown the move to Marjorie. The girl was a fast learner she realised, clutching at her burning, agonized ribs.

But no amount of training could make up for a weak body and Robin's young sibling was wheezing already, her sword by her side rather than held up defensively as Matilda had shown her.

The girl would never be a match for a good swordsman in a fair fight, Matilda knew.

But not all fights were fair...

She waited until Marjorie had come to check she wasn't injured then slashed her own practice-sword around and into the girl's calf.

"There's your next lesson," Matilda grinned as she stood, glaring down at her fallen young foe. "Never underestimate your enemy!"

* * *

After Gisbourne's failed attack, Robin had led the men to a new camp-site, on the other side of Wakefield. As ever, it was well hidden by the foliage and terrain, and close enough to a stream that they could collect fresh water for cooking and washing.

Friar Tuck had gathered his meagre possessions that morning and now he sat by the fire with the rest of the men, chewing a piece of bread. A few days earlier he had made the trip east to St Mary's church in Brandesburton where he'd met with Father Nicholas de Nottingham. The priest – 'rightful' owner of the holy relic Tuck was taking back to Lewes with him – had been peeved to be losing the artifact which he'd only loaned to Robin Hood. The friar had explained things to him, though, and donated a sizeable sum of money as compensation.

Father de Nottingham had been impressed by the likeable Franciscan, and thought he might be right in thinking God had returned the holy relic to him for a purpose so, eventually, had given Tuck his blessing to take the exquisite little box back to Prior de Martini.

A good man, de Nottingham. One the big friar would have liked to share a few ales with, but, with the rumours of Gisbourne being on the hunt again, he'd wanted to get safely back to camp as soon as possible. Maybe sometime in the future Tuck would get a chance to spend more time in Brandesburton with the priest. He'd like that...

Robin had tried to persuade Tuck to stay but he would have none of it.

"I must leave Robin, today. God has sent this relic as a sign. Maybe it was returned to me because I've to go back to Prior de Monte Martini and save his soul... I don't know. I *do* know my body can't take any more of this life though. I'm old" –

"You're not much older than me!" Stephen, the former Hospitaller sergeant-at-arms muttered. He'd not been with the outlaws for as long as the rest of the men, but, like all of them, he'd grown to like and value Tuck's calming presence around the camp.

"Maybe not in years," Tuck agreed, with a small sigh. "But I feel old in my bones."

Will Scarlet shared a look with Robin. The Franciscan had been trapped in Nottingham with them just a few months ago – not long after he'd been shot by Gisbourne and almost drowned in the Don too – and he'd seemed hale and hearty then. In the months since he'd regained most of the weight he'd lost back then and, looking at him now, it seemed like he could offer any of them a challenge in a fight.

Robin knew better than anyone how being close to death could alter a man's perception of the world, though. He had almost given up hope when Gisbourne had captured him, beaten him within an inch of his life, then thrown him in a cell under Nottingham Castle. Although the young wolf's head had come back stronger than ever, Tuck, with his advanced years, clearly felt the after-effects of his own ordeal more keenly than Robin did his.

"You're not even a Benedictine, like the prior and all them in Lewes," Peter Ordevill, the old sailor from Selby grunted. "You're a Franciscan. De Monte Martini won't let you – a greyfriar – live amongst his Black Monks will he?"

Tuck shrugged and got to his feet, ready, at last, to make a move. "I don't know. Before I joined you lads I didn't really have a settled home. I was sent from place to place, escorting important people and relics and money and the like. Lewes Priory was where I spent most of my time though – de Monte Martini needed my services a lot so it became the closest thing I had to a home, despite the fact I wasn't one of their order." He shrugged again, uncertainly. He really wasn't sure what would happen when he reached Lewes. He didn't think he'd be much use as a bodyguard for the Church's shipments any more, but he knew he had to placate Prior de Monte Martini or he would never be a free man again.

"This is pointless," Little John broke in, his rumbling voice filling the small clearing where they'd set up their new camp. "He's made up his mind." He strode over and grasped the surprised friar in a massive bear hug which made his face flush red, from the giant outlaw's strength and embarrassment at the unusual show of emotion. "You look after yourself," John warned. "That bastard prior is one for the watching. If you think you're just going to walk back into his monastery, hand him his relic and all will be forgiven you should think again. He's going to make life hard for you."

It was true of course, but the thought of being a free man again brought a smile to Tuck's lips.

He moved among the men, clasping hands and sharing smiles then, with a final wave of goodbye, he disappeared into the trees.

* * *

Edward of Caernarvon, King of England tapped his fingers on the arm of his high-backed wooden throne and sighed loudly, drawing looks of disapproval from his courtiers, although they were careful not to let the king see them.

Another day of politicking, in Knaresborough Castle that day, which his father had paid a small fortune to rebuild, and he was already bored even though it wasn't yet midday. He could think of lots of better things to be doing on a fine spring day; rowing, or horse-riding, or just

25

listening to his minstrels playing music would be infinitely preferable to this nonsense.

But he had his duties to attend to, so here he was, stuck indoors again. Although he was the most powerful man in the country – and there was no question of that since he'd put down the Lancastrian revolt so successfully the previous year – he still couldn't do whatever he wanted, curse his luck.

He'd been crowned king at the age of twenty-three, when his father, also Edward, had died but his reign had not been a particularly good one, or so the people of England seemed to think. The Welsh appeared to have an affection for him, even now, but his English subjects didn't think much of his rule. He had tried his best but the simple fact was, he wasn't really interested in the things a good king was supposed to do.

He enjoyed the company of commoners, for example, which scandalized most of his nobles. He'd even learned how to shoe a horse along with thatching, hedging and ditching – all necessary tasks, to be sure, but not ones to be performed by a king! Even his much-admired physique was mostly thanks to his love of rowing and swimming which were, again, seen as scandalous pursuits for a royal to be so involved in.

The truth was, Edward enjoyed such rustic pastimes so much because he felt lonely at court. Lonely and bored. It wasn't easy being the king and something as simple and good as repairing the thatch on a cottage brought him a great sense of peace.

"Sire..?"

The petitioner before him, a minor noble from Harrogate, looked embarrassed to be, essentially, upbraiding the king for his inattentiveness but it was clear Edward was lost in his own little world and wasn't paying the slightest notice to what was being said.

"Yes, yes, carry on, my lord, I'm listening," the monarch lied, waving a hand and forcing himself to sit straighter as the man blabbered on about some bridges needing repairing. Why the king had to know about it

Edward had no idea, but he watched the petitioner and tried to look as if he was listening.

It had been good to put down the Contrariants, especially his cousin the Earl of Lancaster. For years they had been trying to undermine him – they had even killed his first and greatest friend, Piers Gaveston. He sighed again, remembering the handsome, charming young man who he had loved yet everyone else seemed to hate. But he had avenged Piers's death when he'd crushed that rebellion and executed the ring-leaders and, now, at last, the country was at peace.

The petitioner finished speaking and bowed his head before looking expectantly at the king for his decision.

"You make a good case, sir," Edward nodded, a genuine smile creasing his bearded face, glad that the man was finished at last. "I agree with the points you make." He waved a hand towards his treasurer, Walter de Stapledon, Bishop of Exeter. "Your Grace, please see to it. We can't have bridges collapsing, can we? The country would grind to a halt."

The nobleman smiled, pleased to have been granted the funding he'd travelled to Knaresborough to ask for. It had been a stressful morning for him too – the king almost never saw anyone these days, leaving much of the country's administration up to his new favourite, Sir Hugh Despenser the younger. But Despenser, the king's chamberlain, was away in Wales at that time and so the monarch had decided he must see to business himself that day.

It was a mistake Edward rectified now, as he stood up and smiled around the room. "I think that's enough for one morning. I will retire to my chambers."

Without another word, and followed by the disapproving stares of his subjects, he strode out of the throne room. The morning was gone, but it was still warm outside; he'd spend the rest of the day with his friends on one of his boats on the River Nidd which ran right past the castle. Sir Hugh would join him soon enough – then *he* could take care of the country.

Henry de Faucumberg, High Sheriff of Nottingham and Yorkshire, was angry. That morning, one of Robin Hood's men had strutted into the city as if he owned the place and offered his services as a bounty hunter.

As far as the sheriff knew, the outlaw had never been pardoned so was still a fugitive. De Faucumberg had ordered his men to arrest the man as soon as he'd realised who the hell he was. Then Sir Guy of Gisbourne had intervened.

The black-armoured, one-eyed, king's man had stepped in to stop the sheriff's guards from throwing the outlaw into the dungeon. Although de Faucumberg was the most powerful man in Nottingham he knew King Edward II expected him to work together with Gisbourne to capture or kill Robin Hood and his men.

It was an uneasy relationship that had only got worse since Sir Guy's defeat – and mutilation – by Hood.

Before, the king's man had been arrogant and unfriendly but he'd obviously enjoyed life. He enjoyed sparring with the sheriff's guards, defeating every one and brutally injuring some of them in the process. His legendary skill with a blade had been the one thing he was most proud of. He rose early in the morning to practice, and spent any spare moments going through combinations and tactics in his head, revelling in the knowledge he was the best swordsman in England.

Then Robin Hood had beaten him. And not only that, the wolf's head had torn off half of his face, leaving him with only one eye and a scar that made him look like a monster.

It had been a fair fight and Gisbourne was winning easily enough – toying with his younger foe – but sometimes the best man doesn't win and, when Sir Guy had slipped on a muddy patch of grass Hood had made the most of his opportunity.

The king's bounty hunter – who had been sent north specifically to deal with the problem of Robin Hood and his outlaw gang – had been left incapacitated for months, his lust for life lessening with every day he was forced to spend confined to a sick bed, while his hatred for Hood grew like a cancer inside him.

The damned wolf's head hadn't just bested Gisbourne though, his men had killed the bounty hunter's second-in-command, Nicholas Barnwell. The man had been the closest thing Gisbourne had to a friend – they'd worked together bringing outlaws to justice for the best part of three years and had shared much together in that time. Barnwell's death was a real blow to the Raven.

Although Gisbourne excelled at leading men in combat, he wasn't much good at dealing with the normal day-to-day problems and personal issues that affected any group of men, being aloof, arrogant and clearly considering himself superior to everyone beneath him. Barnwell had been a good go-between, with his earthy, sometimes sadistic humour endearing him to the men who saw him as "one of them", with no airs or graces.

Gisbourne knew he had to find someone to take Barnwell's place but none of the men in his current command were suitable, being mostly loyal to the sheriff, Henry de Faucumberg, or the king himself.

After his recent failed assault on Hood's camp Gisbourne also knew he'd need to try a different tactic to catch the outlaws. Perhaps find someone who knew where the wolf's head's camp-sites were. Someone who knew the secret, hidden trails in the forests. Someone, in short, that knew exactly where and how Hood's men lived.

It seemed divine providence then, when Matt Groves appeared in the city, looking for employment.

Sir Guy didn't know much about the man, having only met him on a couple of occasions – breaking his nose the first time – but he knew Groves had spent a long time as part of Hood's gang and, more importantly, hated the young wolf's head with a vengeance. His knowledge of Barnsdale Forest would be invaluable too, so, when the sheriff had wanted to hang the man, Gisbourne had stepped in to save him, offering the grizzled outlaw the position as his own sergeant.

"You remind me of my previous second-in-command," Sir Guy had told Groves as de Faucumberg shook his head in disgust and waved them from his great hall. "He was a sour-faced, weather-beaten bastard too."

A rare smile cracked the corners of Matt's lips at that. "You won't regret this, my lord," he vowed. "I know Yorkshire like the back of my hand. Hood never listened to me when I offered advice – thought he knew best, or asked Little John or Scarlet what to do instead. Arseholes, the lot of them. You can count on me, though, I won't let you down, in God's name, I swear it. You took a chance on me when no-one else would and I mean to repay you for it."

Gisbourne didn't like the fawning tone in the man's voice or the angry, darting eyes when he spoke but it was done now, the outlaw was his new sergeant. Whether he was useful or not remained to be seen. If he helped him kill Robin Hood – perfect. If he turned out to be a liability though, he would kill Groves himself without a second thought.

Praise be to God, it was good to be back in the hunt.

* * *

Robin sat nursing a mug of ale, gazing into the fire wistfully, thinking back to the day they had first met the now departed Friar Tuck. So much had changed since then and yet here he was, still a wolf's head hiding from the law.

Allan came over to sit with his brooding young leader. "I don't know for sure," he began thoughtfully, "but I think Matt Groves was riding with Gisbourne in Pontefract when I was there earlier today."

Robin's sat up, his eyes flaring and the minstrel held up a hand defensively, almost feeling the force or his friend's hatred like a physical blow. "I'm not sure if it was him or not! I was in a hurry to get the hell out of there before they found me so I didn't take the time to look too closely. It looked a lot like him though."

Without realising it, Robin's hand fell to the sword hilt at his waist and he snorted furiously. "It wouldn't surprise me if he's taken up with that bastard Gisbourne. Bitter old prick would love nothing more than seeing me hanged."

Allan nodded, then his eyes widened in surprise as Robin continued.

"This is the best news I've heard for a while. Aye, I hope it *was* Matt you saw," he said, in response to the look on Allan's face. "It means I don't have to go looking for the bastard – he'll come straight to me, and then..."

CHAPTER FOUR

April came, filling the trees with thick green leaves and the rains slowed, allowing the ground in the forest to dry out and become less treacherous. The sounds of nature reawakening after the chill of winter filled the air, as insects began to build their nests in dark, hidden places and many of the animals and birds that populated the undergrowth gave birth to their little ones.

"Here, listen to this!" Young Gareth hurried into camp one afternoon, red-faced and puffing, apparently from excitement more than exertion. He was followed by the Hospitaller sergeant, Stephen, who looked bored and irritated by his younger companion. The unlikely pair had been visiting the village of Tretone that morning to collect supplies.

"What's up?" Little John wondered, raising an eyebrow at Stephen who gave a disgusted wave and sauntered to the big cooking pot over the camp-fire to help himself to some of the thin soup bubbling away inside as the other outlaws who were around came across to hear Gareth's news.

"The sheriff's holding a tournament in a couple of weeks."

Silence greeted his pronouncement and the Hospitaller snorted with laughter as he spooned some of the hot food into his mouth.

"So what?" Allan-a-Dale asked. "What's that got to do with us?"

"There's to be games and prizes and stuff," Gareth replied, smiling as he moved over next to Stephen and lifted a bowl of his own which he filled with the – mostly cabbage – soup.

"Are you pissed again, boy?" Will Scarlet demanded.

"No, I'm not!" Gareth retorted, the watery broth dribbling down his chin as he glared at Will indignantly.

"There's going to be an archery competition, and the prize is a silver arrow. An arrow made from solid silver."

There were gasps and whistles of appreciation from the men as the value of such a prize sunk in.

"That's impressive," Robin agreed, shrugging his enormous shoulders. "But why are you so excited? None of us are going to be winning the arrow."

"Why not?" Gareth replied, looking at Robin as he continued to eat. "You could win." He glanced over at John. "Or you." His eyes moved around the outlaws who listened to him in bemused silence. "You're all deadly with a longbow, you could beat anyone in England. Christ knows you spend enough time practising."

"You seem to be forgetting one thing," Scarlet growled. "We're fucking outlaws. The moment any one of us sets foot in Nottingham we'll be arrested and hanged. Particularly me or Robin, since some of the guards know what we look like and, as for him..." he pointed at Little John. "He stands out a bit, don't you think? Being the size of a fucking bear and all."

John laughed merrily and clapped Gareth good-naturedly on the back. "Ah, the innocence – and stupidity – of youth."

"Aye," Stephen muttered. "And if you think that silver arrow is going to be anything more than a normal wooden shaft with some paint on it, you're more than stupid."

The men began to drift off, back to whatever tasks they'd been involved in before the Hospitaller and his teenage companion had returned, laughing at the preposterousness of Gareth's suggestion.

Allan-a-Dale remained by the fire with Robin, strumming his gittern and thoughtfully eyeing the longbow which lay on the grass by his side.

"Maybe it's not such a bad idea of the lad's after all."

"Eh?" Allan was only half-listening, absorbed in the music as he was. "What idea?"

"The arrow," Robin muttered, plucking strands of grass from between his legs thoughtfully. "I'd have a good chance of winning the competition *if* I could hide my identity. Think how much money that arrow would be worth." He looked up, eyes shining. "Enough to buy us all pardons. All of us. We'd be free at last."

Allan nodded slowly. "That's true. But you'd be recognised as soon as the first guard saw you. Every lawman in the north of England knows what you look like by now and, you know yourself – this whole thing is probably a trap specifically to catch you."

Robin sighed. "Aye, you're right, of course. But..." he tossed the little strands of grass he'd been fiddling with into the air angrily. "I promised you men pardons but I don't see how I can ever fulfil the vow."

He fell into silence again for a time, but was soon startled from his reverie by the sound of another of the outlaws crashing through the undergrowth into camp. This time it was Arthur, the powerfully-built lad from Bichill who waved the rest of the men across, his near-toothless mouth split in a cheery grin.

"Keep it down," Allan hissed angrily. "You should know better than to come charging through the trees like a hunted boar."

Arthur waved a hand irritably and addressed Robin who had come over, brown eyes gleaming with interest.

"Two Franciscan friars on the road to Nottingham. No guards."

"If they've no guards they probably have nothing worth stealing," Little John grumbled.

Robin nodded, but the men murmured together, knowing travellers were often the best way to find out news from the wider country, even if they carried light purses hardly worth removing.

"Let's invite them to dinner," Robin laughed, strapping on his sword-belt and collecting his great war-bow. "It would be rude to let them pass without offering our hospitality."

He waved to Arthur to lead the way and followed the lad. "Make sure there's enough stew for our visitors," the young leader smiled to Edmond who nodded and waved farewell.

It didn't take long to find the two friars. Although it was a dry day, there had been rain in the night and it made the remnants of the previous autumn's leaves slick, slowing the travellers' progress to the city.

"Hail, and well met," Robin stepped into the road from behind a twisted old birch tree, raising a hand in greeting and smiling at the two friars who stopped in surprise, their faces registering fear and dismay at the sudden appearance of the large young warrior who greeted them.

"God give you good day, my child," the elder of the two churchmen replied, his eyes searching the undergrowth for signs of anyone else. His shoulders slumped as he caught sight of Arthur, hand gripping the hilt of the sword he wore. Clearly these men were outlaws. "We have nothing of value –"

"We're no robbers," Robin broke in, shaking his head and moving forward to stand before the friars, his gaze steady, searching for any signs that the men might try and offer some resistance. "I'm Robin Hood," he went on, noting the older friar's involuntary step backwards as he recognized the name of the infamous wolf's head. "This is our forest."

The friar opened his mouth to deny Robin's claim to the land but the young outlaw carried on, giving him no chance to speak. "We merely wanted to invite you to dinner. You look like you could do with some food."

The younger friar – no more than fourteen summers at the most – certainly appeared to be in need of a hot meal, being almost skeletally thin. He either hadn't heard of Robin Hood or simply found the idea of food so appealing that it was worth a trip into the lair of a gang of violent criminals. He glanced up at his older man, his eyes hopeful.

"I think not, although we thank you *in the name of Christ* for your generous offer. We are simply in too much of a hurry to be sidetracked."

The man made to move along the path, gesturing for his young companion to follow.

"I insist."

Robin placed himself directly in front of them and the smile fell from his lips, hand dropping to his sword hilt as Arthur stepped into the road behind the churchmen.

"Our camp is this way. Follow me."

"No, wolf's head!" The friar stood his ground, even stamping his foot like a petulant child. "We won't follow –
"

"What food do you have?"

Robin turned at the younger friar's voice, meeting his hopeful gaze with a reassuring smile.

"We have cabbage soup, and our cook has just started making a big pot of venison stew," he replied, watching the skinny youngster's mouth working as saliva formed unbidden and the grumble of his empty stomach seemed to echo back from the sparse spring foliage around them.

"Hubert, get back here, boy. The abbot shall hear of this, you little bastard!"

The novice ignored his superior, following Robin as he set off along the trail again, and Arthur shoved the older friar in the back with a curt, "Move it, priest, or I'll knock you out and carry you."

It didn't take them long to reach the outlaw's camp and they were all glad to return, the grousing friar barely stopping for breath the whole way as he lambasted Robin and Arthur, promising them eternal torture and a place in hell beside the great tyrants of history.

"Two bowls of stew for our guests," Robin shouted over to Edmond. "Make the lad's bowl a big one." He grinned at the young page and bade him sit, which the lad did gladly, looking around at the other outlaws with interest rather than the fear his elder displayed so obviously.

"Be at ease." Robin laughed at the friar as Edmond handed him a steaming bowl and a crust of black bread. "We mean you no harm. You've surely heard of me and the rest of these men; you know we don't murder for pleasure. Be at ease," he repeated. "In the morning you can be on your way with a full belly and a tale to tell your brother friars."

The sun moved into the west and slowly fell, leaving only the crackling camp-fire to cast light on the outlaws and their two guests. The younger of the pair, Hubert, proved to be a friendly boy, who told them they were travelling to Nottingham for the tournament the sheriff was holding in a few weeks. Their abbot had sent them north to the city from Gloucester Greyfriars to bring the word of God to the great number of people who would surely be congregating there to watch or take part in the tourney.

The promise of a near-priceless silver arrow as a prize had sent ripples of excitement all around the north of England and Custos William de Bromley wanted to make sure the masses gathering in Nottingham would dip into their pockets and contribute alms for his church's upkeep.

The older friar, Brother Walter, refused to engage in conversation with the men. He shrank back from any of the outlaws if they came near to him, as if they were flea-ridden dogs or lepers and shouted at Hubert to hold his peace as the youngster spoke with Robin and the men, imparting what news he had from Gloucester and beyond. Still, Walter managed to eat two bowls of Edmond's venison stew and more than his share of ale before falling asleep with his back against a tree stump close to the fire.

"He says it's a sin to eat too much," Hubert grumbled, glaring over at his sleeping superior. "But whenever we stop at an inn he eats enough for a horse while only paying for a small bowl of porridge for me." He sighed. "I suppose this is God's way of teaching me humility before I become a proper friar."

Will Scarlet shook his head in annoyance. "Well, lad, you can eat as much as you like tonight. Eat until you throw up if you want."

Hubert smiled and took the piece of bread Will held out to him with a grateful nod.

When they awoke in the morning, Brother Walter was glad to see most of the outlaws were absent – gone off hunting or fishing or, more likely he thought with a scowl, *robbing* people.

Robin came over to him and helped him up. Young Hubert was already awake and mopping up the last of a bowl of porridge with another piece of bread.

"Here," the outlaw captain handed some of the steaming breakfast to the sour-faced friar. "Eat up, and you can be off."

"As easy as that?" Walter shovelled the porridge into his mouth with his hand, licking oats from his fingers as he looked warily at Robin, as if he expected the big man to skewer him any second.

"As easy as that," Robin agreed, watching the friar devour the meal with a twinkle in his eye. "Once you pay us for your bed and board."

Walter spat in fury and a mouthful of food dribbled down his chin.

"Whatever's in your purse will be enough to cover your debt I'm sure."

Before the outraged Franciscan could react the outlaw stepped in close and, with a knife that seemed to appear in his hand from thin air, sliced through the leather thong that held his purse onto his belt.

Moving back to sit by the fire Robin tossed the purse up and down, feeling the weight with a satisfied nod. "Yes, this'll be just enough I'm sure. I trust you enjoyed your stay here in Barnsdale?"

"You heathen scum –"

Little John and Allan-a-Dale appeared behind the protesting friar and shepherded him from the camp, back towards the main road, screaming for God to rain hell-fire and brimstone on the wolf's head.

Robin, grinning wickedly, clasped young Hubert by the shoulder and pressed the coin purse into the youngster's hand surreptitiously. "There you go lad, keep that hidden under your cassock and buy yourself a pie whenever you get a chance. You best be off or Brother Walter will tell the Custos on you."

Laughing, the skinny page made the sign of the cross, blessing the wolf's head, before stuffing the remainder of a loaf into his mouth and running into the trees after his elder.

* * *

"You really think this will work?" Gisbourne placed his black crossbow on the table beside him and rubbed irritably at his ruined eye-socket. Most people would have worn an eye-patch but the bounty hunter understood the power of appearances and liked to seem as menacing as possible. The sight of his weeping scar was enough to frighten most people.

Matt Groves nodded confidently. "Aye, I do. Hood himself isn't reckless, or stupid, enough to fall for it. But one of the gang members will want to win that silver arrow and they'll enter the competition. Then it's just a matter of capturing the fool and waiting for Hood to come and rescue them. The loyalty he shows to the men is admirable. And stupid."

Gisbourne grunted non-committally. It seemed a hopeful plan to him, but, even with Groves's knowledge of the outlaws and their habits, they'd not managed to come close to finding the wolf's head and his followers in the past few weeks. If Matt's idea flushed them out into the open it would certainly make things a sight easier. Going back into the dense undergrowth of Barnsdale didn't appeal to Gisbourne – his depth perception, and, as a result, his fighting ability, had been hopelessly damaged with the loss of his eye. So, he now had to rely on strategy and cunning more than simple brute force if he was going to kill the wolf's head and his followers.

Besides, Groves's suggestion that Hood was too smart to fall for their ruse was something the bounty hunter questioned. He had a good idea how the wolf's head's mind worked. The man was proud, and he wanted the

39

people to love and respect him. That was why he'd turned up to fight Gisbourne one-on-one on the bridge at Dalton, even though he must have known he had next to no chance of winning the duel. Yes, his reputation meant the world to Robin Hood, and winning a silver arrow from his hated enemies would truly make him a legend. Could he pass up such an opportunity?

Maybe the young archer would turn up in person to enter the tournament after all. Only time would tell.

Sheriff de Faucumberg had, surprisingly, been quite open to the idea of a tournament with a silver arrow as the prize for the best archer when the bounty hunter had approached him in the great hall. Gisbourne had expected he'd have to persuade, argue or even fall back on the king's name to get the man to agree to Groves's plan, but de Faucumberg was almost as sick of the outlaws plaguing his jurisdiction as Gisbourne was. Anything that might get rid of them once and for all was worth a try. God knew, they'd tried everything else in the past few years, without much success.

"Yes, it seems like a reasonable idea. We can simply paint a normal arrow with silver paint; no one will be able to tell from a distance," de Faucumberg had suggested, rolling up parchments on the great oak table that separated him from the Raven and taking a sip from the silver goblet by his right hand.

Gisbourne had been adamant though. "Out of the question, sheriff. People are going to come and see it before the tournament – they'll be able to tell immediately if we just paint a normal, wooden arrow. No, we must have the local smith make us the real thing if we're to entice the wolf's head into coming here for it."

"And where are we going to find the silver to make this precious missile?" de Faucumberg wondered.

Gisbourne had laughed mirthlessly. "Come, now, sheriff. There's more than enough coin from taxes in your coffers to make something as small as an arrow. Melt some of it down. We're going to have a city full of soldiers on the lookout for Hood and his men, there's no chance they'll be able to ever get the arrow out of the city, so it's not like you'll be risking your silver."

The sheriff snorted angrily. "We had a locked city full of soldiers looking for the bastard just a few months ago, yet he managed to escape from the dungeon and walk right out through the gates. I wouldn't be so confident if I were you."

Gisbourne waved a hand dismissively but de Faucumberg carried on.

"Besides, what if none of the outlaws turn up? Or, say they do turn up, but someone else wins the competition? What then?"

"We give them a small bag of silver and send them on their fucking way!" Gisbourne barked, shaking his head. "You're the king's representative here, you wield more power than you seem to realise. Use it, man."

De Faucumberg took the rebuke with a frown, realising the bounty hunter was right. Hood and his outlaws had been allowed to do as they pleased in his forests for too long. Maybe it was time to play a little dirty.

"Fine," he agreed. "Take just enough silver to make your arrow. But you better make damn sure you and your men guard it with your lives, because if you don't... your lives won't be worth the dog shit I stepped in this morning, Gisbourne, trust me."

The Raven threw the sheriff a smug grin, the scar tissue that had healed around his missing eye wrinkling horribly as he raised a hand in mocking salute and strode from the room with a laugh, his black boot-heels echoing as he went. "I trust you, de Faucumberg. It's time you placed some trust in me. The wolf's head is as good as dead."

CHAPTER FIVE

Robin had ordered the men to move camp again on hearing Allan's news that Matt Groves might have taken up with the feared Gisbourne. Matt knew all of their usual camp-sites, having been a member of the outlaw gang for longer than most of them and Robin didn't want to make it easy for the turncoat to lead their doom straight to them.

Their usual hiding places had been chosen years ago by Adam Bell who, as an ex-Templar knight, had a great understanding and knowledge of how to use terrain to his advantage, be it to hide his own men or to mount attacks on others. But they needed to find completely new places to hide in now. Thankfully, Robin, although he didn't have the martial training of a knight, had an instinctive understanding of the forest and how to use it properly.

As ever, Will Scarlet and Little John helped advise their young leader when he found a spot, making sure they had easy access to a little stream for fresh water, while being well hidden amongst the thick foliage of beech, oak trees and lower level bushes, ferns, or long grass. It was not too far from the road between Penysale and Penyston and seemed ideal as there was a local market held close by every Tuesday which would allow the outlaws to collect supplies without having to travel too far afield. The stall-holders and patrons would also, no doubt, be a good source of information on rumours of Gisbourne's whereabouts.

"We should have stopped using those old camping grounds long ago, when Robin killed Adam," Little John murmured, lying back contentedly on a brown patch of grass in the middle of their new home. "It feels good to be somewhere different. Even if we're still not in soft beds, with a nice pair of tits to cuddle into."

It was an overcast, muggy, spring afternoon, with heavy black clouds covering the sky that threatened to burst and soak the land at any time, but the men had a cosy fire going and the new camp-site gave them a sense of security and safety. The thick trees which encircled them felt more homely than any grey castle wall ever could.

Robin laughed wistfully at his huge friend's words, appreciating the blunt language and pleasing imagery it conjured. "True, big man, true."

"True, perhaps," Will interjected. "But the men – including me, I admit - wouldn't have taken kindly to Robin ordering us to give up our old haunts back then. It's a mark of the respect we all have for you now, lad, that you can get us to follow you somewhere new without a shouting match."

Not so long ago Robin would have blushed crimson at the praise from the hugely experienced Will, a man who had fought as a mercenary in the Holy Land and seen much death and horror in his thirty-seven years. Now, the outlaw captain simply accepted Will's words with a grateful nod.

"Pah, I would have followed him if he'd suggested it," John snorted, his mouth twitching mischievously. "You lot just like an argument. Bunch of sour-faced lack-wits."

Allan-a-Dale and some of the other long-term outlaws bristled at that, shooting insults back at the bearded giant, while the newcomers like Stephen and Edmond, the fish-lipped former tanner from Kirklees, grinned and hoisted their ale mugs aloft in a cheer, enjoying the banter.

Robin threw John a thankful smile, knowing his friend, despite the humour, spoke the truth. Before he became their leader, the men hadn't completely trusted Robin. John had taken his side right from the start though and the young man would never forget that loyalty.

"Dinner's ready!" Edmond shouted, taking a last sip of his ale before swapping the wooden mug for a ladle. "Come and get it, lads."

Edmond had found it hard at first to settle amongst the close-knit outlaws, who were more like a military order than a random collection of violent criminals. The lads had been welcoming but a lifetime of being bullied and abused by his peers had made it hard for the tanner to lower his defences and build friendships. Men like Robin and Little

John had gone out of their way to make the young man, with his thin beard, stumpy limbs and thickset body, feel like one of them.

More than any of them, though, Friar Tuck had helped Edmond come to terms with the fact he had captured Stephen's master, Sir Richard-at-Lee, and led him to his death on the gallows in Nottingham. Although he had now begun to feel at ease with the outlaws, the tanner felt Tuck's absence from their group keenly.

"How do you think the friar fares?" he wondered as the men settled down happily to eat the stew he'd made for them. "Will the Prior take him in again?"

"Ach, he'll be fine," Will waved his spoon confidently. "Tuck knows how to look after himself."

"I hope you're right," Allan-a-Dale replied, wincing as the hot food scalded the roof of his mouth.

"I wish he was still here," Edmond mumbled, eyes downcast, chewing on a hunk of bread that he'd dipped into his stew.

The comment was met with silence, the rest of the men agreeing whole-heartedly with it.

"I wish he was still here too," John growled, after spooning some of the food into his mouth. "Tuck could make much tastier stew than this piss-water you've cooked up for us."

Everyone laughed, even Edmond, glad to avert the melancholy that was so easy to fall into living out here in the forest as a wolf's head.

"He'll be fine," Robin said authoritatively. "Honestly, have no fears for Tuck. He used to earn his living as a wrestler; he can take care of himself."

Talk turned to other things as the stew – rather more appetising than John had suggested – filled their hungry bellies and a new cask of freshly-brewed Penysale beer was broached. Robin felt instinctively that he was right: Tuck would be fine. The portly friar could fight like a Templar, yes, but he also had a likeable charisma that often acted better than any heater shield or buckler.

The outlaw leader stood and made his way over to the big cooking pot to help himself to more food, smiling in thanks as Edmond grabbed his mug for a refill. Aye, Friar Tuck would be fine.

He wondered how his family fared, though.

* * *

It had been a while since Marjorie and Matilda had been able to spend some time training together. They both had chores to do at home and at work helping their parents in their own occupations.

That morning had dawned cool and misty, but Marjorie knew that the sun, once it was fully up, would burn the haze away and it would be a fine afternoon, perfect for sparring.

"Can we finish our jobs as soon as possible today," she asked Martha, her mother. "I'd like to go fishing later on, if it's nice."

Martha smiled. She was very close to her daughter, especially since Robin wasn't around much any more. "Of course, that sounds like a good idea. Let's get it all done and make the most of any sunshine – God knows we haven't had much of it lately. Here." She handed the girl an old basket. "Fetch some fresh rushes for the floor. Try and cut some sweet flowers too – they make the place smell nice."

Marjorie grabbed the basket and a knife from the table and hurried off.

It was still early but the men were already off ploughing the fields or mending the fences that penned in their livestock.

She waved cheerily to one of the neighbours, a pleasant old woman with small eyes that the children called Hogface, and shooed a barking dog that ran along after her for a time hoping for scraps.

She reached Ings Beck, breathlessly startling a kingfisher which took flight, then brought out the knife to collect the long green rushes that grew in abundance there.

The blade was fine and sharp and it didn't take her long to fill the basket. As she made her way back home she kept an eye out for wildflowers or herbs which she plucked and tossed into the basket.

Her favourite was lavender, and she knew where some grew not too far off, but she wanted to finish her chores so made do with the daisies and buttercups that were so readily available along the road. They might not have strong, sweet odours, but at least their colour would brighten the room.

Her mother had swept the dirty old rushes out by the time she returned so, together, they spread the fresh ones on the floor of the house, smiling contentedly at one another when they were done.

"Your da will be happy when he gets home," Martha nodded. "Now. Since it's going to be such a nice day, according to you, we should wash the bedding and towels so they get a chance to dry off in the sun. Come on."

Not long after midday the pair had finished the laundry, eaten a small meal of salted ham, bread and ale, and it was indeed fine and sunny.

"All right, you've been a good help this morning," Martha grinned. "Off you go and catch us some fish then. Be back in time that we can have it ready for dinner. I'll feed the chickens then sit outside and do some spinning."

When her mother went out the door Marjorie collected her fishing pole.

"I'll catch us a big one," she shouted, waving as she hurried off towards the fletcher's workshop.

Matilda was busy, surrounded by baskets of swan's feathers and wooden arrow shafts, but she gladly agreed to take a break for a time.

Recently, Marjorie had been working on her own with the wooden sword, just going through different moves that Matilda had shown her, both defensive and offensive. She'd also been trying to eat more and even managed to do a few exercises to strengthen her muscles every day. She wasn't able to run for long, but she had been sprinting over short distances and, although she had no way to be sure, she believed that her speed had improved.

As a result of all her hard work she really thought she had grown stronger not just physically, but mentally too. She felt *good* when she was exercising, which had come as a real surprise. Yes, it was hard, and her lungs would burn for a long time afterwards while her muscles ached from all the new stresses and strains, but somehow she felt happy when she was training.

She was still slimmer than almost any of the other village girls, but as they walked to the little shaded clearing where they practised together Matilda noticed a distinct change in the younger girl's carriage. She held herself erect, her chin up and her shoulders back, where before she'd had a hunched, downtrodden look about her. Matilda smiled, pleased at her charge's new-found swagger and made a mental note not to damage Marjorie's confidence by beating her too easily today.

They reached the clearing, glad no-one was around since they didn't really want people to know what they were doing. Their fellow villagers would probably laugh at them – women weren't supposed to be soldiers.

"All right, ready?"

Marjorie nodded and they did a few limbering up exercises to get their muscles warm before Matilda produced their practice swords from the bundle she'd brought from home. For now the swords were all they had to work with; Marjorie couldn't draw a hunting bow and, although she desperately wanted a crossbow she had no way of getting one. Her big brother would, no doubt, have brought her one if she'd asked him but, for now, she didn't want even Robin to know what she was doing. He loved her dearly, she knew that, but he'd not look kindly on the idea of her learning how to fight in case she got hurt. Besides, where would she hide such a weapon from her parents?

"Ha!" Matilda noticed her student apparently lost in thought and lunged forward, ready to rap the girl on the knuckles to teach her to stay alert, but, surprisingly, the blow whistled through empty air. Marjorie had seen her opponent's muscles tense, a tell-tale sign of imminent attack, and had danced back before the wooden sword could catch her.

Matilda found herself on the back-foot instantly, as Marjorie tried to turn defence into an attack of her own. Their swords met with a sharp crack and they held them there, teeth gritted, until the older girl's strength won out and Marjorie had to draw back, panting, and angry at her puny muscles.

"What's wrong?" Matilda asked, seeing the fury burning from her sister-in-law's eyes and thinking she'd done something to hurt the girl. "Are you alright?"

"No, I'm not, and I never will be, will I?"

The practice sword was thrown to the ground in disgust and Marjorie sank onto the grass beside it a moment later, her knees drawn up to her small chest. She looked like a child, despite her fifteen years and pity filled Matilda who began to move forward, to cuddle the girl, reassure her.

Then she stopped herself, pulled her hand back. Marjorie wanted to learn how to fight didn't she? Self-pity wasn't something that should be encouraged; it wasn't the way to engender a winning mentality in a soldier.

"Oh, poor you," Matilda spat, glaring down at the surprised girl. "Little Marjorie, the runt of the litter, never able to eat more than a morsel of bread and half a cup of beer. Always destined to be the weakest girl in Wakefield. What a shame for you."

Sarcasm dripped from her words and Marjorie's eyes flared, but still she didn't get back to her feet. "What would you know?" she started, but Matilda broke in, not allowing the girl to launch into a self-pitying monologue.

"What would I know? I know that you were a twin. Rebekah wasn't strong enough to survive the famine. But *you* were. God saw fit to spare you for some reason, and now, at the first hint of hardship you're ready to throw away your sword and just give in?" She could see that her mention of Rebekah had struck right to Marjorie's heart but before the girl could react, Matilda carried on. "You're good with the sword – you clearly have the skill for it running through your blood. Blood which you share with Robin Hood, the legendary archer and swordsman." She held up a hand to halt any objections. "Aye, I know you haven't been blessed with his shoulder muscles or the stamina that lets him run from one village to another without stopping, but so what? Should we all just give up because we're not as strong as someone else? Get up. Now!"

Matilda held out her hand imperiously and dragged Marjorie to her feet. The girl was still angry but her dressing down had left her cowed and ashamed at her petulant behaviour.

"Look at you. In the few weeks that we've been training your posture's improved, your appetite's growing and your skill with the sword gets more impressive every day. Not so long ago you wouldn't have spotted my first blow coming – you'd have been left with rapped knuckles and an angry curse on your lips." Matilda stepped in close and grasped her student by the shoulder. "Aye, it's harder for you because of what happened to you as an infant. But you have to face your body's limitations and either work with them or break them down." She released the girl and stepped back, sword raised. "So, what's it to be? Are you going to pick up your weapon and continue sparring, or are you going back to the village to live the rest of your life as a whining cur?"

For a second Matilda seriously feared she'd gone too far with her verbal assault and Marjorie would feel too humiliated to do anything other than walk away. But the girl had an inner strength and Matilda smiled in satisfaction as she grasped the fallen sword and climbed back to her feet to stare into her mentor's eyes.

"You're right," she admitted. "I can't give up now. But I'm going to make you pay for your words."

The young girl charged forward, launching a blistering attack and Matilda genuinely had to use all her skill and speed to defend herself. It didn't last very long, as the attacker's stamina again failed her and they separated, Marjorie breathing heavily and, as before, looking frustrated by her weakness. This time, though, she didn't throw away her sword, didn't thrust out a petulant lower lip, she just stood in a defensive stance, watching her opponent circling, prepared to fend off any thrust or swipe that might come her way.

They sparred for a while longer then Marjorie held up a hand, bending over to try and catch her breath.

"Enough!" she wheezed. "I promised my ma a fish for the table. You get back to your work; I'll try and get one for you too."

Matilda grinned, feeling like an important bridge had been crossed that day. Maybe Marjorie had the temperament to be a decent swordswoman after all.

CHAPTER SIX

"Quiet this morning," Robin yawned, rubbing sleep from his eyes with his fingers. "Where's Allan?"

The minstrel's voice was often the first thing the outlaws heard each day, as he went about getting ready for the day whistling a tune or singing, depending on how hungover he and the rest of the men were. Today though, there was silence around the camp, broken only by the back-and-forth tweeting of a pair of blackbirds hidden in the trees overhead.

"Dunno," Little John grunted, shoving a lump of bread into his mouth, crumbs already lacing his unkempt brown beard. "Must have gone off hunting or something. I haven't seen him."

"Gone off?" Robin helped himself to some of the ale from the barrel they'd broached the previous night and sat on one of the fallen logs next to John and a couple of the other early risers. "That's not like him."

The giant shrugged, but Will Scarlet had learned from bitter experience not to ignore Robin when he made an observation about one of their men acting out of character. He stood up and moved around the camp, counting heads.

"Gareth's not here either," he reported, returning to the rest of the men and grabbing some of the loaf John had almost devoured already. "Where d'you think they've gone without telling anyone?"

"Maybe they did tell someone," Stephen suggested. "You'll need to ask the rest when they wake up." He took a sip of his ale, not being overly fond of the brew this close to dawn. "You think something's up?"

Robin shook his head with a confidence he didn't really feel. "No, Allan's a big boy. I just don't like it when anyone leaves the camp without letting one of us know."

"Allan might be able to handle himself," Will growled. "But Gareth can't, and if he's been on the drink again he could stir up a lot of mischief we could do without."

Robin momentarily held his palms up in resignation. "We've no reason to think anything's amiss yet," he told them. "They've probably just gone off hunting as John says."

"Aye," the big man nodded. "Gareth might be a skinny wee bastard, but even he can set a rabbit trap well enough. Give it till lunchtime; they'll be back with something nice for Edmond's pot later on."

Robin smiled but he remembered the look on Allan's face when they'd talked the day before about the value of the silver arrow. He prayed the minstrel hadn't decided to try and win them all the pardons they craved...

* * *

"Why did you want to come anyway," Allan-a-Dale asked his companion, who shrugged and looked away evasively.

"I'm fed up with the forest, feel like seeing the big city for a change," Gareth replied, fingering the coin-purse he carried hidden under his gambeson.

"Hoping to find some of that grain drink you got from the barber in Penyston, eh?"

"Nah," the younger outlaw shook his head nonchalantly. "Can't handle that stuff, I'll stick to ale. At least I don't get cramps in my guts with ale." He grinned over at the minstrel but Allan saw through the protestations.

Gareth wasn't much of a travelling companion, and he wouldn't even be entering the tournament since he was too weak to draw a longbow or wield a sword very well, but Allan hadn't wanted to head into Nottingham by himself so he was glad when Gareth had offered to come along to keep him company.

"What d'you think Robin'll do when he finds out where we've gone?"

Allan had wondered that himself, but he wasn't sure of the answer. "Either he'll go crazy that we've not followed his orders to stay in the camp, or he'll accept that we're all our own men and can do what we want."

Gareth didn't reply as they hurried along the road towards Nottingham.

"He'll cheer up when he sees the silver arrow I've won, though. Then we can sell it and win pardons for us all!"

The two men grinned at that. It wasn't such a fanciful idea – Allan was an excellent shot, his skills honed to a fine point by the hours of practice Robin insisted the fighters in the group performed each week. He had a very good chance of winning, should they be allowed to enter the competition without anyone realising they were wolf's heads. That didn't seem too big of a threat: neither had been to Nottingham any time recently so the guards wouldn't recognise them and both were unremarkable looking so they could lose themselves in the crowds.

Gareth might have wanted to head into the city to look for strong alcohol, but Allan was looking forward to performing in front of a crowd again. It had been nearly two years since he and Robin had entertained Lord John de Bray's guests in the great hall of Hathersage manor house. He missed the excitement, the nervous tension, that feeling of uncertainty that even the most experienced of minstrels felt when they put themselves in front of an audience. Shooting in the archery competition, before what would surely be a huge gathering of locals, would be much like playing the gittern for a hall full of rowdy nobles.

He smiled and revelled in the warm spring breeze as they walked.

This was going to be fun.

* * *

Tuck had ridden at a leisurely pace when he left the outlaw's camp, not being in any great hurry to return to Lewes like the prodigal son the prior had never expected to see again...

The friar was no fool. He knew de Monte Martini wouldn't look kindly on him when he showed his face there again. Not only had he 'lost' the prior's priceless artefact years earlier, but he'd then allowed outlaws to steal his superior's cart full of money and, to add insult to injury, Tuck had *joined* the outlaw gang who had gone on to further humiliate de Monte Martini when he and the Sheriff of Nottingham had tried to capture them.

The kindly clergyman grinned. Ah, but it had felt good to get one over on the nasty prior, it truly had. The smile fell from his fleshy lips, though, as he contemplated the welcome de Monte Martini would have for him when he appeared unexpectedly in Lewes. The fact that he was returning the lost relic – something the prior had paid an obscene amount of money for – would, he hoped, mollify the senior churchman and allow him to stay with the Benedictines at least until the Church found some other place for him, within his own order perhaps.

At the very least, Tuck hoped he'd *survive* the reunion.

"Hey, priest! Get off the fucking horse, now."

The harsh voice jolted Tuck back in his saddle and his hand strayed instinctively to the heavy cudgel he habitually carried within the folds of his grey cassock.

He pulled gently on the palfrey's reins, bringing it to a halt, his eyes scanning the area as he calmly assessed the situation. He'd gone along with Robin and the others often enough on robberies just like this to have a good idea of how things worked, so he knew urging his mount into a gallop would probably result in an arrow in the back.

He remained in the saddle, waiting for the would-be thieves to show themselves. Moments later, three men appeared from the thick foliage on either side of the road, while at least one other man coughed from behind him, letting the friar know he was covered on all sides.

"I told you to get off the fucking horse!" the man in the middle of the trio on the road ahead spat. He was a small man, bearded and dirty looking, with a slight build while the two that flanked him were much larger. Tuck had met men like this outlaw before – the maniacal gleam

54

in his dark eyes suggested what he lacked in physical stature was made up for in violent lunacy.

Although his comrades were much bigger, they deferred to the little dark man. Tuck knew he had to be very careful if he didn't want to lose the coin-purse he carried inside his habit. Or his life. He dismounted, making a show of his clumsiness and clutching his back as if he was in great pain from riding.

"What can I do for you, my son?" he asked, smiling deferentially at the little man. "A blessing? Do you seek –"

"Enough, priest," the robber growled, sidling over and standing to look up at the palfrey whose ears were back as it sensed something was wrong. "We need no blessings in Sherwood. What we need is silver and gold. And food. And judging by the belly you're carrying around on you, you've got enough of everything to share with me and my companions here." He raised the sword he carried, unusually, in his left hand, brandishing it menacingly, and Tuck noticed the man was missing more than one finger from his right hand. Punishment for being caught stealing before perhaps, although that method of justice had – mostly – been done away with years earlier.

Dangerous, but hopefully stupid.

The friar looked back across his shoulder to see a tall young man holding a longbow with an arrow already nocked. His hands were steady, but the expression on his face was one of distaste. Not at the clergyman, no... the big man's eyes flicked to his leader for a moment and Tuck knew the youngster wasn't happy to be here doing this.

"Aye, he's got you covered, old man," the robber leader grinned, showing a mouthful of surprisingly complete teeth. "And the rest of us'll split you wide open – priest or not – if you don't hand over what you've got. Including that nice horse."

There was little point denying he was carrying money, Tuck thought. The robbers would know he'd need coin to pay for food and board as he travelled.

"Will you let me be on my way if I give you what I have?" he asked in a trembling voice, moving towards the small man and fumbling in his cassock. As he reached the robber, he smiled, remembering a similar scene a couple of years earlier when he'd first met Robin and the men.

"Here you go, have the lot!"

The two robbers further back on the road stood in stunned silence for a moment as their leader collapsed in front of them. Tuck had whipped the cudgel concealed in his robes up and into the jaw of the robber, then, as the man stumbled backwards, the friar brought it around in a tight arc into the side of the man's neck, sending him flying across the road, senseless.

Before anyone could react, Tuck turned and jumped forward, ramming the cudgel into the man on the left's face, feeling teeth crunch as his target reeled back and landed on his backside with a furious howl of pain.

By now it was obvious this was no normal priest and the final swordsman struck out with the battered old blade he carried, a killing blow aimed right at the clergyman's neck.

Tuck had been fast when he was young, but now... he twisted sideways, lashing out with his own weapon which hit the back of his opponent's skull with a shocking crack, sending the robber crashing to the hard earth of the road. The friar let out a breath of relief as he realised his flesh was unbroken – the oaf's blade had only slightly torn his cassock.

He made sure the three downed robbers were incapacitated then glanced back to the bowman and was relieved to see the youngster staring at the scene before him, mouth open in surprise, bowstring not even drawn taut. Still with one eye on the archer, Tuck moved over to the man with the wounded mouth and kicked out at the side of his head, hard enough to send the man reeling.

"What's your name, son?"

The young man watched the friar return to his horse and pull himself back into the saddle, longbow still held low at his side.

"James."

"And where are you from?"

"Horbury."

Tuck shook his head with a frown.

"I can tell just from looking into your eyes that you're not like these men. You don't have the violence burning inside you that they do, especially the little one." He glanced at the unconscious robber leader and crossed himself before turning his gaze back to the young archer. "He's got the devil inside him, that one. You'd do well to get away from him now, before he leads you into trouble you can't escape."

James removed the nocked arrow from his bowstring and stuck it back into his belt with a grunt of agreement.

Tuck nodded in appreciation.

"The Lord's blessing on you for not shooting me. Perhaps one day I'll be able to repay your mercy." The friar grasped the pommel of his horse's saddle, placed his right foot into the stirrup and, with a grunt, hauled himself ungracefully onto the palfrey which danced nervously beneath him. "Take yourself home to Horbury. Stop robbing people with these men but, if ever the law are after you and you have nowhere to turn – seek out Robin Hood. Tell him Friar Tuck sent you."

James's eyes widened. "I knew you weren't just some fat clergyman."

"That's where you're wrong," Tuck replied with a smile, kicking his heels into the horse which trotted back towards the road. "I'm on my way back to Lewes exactly because I *am* just a fat clergyman."

CHAPTER SEVEN

Allan and Gareth were nervous as they approached the Carter Gate into Nottingham. They'd met some other travellers on the road – a bald little merchant who rode a fine-looking horse, with his two bodyguards – and joined their party. Now they all stood in the short yet slow-moving queue waiting to enter the city. The guards were checking everyone who sought entry and the outlaws could both feel the sweat trickling down from their armpits despite the chill afternoon air.

"You lot, move up!"

The merchant took the lead, smiling at the gatekeepers as he submitted to a perfunctory search for concealed swords; citizens as well as visitors being banned from carrying them during this period. Gareth and Allan only had daggers with them, which they were allowed to keep, but the merchants two bodyguards were made to hand over their long-swords, for safe-keeping until they left the city. There was much cursing and huffing at this which Allan understood. Although the blades the mercenaries wielded were poor quality they marked them as men of a certain class and a soldier felt as good as bollock naked without his sword.

"What you all here for?" one of the guardsmen asked, his voice betraying the boredom he felt at this repetitive task.

"These men are my bodyguards," the little merchant replied in a surprisingly powerful voice, waving a hand at his henchmen. "I'm selling fine gemstones. Here, take a look" –

The guard waved the merchant away with a scowl as the man opened his coat to display his wares.

"What about you two?"

"I'm here to enter the tourney." Allan brandished his longbow to illustrate his point. "That silver arrow the sheriff's offering as a prize is as good as mine." He winked at the guardsman confidently. "Seriously, mate, get your money on me."

"Aye, I'll be sure and do that," the guard nodded with a disinterested frown. "I'm sure you'll be able to beat that French archer that's been practising in the town centre for the past week." He glared at Gareth, taking in the young man's skinny arms and red-rimmed eyes. "What about you, boy? You ain't here for the silver arrow are you? You don't have the shoulders of your mate here. You don't look strong enough to peel the hose off one of the whores at the Maidenshead, never mind shoot a longbow."

The merchant roared with laughter at the guard's simple joke while his bodyguards grinned at the outlaw, daring him to make a smart reply to the old guard.

"I'm just here to watch the tourney," Gareth grunted, his face flushing scarlet in embarrassment. His lack of stature made him feel inadequate every day, especially living with a gang of outlaws who were, to a man, built like the trees they used to conceal their camp-sites. "So you can fuck off," he added angrily, but under his breath so the guard wouldn't hear.

"Wait! That one – hold him there. I know him."

A voice carried to them from the tower doorway behind the guards and Allan shared a worried glance with Gareth. The merchant surreptitiously inched away from them as another blue-liveried guard pushed past his fellows and stared at Allan.

"I know you."

* * *

Matilda wiped her brow and reached for the cup of fresh water her mother had brought her a short time ago. Her young student, Marjorie, had visited earlier on, asking if they could go hunting again but Matilda was too busy. Her father had been commissioned by a wealthy merchant in Sheffield to make a large batch of arrows. Not just any arrows though – these were to be the finest: birch fletched with eagle feathers.

59

Henry had managed to procure some, but eagles weren't common so he'd told Matilda to use sparrowhawk and peregrine falcon feathers as well. The merchant would just have to make do.

The young woman had helped her mother tidy the house in the morning and now sat outside in the sun, sorting the feathers into piles – left wing or right. Little Arthur was playing with some discarded, poor-quality feathers and he'd occasionally sing to himself or shout random noises which brought a big smile to Matilda's face. The boy's sweet voice certainly made chores more enjoyable.

Once she'd separated a batch of the feathers she shaped them then glued and bound them onto poplar shafts her father had already prepared. It was simple enough work but required nimble fingers and concentration. Thankfully her infant son was well-behaved and only rarely tried to wander off when he thought his ma wasn't watching.

This was her usual day, although, normally, she'd be using goose feathers and working much faster. Every now and again, though, her father would pick up an order from some nobleman who wanted fancy feathers or exotic woods for his shafts and production would slow. Her fingers ached after a day's work, even now when she'd been doing it for years, but it brought a decent wage and could be done inside in the winter months.

It wasn't a bad way to make a coin, not at all. Especially in this fine weather. Still...

She would have liked to go hunting with Marjorie, even just for a short time to break up the monotony of her work, but the merchant had ordered a large number of arrows and they had to be completed quickly or he'd pay them less.

It would do the younger girl good to catch a few hares on her own anyway. Assuming foresters didn't catch her again...

"Get down from there, right now!"

Arthur turned round guiltily, halfway up the stone wall that separated the Fletcher's from the field next to them.

"Now!"

The little boy slowly dropped back to the ground and ran to her, laughing, and she couldn't help joining in even though she knew she should scold him and beat him like all the other young mothers in the village did with their children.

She put down the shaft she was working on and stood to scoop up her squealing son, spinning him round and hooting herself before dropping onto the grass, gasping.

"Never caught anything. Not one bloody hare."

Marjorie walked into the garden and slumped onto the stool Matilda had just vacated.

"Off you go, little boy," Matilda grinned, kissing Arthur on the cheek and shooing him off towards the house. "Go and play with the wooden soldiers daddy brought you from the market in Barnsley. No more climbing or I'll smack your arse."

She watched him toddle off, then sat down on the ground next to Marjorie, lifting her unfinished shaft and starting work on it again.

"I set those snares days ago. Should have caught *something* by now."

"Maybe the hares are too smart for us now," Matilda shrugged. "I wouldn't worry about it."

"No, you wouldn't worry about it, because you always catch something." Marjorie growled, staring at her sister-in-law as if it was her fault she hadn't been able to catch anything for her family's dinner pot. She sighed, again.

Matilda could see Arthur inside the house, trying to climb the ladder that led to her parent's bed and, exasperated, she jumped to her feet. "Get down from there, right now," she shouted, flailing her hand angrily. "Down. Now!" She suddenly rounded on Marjorie.

"Look, you're no good at hunting. Tough. I'm trying to work here, while making sure my son doesn't break his

61

neck at the same time. Why don't you go and make yourself useful instead of trying to be your brother?"

She regretted her angry words instantly, as tears welled up in Marjorie's eyes and the girl stood, knocking the stool onto the floor, before running off without a word. There was no time to chase her though.

"Arthur, get *down* from there right now!"

* * *

"Everything all right?" the gate guard demanded, glaring at the newcomer. "We've got a queue a mile long here, Thomas."

"Just trying to remember where I've seen this man. Let the others move on."

The merchant waved them farewell, a look of relief plain on his face as the queue began to move into the city again. From the corner of his eye, Allan could see Gareth's head swivel as if searching for the fastest escape route and a cold bead of sweat dripped slowly down his back, making him shiver.

Allan's clasped his hands, preparing to grab the dagger he carried hidden in his belt. They would not escape when the guard realised who he was; the crowd was too thick and the guards too many. The burly archer wouldn't go down without a fight, though.

At last the guard's eyes flared in recognition and he grabbed his older companion's arm roughly.

"I remember now! He's a minstrel. You played for us in Hathersage – Lord de Bray's manor house."

Allan's face creased in a huge grin and he moved his hand away from the hidden blade to pat his gittern case, relief flooding through him.

Thomas smiled at the other guard who looked irritated rather than impressed as he continued checking any visitors who looked like they might be coming into his city to cause trouble.

"Him and his mate – they looked like soldiers but played and sang like minstrels. It was a fine night." He

62

glanced at Gareth then looked back at Allan. "After Lord de Bray was ruined I left to take up a job here in Nottingham. Strange business it was..." His voice trailed off as he remembered his former employer's downfall which had, unbeknown to Thomas, been brought about by Robin Hood and his men. "Anyway," he went on, face brightening again. "What brings you here? You and your little mate going to play music for Sir Henry?"

"Nah, I'm here to enter the tourney. I'm almost as good with the longbow as I am with the gittern. The sheriff might as well give me that silver arrow right now."

Thomas grinned then looked back over his shoulder at the guardhouse. "Well, good luck, lad. It was good seeing you again. I better get back to my post or the sergeant will kick my arse." He clapped Allan on the arm then turned away. "If you're bored and looking to earn an extra coin or two, make your way to the Cotter's Rest. That's where most of us guards go for a drink when our shifts are done. The landlord, Fat Robert, will put you up in return for a few songs. Farewell!"

At last the old gate-guard gestured impatiently for them to move on through the gates and Allan blew a long breath of relief as they left the gatehouse behind.

"My lord," a young lad of no more than fourteen years grinned at them from behind a stall stacked with oatcakes and loaves. "Freshly baked. Finest in the city, I swear it."

Allan produced a coin and tossed it to the boy, lifting a couple of the oatcakes from the display and handing one to Gareth as he bit into his own, crumbs spilling down his gambeson.

"We need a place to stay," the minstrel mumbled, eyeing the savoury snack in appreciation. "Somewhere far away from the Cotter's Rest."

The boy nodded and winked knowingly. "Want to avoid the law eh? I don't blame you – when they've had a skinful they cause more trouble than anyone." He pointed to the east side of the city and gave them directions to The

63

Ship – an establishment he assured them was one of the best in the whole city.

Allan handed him another coin in thanks and the outlaws moved off into the crowd again.

They'd taken some money from their own funds back at the camp-site; not enough to draw attention to themselves should guards like the ones at the gate take an interest in them, but enough to pay for food, ale and lodging for a while. Maybe enough even for a visit to the fabled Maidenshead – Prior John De Monte Martini's own establishment – or one of the other brothels in the city, Allan mused, grinning to himself at the ease of their passage into Nottingham.

They moved from one inn to another, checking the quality of the accommodation and sampling the ale in each one. Although they were, to all intents and purposes, simple peasants – yeomen at best – they were rich men by the standards of most of Nottingham's populace, thanks to the success they'd enjoyed as part of Robin Hood's gang. Although they couldn't flaunt their wealth without drawing unwelcome attention to themselves in the potentially hostile city, they *could* afford to pay for some half-decent lodgings for the few days they expected to spend there.

"I like this place," Gareth smiled, his bony fingers curled around a wooden cup of cheap wine when they eventually reached The Ship and found a table to share. It was a pleasant enough place, with fresh rushes on the floor and a newly painted sign above the door which suggested the landlord took pride in his establishment.

Allan eyed his young companion sceptically. "You mean you like the drink they're serving up."

Gareth was past caring whether Allan knew about his taste for strong drink or not. "Aye, I do," he nodded, "it's not the barber's grain drink, but it's better than that piss-water you all drink. Ale. Pfft. This stuff," he held his cup aloft with a crooked smile, "is all right."

Allan paid the inn-keep the three shillings he demanded for a few nights room and board the next time the man passed their table, wondering if he'd made a wise decision coming here with Gareth. None of the other outlaws had shown any interest in taking part in the tourney, which had surprised the minstrel who knew better than anyone how good they were with longbows, long-swords or quarterstaffs. He'd expected some of them would want to test themselves against the best men the Sheriff's tournament would attract, but no... they were all content to sit around that God-forsaken forest, day after day, eating rabbit stew and talking about a time when they'd be free men again.

Well, Allan mused, Robin was right. Once he had the silver arrow he'd be able to sell it and bribe some powerful nobleman to grant them all pardons.

"More wine," Gareth demanded with a grin as he gazed at the buxom serving wench who came to clear their empty cups. "Bring me more, my beauty."

The girl looked amused as she carried the empties away and Allan sighed. Maybe it would have been better to be lonely than bringing this young sot along after all.

It'd be an early night for them both tonight, even if he had to drag Gareth away from the bar by his hair.

* * *

In the morning Allan asked the inn-keeper if he knew anything about the upcoming tournament.

"Aye," the red-faced man replied, nodding. "They seek to sort the wheat from the chaff. Anyone that wants to enter an event has to go to the castle to prove their skill in qualifying heats. What're you doing?" He took in Allan's wide shoulders and nodded. "Archery, eh?"

"Aye," the minstrel replied. "I'm not bad with a blade as well, but I don't think I could match the best in the shire. Shooting a longbow though..."

"A match for Robin Hood himself, eh?" the inn-keep smirked, one eyebrow raised almost mockingly. He'd heard these tales before countless times, and learned to take them all with a healthy pinch of salt.

Allan was just glad Gareth, who stood at his side, hadn't been drinking yet that morning. No doubt the youngster, if he'd been inebriated, would have told the barman all about their friend Robin.

"Aye," the minstrel returned the man's condescending smile. "I'd say I can match the famous wolf's head. But he won't be entering this tournament will he? Not if he's got any sense – the law would be all over him. So I reckon I've as good a chance as any of winning the silver arrow."

"Sure you have," the man shrugged in boredom. "If you want to enter, you'd better get yourself to the castle. If you're as good as you think you are, they'll let you enter the tournament." He moved away to continue cleaning up the worst of the mess from the previous evening's revelry, leaving his two guests to their conversation.

Gareth had decided to stay at the inn, rather than going to the qualifying heats. "All those soldiers? Someone might recognise me," he said. "Besides, I'm shit with a bow, I'll just get in the way. I'll hang around the inn. Might even take a walk about the town."

"Someone might recognise you," Allan growled sarcastically, fixing the younger man with a stern look.

"I'll keep my head down," Gareth replied, pulling the hood on his cloak up over his head to show how well he could hide in its dark shadows.

Allan moved to stand right in front of his companion and gazed at him. "I'm not joking," he said. "Don't sit around here drinking all day, mouthing off to anyone that'll listen. You'll get us both in trouble, and if you say enough, you'll bring hell down on Robin, Will, John and all the rest of our friends."

Gareth shook his head angrily. "I won't even be drinking," he muttered.

"I'll be back soon enough. There's no doubt I'll qualify for the tourney. After that I'll head straight back here. We can get a drink then, all right?" Allan patted the youngster on the arm reassuringly. "And don't go showing off your coin either, unless you want some thief to take it from you."

Lifting his longbow and checking the little pack he carried on his belt to make sure the hemp string was safely inside, Allan gave a last nod to Gareth and left The Ship to make his way to the qualifying rounds at Nottingham Castle.

* * *

Sure enough, Allan qualified for the archery section of the sheriff's tournament without any problems.

Getting into the castle was easy enough, although the guards did look closely at every entrant's face before granting them access to the courtyard where the heats were being held. The minstrel knew Robin would have been recognised immediately by the guards under such scrutiny – his description would have been well known to the soldiers and a fat purse would be the reward for any who spotted the notorious outlaw so despised by Sir Guy of Gisbourne.

Allan, on the other hand, was known to few of the lawmen although, in his younger days he had performed as a minstrel in many places and secretly hoped someone or other would shout, "You! You're that fine gittern player," just as the gate-guard had done.

It would certainly be preferable to being recognised for the outlaw that he was, but no-one gave him a second glance as he made his way to take part in the qualifying rounds.

The castle was, of course, home to a variety of equipment used in the training of soldiers, and it was all seeing action that morning as Allan walked to the big targets that would separate the skilled archers from the talentless.

The wolf's head was surprised at the number of entrants; the courtyard was full of them, all hoping to win the magnificent silver arrow that the sheriff had, perhaps foolishly, placed on display atop the battlements so the competitors could all see what they were striving for.

"Christ, that thing looks heavy," the middle-aged man in line next to Allan muttered, glancing at the minstrel with wide-eyes. "We'd never have to work another day in our lives if we won that."

Allan smiled. In all honesty, he was already a fairly rich man, as were all the members of Robin Hood's gang. The gold and silver coin they'd taken from the obscenely wealthy nobles and clergymen travelling through Yorkshire over the past couple of years had made them all financially secure. Set for life, they were.

It was just unfortunate they were all outlaws so could never enjoy the fruits such wealth might bring.

That arrow, though... It must have been worth a fortune, Allan guessed. Truly, such an amount of silver... It could be melted down or small slivers could be shaved off to barter with and there'd be enough to truly set a man up for life – even an outlaw like him. He could make his way to France, bribing lawmen and officials along the way to allow him safe passage. Then he'd build a house somewhere in Normandy or Brittany, buy the fanciest gittern he could find, and settle down to a life of wine, women and song, safely away from Gisbourne or the sheriff or anyone else. He'd have to learn to speak their language but...

"You lot! Move up!"

The sergeant's bellowed command startled Allan from his pleasant reverie and he moved forward with about twenty other entrants to take aim at the big targets lined up in front of them.

"Good luck!"

Allan grinned at the man next to him as they fitted their bowstrings, pulled arrows from their belts and took aim, ready for the burly sergeant's order to shoot, which seemed to take forever as the soldier peered along the line of bowmen, looking for any sign of obvious weakness in their stance. Finally, he stepped back, satisfied and roared, his shout reverberating off the great stone walls.

"Loose!"

Three times the archers shot, before the sergeant checked the targets and then informed them who'd qualified and who hadn't.

Allan knew this exercise was merely to weed out those who were truly unskilled, so he made sure to hit the centre of the target with only two of his shots, although he surely could have managed all three, as the distance to it was quite short and the target itself rather large.

Still, a few of the men in his qualifying group failed to hit the centre even once, and one competitor failed to strike the big round board at all, his missiles clattering harmlessly into the wall behind the target pitifully and sending some of the idly spectating guardsmen running, with angry curses spilling from their mouths.

"The next heat will be in two days!" The sergeant shouted, addressing Allan and the rest of the men who had successfully qualified. The man pointed at another soldier seated at a table close-by. "Collect a token from the clerk there, and make sure you bring it when you return or you won't be granted entry. Now get out of the fucking way, so the next lot can take their turn."

Thirteen remained from the original group of twenty and, as they all cheerfully made their way to collect their qualifying tokens Allan could see no threat from any of them. None had performed spectacularly, although one man did manage to hit the red circle in the centre of the target with each of his three shots. He was an older man though, and his arms would surely weaken and give out during the tournament itself. No, Allan didn't think any of the men from his qualifying group posed a threat to him.

Then again, some of them might be hiding their true ability just as he was...

Grinning, he collected the wooden token that would grant him entry back into the castle in two days and, with a cheery wave to the next row of nervous qualifiers, made his way out the castle and through the bustling streets to The Ship, hoping he wouldn't find Gareth in his cups telling the entire common room about his adventures with Robin Hood and Little John.

He heaved a small sigh of relief when he made it back to his room in the inn and found Gareth there, mending some of his clothes with a bone needle and some thread. His face was a little flushed, suggesting that he'd spent a few coins on wine that afternoon but he was by no means drunk.

"How did you get on?" the young man asked, eyes lighting up as his companion strode into their sparsely furnished room. "Did you beat everyone?"

Allan shook his head and slumped onto the flea-ridden bed, stretching out happily. "Nah, I got through to the next round, but if I'd been too good it might have drawn attention to me. I only want to do enough to get through the qualifiers and into the tournament itself. Then I'll show them what a lowly wolf's head can do."

Gareth jumped up and pulled on his worn old leather boots. "Come on, don't go to sleep, it's still early. I've been on my own all day, I'm bored. Let's go and get that drink you talked about this morning, and some of the inn-keep's food that I can smell cooking up."

There *was* a very meaty aroma wafting through the inn, Allan had to admit, and his stomach rumbled loudly as if in response to Gareth's request.

"Alright, let's go," he agreed, standing up and straightening his brown jacket. "But no mentioning Robin."

Their night was a pleasant one, and Gareth behaved himself well enough. The inn-keeper brought them bowls of beef stew with spring vegetables which was excellent if a little short on meat. Then they had a few ales, listened to some of the locals singing and eventually retired to their room.

Robin had been worried about nothing, Allan thought. Even if he didn't win the tournament, and the silver arrow, this was going to be an enjoyable few days. Who could possibly recognise him or Gareth in a city full of strange faces?

CHAPTER EIGHT

The next round of qualifying in the castle courtyard was a little harder than the first one, with the very worst of the entrants now gone and only those competent with the longbow left. Some of them were very good, Allan noted, as he stood waiting to take his own turn, watching the other competitors firing arrow after arrow into the worse-for-wear targets which hadn't been replaced or repaired in the past few days.

Three times Allan and his group shot, with three arrows each time, and the scores were tallied by the same sergeant that decided who progressed on the outlaw's earlier visit to the castle.

Allan made sure to hit the red-painted centre section on six of his nine shots. The other three he aimed close but hit just outside the middle. It was enough to see him through to the tournament itself, without drawing any unwanted attention from the guards or, indeed, the other competitors.

He enjoyed the afternoon's shooting, relishing the chance to stretch his great shoulder muscles, and he made mental notes of the best of the other archers, so he'd know who to watch out for when the tourney started for real in a few days.

Then he strolled back to The Ship with a swagger, pleased with how things were going and catching the eye of a group of young girls who were washing clothes on the banks of the River Leen. Their giggles and whispers as they watched him pass made him smile – he hadn't enjoyed female attention like that in such a long time.

Exiled to the greenwood as he was, living with only hard, hairy-arsed men for company, could be a lonely existence at times and he vowed to pass along this road again tomorrow, only next time he'd stop to drink from the well. Maybe even strike up a conversation with one or two of the pretty girls...

His thoughts came back to reality as he reached The Ship and remembered Gareth.

Again, he prayed the young man wasn't drunk but, as before he needn't have worried. Gareth was in the common room of the inn, and he had a mug of wine before him, but he was sitting alone quietly, observing a couple of the locals singing for the rest of the patrons.

"You made it through?" the skinny youngster demanded when he caught sight of his broad-shouldered mate coming towards him.

"Of course!" Allan grinned, gesturing to the serving girl to bring him an ale and settling his bulk into the wooden chair to watch the singers. "No problem. I'm in the tournament for real." He handed over a small coin, nodding his thanks before taking a long pull of the freshly brewed ale. "And I'm sure I've got a good chance." He wiped froth from his upper lip absent-mindedly, engrossed in the surprisingly good rendition of "Man in the Moon" that the two locals were belting out.

It was a song that brought back fond memories for Allan, who had performed that very tune with Robin a couple of years ago when they'd passed themselves off as travelling minstrels to gain access to a rich nobleman's house. They'd impressed Lord John de Bray's guests that night, before rescuing Will Scarlet's daughter Beth from a life of slavery the next morning.

The minstrel lifted his mug to his lips and drained the lot in one go, the glow from the alcohol and the happy memories spreading throughout his body almost instantly and he grinned to the serving girl, waving his empty mug for a refill.

As the singers finished their song Allan turned and fixed Gareth with a stony glare. "I feel like having a few ales here tonight to celebrate getting into the tourney but I'm warning you – keep silent about who we are, where we came from and who we know. You understand?"

Gareth gave a sullen nod and fiddled with his mug like a naughty child.

"I mean it, lad," Allan continued. "We can have a good time here this evening, but if you so much as mention Robin I'll fucking knock you out. Your tongue loosens when you've had a few drinks and it could get us all killed so..."

"Alright!" the younger outlaw shouted, slamming his mug onto the table angrily. "I'm not an idiot." He met Allan's eyes but continued in a much quieter voice as people turned to see what the commotion was about. "I won't say a word about anything. Alright?"

The minstrel felt guilty for upsetting his companion. "Good lad," he smiled, gripping Gareth's wrist. "Get yourself another cup of wine, then, and we'll order some food. Tonight we celebrate!"

* * *

Afternoon gave way to evening and The Ship began to fill up as Gareth and Allan enjoyed the drinks, the food and the banter. The minstrel watched his younger friend like a hawk in case Gareth mentioned Robin or the fact they were outlaws but the evening went smoothly and, as darkness drew in outside, the inn-keeper banked the fire in the old stone hearth and the low-ceilinged room was filled with light, laughter and music.

As they joined in with the rest of the inn's patrons on yet another sing-along Gareth shouted into his friend's ear.

"You brought your gittern, didn't you? Go and get it. We'll give this lot a tune to remember!"

Allan shook his head. "We can't draw attention to ourselves," he shouted back, cupping his hands against Gareth's ear to be heard over the raucous singing.

The wine and ale flowed as time wore on and the two outlaws had the best time they'd had in months. Their bellies were full of the inn-keeper's tasty stew, they had plenty of alcohol to drink and the locals had welcomed them warmly into their company. There were even some good-looking older ladies throwing them suggestive glances.

They were having so much fun, and the drink was flowing freely. Too freely. As always, tongues were loosened...

"Aye, I'm Robin Hood's right-hand man. We're like brothers!"

The woman fluttered her eye-lashes and smiled at the story, not really taking it in. The singing was loud and the man beside her was too drunk to be believed, but he had a purse full of coin and she planned on making the most of it tonight.

"I'm telling you," he went on, seeing the blank look on her face. "We've had lots of adventures. I'm only here in the city for this tournament. Keep it to yourself, but..." He leaned in close and tried to whisper in her ear, although in his inebriated state it came out as a bellow. "I'm an outlaw!"

Thankfully the music drowned out the confession. His companion heard him though.

"What are you doing? You'll get us both jailed!"

Allan shook his head with a snort. "Shut up, Gareth," he slurred. "No one's listening. Why don't you go an' get my gittern from our room?" The big outlaw stood up, a broad, drunken smile on his face. "I'll show these people how a true minstrel performs."

"Fucking sit down!" Gareth grabbed Allan's arm and hauled him back into his seat, looking around nervously to see if anyone had heard the confession.

Reality hit the minstrel, even through the alcoholic haze, and he grinned sheepishly, lifting his mug ostensibly to take another drink but in reality to try and hide from what he'd just done.

He looked blearily around the room but all he could see were happy revellers enjoying the singing. The ladies that had been sitting beside them shared irritated glances and wandered off into the crowd to try and find some other, less inebriated, drinkers to take advantage of.

"Ah, fuck 'em," Allan waved a hand after them, staring at Gareth who shook his head in return.

"You've got a cheek talking about me," the younger man hissed. "You're the one that's going to get us into trouble with your shouting about Robin Hood."

No one was taking the slightest bit of notice of them as far as Allan could tell. He shrugged, smirking like a naughty boy and drained the last of the ale in his mug.

"I'll get us another," he mumbled, fumbling in his pouch for coins.

"No you bloody won't," Gareth retorted. "You've had plenty. Just sit there and watch the singers until I finish my wine. Then we're going back to the room so you can sleep it off." He shook his head again in irritation. "And you were worried about *me* acting like an arsehole..."

* * *

Friar Tuck smiled at the bald old Benedictine monk that opened the large wooden door to the priory. "God be with you, brother."

The man's rheumy eyes glared at him for a moment, taking in Tuck's grey cassock that marked him as a member of the Franciscans.

"What d'you want?"

Tuck laughed; a genuine, happy sound, filled with affection and pleasure to be in a familiar place with a familiar face. "It's me, you old sod. Robert!"

He gave his real name, Tuck being merely a nickname shared by many friars on account of the way they sometimes wore their cassocks, with the material tucked between their legs for freedom of movement.

The gate-keeper narrowed his eyes in confusion, leaning out of the doorway to gaze at the man before him. "Robert? Is it you, truly? I remember you having a lot more meat on your bones."

The door was hauled open by a second, much younger Benedictine, and Tuck moved forward to grasp the older fellow's arms. "It's me right enough, Edwin," he grinned. "I lost some weight recently – nearly died, in truth – but the good Lord saw fit to return me to life, and to you too now." He nodded towards the second, younger monk, who returned the gesture.

"Well met, Osferth."

Finally, the old gatekeeper smiled and squeezed Tuck's arms happily. "It is you! Oh, Robert, it's good to see you again, the place has been quiet without you around. Come in, come in!"

They moved inside and Osferth shoved the heavy door closed, drawing the great iron bolt into place. They were safe enough these days, but old tales of marauding Vikings had left their mark on many clergymen who were happy to make themselves as secure as possible behind their thick stone walls and stout doors.

"I'll leave you to it," the younger monk said as he turned and made his way along the corridor. "I have chores to do."

"It's good to see you, Robert," the old man repeated, paying no heed to the departing Osferth. "But... why have you returned?"

Tuck shook his head. "I know the prior –"

"You *don't* know," Edwin interjected. "The man hates you. In the name of Christ, Robert, he'll have your balls for dinner when he sees you've returned. What possessed you to come back here? His hatred for you has barely dulled in the time you've been gone."

Tuck nodded and clasped his hands within the folds of his voluminous grey cassock. "I have my reasons," he replied. "Hopefully what I bring to the prior will go some way to restoring me in his favour."

Edwin snorted, an incredulous look on his face. "I'll give you one last chance, Robert. The brothers here all miss you, as do I, even if you're not one of us. But I'd rather you left than suffer de Monte Martini's wrath. Go now – back to your outlaw friends – and I'll not tell a soul you were here." He grasped Tuck by the forearm and stared into his eyes earnestly. "Go, my friend."

Tuck had expected Prior de Monte Martini to hate him after everything that had happened. De Monte Martini was a vindictive, petty man who liked to throw his weight around at the best of times but Tuck had done much to earn the man's hatred, even if he didn't deserve it. He had done his best to protect the prior's belongings – it hadn't been his fault they'd been stolen. Twice...

He smiled, trying to appear more confident than he felt.

"It'll be fine, Edwin. Prior de Monte Martini will be glad to see me, trust me."

The gatekeeper shook his head sadly, a heavy sigh escaping from his thin old lips. "If you say so, old friend, if you say so. Let me take you to him then."

He turned and hobbled off along the chilly corridor which seemed to press in on Tuck who had become so used to the open spaces and bright, natural beauty of Barnsdale Forest.

They passed one or two of the brethren who looked across in astonishment as they went by, and the prior's bottler, Ralph, who gaped open-mouthed then hurried back down to his cellar, before Edwin stopped in front of another great door made of dark, varnished oak and gave Tuck a final look.

"If you're sure about this, Robert, I'll tell the prior you've returned." He shook his head, again, at Tuck's firm nod and grasped the cast-iron handle. "If you insist, then. May God be with you."

* * *

"Oh, fuck."

It was a sign of Allan-a-Dale's advanced inebriation that he never even raised his head from the table at Gareth's muttered oath.

"Wake up!"

The skinny young outlaw grabbed his big friend's arm and shook him until Allan looked up with bloodshot eyes. "We've got trouble. Probably because of your big mouth." He nodded towards the bar and the minstrel looked around to see one of the city's guardsmen in conversation with the

77

inn-keeper. Three more soldiers followed their leader, all clad in light armour covered by the blue surcoat the sheriff's men wore as their uniform. Behind them stood two grey-robed friars: Brother Walter, smiling nastily while his charge, the oblate Hubert, looked about unhappily.

"Oh fuck," Gareth repeated, the panic evident in his voice. "The guards are coming over. What do we do?"

"Sing them a song?" Allan smiled, watching the oncoming soldiers who threaded their way through the inn's patrons, most of whom moved aside to clear a path although some of them stood their ground and stared sullenly at the lawmen pushing past.

"You." The guard sergeant stopped behind Allan's chair and glared down at them, his hand resting on the pommel of his sword.

"Sit, my lord!" Gareth grinned nervously. "What can we do for you?"

"We were given a tip from someone that saw you in the street earlier today," the soldier replied. "He says you're Robin Hood's men." The sergeant shrugged, as if sick of hearing these tales that inevitably turned out to be nothing. "I don't care if you are or not, but you're coming to the castle with us –"

Before he could finish his sentence Allan stood up and rammed the back of his head into the guard's face, sending the man reeling, nose shattered and bleeding before he collapsed onto the filthy rush-covered floor in a daze.

The remaining three guardsmen, used to dealing with rowdy drunkards, moved in to restrain their leader's broad-shouldered assailant, but, belying his inebriation, Allan side-stepped the first man's grasp and hammered a meaty fist into his opponent's cheek, sending the man sprawling into another table, drinks and outraged patrons scattering all about the place as screams of fright and roars of anger filled the air.

"I told you I was one of Robin Hood's men!" The minstrel shouted towards the middle-aged lady he'd been trying to seduce earlier. "You didn't believe me but –"

He was cut-off mid-sentence as the two remaining guards came at him. One rammed a wooden cudgel into his midriff and, before he could even bend over in deflated agony, the other tackled him to the ground and began to rain blows down on his head.

As the two guards battered his friend senseless, Gareth – bloodshot eyes wide in fear – fell to his hands and knees and pushed his way between the legs of the rest of the drinkers who stood watching the confrontation with glee.

"That's enough," the guard sergeant mumbled, pulling his men away and holding his broken nose gingerly. He aimed a final kick at Allan who lay, battered and unresisting amongst the vomit-and-ale-soaked rushes on the floor, before looking around the place in anger.

"Where's the other one?" he shouted. "This one's mate. Where is he? Tell me, now!"

The inn's patrons looked about the room innocently. Like drinkers everywhere they had no intention of helping the law capture one of their own, even if they didn't know who the fugitive was, or what he was supposed to have done to warrant arrest by the local militia. Many of them had been in the tavern all day and had shared a laugh and a joke with the thin young man who'd said he came from the nearby village of Wrangbrook.

The front door closed quietly behind him as Gareth slipped out and sprinted into the shadows, praying desperately that the furious soldiers hadn't beaten his friend to death.

Now what was he supposed to do? He was no fighter, he couldn't batter his way through the guards manning the gatehouse, and he was no charismatic charmer that could simply talk his way out of the situation either.

Christ above, he thought fearfully, *how do I get out of this one with my hide intact?*

CHAPTER NINE

In the end, Gareth's lack of charisma and nondescript appearance proved to be his salvation. He was able to join the steady flow of people leaving the city, having made his way hastily to the Chapel Bar gate before any alarms were raised and he simply walked right out as if he was a member of a noisy family who didn't even notice he'd latched onto their party.

The guards didn't give him a second glance, and, for once in his life he was glad to be such an unremarkable fellow.

He knew his luck might run out though, when the sheriff's men circulated his description. It was possible someone at the gate would realise he'd passed through not long ago and the chase would be on. One of Robin Hood's gang was a prize the soldiers would spare no effort to claim.

With a glance over his shoulder he sucked in a lungful of air and broke into a run again, leaving the main road and shoving his way past bushes and low-hanging branches, his eyes able to pick out a way through the foliage thanks to the many months he'd spent living in the greenwood with the outlaws.

After a while he relaxed his pace, chest heaving and throat burning, the sweet smells of spring filling his nostrils as he hawked and spat out a thick glob of phlegm. Even if the law did come after him, they'd never manage to catch him now, he was sure.

When he ran, gasping, into the clearing the outlaws were using as a camp-site the men that were there turned in surprise at his sudden appearance. If enemies were to try and sneak up on them the lookouts that were posted day and night should alert them to their approach, but Gareth knew exactly where he was going and had managed to get past the sentries and to the camp without the alarm being raised.

"It's Gareth!"

Little John appeared from his camouflaged shelter at the cry, a pair of worn brown trousers in one hand and a bone needle in the other. "Where the fuck have you been, lad? And where's Allan?"

More of the gang started to appear, anxious to hear the young man's news.

"Taken," he gasped, bending to place his hands on his thighs, gasping for breath.

"I knew this would happen," Robin shouted, pointing in anger at Gareth who winced at the force of his leader's ire. "You should never have gone off without saying anything to the rest of us. I assume you went to Nottingham for the tourney and the sheriff's men took him?"

"It wasn't my idea, it was Allan's," Gareth protested, his voice high and reedy, like a scolded child trying to shift the blame to a naughty playmate. "That friar you robbed, Brother Walter – he must have seen us going into the inn and told the guards. I was lucky to escape. Allan took a hell of a beating..."

"Ah, bollocks," Robin slumped heavily to the ground, staring at the dead embers of the previous night's cooking fire, his expression unreadable.

Allan was one of the men Robin was closest to in the group. They had become firm friends when, together, they'd rescued Will Scarlet's daughter from her enforced servitude in Hathersage. They had been blood brothers ever since. The idea of the cheerful minstrel being imprisoned in the city jail made him feel physically sick; he'd been captured and held there himself the previous year. It had been a horrible time that had almost broken the outlaw leader's spirit.

He hated to think what an experience like that would do to his friend. And he knew the sheriff would take no chances with his captive this time around; there would be no repeat of Friar Tuck and Will Scarlet's daring rescue of Robin the previous summer. Allan had no chance of escape.

"What d'you think'll happen to him?" Gareth asked.

Will gave a snort. "What do *you* think? They'll hang him as part of the tournament, won't they? More entertainment for the crowd."

"Never mind that," Little John rumbled. "The question is: what are we going to do about it?"

Robin didn't answer and neither did anyone else. They knew there was nothing they could do to help Allan.

"He's as good as dead..." the Hospitaller sergeant, Stephen, muttered ruefully, shaking his head. "Good lad too." He crossed himself and glared at Gareth, silently accusing the youngster for the minstrel's predicament.

"It's not my fault – he was going anyway. I just went along to see how he got on, so you can stop giving me dirty looks you old prick –"

"Enough!" Robin roared, jumping to his feet angrily. "It's done. There's no point in the rest of us falling out."

The men sat in silence for a while before Little John also stood up and moved back into his crude shelter before reappearing with his enormous longbow and quarterstaff, both of which were a foot longer than any normal ones.

"I know we can't storm the castle," the giant said to Robin as the rest of the men looked on in surprise. "And I know we can't sneak in through the latrine like Will and Tuck did. But I can't just sit around here waiting on news of Allan's hanging to reach us. I'm going to the city."

Robin shook his head in disbelief. "You can't – the guards will shoot you on sight. You stick out like a nun in a brothel for fuck sake!"

John shook his great bearded head. "I'm not going on a suicide mission. I just want to go and see if I can hear what the local gossip is. The travellers coming out of the city might be able to tell us what's happening."

He looked around at the rest of the men. "I know it's pointless, but it's better than sitting here doing nothing. I'm going."

It was a futile gesture but Robin understood his big friend's feelings.

"Fine," he nodded after a moment's thought. "Let me gather my own weapons and some food. I'll come with you. We'll go to Penyston and buy a couple of horses for the journey first, though. Might come in handy." He was rewarded with a grateful look from John before he turned to Will Scarlet. "You look after things here while we're away, all right?"

Will shrugged in resignation. "Might be an idea for us to move to a new camp," he said. "Just in case they –" he broke off, not wanting to voice his fears for their captured friend. "Just in case Allan tells them where we are."

Robin agreed. "Good point. Why don't you lead the men back to the old camp near Selby? You know, the one we were used for a short time last year? Seems as good a place as any. We haven't camped there for a while. There's no reason Allan would even think of telling the sheriff we were hiding out there again. And Groves doesn't know anything about it since he'd left us by the time we were camping there."

Robin collected his weapons while everyone else moved to gather their things for the move. They'd done this so many times over the years that it was second-nature to them – like a well-rehearsed scene from a play.

Before he left with John, Robin took Stephen aside.

"Will's calmed down a lot in the past year or so," he told the Hospitaller. "But he's still prone to moments of madness if his temper gets up. He's the obvious person to lead you all when me and John aren't around, but he needs someone to make sure he doesn't react in anger if there's trouble. Someone to keep a cool head."

Stephen nodded. "I'll keep an eye on him," he promised. "I never wanted to be a leader myself – I've always been happy to be a sergeant. But even Sir Richard needed someone to tell him to calm down at times." He smiled wistfully, the memories of his former master, hanged a few months before by the sheriff, coming back to him in a rush. "You and John go to Nottingham and see if you can stop Allan suffering the same fate as my master did. Don't worry about us, we'll be fine."

Robin grasped the Hospitaller's arm in farewell before shouting goodbye to the rest of the men and haring off into the undergrowth.

"God be with you," Stephen mouthed, with a final, hopeful wave to the two departing outlaws.

* * *

"You? In God's name, I can't believe it. You dare show your fat face around here again? After what you've done?"

Prior John de Monte Martini raged at Tuck, obviously forgetting the flabby shape of his own lined red visage in the astonishment of the friar's unexpected return as Edwin, job done, backed from the room and closed the door gladly behind himself.

Tuck stood, head bowed, as de Martini continued his tirade for a while longer, listing the friar's transgressions against him, punctuating his verbal stabs with a fist that he slammed every so often onto the table that separated them.

"Eh? You Franciscan bastard. I should have had you excommunicated. How dare you show yourself in my priory again, as if nothing had happened?"

Tuck spread his hands wide, not seeking forgiveness, but time to explain his side of the story.

"Go on then, man," the prior gesticulated towards him. "Let's hear it. Let's hear why I shouldn't have you burned at the stake like the heretic – nay, *wolf's head* – that you are."

Tuck nodded into the expectant silence and placed a hand into the folds of his cassock before drawing out the little ornate reliquary that he'd obtained from St. Mary's in Brandesburton. He was rewarded with a small spark of interest that flared in de Monte Martini's eyes.

"I have it."

The prior stared hungrily at the reliquary, knowing it was somehow significant and knowing too that he coveted it. But the man had never seen it before, the friar remembered. It had been stolen from Tuck years ago by one of his own mercenaries, before he had a chance to give it to de Monte Martini.

"The relic you sent me to Eze in France to collect. The one that was purloined from me just as I'd returned here."

It took only a moment for the prior to recall exactly what the former wrestler was talking about. He had given Tuck a huge sum of money to buy the artifact; its loss wasn't something a man as driven by worldly wealth as de Monte Martini could ever forget.

"Christ's beard!" He stood up, fingers grasping the edge of the table spasmodically. "You have it? Truly?" His voice dropped and he looked at the little box in Tuck's hand longingly before his tone hardened again. "How?"

The prior knew Tuck had been living amongst the outlaws in Barnsdale so the friar saw no reason to hide the facts of his story; besides, he didn't want to lie on holy ground to his superior. Even if the man *was* a wicked bastard that cared more for coin than he did for God.

When he finished his tale the prior simply stared at the reliquary hungrily before demanding the friar hand it over to him.

Tuck did so, then allowed the sweating, flushed prior to struggle for a while before he leaned forward and flicked the hidden switch that popped the box open and revealed the sandy-coloured hairs inside.

Christ's beard.

Both men held their breath and gazed in awe at the sight before them. They beheld a part of their saviour's own body; something that had miraculously healed Tuck when he had been thrown into an unnatural deathly sleep by the crossbow bolt of Sir Guy of Gisbourne and the icy-cold waters of the Don. Something cut reverentially from Christ's face when he'd been taken down from the cross, before his resurrection and ascension to heaven days later.

Tuck wondered, as he always did on looking inside the reliquary, why the hair wasn't darker as he'd have expected, coming from a Judean as it supposedly did, but... who was he to question God's holy relic?

"It's incredible." Prior de Monte Martini breathed in excitement and Tuck could almost see the gold coins flashing in the man's eyes as he contemplated how much money this sacred object was worth. Fortunes, no doubt. More than he'd given Tuck to pay for it years earlier for sure. Relics like this only ever appreciated in value.

And here was this wolf's head, outcast from the prior's own service, returning to the fold like the Prodigal Son and handing it to him to do with as he pleased.

He clasped his hands and offered a prayer of thanks, eyes raised skywards, a grin on his jowly face.

"Truly, God works in mysterious ways, Brother Stafford. Welcome back to Lewes."

Tuck smiled in relief, glad that his gift had pleased de Monte Martini but knowing the prior wasn't likely to just allow him to settle into an easy life amongst the Benedictines here.

Although de Monte Martini's face glowed with pleasure as he waved Tuck out of the room the friar couldn't miss the sadistic spark that still burned in the man's eyes when he watched him depart.

Still, it was a start. He was back in the Church again, no longer an outcast, with good men he called brothers even if they were from a different order. Not the type of brothers he'd spent the last few months with, like Will Scaflock, John Little and Robert Hood of Wakefield but his brothers just the same; brothers in God's service. Edwin the gatekeeper and Ralph the bottler and all the other acquaintances he'd missed during his time in Barnsdale.

He was looking forward to spending his days praying, reading the bible, tending the vegetable garden that lay inside the priory walls and having a pallet and a roof over his head every night even in the harshest of weathers. Thick stone walls were much better than trees for keeping the ice-cold winds of winter at bay.

It was no life of luxury in the priory, for sure, but it was a sight more comfortable than sleeping rough on the frozen earth of the forest, when the leaves had blown from the trees and the icy rains and bitter gusts battered the greenwood as it did every single year without fail.

Aye, he was glad to be back in Lewes, even if he would badly miss his friends in Barnsdale. He just hoped the prior wouldn't make his life *too* miserable.

* * *

"You think you could take me, minstrel?"

Allan stood, watching Sir Guy of Gisbourne warily, wondering what was happening but knowing whatever it was wouldn't be pleasant.

"Eh? A man with one eye? Look at you." The Raven had appeared almost silently inside Allan's gloomy cell and now moved to grasp the minstrel's great arms firmly. "Strong. Younger than I am. Angry."

Allan remained silent, warily watching his despised enemy but not wanting to bring any more trouble down upon himself. Robin's stories of his time in this very dungeon last year had been sickening, and the minstrel knew the bounty-hunter could turn violent at any moment if provoked.

"What do you want?" he asked, trying to keep Gisbourne in sight as the man continued to walk slowly around the cell, losing himself in the shadows where the light from the softly guttering torch he'd placed in the sconce on the wall didn't quite reach.

"I want to prove myself. Your friend hurt me badly not so long ago, and I'll never be the swordsman I was before Hood took my eye. I may never be able to shoot my crossbow very accurately either." His hand caressed the stock of the weapon. "I was very fond of this crossbow too – it got me out of trouble more than once. Almost killed your friar companion too."

Still he kept circling Allan, as if his feet were bewitched and he couldn't stop them moving.

"So what is it you want from me?"

"I want you to fight me, wolf's head. It's as simple as that."

87

It had to be a trick. Allan wanted to grin and tell the king's man he'd be glad to beat the shit out of him but he knew Gisbourne was no fool and, despite the loss of an eye, was probably still deadly. He held his tongue and at last the black-armoured Raven stopped walking and glared at him.

They were about the same height, although the lawman was slimmer – wiry where Allan was broad-shouldered and brawny, so their eyes met across the dank cell although the smoke from the torch made the minstrel blink and Gisbourne nodded.

"I'm not supposed to be down in the dungeon – the sheriff's worried I'll try and carve you up like I did to Hood when he was here. But I don't have any intention of doing that. Your leader was, supposedly, a worthy opponent for me. The best swordsman in all England, people said of him. They were wrong – I was the best. But I had to prove it by facing Hood, blade in hand, one-on-one. I had the chance to do that when we captured him and brought him here."

He shook his head. "I had him then – he was no match for me, despite what the ballads said about his skill. The sheriff stopped me from killing him but I proved I was the better swordsman." He stepped in close again. "This isn't about that. I simply want to prove that I can still win a fight with a man that genuinely wants to murder me. Sparring with the guards here is pointless – they're frightened of hurting me, even when *I* hurt *them*."

He moved back and looked out into the corridor, nodding to someone out of sight – presumably a guard – then turned back to face Allan.

"I have no real desire to kill you. De Faucumberg wants to hang you as part of the tourney's entertainment and who am I to deny the crowd their fun? No, I simply want to best you, man-to-man. No weapons other than those the good Lord gave us."

Allan clenched his fists, mind whirling.

"If you win, you go free. You have my word. The guard outside has his orders to see you escorted safely to the Carter Gate. I'm afraid you'll have to climb a rope down into the latrine, just as your friends did not so long ago. Most unpleasant, but better than dying, no? The door to the outside has been replaced since Hood's escape through it, but the guard has the key to it."

He began to swing his arms and stretch the muscles in his legs. "It's dark outside, you won't be spotted if you and your escort keep to the shadows."

Allan didn't know how to respond. He still felt it had to be a trick but, as he stood looking at the door a blow suddenly rocked his head back and he stumbled, cursing and lifting his arms to ward off any more attacks.

"You have no choice, really," Gisbourne growled, dancing from side to side and keeping out of Allan's reach. "Fight me or stand and be pounded into a bloody mess."

He darted forward again but the outlaw flinched to the side, bringing up an arm in time to deflect the punch.

"You swear in God's name I'll be set free if I win?"

"In the name of God, the Christ and all his saints, I swear it," Gisbourne replied, aiming another blow at the big longbowman who, again, managed to evade it easily enough.

Freedom was his. All he had to do was deal with this one-eyed bastard and he'd be in Barnsdale by the following evening. Of course, he'd been stuck down here for days with very little food or drink and he'd barely slept but...

He bared his lips in a feral grin and, as his opponent drew near once more, threw a haymaker of his own which just missed its target. "You have a deal, Gisbourne, you whoreson. I'm going to make you pay for all the shit you've done to us. You might not want to kill me, but I'll gladly crush the breath from you with my bare hands."

The cell was only dimly lit and small too. Gisbourne had to be mad if he thought he could best the powerful wolf's head in here.

But he is *mad,* Allan thought. *I need to finish this and get the fuck out of here.*

Knowing the Raven was faster than him, he charged straight forward, hoping to crush the man against the wall where he could use his superior strength to hold Gisbourne in place and rain blows down on him.

As he began to move, though, he tripped over the lawman's foot and bright stars burst upon his vision as a punch landed on his cheek. Then another, as his attacker switched fists.

"I'll make up a good song about this, once I'm back in the forest," Allan growled, raising his arms as Sir Guy stepped back and they faced off again. "I'll make sure everyone knows how easy it was to beat you, and how you shit your breeches when I throttled the life from you."

He aimed a kick but Gisbourne caught it and jerked, throwing him off balance before battering his own foot into the minstrel's knee, dropping Allan to the floor with a shocked cry.

It hadn't done any real damage but the Raven followed it up with another boot, this time to his downed opponent's face.

Even with only one eye Gisbourne was fast. Allan hauled himself upright, flailing his muscular arms to avert any more attacks.

"I'm getting used to it now," the bounty-hunter smiled, to himself more than Allan. "I thought I'd never be able to fight well without both my eyes but..."

He crouched as the outlaw roared and charged towards him, aiming a left uppercut that rocked Allan again although this time he did manage to grab hold of his tormentor.

Furiously, and with a sense of real fear beginning to set in, the minstrel put all of his weight into his knee, ramming it into Gisbourne's midriff. The blow hit home and he tried again, repeatedly, using both hands to try and keep his target in one place.

The Raven was as agile as a cat, though, and managed, after the first hit had knocked most of the wind from him, to keep his body away from the follow-up strikes before, finally, he twisted out of Allan's grip and poked a finger into his eye.

Dizzy from the blows he'd taken and the effects of his captivity, Allan knew he couldn't afford to give ground so, squinting desperately, he tried to regain his hold on Gisbourne, kicking his legs out in the hope of catching the bastard a sore one.

Suddenly, he felt an excruciating pain that started between his legs and quickly seemed to grow to fill his whole being.

Gisbourne grinned at him as he mercilessly tightened his grip on Allan's testicles, then he smashed his head forward and watched in triumph as the wolf's head fell to the floor making pitiful noises.

"Looks like you won't be going free today after all, minstrel."

With a laugh, the Raven strode breathlessly from the room. As the lock clicked inexorably back into place it was all Allan could do to roar, "Bastard!" before he leaned his head back on the ground and prayed for the pain between his legs to subside.

CHAPTER TEN

The outlaws back in the camp near Selby carried on as normal while Robin and Little John were away. Will Scaflock naturally assumed command, being the obvious man for the job. Before Robin had joined them Will had been their previous leader's second-in-command. The men all respected him and even feared him a little, although the volcanic temper that had given him the nickname 'Scarlet' was, mostly, gone nowadays.

Still, for all that, to some of the outlaws their young leader's absence seemed something of a holiday for them; a time to relax and let down their guard a little, despite Will's watchful eye. It wasn't as if Robin was ever hard or unfair on the men – he was more like a friend than a commander to them all but, as ever when the person in authority goes away for a time, things became just a little more open than usual.

One person who took advantage of the more relaxed atmosphere was young Gareth. Of course, he was his own man and could do whatever he liked pretty much, but he didn't like to drink too heavily around Robin. His captain's disappointed gaze always made him feel ashamed and, as a result, he tended to keep his drinking to a more manageable level, so he wasn't stumbling around camp walking into the fire or tumbling into the nearby River Ouse.

But, with Robin and John away to God-knew-where and for who-knew how long, Gareth became more open in his inebriation.

Will tried to warn the lad about it, but the steely glare from the ex-mercenary wasn't as effective as the pitying look Robin gave him whenever he was obviously too drunk. Will simply didn't care as much as Robin.

It was with some exasperation, then, that Scarlet found the skinny youngster by the riverside on his own one evening, a half-empty ale-skin by his side and tears streaking his grubby face.

"What's the matter with you, lad?" Will's voice was gruff although he was trying his best to sound friendly. He really couldn't be bothered with other people's problems – he had enough bad memories of his own to deal with after all.

Gareth didn't even look up, just placed the ale-skin to his lips and took another long pull, careful not spill a drop as the older outlaw dropped down onto the grass next to him.

"You're going to kill yourself if you don't watch your drinking. That's up to you," Will shrugged. "You're a big boy now, you can do what you like to yourself."

Gareth turned his damp eyes to look at Scarlet, sensing the 'but' before it came.

"But you keep this up and you'll do something stupid one day, and bring trouble down on all of us."

They sat in silence for a while, Gareth not too far gone to accept the rebuke without getting angry. He knew Will spoke the truth anyway, it was pointless disagreeing. He didn't *want* to drink every day; he just couldn't help it any more. Since he'd acquired a taste for the grain drink the barber in Penyston had given him he'd found solace in the cosy fugue that alcohol produced.

Recently his need had grown even worse.

"My ma's died."

Will looked at the younger man in surprise. Gareth hadn't visited his home in Wrangbrook for weeks as far as he knew. The lad must have kept his bereavement to himself all that time. No wonder he'd been drinking more than ever – his mother was the only family Gareth had left. Now he had no-one.

"She had a shit life," the young outlaw muttered distantly. "My da died when I was only about six or seven, I can hardly remember him. She always talked about him; they really do seem to have been good together, not like some folk in Wrangbrook. Or anywhere else for that matter, I suppose. She missed him badly although I think she was happy that I was around. Just as I was happy to have her." His voice tailed off and a sob shook his thin frame.

"She had a job working in the fields in the summertime and did odd-jobs around the village in the winter months – mending clothes, brewing ale, things like that. We were all right, although we never had much to eat."

Will watched Gareth speak but remained silent as he took in the spindly arms and legs the boy had been cursed with as a result of that childhood malnutrition.

"Then, one day when she was carrying a cask of ale to the inn she tripped and broke her arm. I mean, really broke it... the bone came right out through her skin, it was terrible." He shook his head sadly. "We didn't have a surgeon in Wrangbrook, just the barber. He did his best but he didn't know much about injuries like that. My ma's arm knit together twisted and she couldn't work properly with it any more. She was in constant pain. I was about twelve then. I did my best to find work to put food on the table for us but, well... I'm not much good at physical labour. We had to survive on handouts from other villagers."

He met Will's gaze, anger flaring in his tear-filled eyes. "It was humiliating! The people were kind and tried to help us but... it was so humiliating."

"Is that why you stole the food from the chapel?" Will asked softly, knowing some of the lad's story although he'd never heard it in as much detail before.

Gareth nodded. "When I was fourteen I started stealing food whenever the neighbours hadn't given us enough to fill our bellies for the day. I could have just asked them, they would have given us more I expect, they were good people, but it was too embarrassing. So I would lift a loaf from the baker's shop or a pie from the butcher's. I was always careful and never got caught." He stopped and stared thoughtfully at the dark waters of the Ouse. "Perhaps the baker and the butcher knew what I was doing and turned a blind eye."

Will thought that likely, since Gareth, despite his small stature, was never that light on his feet or particularly nimble, but he held his peace, not wanting to hurt the lad's feelings.

"We had a visitor one day – some important priest or bishop or something like that. There was a big fuss in the village and everyone came out to watch this churchman ride into the place like he was the king or something. I used to be very pious and I'd already been to the church that morning to say my prayers. The church was only a small building with one main room, so I could see the priest laying out a table with all sorts of fancy foods: roast chicken, fresh bread, apples, eggs. I didn't even know what some of the stuff was – I'd never seen it before."

Will's stomach rumbled and he cursed it silently but Gareth didn't seem to hear the gastric growling. "I sneaked back in when everyone was out welcoming the bishop and shoved some of the food inside my pouch. I didn't take any of the really fancy stuff, just things that I thought wouldn't be missed as much. Bread and eggs and the like. There was someone in the shadows though, one of the local men. He was praying silently at the back of the building and he saw me take the food. He shouted at me and chased me out the door straight into the mob."

Will could imagine the scene in his mind's eye. It would be nice to think the villagers would have shown the poor boy some compassion but it didn't always work like that, especially when a bishop was around.

"I don't know what they were going to do to me. I tried to tell them I needed the food because my ma was poorly but the churchman was shouting and stuff, like they do, and I was frightened. I managed to break through the crowd – some of them, I'm sure, moved aside to let me pass – and I ran into the forest where I eventually found you lot."

Will remembered the day. The lad was even skinnier than he was now, having been hiding out in Barnsdale for over a week before the outlaws had come across him.

And now his mother was dead and he was all alone in the world.

They remained seated in silence for a time before Will got to his feet and extended a hand to help Gareth up.

"Come on, let's go back to camp. I know it feels like you don't have much to live for and it's all too easy to lose yourself at the bottom of that ale-skin but you're not alone. We're here for you, all of us. You're our brother, lad, never forget it."

They made their way back to the rest of the men and Gareth lay on his pallet by the fire, falling asleep almost straight away.

Will sighed and shook his head. The lad's life had been a hard one, that was certain. But so had all of the outlaws – they had to deal with it, and so would young Gareth.

Will wasn't sure the boy had the strength; he just prayed the rest of them didn't go down along with him.

* * *

He'd known it wouldn't be easy when he returned to the priory, but Tuck hadn't expected it'd be so hard to take as it was turning out.

Prior de Monte Martini made sure Tuck was given the worst chores around the place – chores that would normally be done by new, young novices, not a veteran like himself who had just returned a priceless relic to the craven bastard.

Being made to clean out the latrine was the worst, the portly friar thought, as he shovelled a large pile of shit through the opening that would take it outside and down the slope, preventing the waste from building up too much. He grinned in spite of the stench as he remembered Will Scaflock climbing the wall of a similar latrine not so long ago when they'd rescued Robin from his imprisonment in Nottingham.

The smile dropped from his face soon enough though, the smell pervading even the dampened rag he'd tied around his mouth and nose to try and hold the evil vapours at bay and he gagged again, shaking his head, eyes watering.

There was a noise from above and, with a curse, he jumped back just in time as another turd dropped into the rancid pile.

Eventually he'd shifted most of the detritus and gladly left the latrine, wiping sweat from his tonsured brow and tearing the rag from his face irritably as he closed the heavy door behind him to try and block out the worst of the fumes.

If de Monte Martini thought he could break him by giving him the worst chores in the priory he could think again. Tuck was a man of the cloth and his place was in God's service. He'd been forced to leave his rightful place once before... it'd take more than a latrine full of shit to push him out again.

He tore off the filthy leather boots the friars used when they had to clean out the latrine and left them by the door, pulling on his own worn out sandals with a sigh of relief.

He'd earned a rest.

He began to make his way to the priory's larder where he hoped the bottler, Ralph, would share a cup or two of ale and some bread with him. As he walked he smiled and breathed deeply, imagining the smell of the freshly baked loaf that awaited him. It would be a lot nicer than the stench from the mound of faeces he'd just been shovelling.

"Go and tell him to sweep the leaves from the front path now," Prior de Monte Martini told his dean, Henry of Elmstow, as they stood watching Tuck from the opposite end of the corridor.

"But it's pouring with rain –"

"I know!" The prior smiled. "Blowing a gale too. Good enough for the bastard." He waved a hand irritably at the old dean who scurried off to give Tuck the bad news.

De Monte Martini hadn't forgotten the trouble Robin Hood had caused him. He still couldn't breathe properly after the wolf's head had smashed his nose all those months ago in Wakefield. And on top of that was the vast sum of money the despicable outlaw and his friends had stolen from the prior when they'd ambushed the cart full of silver that Tuck had been supposed to escort to Lewes not long afterwards.

Yes, he'd make Tuck's life a misery for a while, make him wish he'd never returned to Lewes. Then, when he was close to breaking, de Monte Martini would find some way of using the man. Perhaps he'd relent, and make a show of forgiving the friar.

The fat idiot would be so glad to escape his life of drudgery he'd tell the prior everything he knew about Robin Hood and his men. Then de Monte Martini would pass the information on to Sir Guy of Gisbourne.

The wolf's head had, so far, got away with breaking his nose and stealing his money, but God had been kind enough to deliver one of Hood's best friends into his grasp. He meant to use the good Lord's gift to destroy the outlaws once and for all.

And, if his little ruse to win Tuck's confidence didn't work, there were other ways to make someone divulge information...

For now, though, he'd just sit back and enjoy watching Robert Stafford shovelling shit and sweeping leaves in the pissing rain. There'd be plenty of time to make the friar's life even more painful soon enough.

* * *

"I need a favour."

Robin and Little John had stopped in the village of Mansfield for some provisions, but also because John had a friend that lived there. They sat in a small dimly-lit dwelling now, the shutter pulled over as protection against the cold night chill as much as against prying eyes, and the householder tossed another log into the fire, causing the small blaze to spit and crackle merrily.

"Anything," the man replied. "I owe you my life, or at least my hand, friend."

Three years earlier John and some of the other outlaws had been out hunting and stumbled upon some foresters who had arrested this fellow, Luke, a butcher, who'd been caught poaching. Although the penalties for such a crime weren't as severe as they'd been two-hundred years ago, when transgressors might be sewn into deer-skins and hunted to death by packs of dogs, Luke had still faced a hefty fine or even the loss of his hand.

But the outlaws had chased off the lawmen and set Luke free. He'd returned to his home here in Mansfield, promising to repay his debt if ever John had need of him.

"We'd like you to go into the city and find out what's happening to one of our friends – a minstrel, name of Allan-a-Dale. I'm not asking you to place yourself in any danger or to make yourself conspicuous; just go to the inn Allan was staying at – The Ship it's called – and see if you can learn anything about his fate."

Luke nodded and placed mugs of ale before John and Robin with a small, nervous smile. "Of course," he agreed. "I'll ride out in the morning. With God's blessing I'll return in the evening with good news. In the meantime, drink, make yourselves at home and tell me about your adventures in the greenwood."

Luke was as good as his word. He owned an old, but still healthy, horse which he normally used to pull his cart, and so he made the journey to Nottingham and back much quicker than he could have done on foot.

"How did you get on?" John demanded as Luke came into the little house. The giant and his young leader had remained cooped up inside all day, for fear of being spotted and reported by some local busy-body. Apart from the danger to themselves, they had no desire to bring trouble to the butcher.

"Good and bad news," Luke reported, pouring himself a drink and draining it with a gasp before splashing some tepid water from a big bowl onto his face to wash the grime and sweat of the road off. "Your mate's being held in the castle dungeon right enough. The sheriff plans to hang him."

John groaned but Robin spread his hands and glared at the butcher. "What's the good news then?" he demanded.

"Ah, well, the sheriff has sent messengers to London to see the king. He wants the king's permission to hang your friend, you see, so... I don't know if you plan on trying to rescue him or what but you have at least some time to try it before the friars return with the king's seal."

"Wait," Robin sat down opposite Luke. "Why would de Faucumberg need the king's permission to hang an outlaw?"

"I don't know, but that's the rumour." Luke shrugged.

"What about these friars," John demanded. "What've they got to do with it?"

"The sheriff asked the two Franciscan friars that informed on your mate if they'd go to the king and they agreed. They must be on the road right now."

John gripped Robin's shoulder. "That old bastard Walter. It wasn't enough for him to see Allan captured, he's going to make sure he hangs too."

Luke stood and helped himself to another mug of his ale with a sigh of exhaustion. "Well, lads. You can bed down here again –"

"No." Robin moved to gather his things, gesturing John do the same. "We're leaving right now. If De Faucumberg needs the king's seal to hang Allan he'll want it as soon as possible, so he'll have provided the Franciscans with horses. We don't have time to waste – we need to catch them and find out what's going on. Something doesn't add up."

A short time later Luke waved as the grim outlaws kicked their mounts into a canter along the road to Nottingham, the sound startlingly loud in the dark, silent village, like Gabriel's hounds or the Wild Hunt.

"I wouldn't want to be those friars when that pair catch up to them," the butcher muttered before he made his way back inside, shoved the bolt across the door and, with a shiver, tossed another log onto the hearth.

* * *

"I think we should get moving," Hubert said to Brother Walter as they dressed in the sparsely furnished but comfortable enough room they'd paid for in the inn.

The older friar waved a hand irritably at the young novice and took his time as he pulled on his worn old sandals, cursing the calluses and corns that beset him and wondering why clergymen were never allowed to wear socks. His head was pounding from the ale he'd consumed the previous evening and all he wanted to do was go back to sleep for a while.

No chance of that with Hubert around though.

"The sheriff said we should take his news to the king as fast as possible. If he finds out we've been tarrying he'll be angry."

Again Walter waved a hand in annoyance, this time spitting an oath at the youngster as well. It was true, Sir Henry de Faucumberg had asked the Franciscans to travel to London with all haste, even giving them a purse filled with silver coins to pay for their expenses. When Brother Walter had told the sheriff of their run-in with Robin Hood de Faucumberg had given the friar even more money to hire a couple of mercenaries to deter any other would-be robbers on the road.

Walter had every intention of travelling to the king but he saw nothing wrong in enjoying the sheriff's money on the way there. He also saw no point in racing to London as if the devil himself were after them. The outlaw – Allan-a-Dale – wasn't going anywhere.

The Franciscan made himself ready and muttered for Hubert to follow him as he left the room. The mercenaries he'd hired in Nottingham were waiting outside their door, bright and eager to earn their fee.

"We've already broken our fast," one of them said. "If you would like to get on your way?"

"In the name of Christ, you're as bad as this one," Walter groused, gesturing at Hubert who flinched back from his elder's ire. "All right, let's get some bread and cheese – and ale! – from the inn-keep and we'll be on our way."

The road was quiet when they eventually set out on the next leg of their journey to the capital, a hard, driving rain beating down on them as they huddled into their cassocks and prayed for clear skies. Walter knew Hubert was right about the sheriff being angry if they didn't get to their destination in good time so he kicked his heels into his mount and his three companions followed suit to keep up.

They moved at a stead pace through the sheeting downpour, but not too fast for fear of one of their horses slipping on the wet road. A lame nag was no use to anyone.

"God's bollocks, priest," one of the mercenaries, Philip, shouted over the sound of the drumming rain after they'd been riding for a while. "Can you and your boy not ask the Lord to stop the rain for a bit? I'm soaked to the skin – we'll all end up with a fever if we don't get dried out soon."

Brother Walter didn't like the blasphemous nature of the man's words but he agreed with the sentiment. Besides, it would be a good excuse to stop at the next village where he could warm himself by the fire of the local inn with an ale or three.

As he opened his mouth to tell the mercenary as much Hubert shouted happily. "It's stopping. Look, there's even a rainbow on the horizon!"

"Praise be to God," Walter muttered through gritted teeth, glancing up and seeing the clouds beginning to thin as the sun tried to force its way between their heavy grey bulk.

"Indeed!" Hubert agreed, oblivious to his elder's annoyance at missing out on another chance to spend

102

Sheriff de Faucumberg's silver. "God sends us clear skies for our journey."

"That ain't the only thing he's sending us," Philip growled, turning to look back along the road behind them. "Look. Riders. And they don't look like they're filled with the love of Christ."

CHAPTER ELEVEN

Robin knew Brother Walter had recognized them as they approached, from the fearful look on the man's lined face. The friar reined in his horse, knowing they couldn't escape, and shouted at the two mercenaries to draw their weapons and defend them.

Swiftly, the two hired soldiers did so, hauling their mounts around to face the oncoming threat and setting themselves to ward off whatever attack was imminent. However, the sight of the heavily built men riding towards them, particularly Little John with his quarterstaff that seemed almost as long as a knight's lance, made the mercenaries baulk.

"Who the fuck are these two?" Philip demanded of the friars. "You never said anyone was after you. Look at the size of that one, he's a fucking giant."

His companion, Edwin, a stocky, ginger-haired man of advancing years nodded silent agreement but the pair were honourable men and they'd been paid good coin to do a job. They raised their swords, ready to defend the churchmen as the two riders approached, grim-faced, the threat of violence emanating from them like a wave.

"Hold!" Philip commanded as the two men came closer, their intent obvious as they glared murderously at Brother Walter.

Robin and Little John hauled on their mounts' reins, bringing the beasts to a halt just outside the reach of the mercenaries' blades and the bigger of the two glared at them from beneath his shaggy brown fringe.

"You know who I am?" he demanded, simply.

There was only one giant in the north of England that everyone told tales of.

Philip swallowed, eyeing the enormous staff that was aimed in his direction. "John Little?"

"That's him," Robin growled. "We have no quarrel with you two. But we want a word with that one there," he pointed his blade at Brother Walter. "So you can either stand and be cut down or you can fuck off. Either way, that friar is ours."

For a moment there was silence as Philip tried to take in what was happening. He'd been paid to protect the friars, and, although the two men facing him were notorious killers, the mercenary took pride in his job.

He glanced across at his companion, Edwin, and knew there would be no help from there. The man was gazing, awestruck, at the celebrated outlaws.

Philip looked at the younger Franciscan and shook his head sorrowfully. In truth, the mercenary cared little for the older clergyman, but Hubert seemed a decent enough young lad.

"Have no fear for the novice," Robin said, watching the mercenary's eyes and guessing what was going through the man's head. "We only want to speak to the older friar – Hubert can be on his way if he wants." The wolf's head jerked his head back along the road, indicating the direction the page and the mercenaries should go if they wanted to stay alive. "Move it, the three of you." His demeanour was calm, but young Hubert was shocked at the violent intent that flared in the big outlaw's eyes.

When Robin Hood had 'invited' them to dinner not so long ago the wolf's head had been good-natured and affable, even in the face of Brother Walter's incessant grousing. But now, Hood wore a mask of barely controlled rage.

"You go," Hubert nodded to the mercenaries who, although surprised at the command from the youngster, gladly followed his order and, with respectful nods towards the legendary outlaws, kicked their steeds along the road to Nottingham without a backward glance.

"I'll stay here with Brother Walter," Hubert finished in a small voice, feeling inside his pouch for the weight of the purse Robin had given him at their last meeting. That purse told him Hood wasn't a wicked man, and the young novice felt a duty to help his elder, even if the friar was a moaning, selfish old sot.

As the mercenaries rode off Little John walked his horse forward and poked his great oaken quarterstaff into Walter's midriff, sending the friar flying, to land with a heavy thump in the grass by the side of the road, where he lay cursing and crying like a smacked child.

The rain came back on then, mirroring the tears that sprang from Brother Walter's eyes as he lay, face-down on the ground, expecting a sword thrust to send him into God's arms in heaven at any moment.

Robin dismounted and moved to grasp the prone churchman by the scruff of the neck, hauling him up and glaring into his moist eyes.

Hubert moved to try and protect his elder but Little John was beside him and held him back, shaking his head slightly.

"You gave our mate Allan over to the sheriff," Robin said, his voice rising as he shoved Walter backwards until his shoulders hammered painfully against the trunk of a young silver birch. "You've condemned him to die! And for what?"

"Your friend is a wolf's head," the friar managed to reply, his anger enough to overcome his fear. "As are you, and your pet bear." He spat in John's direction. "May God strike the pair of you down where you stand."

"Where are you going?" Robin demanded, ignoring the jibe. "What did the sheriff ask you to do?"

"I don't know what you mean," Walter replied. "We're returning to Gloucester Greyfriars. When you stole our money we couldn't afford to stay in the city." He fixed Robin with an indignant glare but the young outlaw was in no mood for the friar's lies.

"I asked you where you were going," Robin asked again, cuffing the friar hard across the face and allowing the dazed man to sag to the ground, mewling like an injured cat. "And until you tell us, what remains of your miserable life is going to be filled with pain."

"Stop it!" Hubert pulled away from Little John and brushed past Robin to kneel beside the elder Franciscan, placing a hand reassuringly on Walter's arm. "We're going to the king," the youngster admitted, looking up at the outlaws as the rain streamed down from his thick brown hair into his wide eyes. "The sheriff gave us a letter to take to him."

"What letter?" Little John rumbled, his voice seeming like distant thunder to the sodden young page. "What does it say?"

Hubert shrugged. "The sheriff seeks the king's permission to hang your friend. We're to return with the royal seal."

Robin looked across at his huge friend, not quite believing the youngster's story. Why would de Faucumberg need to ask Edward's permission to hang a common outlaw? It made no sense – as the king's representative in Nottingham and Yorkshire the sheriff had power enough to mete out justice to the likes of Allan-a-Dale.

There had to be more to this letter than Hubert knew.

"Give it to me," Robin demanded, gesturing to Walter. "The letter – give it to me now."

For a moment the friar lay on the soaking grass, a murderous look on his face as he gazed up at the wolf's head, then, nostrils flaring, he grasped Hubert's arm and hauled himself to his feet before reaching inside his cassock.

"Come and get it if you want it."

Before either of the outlaws could react, Brother Walter had pulled out not the letter but a small knife, and pressed it against his novice's throat. "If either of you come any closer I'll kill this little sinner," the friar grated, holding Hubert's arm tightly.

John spat in disgust onto the ground. "Call yourself a man of God? You make me sick. That lad has more of the Holy Spirit in his little finger than you have in your black soul, damn you."

Walter was backing away towards his horse which had wandered from the road and found a thick patch of grass where it stood grazing, uninterested in what was going on behind it.

107

"You'll not get away from us," Robin vowed. "Give us the letter now or we'll take it from your dead fingers."

Walter shook his head. "I may not be the fastest rider on God's green Earth, but the next village isn't far. I'll be able to make it there before you – the people won't allow two criminals to murder a clergyman."

Robin cursed inwardly. The little prick was right. Yet he knew there was something important in that letter; something that might be the key to more than just helping Allan avoid the gallows.

There was little he or John could do it seemed. Young Hubert's face betrayed confusion and fear, as his companion's blade pressed against his windpipe and they slowly but surely inched their way back towards the big palfrey that still ignored their approach.

Allan was their friend, yes, but they wouldn't endanger the innocent young novice; Robin wasn't sure if the fear-crazed friar would actually harm Hubert but he couldn't take a chance with the boy's life.

The rain, already heavy, suddenly became a hammering torrent and Robin pulled his hood up to keep the deluge from running into his eyes as it bounced off the ground, forming deep brown puddles in a matter of moments.

The Franciscan finally reached his mount and, with a victorious smile, lifted his left hand to take the horse's bridle. As he did so, the palfrey stepped to the side nervously and Walter's foot slipped in the mud.

Robin and John watched in disbelief as a thin red line appeared on young Hubert's neck, stretching from one side to the other. The older friar regained his balance and, not even realising what he'd done, shouted triumphantly and dragged himself atop the palfrey, leaving go of the young boy as he did so.

He kicked his heels into the horse and galloped away with a laugh while the torrential rain turned the wound in Hubert's neck into a grotesque river of crimson and the youngster slumped face first into the grass.

"He's already dead!" Robin screamed as his shocked friend made to help the novice. "Leave him – we need to stop the friar before he reaches Chesterfield."

They pulled themselves gracelessly into their saddles – neither was much of a rider – and, with a last, helpless look at the pitiful, soaking corpse in the grass beside them, chased after Brother Walter.

* * *

The cell was cold, despite the time of year, and the floor was sodden with piss and God knew what other filth. The sunlight didn't reach down here under Nottingham Castle but the rats and insects did and, after his beating from Gisbourne, Allan felt like he was going crazy. The smell wasn't an issue any more; he'd grown used to that, which was surprising given how hellish it was. No, the disgusting little sounds of rats and mice and – he shuddered – whatever else was down there with him, *crawling* about the walls and floors of his cell tortured him. He was a minstrel – he wanted to hear the open chords of a gittern, the perfectly tuned strings of a fine citole or the sweet singing voice of a young girl singing.

"Let me out you bastards!"

Allan groaned and dropped his head into his knees at the crude, echoing shout from one of his fellow prisoners somewhere along the gloomy corridor. If it wasn't dark slithering and scratchings it was half-mad rants from the other poor unfortunates that were imprisoned in the inky blackness alongside him. And now, the ever-present fear that Gibourne might return for round two...

Ah, well, at least he had a cell to himself. Praise God for small mercies.

"In here, dickhead."

The iron-strapped door swung open and Allan shrank back against the wall, drawing his legs up against him, eyes burning in the light of the torch that was carried by one of the sheriff's guardsmen.

An old, old man was pushed into the cramped room, falling to his knees with a whimper, and the door was slammed shut again, the lock clicking into place with the finality of a tomb.

The minstrel said nothing, just stared, unseeing, at the dark spot where his new cell-mate had been deposited. The man breathed heavily but there wasn't enough light to make him out and Allan sighed.

"Stay away from me."

The newcomer shrieked and Allan could hear him scrabbling away on his hands and feet into the far corner.

"Please, don't hurt me."

"Relax, old one. We're all in the same boat down here. Our time will come soon enough."

The harsh breathing softened eventually and Allan, starved for company asked the man's name.

"Edward," came the reply and Allan smiled in the darkness.

"Pleased to meet you, Edward. Shame it wasn't in happier circumstances."

The old man grunted self-pityingly. "You?"

"Allan-a-Dale."

There was another grunt, although this one was more like laughter. "Funny name." The prisoner must have realised laughing at someone down here wasn't a good idea, as he hastily added, "No offence, mind."

"None taken," Allan replied in a voice that suggested the exact opposite. "You might have heard the name before?"

There was silence from the opposite end of the cell and Allan sighed. Everyone knew Robin Hood and Little John and Will Scarlet, thanks in part to Allan's own songs. Yet few knew of the minstrel himself.

"What you down here for?" the old man wondered, his voice growing stronger, more confident as time passed and his companion hadn't stove his head in. "They caught me stealing a sheep. Bloody shepherd claimed he saw me having relations with it but he's a damn liar. I just wanted to eat the woolly bastard, not hump it."

Allan sat in silence for a long while wondering what in the name of Christ the guards had put in his cell with him then, eventually, he shrugged. He was bored, and an audience was an audience.

"I'm a minstrel," he began, his voice rising and seeming to fill the little cell with its power.

"Alright, no need to shout," his new cell-mate grumbled. "I'm only over here."

"I'm also one of Robin Hood's men," Allan went on, in an imperious voice, angry at the man's interruption. It seemed to do the trick – the old sheep... thief, held his peace after an almost imperceptible indrawn breath and the minstrel nodded into the dark in satisfaction before continuing.

"I've always been a musician – I was born to it. My mother and father were part of a big troop that travelled all around the country performing for lords and ladies. Sometimes they even went to France although I must admit I've never been there myself." He coughed, the foetid air clogging his lungs, then went on with his tale.

"We made a decent living and it was a fine life. Better than toiling in the fields that's for sure. I had an older brother, Simon and we'd often perform together, just the two of us, both playing the gittern. We worked out how to play different harmonies and things, you've never heard anything like it before. People loved it."

"How'd you end up in this shit-hole then, if you were so good?" the old man demanded.

"We played in Hull one night, at the lord's manor house. We went down well; everyone loved us. But the lord, I forget his name now... Christ I remember what he looked like though, lanky prick. Wish I could have five moments alone with him... Anyway," Allan growled, remembering where he was, "the lord tried to underpay us. He only gave my father half the agreed fee and, well, our troop didn't take it too well."

Allan sighed heavily, remembering that morning almost as if it had been a week rather than over a decade ago.

"A fight started and the lord was badly injured. My brother and I were in the thick of it – I think it might even have been me that stabbed the nobleman but everything was happening too fast. It was all a blur. We were well outnumbered by the guards though, so we forced our way out of the manor house, the women and children jumping into our wagons and riding them off as fast as they could. We made our way along the road to the next town, pissed off that we'd been underpaid but, God's bollocks, our blood was up from the fight – we'd shown that fucking lord not to mistreat us."

"Did they follow you?"

"Aye," Allan nodded. "Some of them did. The more vicious of them; the ones that couldn't accept defeat at the hands of some minstrel band..." His voice trailed off and there was silence for a time, unbroken even by the skittering of rats. "There wasn't enough of them to stop us and mount a proper attack so they just hit us once from the rear and rode off, shouting and laughing. Me and my brother were riding rearguard – I did my best to fight them off but Simon... he was cut down like wheat under a farmer's scythe."

A prisoner's maniacal laugh echoed along the corridor incongruously and Allan, finally giving in to the fear and stress that had been slowly crushing him ever since Gisbourne's beating, sobbed loudly, burying his face in his legs again.

"My mother and father never forgave me for not saving Simon," he whispered, wiping his eyes with the backs of his hands. "I was only thirteen and he was a grown man but Simon had been their favourite. I could play gittern but I couldn't sing in harmony with the rest of them very well whereas he could do it all. I think my ma wished it had been me that had died... I ended up heading off on my own. Tried to live lawfully but, you know how it is."

The old man slapped something crawling up his calf, feeling it crunch under his palm. He knew Allan's tale was done and wondered what to say after such a depressing story. Finally he cleared his throat and asked the only question he could think of.

"We're going to die here aren't we?"

"Aye," Allan laughed through his tears. "I believe we are."

* * *

The friar wasn't a skilled rider, that much was obvious as the two outlaws chased after him. Yet neither were they, and it was hard going as they urged their tired mounts on through the torrential rain, desperately hoping they'd catch Brother Walter before he reached the safety of Chesterfield, a market town of a fair size with, undoubtedly, a large tithing to enforce the law...

The sun, already well hidden by the dark grey thunder-heads, had now begun to set and the countryside was a blur of lengthening shadows as the riders neared the town.

"We won't catch him in time," Little John roared over the drumming of hooves and rain.

Robin could see John was right, but he kept his head down, close to his palfrey's neck, and willed the beast onwards, cursing his lack of riding experience. He had his longbow and half-a-dozen arrows tucked into his belt but knew he'd fall off the galloping horse if he tried to use them. They couldn't let the Franciscan escape though – whatever was in the sheriff's letter was vitally important. They *had* to take it from the fleeing clergyman.

Not only that, the wolf's head despaired as he thought of young Hubert, lying dead in the grass, his throat slit like an animal sacrificed to some crazed pagan god. He'd be blamed for it, Robin knew. When tales were told of this day, the minstrels would assume he, the notorious outlaw Robin Hood, had killed the novice.

After all, who would believe the pious friar had torn the young boy's throat open accidentally?

Sometimes a dark reputation was a handy thing to have, but the idea of people seeing him as a murderer of

113

the friendly young novice made Robin seethe and he kicked his heels into his mount's side, willing the big animal onwards.

"We don't know the people in that town," John shouted, waving a big hand forward. "We're not going to catch the little prick in time, and he'll have the law on us once he blurts out his story. We should turn back now."

"No!" Robin replied, his voice whipped away by the wind that tore at them as they flew along the road. "Not until he enters the town. I won't give up."

They continued, gaining on the friar who would occasionally turn in his saddle to look back at them, his face an angry mask as he lashed his feet into his own mount's heaving, steaming, sides, but he was almost there. Almost at the safety of Chesterfield.

The town lay beyond a swollen river and Brother Walter laughed wildly as he spotted the bridge that would take him to safety. Then his joy turned to dismay as the pounding hooves of his mount carried him towards the stone structure and he cried out a most unholy curse.

The bridge had collapsed.

The horse raced on towards the damaged structure, the friar unable to decide what he should do. To stop meant certain death at the hands of the pursuing outlaws. Yet the river looked much too wide for his horse to jump across, even if he knew how to make the palfrey perform the feat.

"Christ protect me," he murmured, looking skyward as he kicked his heels in again and gritted his teeth in terror, knowing he had to make it to the other side of the swollen river if he was to survive.

His horse had better sense than Brother Walter though. It dug its shod hooves into the slippery wet ground and slowed to a sharp stop, so abruptly that the Franciscan was thrown forward to land face first in the grass at the edge of the raging water as his pursuers charged up behind him with triumphant howls.

"Where's the letter?" Robin shouted, dropping to the ground and running over to grasp the stunned churchman by the throat. "Give it to me or, so help me God, I'll strip you naked and search your clothes for it."

The friar knew there was no point defying the furious wolf's head now. He pulled the sheriff's letter from its hiding place inside his grey habit, handing it over shakily, his eyes wide with fear.

"You know you killed Hubert?" Robin demanded, shaking the friar viciously. "He's lying dead, face-down in the dirt a mile back along the road. Your knife opened his neck, you evil sack of shit."

The clergyman, already trembling from fear, and the damp that the rains had brought, shook his head in disbelief. He was a moaning, cranky old bastard, he knew that himself, but he was no murderer. He was a man of god, a friar, there was no way he'd ever take the life of another human, even that irritating young novice he'd been saddled with.

"You're lying," he shouted, almost hysterically, the rain running down his face and mingling with the tears of terror that spilled from his red-rimmed eyes. "*You* killed young Hubert, and now seek to lay the blame on me. As if anyone will believe that, you murdering wolf's head."

Robin punched the friar hard in the face, sending the man flying as he broke de Faucumberg's seal and tore open the letter.

Little John dismounted and grabbed Walter by the belt as he tried to scrabble away, sobbing, into the undergrowth by the river's bank. Robin was engrossed in the letter.

The young man had been taught how to read a little by Friar Tuck, but it took him a long time to make any sense of the sheriff's words, and Walter struggled against the giant's implacable hold as the wolf's head read and re-read the parchment in disbelief.

"Well?" John demanded, shaking water from his hair like a great, sodden hound. "What does it say?"

Robin looked up at him with a small smile. "We need to go to London to see the king," he replied. "If it says what I think it does, he has to read this."

John grunted and shook the friar again. "What about him?"

"If we let him go he'll give us away –"

"I won't! I swear in the name of God and all his angels. I won't!"

Robin shook his head sadly, thinking of the Hubert – a mere child – lying dead by the roadside and fixed Brother Walter with a hard stare.

"Take his clothes and valuables so no-one will know who he is. Then throw him in the river."

CHAPTER TWELVE

Although Robin couldn't read all that well, especially the Latin that the sheriff's letter to the king was written in, he was able to make out a few words; enough to make him think the document could be incredibly important to him and his friends.

After they'd stripped the friar of his robe, brass pectoral cross and the coin purse de Faucumberg had given him, Little John had thrown the screaming man into the raging torrent of the River Rother. "If you're so close to our Lord he'll fish you out, or send one of his saints to do it," the giant roared as the skinny white figure was carried away by the swiftly moving waters. "Somehow," he growled to himself as the figure, and its cries of terror, receded into the distance, "I doubt God will be much interested in you."

They made their way back to young Hubert's pitiful corpse and, with heavy hearts, stripped him too of his clothes and valuables before carrying his body back to the river and tossing him into the churning waters. They watched in silence, heads bowed in prayer, as the boy's pale, lifeless cadaver was washed away.

"We'll stop at the next town," Robin said, climbing back onto his horse which looked fed-up as the rain streamed down its long face. "Dry out, get some food and, maybe, buy ourselves Franciscan friar's outfits since these ones are too small..."

John mounted his own palfrey, throwing his leader a look of disbelief. "You think the two of us will pass for friars? We're much bigger than any of the pious bastards I've ever seen. No-one will believe it."

Robin shrugged, kicking his mount into an easy canter back onto the road south. "A lot of old soldiers – sick of the death and killing and looking to atone for the things they've done in their lives – become monks or friars. Just because we haven't seen anyone as big as us doesn't mean much. Neither of us is very well-travelled."

John shook his great head like a hound, rain spraying off him. "Maybe," he conceded. "Perhaps Will or Tuck could tell us more if they were here."

They made good time, only stopping for a short while to burn the incriminating Francsican cassocks, and reached Chesterfield by early evening. The rain had stopped and the spring sun had even made an appearance, drying the worst of the damp from their clothes although it was sinking into the horizon as they rode past the lone gate-guard and into the town.

"No riding in the streets," the guard, a middle-aged man with a head cleanly shaven, shouted at them, nodding in satisfaction as the two men dismounted with apologetic waves.

"We seek an inn," Robin said to the man.

"Mercenaries are you?"

The outlaw nodded, noting the older man's look of appraisal. "Aye, on our way south to seek work for one of the lords in the big city."

"Used to be a sell-sword myself, in my younger days," the guard replied. "Before I met my wife..." He shook his head with a rueful smile. "But you lads don't want to hear about my troubles, you look like you could do with a few ales and a warm fire." He pointed along the street to the west of the town. "Follow the road there, not far along it you'll find the Hermit's Arms. Stupid name, I know, but the landlord's wife brews a fine ale and there's a stable for your mounts."

The outlaws waved their gratitude and Robin tossed the man a silver coin for his trouble which the guard caught and bit into before grinning and turning back to watch the gate.

The Hermit's Arms proved to be a goodly-sized establishment with two stories and, as the guard had promised, a well-appointed stable where they left their palfreys in the care of a young lad no more than ten years old. Another small coin was enough for the boy to promise he'd take special care of the horses as Robin followed John into the inviting common room of the inn.

A serving girl warmed a couple of ales for them using the pokers that sat by the fire for the purpose, took payment for a room and promised to bring them some of the stew they could smell cooking.

The pair then spent an enjoyable night in the tavern. It was hard to believe, but Robin realised this was the first extended period of time the two friends had ever really shared on their own together.

In the past two years they had often fished by the River Calder, sat by the camp-fire sharing stories and robbed rich merchants in each other's company but there had always been one or more of the other outlaw gang somewhere nearby, and the threat of capture or death at the hands of the law hanging over them.

They felt safe here in the inn though.

The ale was indeed good, the fire cosy and bright, and the companions enjoyed a fine evening before making their way to the room they'd paid for. Once there they collapsed, exhausted, on the crude but comfortable beds and forgot about their troubles for a time.

In the morning, they downed some more of the landlord's ale to take the edge off their hangovers and left, with a wave to the man and his wife, who furnished them with bread and hard-boiled eggs for their breakfast.

The inn-keeper had pointed them in the direction of the nearest tailor with a puzzled look on his face, but he knew better than to ask questions of guests. Sometimes it was safer not to know certain things...

The outfitter was, like the inn-keeper, surprised when the two enormous, hard-looking men had walked into his shop and asked to buy the biggest grey cassocks he sold.

"Are they for," the man eyed them suspiciously, "yourselves?"

"Aye, they are," Little John nodded. Despite his great size, the giant had an open, honest face and his smile could disarm almost anyone. "We're heading to Manchester to visit a friend of ours. He heard a rumour we'd become friars so we thought we'd turn up dressed in cassocks to see the look on his face." He laughed, the infectious sound filling the small premises. "Can you imagine? Us? Franciscans? It's hilarious!"

The man smiled, not entirely convinced by the story, but the younger of the two men pulled a purse from his belt and opened it to fish out some coins. Clearly these two men – soldiers from the look of them – had earned enough money to throw it away on something as frivolous as a jest. And who was he to care who he sold his wares to? Their silver was good as any man's.

Sizing up Little John the tailor nodded and slipped into the back of the shop where he could be heard rummaging around for a short while. Eventually, he returned with two massive dark grey cassocks, shaking them out and holding them high up to show their length.

"They look ideal," Robin nodded approvingly. "We weren't sure if you'd have any big enough to fit us."

The man held one against John's great frame with a practised eye, murmuring to himself. "Oh, yes," he said. "Clergymen come in all shapes and sizes, they're not all thin old men. That being said," he looked up at John again, "I've never seen one as tall as you. But then, I've never seen *anyone* as tall as you; I'm afraid this will be rather short. You realise that, to complete the disguise, you'll have to shave your heads?"

John threw Robin a venomous look at the idea of wearing the clergyman's hairstyle but his young leader simply shrugged and grinned. The tailor was right – they'd need to lose their unruly thick hair.

They paid for the garments, promising to tell the tailor how their trick worked if they were ever back in Chesterfield again before collecting their horses from the Hermit's Arms and riding south again.

To London. And the king.

* * *

"Get that filth cleared, you two!" The dean hooted at Tuck who had, again, been sent to clear out the latrines with his companion for the morning; Osferth, the monk that had helped Edwin open the door when he'd first returned to the priory.

The big friar ignored the mocking laughter from the prior's right-hand man, using his shovel to throw the human waste out of the building and down into the ditch far below, wishing Henry of Elmstow was lying suffocating underneath the mound of shit.

Not only had the former outlaw been made to do the filthiest, most menial tasks since his return to Lewes, but he'd also been told to take his meals – reduced in size under de Monte Martini's orders no doubt – with the novices, and the Benedictine monks had clearly been told not to converse with him. That was the worst penance; he didn't mind shovelling shit, or sitting with the youngsters, or even having less to eat than he was used to... no, it was the lack of companionship that really got to him. He was a sociable fellow and some of the brothers here had been friends of his before he'd joined Robin Hood's gang.

At least today he had someone to share the work with. Brother Osferth must have annoyed the prior too, to be given a task like this, although the younger man hadn't said a word to him since they'd started work that morning.

With a grunt that was half a sigh Tuck threw out another spadeful of watery, stinking muck and resolved not to let the prior grind him down. God had placed de Monte Martini's missing holy relic in Tuck's hand for a purpose he believed; he was meant to return here for some reason.

He'd just have to ignore the harsh treatment and pray the prior got bored with tormenting him soon.

As he worked he contemplated the idea of returning north to rejoin Robin and the rest of his outlaw friends but he rejected the notion sadly. His body was past it – the illness he'd suffered the previous summer after Sir Guy of Gisbourne had shot and nearly drowned him had taken its toll. Although he'd put some weight back on over the months, he now *felt* old; his bones ached. It was a hard thing to accept but it was true. The noisome fumes in the latrine made it difficult for him to breathe too, even

121

through the damp rag, and he'd recently developed a racking cough that occasionally saw him bent double with the force of it.

His days of living in the greenwood were over; that chapter of his life was done. He knew when he returned here that the prior – an unpleasant man at the best of times but with a grudge against Tuck to boot – would make his life hard. It appeared the prior's steward had also made it his personal task to mete out Tuck's penance.

He mouthed silent prayers to God, sweating freely from the hard work in the confined, foetid space and asked for the Lord's strength and guidance.

Or at least a few days rest from shovelling human waste...

* * *

Marjorie avoided Matilda after their falling out. Any time the older girl tried to talk to her, to set things right, Marjorie would ignore her and leave to collect berries, or firewood, or flowers to decorate the house. Anything to get away from her sister-in-law.

It couldn't go on forever though. Matilda came into the Hood's house one morning when Martha and John were out, closing the door behind her and blocking it with her body.

"I'm sorry, Marjorie. Truly, I am. You have no idea how stressful it is trying to finish your work on time while watching an infant that has no sense of danger."

Marjorie glared at her, but said nothing.

"Look, you have to stop trying to be something you're not. Accept yourself for who you really are. Aye, you're no good at hunting – so what? Not many local girls are. Why should you be any different?"

Marjorie sighed and sat down in one of the chairs beside the trestle table the family used to eat their meals at. It was a fine table, well-made, and the family folded it away every evening to save space in the small dwelling.

"I have to be good at something," the girl said. "Everyone is good at something."

Matilda sat down next to her, relieved to have finally broken the barrier between them.

"You're young yet. I know, I'm not all that much older than you, and when I was your age I wasn't sure what I wanted to do with myself either. The thing is, life has a habit of leading you wherever it is you need to go – wherever you're needed."

Marjorie looked unconvinced as Matilda forged on.

"You're not a hunter, and you'll never be the greatest sword-fighter in England, right. But neither will I. Look at you – the training you've been doing has toughened you up – put meat on your bones. It will come in handy one day, just wait and see."

They sat in silence for a time but it wasn't an awkward silence. Their old friendship was back, and Marjorie was glad of it.

"I have to get back," Matilda said, standing up and smiling at her young companion. "We still haven't completed that order for the merchant. My da keeps finding loose fletchings and making me redo them. Feels like my fingers will be nothing but bloody bones by the time we get the order all done."

She opened the door, sunlight streaming into the gloomy house. "Come over to mine later – Arthur's been asking after you."

Marjorie smiled and promised she would visit sometime, but, when the door had closed again and she was left by herself she stared, unseeing, into space, wondering where her life was going.

She was only young but she felt very old. She'd seen so much in her short life and it got to her sometimes. She had to admit, though – training with Matilda had made her stronger in every way. She liked the feeling; enjoyed the sense of purpose the exercises gave her.

"Time to get back to work."

She stood up, feeling not quite as if she'd found her true calling but realising life would go on whether she wallowed in self-pity or chose to get out and make the most of things.

Matilda was right – life would find a use for her eventually.

CHAPTER THIRTEEN

The journey south took Robin and Little John the next three days but they enjoyed the ride despite its ultimate purpose. Spring was in full bloom so the fields were green with barley and rye, the grass and foliage that blanketed the countryside was thick and lush and the sun cast a warm light on the countryside meaning the night they camped out was fairly comfortable.

"Aye, England truly is a green and beautiful land," Robin said, watching the unhurried passage of a large black and orange butterfly with a contented smile.

"It is," John agreed. "When it's not pissing down or some ugly forester's trying to smash your teeth into the back of your skull."

"I've never been this far south before. In fact, before I was outlawed I don't think I'd ever even left Yorkshire."

John nodded. It wasn't uncommon for people to spend their whole lives within their own county – there wasn't any need for a peasant or yeoman to travel to a city and, even if they wanted to, the price of an inn was enough to discourage most.

"I've been here before," Little John said, looking around thoughtfully. "At least, I seem to have a memory of some of the landmarks we've passed today. My family travelled to the capital once, when I was very young, on a pilgrimage. My grandmother was ill, and the priest in St Michael's suggested we come away down to pray for her in St Paul's Cathedral. I don't remember much about it to be honest."

Robin was impressed that his friend had travelled so far in his life. "Did your prayers work? Did your grandmother recover from her illness?"

"No. She died a week later." The giant shook his head ruefully then his smile returned. "Waste of bloody time that pilgrimage."

It was unusual for John to mention his family, even now that they'd been friends for a couple of years, and

Robin wanted to take the opportunity to find out something of the big man's past.

"Did you never travel with Amber and wee John?"

"Nah. My wife was a maid for one of the merchants in Hathersage – still is, in fact. She couldn't just take weeks off to travel to no good purpose." John's eyes stared fixedly on the road ahead as thoughts of his wife and son came to him. He sighed heavily. "I have more than enough money now that I could travel anywhere I like. Even Rome, or one of those other famous old places the minstrels sing about. I bet John would have a great time climbing those big monuments – you remember the ones Allan goes on about? The colloso... collosem or something I think one's called." His hand disappeared inside the grey cassock and touched the cheap amulet he wore on a thong around his neck that had been a gift from Amber long ago. "I have all the money to do what I want with my family and no chance to do it."

"You will," Robin assured him, meeting the giant's eyes. "I promise you. Somehow we'll win a pardon and you can take your family to Rome."

John grinned and looked back at the road ahead. "Ach, my wife would be just as happy travelling to Sheffield to visit her sister. Speaking of which, how's young Marjorie? Not so young now I suppose, she'll be nearly a woman eh?"

"Aye," Robin said, thinking fondly of his younger sibling. "She's well enough, although she'll never be as sturdy as my ma, or even Matilda. I expect my da will be looking for a husband for her soon enough – hopefully whoever it is looks after her. They'd fucking better or else..."

The pair fell into a somewhat maudlin silence as their thoughts lingered on loved ones far away and their mounts carried them towards the city. The light began to fail before they could get there though, so, as the sun slowly set and the road became treacherous for their mounts, they chose to spend the night in another small town, not that far from the capital's walls.

Before entering the place they found a small stream and, using their eating knives, shaved one another's heads in the same way Friar Tuck did, with the crown bald and the back, front and sides left as they were.

"You look like a right fucking oaf," John giggled, squinting at his friend in the dim light while running a hand over his own scalp and looking down at the bloodstained fingers ruefully.

Robin laughed. "Aye, I bet I do," he agreed, trying vainly to see his reflection in the stream before cupping some of the chill waters and using it to wash the crimson from the pores of his own head. "But at least we look more like friars now. Wait, you're not finished, you need to shave that beard of yours."

"My beard? I've been growing this for years."

Robin grinned. "Can't be a friar with a beard."

When they were finished even their friends wouldn't have recognised them straight away and, in Little John's case, maybe not at all.

They made their way into the town and, since they had coin enough to pay for decent lodgings were able to spend a comfortable evening in the local inn's common room. There was plenty of meat and ale to fill their bellies, but the overnight delay irritated the pair as they wanted to reach the king as soon as possible.

What they would do when they came face to face with England's monarch they weren't quite sure yet. Would they even make it in to see the king, or would they be recognised as outlaws and cut down before they even made it past the first guardsmen? Even if they did convince the guards that they were clergymen would they be able to fool the king too? Or would they be found out as soon as they opened their uneducated mouths?

Only time would tell but Robin was confident, as always. All would be well...

They were up before dawn the next day, even before the cockerel – which the landlord had promised was a perfect time-keeper – had crowed to signal the sun's ascent into the eastern sky. After bothering the inn-keep for some bread and cheese to break their fast they set off at a brisk pace, only stopping to hide their bulky weapons in a thick clump of bushes a little way off the road – they wanted to look like clergymen, not soldiers after all. Then, remounting they pushed their horses hard and reached the capital city's gates while it was still morning.

London.

Both outlaws had the hoods drawn up on the grey cloaks that they wore in what they hoped was the Franciscan style and, along with the pectoral crosses they'd taken from Hubert and Walter to hang around their necks, they looked like nothing more than normal – if extremely well-built – friars to the gate guards who watched them pass without a word of challenge.

"We should visit the Franciscan... church or priory or whatever the hell they call it," Little John murmured as they walked their mounts through the unbelievably crowded streets of London. "It's what real friars would do."

Robin snorted making his horse glare back at him with a bulging eye. "We're not real friars, even if we have spent so many months living with Tuck," he said, pulling on his palfrey's bridle. "We wouldn't know how to act like them and the Franciscans would see through our disguise in a moment. No, our best bet is to head straight for the royal palace and seek an audience with the king. We can deliver our letter and be on our way again before the day's out."

Little John smiled although Robin could see the stress of their situation written all over the giant's newly-shaven face. "Aye, straight back to Nottingham to free Allan without a hitch. Piece of piss."

The companions had never seen so many people gathered in one place: foreign merchants dressed in brightly coloured clothes chattered to one another in strange languages; carts laden with eggs and cheese rattled past; workers drove noisy sheep along the road to market and street vendors hailed them continually, with cries of "Hot peascods," and "Sheep's feet, come an' get 'em."

Their mouths watered at the sight of the laden trays but they were in too much of a hurry to stop.

They had no idea of the layout of the city or how to get to Westminster Palace but there were enough people to ask directions, and, once they grew nearer, the imposing bulk of the place stood high above any other building in the vicinity.

Although their initial plan had been to find someone to read Sir Henry de Faucumberg's letter to the king that they'd taken from Brother Walter, in the end Robin had decided against it. Showing the parchment to anyone else would surely draw unwanted attention to them – no real friar or monk would ask a layman to read a letter for them. Especially a letter about the capture of a member of the notorious Robin Hood's band.

Robin felt sure that he'd picked up the gist of the document himself anyway, and he wasn't about to place their lives in danger just to fill in the few Latin blanks that he couldn't make sense of.

"So tell me, then." John grumbled as they neared the royal palace. "What you think the letter says. You've been keeping it a secret this whole time."

Robin looked around in wonder at the enormous stone walls and imposing architecture that surrounded them and threw his big mate a happy grin, his teeth flashing from beneath the cassock's hood.

"I believe the sheriff is telling the king that he's captured Allan, but, if I have it right, he's also complaining about Sir Guy of Gisbourne's treatment of the people of Yorkshire."

John whistled quietly. He hadn't expected de Faucumberg to speak out against the king's own bounty hunter. "I have to admit," he said, "the sheriff comes across as a decent man. Even if he did double-cross us the other winter. And Gisbourne has been even more of prick lately... What d'you think the king'll do?"

Robin shrugged. "What do I know about the workings of royalty? Hopefully the king will listen to his sheriff and call Gisbourne back here before sending him overseas or to Scotland or, well, anywhere other than Barnsdale."

"I take it you have a plan, or at least some idea of what to say once we're in front of the king?" John asked, raising a bushy eyebrow questioningly. "What about the letter's broken seal? How will you explain that?"

Robin shrugged again and laughed. They'd reached the palace and nerves grasped his insides but he pushed them aside, knowing he had to appear outwardly calm or the king's guardsmen would see through their outrageous disguise. "Don't worry, of course I have a plan – don't I always?"

"Aye, always," John agreed, lowering his voice as they approached the gates. "Most of the time they're crazy and suicidal though. I hope this time you have something a bit better because if the king doesn't believe our story, there'll be no escape."

The huge, cold, grey walls loomed high above them, staggering them with their sheer size and Robin felt a lump of bile forming in his throat. He coughed to try and clear it but it stuck, lodged there and he wished they'd stopped at a tavern for a few ales before coming here. At least if he was drunk he wouldn't feel so frightened.

But it was too late for that. They'd reached the great wooden gates to the palace and there was no going back.

The guard captain looked them up and down, taking in their great size and the grey habits they wore with a look of interest on his face before nodding respectfully.

"State your business with the king, brother friars."

Robin took a deep breath, not even noticing the uncomfortable phlegm had disappeared as an icy calm came over him and he began to tell the guard their tale.

* * *

"Bugger this, and bugger the prior."

Tuck smiled at Brother Osferth, his companion for the morning – again – and nodded sad agreement, glad that the fellow was feeling more talkative today. "Aye, God forgive me, but I'm beginning to wish I'd never come back here." He lifted another armful of logs which Osferth was splitting with an old axe and stacked them with the rest of the pile they'd been working on since dawn.

While the rest of the monks had been making their way to the early morning service of Lauds Prior de Monte Martini's dean, Henry, had waved Tuck and Osferth aside and told them the prior needed firewood chopped as there were important visitors coming from London that day. It was obviously nonsense; Tuck had seen the vast stores of fuel that were piled up by the priory's east wall, so even if there *were* visitors they didn't need any more wood for the hearth in the chapter-house but he hadn't bothered arguing with the dean.

Osferth, on the other hand, complained loudly and angrily about missing his morning devotions. The dean simply shrugged and told them it was the prior's orders and they'd better get on with it if they didn't want to miss their dinner as well.

A sharp crack filled the air as the younger monk hefted the axe again before wiping the sheen of sweat from his brow and sitting down on the pile of uncut logs with a heavy, angry sigh.

Osferth was in his mid-twenties, although he looked much younger, and had an open, pleasant face which fitted his personality perfectly. The other monks in Lewes Priory liked the man, but he had a problem taking orders and it had led de Monte Martini to mark him down as a troublemaker.

"God works in mysterious ways," he replied to Tuck, who grunted non-committally. "We all heard about you joining those outlaws up north. Never thought I'd see you here again but... God must have led you back here for a purpose."

Tuck allowed himself to slump down on the grass beside Osferth, a hacking cough bursting from his lips as he did so. "What purpose?" he growled. "To cut logs? To shovel filth from the latrines? To listen to the babbling of novices?" He coughed again, bending over until his head was almost on the ground before wiping his mouth and glaring up at his companion. "To eat even less than I did as a wolf's head in the snow shrouded forests of Yorkshire? Is that my purpose?" He shook his tonsured head irritably. "God be praised then, I've found my true calling."

Osferth smiled before standing up and lifting the blunt axe again. "Someone should really sharpen this bloody thing," he muttered before he placed another piece of timber on the block and brought the weapon down on it, splitting it neatly in two. "At least you're not with the outlaws any more. Once the sheriff knows where they are he'll make short work of them. This might be a harder work than we'd like but it's better than being killed."

Tuck hauled himself to his feet with a grunt, clutching at the sharp pain in his chest where Sir Guy of Gisbourne's crossbow bolt had almost ended his life the previous summer. "The sheriff's been after Robin and the lads for a long time now – years!" He smiled. "They know how to stay one step ahead of de Faucumberg and his men."

Osferth continued chopping wood in a mechanical fashion, occasionally wiping his brow or blowing a curse from dry lips. "Aye, maybe," he finally agreed. "But the prior's information will let the lawmen finally catch up with Hood."

Tuck's head spun round and he almost dropped the pile of wood he was placing neatly amongst the rest of the pile. "What information?"

The axeman's eyes flicked up at the note of surprise in Tuck's voice and he held the implement still for a moment. "You know – the location of Hood's camp."

Tuck dropped the firewood onto the ground and moved across to stand before Osferth, his eyes blazing. "What are you talking about?" he demanded. "De Monte Martini doesn't know where they are. How could he?"

Osferth stepped back, unnerved by the threat of violence that he saw reflected in Tuck's normally jovial features. "I don't know how he found out the location of their camp, but he did. He sent one of the brothers north to

Nottingham just the other day, to tell the sheriff. Did you not know?"

Tuck sagged back onto the stone wall that surrounded the priory, his mind whirling. He hadn't heard anything about this, probably because he'd been made to take his meals with the novices and the other friars had been warned against talking to him by the prior.

"Hood and his men are probably all dead by now," Osferth grunted, swinging the axe to split another log. "I'm sorry," he said, as he placed another, fresh piece of wood onto the block and stepped back to half that one too. "I know you were close to some of them."

Tuck suddenly lunged forward and grabbed the Benedictine's right arm in a grip that shocked the younger man with its strength. "When? When did the messenger leave for Nottingham?"

The axeman shook his head. "I don't remember. A day or two ago I think. Brother Cedric it was. One of the –"

"– Younger men." Tuck finished for him. "Aye, I know who Cedric is."

The big friar leant against the wall and closed his eyes, his mind racing. What was he to do? His friends might be dead already. And yet... What was his life now? To be used and abused by de Monte Martini, a greedy, grasping man not worthy of the title of prior? Surely this wasn't God's plan for him.

No, it was a sign!

Tuck saw it clearly now. He'd known as soon as he'd set eyes on the long-lost holy relic back in Yorkshire with the outlaws that it had been given to him for a reason. He'd been stoic in the face of the prior's harsh treatment but he'd been unable to fathom the divine purpose in it all. Why would God send him back here simply to be treated like a serf?

Now it was clear. He'd been brought here to save Robin and his friends, not that damned prior.

"Brother Cedric only has a couple of days start," he said, turning to meet Osferth's gaze. "I can still reach Nottingham before him." He pushed himself off the wall and, firewood forgotten, hurried past his surprised companion, a fiery gleam lighting his eyes from within. He knew what his purpose was now, and chopping firewood or shovelling shit was not part of it.

"Wait. Wait!"

Tuck waved a hand irritably as Osferth chased after him.

"Stop, Robert!" The younger man shouted behind him. "Let me come with you."

That halted Tuck, although only for a moment. "You can't come with me," he retorted, shaking his head as he hurried back into the priory and along the gloomy corridor to his cell. "I'll be returning to a life as a wolf's head – an outlaw. A criminal that any man can cut down with church and state's blessing!"

Osferth caught up to him and fell into step by his side, a boyish grin on his face.

"So you say," he laughed. "But I'm no outlaw; I can go where I like and I'm coming too. It has to be better than this."

Tuck hurried along the corridor shaking his head. Osferth seemed touched but this was a step too far even for him. "You can't just leave your life here; what about your vows? Besides, the prior will send word to every Benedictine in the country about what we've done."

Osferth kept pace beside the older man for a moment then cocked an eyebrow at the older man in bemusement. "What we've done?"

"Aye," Tuck grinned. "That ungodly womaniser doesn't deserve to keep the relic I returned to him. With the Lord's grace I'm going to steal it and take it back to Brandesburton, where it belongs."

* * *

Another tiresome day listening to men prattle on about minor matters that, to them, seemed like grand problems but ultimately left King Edward II bored and irritated and watching the shadows lengthen as the sun moved across the sky outside, wishing it would move faster so he could get out and see his friends.

Sir Hugh Despenser the younger was his friend, and, as the king's chamberlain, had accompanied him on this trip to Westminster Palace. He was glad his closest friend and adviser was there; although they had put down the rebellion a year earlier, things had not been as peaceful as the king would have wished. The Scots had continued to be a problem and even Sir Andrew Harclay, who'd led Edward's forces so effectively against the Contrariants at the Battle of Boroughbridge, had taken it upon himself to treat with the Bruce. The king had ordered Harclay arrested and taken to London where he was executed for his treasonous actions. Thankfully, the Scots had, provisionally, agreed to a truce which had been thrashed out mostly by Sir Hugh himself and would hopefully sign it within the next few weeks.

For the first time in his reign, King Edward could rule without the threat of war in the north hanging over him. But the defection of Harclay rankled badly and Edward felt a black depression come upon him every time he thought of his formerly loyal general.

He was a lonely king, and he smiled at the younger Despenser, glad he was there with him. His wife, Queen Isabella, hated Sir Hugh, but Edward cared little for that – they hadn't shared the marital bed for months and had never been particularly close anyway, despite their four children. When the rebels had forced the king to exile Despenser two years earlier Edward had continued to support his friend financially and, as soon as possible, allowed Sir Hugh to return and reclaim his lands, titles, and position as his closest adviser.

Like Piers Gaveston before him, the younger Despenser was loved by Edward but their friendship didn't sit well with the people of England. Damn them all to hell, a king needed someone that he could trust, why couldn't they accept that? It wasn't as if his confidante and adviser was incompetent – on the contrary, both Hugh and his father, also called Hugh, were capable and ambitious men who had proven their worth to the crown, even in the face of the murderous hostility of the rebel magnates.

Still, there didn't seem to be much Sir Hugh could do about the seemingly endless line of irritating petitioners that waited outside the grand chamber. Edward would just need to get on with things until he and his friend could move on to more interesting pursuits.

"You look in ill humour, sire," Sir Hugh noted, a small smile playing on his thin lips.

"Do you blame me? This is interminable."

"Well, I think you'll enjoy receiving at least a couple of your visitors today." The chamberlain grinned and gestured at the line of petitioners who stood queueing to meet the king. Behind a small, balding man in ridiculously extravagant clothing stood two of the biggest friars the king had ever seen.

"They bring word from Sir Henry de Faucumberg, Sheriff of Nottingham and Yorkshire." Sir Hugh muttered.

Edward watched the clergymen as the bald man was announced and approached the throne, his eyes taking in their impressive physiques which even the shapeless grey cassocks couldn't hide. Sir Hugh was right, these two promised to be much more interesting than the usual mumbling, nervous nobles he had to deal with. Like the little fop that knelt before him now.

Edward sighed. He'd have to deal with this one before he could find out who the huge friars were. He forced what he hoped was a reassuring smile onto his handsome face and gestured at the supplicant before him. "Rise and state your case, my good man."

136

CHAPTER FOURTEEN

The audience room was astonishing. If Robin and John had been impressed by the architecture and sheer grandeur of the capital city before, they were left open-mouthed by the sight of the king's reception chamber.

There was, of course, a high-backed throne, although it wasn't as large or as ornate as Robin expected. It looked rather comfortable in fact, and the wolf's head supposed it had to be, if the king was going to spend extended periods in it dealing with his courtiers.

The walls were lavishly decorated with paintings and tapestries shot through with gold and silver which caught any light and shone beautifully. There were weapons – ceremonial of course although they would doubtless prove as deadly as any other if wielded in anger – displayed in stands in the corners of the room and even the table the king and his advisers sat behind looked as if it had been hewn from one great living piece of oak, with gargoyles and religious motifs carved delicately into the legs and corners.

In short, the room was stunning.

The two outlaws, hunched and hooded in their grey robes, waited in line behind those others who had come to petition the monarch. A wealthy merchant complaining about the activities of pirates in the waters off the coast of Cornwall; a bailiff from Derbyshire pleading for help with a gang of violent outlaws that were plaguing the area; a group of farmers from Lincolnshire demanding something be done about their lord who took too much grain from them in tax and a variety of others, all seeking the king's aid.

Edward looked utterly bored by the whole thing, only occasionally sitting up in his finely carved chair to listen intently when someone's story caught his interest. For the most part he played with the cuffs of his embroidered sleeves and seemed on the point of falling fast asleep. His advisers at least seemed interested; one man with a neatly-trimmed beard sat at the king's right hand, smiling and raising his eyebrows in consternation whenever a petitioner appeared to be upset, but it was clear nothing of any real importance was happening at court that day.

The petitioners took their turn to state their case and, depending on the outcome, passed Robin and John either grinning in triumph or muttering about the king's inattention. John fidgeted nervously as they waited their turn, but Robin stood stock still, taking in everything that was going on to make sure he knew how to address England's most powerful man.

"Pull your hoods down, brothers," a footman hissed in annoyance at the two would-be Franciscans as their time to address the throne approached. "You can't meet the king with your faces hidden."

Robin swivelled his head to meet Little John's wide eyes and the pair pulled back the cowls, revealing their tonsured heads. The footman that had reprimanded them took an involuntary step backwards, the sight of the young, hard faces giving the huge friars a somewhat sinister, threatening look. Had he been manning the gates when this pair had arrived he would have turned them away, but it was too late for that. The man in the line before them, a magistrate from Norwich seeking authority from Edward to seize the lands of a troublesome local baron, stated his case successfully and was waved away, smiling like a sailor in a whorehouse.

It was time to meet the king.

The footman stepped back, warily watching the two massive, grey robed, friars who approached the throne and knelt respectfully.

"You are Franciscans?" The greybeard on the king's left asked politely, his eyes taking in the unusual sight before him as Robin and John nodded. "State your names, and your business here today."

"Brother Hubert –"

"– and Brother Walter," Robin broke in, finishing the introduction and rising at a gesture from the old adviser at the king's side. "From Gloucester Greyfriars." He made the sign of the cross but kept his head bowed rather than meeting Edward's stare and fished inside the grey cassock to retrieve Sir Henry de Faucumberg's letter. The competent, professional-looking soldiers behind the king moved forward, pole-arms raised threateningly as the tall young friar with his enormous archer's shoulders put a hand inside his robe, but Robin produced the rolled-up parchment with a small smile and the guards relaxed.

A servant hurried forward to take the proffered letter and moved to kneel before the king, head down and hand outstretched. Edward, eyes still fixed on the two enormous clergymen before him took the rolled up parchment and finally looked down at it with a frown.

"We bring word from Sir Henry de Faucumberg, sire," Robin said, pleased to hear his voice ring out strong and true despite the nerves that gripped his insides. He could feel the sweat pooling uncomfortably under his armpits and he sensed Little John tensing beside him, ready to fight for his life should the king query the fact the letter's seal had been broken.

"This," Edward growled, looking up and meeting Robin's gaze, "is from the Sheriff of Nottingham and Yorkshire?"

"Aye, lord king, it is. He tasked us with delivering it into your hands. I can only apologise – we encountered some... trouble, on the way here. A pair of craven outlaws tried to rob us. They broke the seal on the letter although, needless to say they couldn't even read." He smiled slightly, confidently. "Brother Hubert and I managed to take back the letter and... chase them off."

The atmosphere in the hall had become strangely tense and Robin prayed silently that it was simply because he and John were much bigger than most other clergymen.

King Edward placed the parchment on the table in front of him without unrolling it and walked around to stand before them.

The outlaws tried to remain calm. This was new: the king hadn't moved out of his comfortable throne all day until now yet here he was, striding over to look into Little John's eyes.

"Stand up straight." As Edward spoke the guards moved in close, weapons held ready should either of the big friars seek to attack the monarch.

Little John's eyes flicked uncertainly towards Robin but he knew better than to refuse a command from England's ruler so he pushed his shoulders back and raised himself to his full height of almost seven feet.

There were gasps from the guards and from the petitioners lined up behind them as they took in the great size of the man – the friar – before them.

King Edward, though, grinned and stepped in closer, to stand so near to the giant outlaw that John could smell the delicate flower-scent that the king daubed on himself each morning.

"You're a big lad," Edward smiled approvingly, using his hand to mark his own height against Little John. The king wasn't a small man by any means – in fact he was just as tall as Robin, who watched the bizarre interchange with one eyebrow raised in surprise – but he only came up to John's neck. "How tall are you?"

John shrugged. "I don't know, sire. I've never measured myself."

The king grinned appreciatively and turned his eyes on Robin. "Friars, eh? I'm sure you did chase off those outlaws," he said, his voice full of wonder. "Excellent!" He returned to his throne and sat down, still smiling happily as he lifted the letter from Sir Henry de Faucumberg again. "I've never seen friars as big as you two before but I suppose you were soldiers at one time before renouncing the warrior's way of life and taking service with Christ. Good. I'd wager any more outlaws in my forests will think twice before they try and rob the pair of you once word gets around!"

Robin let out a nervous breath as the king tore open the rolled-up parchment without inspecting the seal too closely and began to read.

He grunted as he read before, at last, he snorted with laughter and handed the letter to the greybeard by his side.

"How did you two come to be de Faucumberg's messengers? And who is this Allan-a-Dale? What do you know of him?"

The king grilled Robin for a long time, the tall young 'friar' responding to the questions apparently truthfully and thoroughly entertaining the monarch with the tale even as the other petitioners lined up behind them muttered in annoyance at the delay in stating their own cases.

When he reached the end of his story the king looked at Robin thoughtfully, his eyes moving to Little John who tried to stand still but couldn't help fidgeting every now and again like a child apprentice under his master's harsh gaze.

"Do you know what the rest of de Faucumberg's letter says?" the monarch finally asked.

The outlaws shook their heads and Robin replied. "No, lord."

Edward grunted. "No, I don't suppose you would, would you?" He looked at the counsellor at his right hand who shrugged and shook his head, not sure what the king wanted to hear from him.

"The sheriff wants me to recall Sir Guy of Gisbourne. Apparently my bounty hunter has become something of a liability. And a violent one at that." The king threw the parchment onto the table irritably. "De Faucumberg needs a kick up the arse. You two will return to Nottingham with my reply, yes?"

"Of course, sire," Robin nodded deferentially. "We were to return there to continue our mission anyway. It would be our pleasure – nay, our *honour,* to carry your word back to the sheriff."

Edward smiled and muttered, "God be praised," before turning to face his steward who sat taking notes at a small table in the left-hand corner of the huge hall. "Make sure the good brothers are rewarded for their service to the crown," he told the man. "A donation to – where did you say you were from? Yes, Gloucester. Send

141

a donation of fifty pounds to Custos de Bromley on my behalf. In the meantime, take a letter to Sir Henry in Nottingham."

Robin and John bowed their heads gratefully to the king for the donation to 'their' friary as the monarch dictated his reply to the sheriff before the steward placed the parchment in an envelope, dripped a great red candle onto it and Edward pressed his ring into the soft wax.

"Sire," Robin took the letter with a respectful bow. "We will gladly carry this to Sir Henry but... I fear he may not like your reply and..."

The king met the young man's eyes and nodded in understanding. "And he will blame you two. I see." He waved over to the steward again. "Write another letter for the brothers to carry – one that makes it very clear they are under my protection and should be treated with all the respect loyal subjects of mine deserve. Now..." England's ruler smiled at Robin and John. "You two have livened up these dull proceedings and I thank you for it, but you may go. Return to Nottingham and my sheriff. I pray we meet again some day for I've enjoyed your company. Do you row?"

The question was directed at Little John who shook his head. "No, sire, I much prefer dry land."

"That's a pity," the king sighed, pressing his ring again into the wax of the letter of protection his steward had written out for them and looking at the huge man in the grey Franciscan robe appreciatively again. "You would have made a fine addition to my team."

He waved them away with a smile and the pair walked from the room as fast as they could, trying not to appear too relieved to have survived the royal meeting.

"That went well," Little John murmured as they passed the two pikemen guarding the hall doors.

"Aye," Robin agreed, pulling the hood on his cassock back over his head as they made their way towards the spring sunshine that struggled to light the chilly stone corridor. "Now we just need to deliver these letters to the sheriff and pray to God he believes they're genuine. We might not get rid of Gisbourne but at least I managed to persuade the king that Allan wasn't as bad as the sheriff's letter made out... "

* * *

The black-armoured bounty hunter had always made the villagers around Yorkshire nervous, ever since he'd first appeared in the area to work on the king's behalf the previous year. But after he'd suffered the terrible injuries to his face at the hands of Robin Hood he'd become even more frightening and the locals all over Yorkshire now dreaded a visit from Gisbourne and his men.

Patrick Prudhomme, headman of the village of Wakefield, repressed a shudder as the soldiers, at least a dozen of them, walked past him. Even Gisbourne's new sergeant, Matt Groves, a man Patrick knew well enough from his time as an outlaw seeking supplies from the villagers, had a vicious manner about him. Still, even he lacked the air of unpredictable madness that now appeared to surround Gisbourne like a great dark cloud.

Patrick steeled himself, wishing someone else would take over the role of headman, and hurried into the street after the visitors.

"My lord!" he shouted, striding along to reach the front of the small group. "My lord, I bid you welcome to our humble village, it's been a while since you last graced us with your presence."

Sir Guy stopped and turned his remaining good eye on the fidgeting headman with a sneer. The sight of the lean man's ruined face was enough to send small children screaming and, truth be told, Patrick would have liked to join them at that moment, but he stood his ground and returned Gisbourne's malevolent stare.

"Ah, Prudhomme isn't it? Yes, I know of you, although you were nowhere to be found the last time I visited, when Robin Hood and his friends killed several of my men. Robin Hood of *Wakefield* –" The slight emphasis Gisbourne placed on his village's name brought out a cold sweat on Patrick's skin "– also struck me last year, when I was unable to defend myself and, as you can see," he tapped his missing eye. "Ruined my good looks."

The bounty hunter swung away and began to walk along the muddy street again, his soldiers, and the anxious headman, following in his wake although one of Sir Guy's men, at an almost imperceptible signal from the wiry man, made his way back along the road they'd just come along.

"I'm fully recovered now," Gisbourne continued without looking at Patrick. "But, as you can probably imagine – especially after the last time I was in your little village – I'm even more determined to bring that outlaw scum to justice."

The words were spoken softly but Patrick's mind whirled, wondering exactly what the disfigured man-hunter was going to do. He'd heard the rumours from other villages roundabout ever since Robin's band had defeated the lawmen; rumours of Gisbourne and his men's brutality and merciless persecution of those the king's man suspected of giving aid to Hood and his gang.

Before, Gisbourne had been kept on a fairly tight leash by Sheriff de Faucumberg who'd ordered the bounty hunter not to harm the villagers in his pursuit of the wolf's head. But recently the sheriff's authority had not been enough to rein in the man people called The Raven. He was the king's man after all – sent there by Edward himself to do whatever he could to bring down Robin Hood and his gang.

The people of Yorkshire were terrified of the black-clad soldier, but no-one would stand up to him.

"Have you seen Hood lately?" Gisbourne asked the puffing headman who hurried along, trying to keep pace with the tall soldiers. He might as well have been asking after the weather for all the apparent emotion in his voice, but Patrick, a surprisingly perceptive man, knew better. The Raven wasn't just a master swordsman and a wicked bastard; he was also an actor – a showman. You could never take Gisbourne at face value, for everything he did

144

was calculated, and intended to create the atmosphere of fearful competence that he revelled in.

"No, my lord," Patrick replied truthfully. It had been weeks since Robin had left Matilda and their young son, Arthur, to return to life in the forest. "The outlaws must have moved their camp somewhere far to the east, for we've not seen hide nor hair of any of them for a long time now."

Gisbourne turned to look into the headman's eyes momentarily, apparently trying to measure whether he was being truthful or not before, satisfied, the Raven looked away again, continuing his walk towards the Fletcher's house.

Patrick cursed inwardly when he realised their destination. This was bad. Not that many months before another lawman – Adam Gurdon – had come to the village hunting for Robin Hood and had caused more than a little trouble at the Fletcher's house.

"My lord –" he began again but Gisbourne waved a gauntleted hand irritably.

"Shut up, Patrick, you're becoming annoying."

The headman closed his mouth, his lips pressed tightly together in a bloodless line as he fretted over what was to come. He was pleased to see many of the other villagers beginning to gather behind them and he tried to relax.

When the previous bailiff, Gurdon, had come to Wakefield and arrested Matilda, knocking her father, Henry the fletcher, out cold when he tried to intervene, the locals had been outraged. Robin Hood and his men had managed to rescue the girl though, and afterwards the people of Wakefield had complained bitterly to their then lord – Thomas Plantagenet, the Earl of Lancaster – who told Sheriff Henry de Faucumberg in no uncertain terms to leave the villagers alone in future.

To his credit, the sheriff had never sanctioned the arrest of Matilda Fletcher; indeed he'd known nothing about it at the time and, since then, he'd tried to make sure

Gisbourne and the other lawmen in the county left the innocent people of Wakefield pretty much to themselves.

Although Sir Guy's reputation was as fearsome as his appearance, he only had a handful of soldiers with him and, Patrick noticed, many of the villagers carried the tools of their trade: hammers, axes, pitchforks... they could all be lethal weapons in the hands of an angry mob.

There would be no repeat of last year's débâcle, the headman vowed. If the bloody bounty hunter wanted violence the good people of Wakefield would give it to him.

"God's blood!"

Henry's curse carried along the street as the crowd approached the fletcher's workshop and Patrick, trying to act braver than he felt, shoved his way past the soldiers to stand beside Matilda's red-faced father who was finishing arrows with beautiful snow-white fletchings taken from a swan.

"You'll be Hood's father-in-law." The black knight made it a statement rather than a question and the fletcher simply stood, his fists clenched, glaring at the Raven and his companions and snorting in disgust when he saw Matt Groves, another former outlaw who had come to him looking for supplies not so many months ago.

"Another poacher turned forester," Henry spat at Groves's feet. "Just like Adam before you, and you remember what happened to him."

Matt's face burned scarlet with fury and he took a step towards the glowering man but Gisbourne placed a hand on his sergeant's arm and held him in place.

"I've heard the story about Adam Gurdon and his untimely end," Gisbourne nodded. "I've also heard about your daughter and her part in it. Good teeth, I hear..."

Matt sniggered at that although the bounty hunter hadn't been making a joke and the erstwhile member of Robin's gang moved around to stand behind the Fletcher and his daughter.

"I'm not here to arrest anyone," Gisbourne went on, to audible sighs of relief from the watching villagers. "I'm simply here looking for information on the outlaws' whereabouts. The king is tired, you see – as am I – of this gang being allowed to wander around Barnsdale as if they owned the forest."

He turned and addressed the crowd. "Robin Hood and his entire gang are not only outlaws; they're rebels too. They took part in an armed uprising against your king. They also killed a number of my men when we tried to arrest them recently. And that," he turned back to the look at the fletcher, "is something that cannot be ignored."

The villagers muttered nervously amongst themselves, sensing life was about to get a lot harder for every one of them if this Raven didn't get what he wanted.

Still, the simple fact was, no-one in Wakefield knew where Hood or his men were hiding out these days. Patrick had told the truth: none of the outlaws had been to their village since the day Sir Guy's men chased them into the greenwood weeks earlier.

Gisbourne absorbed the silence, his irritation rising and finally beginning to show in his demeanour as he turned his single hazelnut eye on Matilda who stood her ground defiantly despite the presence of Matt Groves, breathing noisily through his nose, close – too close – behind her.

"Lady, I have no interest in arresting you. I have no doubt it would draw out the wolf's head, but without any evidence of wrong-doing on your part I, legally, have no reason to take you into custody. The sheriff would be most annoyed if I were to go around arresting all and sundry simply because I felt like it." He smiled at her and, although it appeared genuine, the expression made her legs feel weak and the fletcher glanced at her in concern but before he could move to steady his daughter Matt Groves grasped her from behind.

It might have been said Groves was trying to help the girl; to stop her from fainting. But, although he did catch her from collapsing onto the grass, his hands came right around the front of her body and roughly squeezed her breasts as he leered into her eyes which met his in fury

147

rather than fear. This wasn't the first time a man had touched her without consent and her blood rose at the filthy lawman's intrusion.

Suddenly, Groves's hands fell away as Henry Fletcher smashed his right fist into the side of the one-time outlaw's face, sending the man crashing sideways. Henry followed up the first blow with another, again to the side of Matt's face, and the unfortunate lawman dropped to the ground like a sack of grain.

The rest of the soldiers moved to draw their swords, and the villagers cried out, moving forward threateningly, but Sir Guy raised a hand imperiously and roared, "Enough!" in a surprisingly powerful voice.

Everyone, even the enraged fletcher, stopped in their tracks to look at the king's man.

"Bastard." Groves spat into the silence, shaking his head blearily and grasping his bruised cheek which he knew would hurt like hell for the next day or so – might even be cracked or broken. "You have your excuse," he grunted at his leader. "Arrest the big bastard for assaulting a lawman."

Henry shouted in outrage and his fellow villagers joined in, their voices clamouring for justice but, again, Sir Guy raised a hand and shook his head for quiet.

"You're newly come to my service," the Raven said to Matt reasonably. "So this can be a lesson for you: I don't disrespect women, and I don't allow my men to do it either. You laid your hands on the lady Matilda and her father rewarded you handsomely for it." He spoke to Robin's wife respectfully. "My apologies, lady."

Matilda bobbed her head in surprise, not entirely sure the whole encounter was real or some strange waking dream, but the bounty hunter continued, turning this time to address Patrick again, although his voice carried to everyone in the village.

"I came here today to give you people fair warning: from now on I expect you to send word whenever you hear news of Hood and his gang. I will return periodically if no messenger from your village is forthcoming and, each time

I'm forced to return an... accident will befall Wakefield. I am a lawman, so I must uphold the law and that means I can't arrest any of you without reason – but that doesn't mean God won't strike your homes and workplaces with his righteous anger."

He suddenly glanced over Patrick's shoulder and pointed. "See there. The good Lord has heard my words and sent his wrath down upon you."

The headman looked around and his eyes widened in fear.

"Fire!" someone in the crowd shouted. "Fire!"

Although there were other buildings blocking the line of sight, Patrick knew it was his house that was burning, and he remembered the soldier that had left the Raven's party when they'd first arrived in the village. He threw a murderous glance at the smiling Gisbourne before running towards the curling black smoke that marked every villagers nightmare. Unchecked it would spread quickly between the wooden houses, the sparks and embers jumping between the dry walls and thatched roofs and, quite possibly, destroying half the village before it could be brought under control.

Everyone except the Fletcher and his daughter raced to gather water from the great butts they kept filled from the waters of Balne Beck to extinguish the fire in the centre of the village.

"Make sure you and your townsfolk heed my words," Sir Guy said to Henry who pulled Matilda in close beside him defensively although the soldiers were turning to leave, Matt Groves still glaring balefully at the fletcher. "No more will the people of Yorkshire harbour outlaws. I *will* bring the king's justice to Hood; in the name of God I swear it."

With that, Gisbourne walked back along the street, his men trailing at his back like a pack of faithful hunting dogs. The fletcher and his daughter watched him go, fear making an icy pit in their guts.

"What are we going to do?" Matilda whispered.

But Henry had no answer for her.

149

CHAPTER FIFTEEN

"Fire!"

The cries rang out in the cool night air and, as the monks blearily hauled themselves out of bed and understood what was being said, panic quickly set in.

It hadn't been Tuck's preferred way to get Prior de Monte Martini out of his bedchamber; he'd tried simply climbing up some handily placed ivy to his superior's window first, but the accursed plant had torn itself free from the wall under Tuck's weight and he'd found himself on his backside with a none-too-Christian oath on his lips.

So, unknowingly echoing Sir Guy of Gisbourne's arson back in Wakefield, Tuck had asked Osferth to go and set alight to one of the small wooden outbuildings within the grounds. It was far enough away that the friars would be able to douse the conflagration before it spread and became truly dangerous, while being just close enough to the main priory building that the sight of the flames licking skyward would be sure to cause havoc, if only for a short time, until the water buckets could be fetched and do their job.

Tuck stood concealed in the shadows outside the prior's private chamber, listening to the muffled shouts from outside. They were punctuated now by crashing sounds, as of timbers collapsing and the burly former outlaw shook his head irritably. Clearly Osferth had set a larger fire than he'd been asked. Tuck should have guessed as much when he'd seen the gleam in the younger man's eyes as he'd crept off to gather a tinderbox and some kindling.

The man's a pyromaniac, Tuck thought just as footsteps came hurrying along the high-ceilinged corridor and he pressed himself further back against the wall so the flickering orange glow coming through the few windows wouldn't reveal his hiding place.

It was Ralph, the prior's bottler, who ran to the sturdy door and pounded his fist on it. "Wake up, father! There's a fire! Fire!"

Still, there was no sound of movement from within the chamber and Ralph began to hammer on the door again, stepping back hastily when it was pulled open and the angry red face of de Monte Martini loomed into the dimly lit hallway.

"Yes, yes, I heard you. St. Peter himself must have heard you at the gates of Heaven, by God. Let me gather – "

"No time, father!" The bottler waved his hands in the air and practically hopped on one foot, causing Tuck to stifle a laugh in his hiding place. "Your safety is more important than any worldly possessions. Come, we must go now – everyone else is outside helping fight the blaze."

De Monte Martini stared at the nervously flapping man and shook his head in disgust before sighing heavily and shrugging his shoulders. He stepped into the hall and used a key to lock the big door then allowed himself to be led away to the nearest safe exit.

As soon as the pair turned the first corner Tuck took a deep breath and charged at the door which gave way much easier than he'd expected it to and he stumbled to a halt, breathing heavily, his eyes taking in the surroundings, searching for the little reliquary that he'd come to know so well.

The prior, of course, didn't clean his own chambers. Lower brothers of the order changed de Monte Martini's bedclothes, dusted his furniture, swept the floor and performed all the other menial tasks to keep the room in good order. The prior had been careful never to allow Tuck into the chamber, not trusting the former outlaw within his own, personal, quarters, but Osferth had sometimes carried out the cleaning chores in the large room.

"It's a fancy place," he'd told Tuck earlier that evening. "There's expensive rugs on the floors, fine tapestries depicting scenes from Christ's life on the walls, and on his chests of drawers he displays all the really fine relics he's collected over the years. That one you're looking for will be there, I'm sure, although I've not been in there since you came back so can't say for sure."

Tuck had been disgusted to learn the prior hoarded religious artefacts to display in his own chamber, for his own private delight. Now, as the friar stood looking around the room his disgust turned to anger.

There was a fortune in holy trinkets dotted about the place, some with fine engraved gold information plates underneath them that were probably valuable enough to be called treasures in their own right.

A towel Christ had used to dry his face; a fine silver cup that had apparently belonged to St Stephen; a glass vial of the Virgin Mary's breast milk; a little jar with some of the clay Adam had been fashioned from; thorns from the crown the Romans had forced onto the Lord's head before he made his final journey to Golgotha...

It was obscene. These spiritual marvels should be available for all to venerate. Who knew how many sick people could be cured by the touch of one or other of these? Yet here they sat, hidden from the world, so de Monte Martini could bask in their glory himself. It was, truly, a despicable sin.

Finally, his roving eyes came to rest on the one particular relic he sought and he hastily grabbed it, shoving the artifact into the pocket sewn inside his grey cassock before turning to leave.

And stopping dead in his tracks.

Prior John de Monte Martini stood, mouth open in shock, glaring at him murderously. "I knew you were wicked," he hissed. "I should have handed you over to the law when you came crawling back here. You must have been right at home with those filthy outlaws, you devil."

Tuck had no idea what to do. If it had been anyone else, he'd have simply knocked them out of his path but... despite the fact de Monte Martini was hardly a beacon of piety, the man was, still, a prior and, in theory, much closer to God than Tuck.

The prior's eyes flicked behind Tuck and noticed the empty space where the ornate reliquary should be. "Ah, so that's it," he smirked triumphantly. "We can add the sin of theft to your long list of crimes."

As the man opened his mouth to shout for help Tuck thought of the hoarded relics and the prior's all-encompassing greed. He thought of the brothels de Monte Martini owned. And he thought of Robin Hood and the rest of his friends whose location the prior's own messenger would, any day now, hand over to the one-eyed bounty hunter known as The Raven.

Before any sound could escape his superior's lips, Tuck balled a meaty fist and punched him on the nose, knocking him backwards into the door-frame which he slid down, to sit on the floor clutching his bloodied face. It had been a heavy blow, with many years of pent-up frustration behind it, and the prior sat, too dazed to move or even say anything. It wasn't the first time he'd suffered a broken nose: that young whoreson Hood had done the same thing to him two years earlier, an action that had, unbeknown to any of them at the time, set all these events in motion.

Unlike Robin though, Tuck had no desire to continue the assault. Indeed, he'd shocked himself by lashing out at de Monte Martini, and he knew now there was no turning back from the path he'd set himself upon. The law would be after him, the prior would see to that, and he'd hang like Sir Richard-at-Lee had – another enemy of de Monte Martini – the previous summer.

With a final glance at the dazed prior Tuck hurried from the room, picked up his quarterstaff and small pack that he'd left in the shadows and left Lewes Priory for the last time.

* * *

Sixty miles north of Lewes where Tuck and his new travelling companion, Osferth, were hastily making their escape from the outraged Prior de Monte Martini, Robin and Little John had just left London. They retrieved their concealed weapons from the thick foliage outside the city then headed back onto the road to Nottingham with the invaluable letter from the king to Sheriff de Faucumberg.

"He seemed a good lad," John said, and had to repeat himself when his words were lost behind their cantering horses as the pair tried to get home as quickly as possible.

"Who?" Robin shouted, looking over in puzzlement before turning his eyes back to the road ahead, the muscles in his thighs burning already as he gripped his palfrey too tightly for fear of falling off. He would never be much of a horseman he thought, trying to relax a little.

"The king! He seemed like a nice enough sort. I'd like to share a few ales with him, I bet he'd be a fine drinking companion."

Robin grinned at his friend's idea, imagining Edward spending a night by their campfire in Barnsdale with the grumbling Will Scarlet and the Hospitaller sergeant, Stephen, not to mention Allan-a-Dale and his ribald songs.

He pulled his horse's bridle gently to the side to slow it without hurting its mouth then let the beast continue at a walk which was much less painful on the young man's inner thighs. John noticed Robin's change of pace and checked his own mount, taking up position beside his friend.

"D'you think Allan's all right?"

John puffed up his cheeks and exhaled softly, brow furrowed. "No idea. You know better than me what it's like in Nottingham's dungeon. The sheriff didn't hang him straight away though, so hopefully that's a good sign."

Robin didn't answer. It wasn't the sheriff he was worried about, it was Sir Guy of Gisbourne...

"Imagine if he'd not been caught and had actually won that silver arrow," John said, watching his leader's sombre introspection. "How much do you think it's worth?"

Robin glanced across at the big man and smiled. "God knows – enough to buy us all pardons though. I suspect that's why Allan went into the city on that fool's errand in the first place. We spoke about it the night before he and Gareth left." He stopped short of blaming himself out loud for the whole mess, knowing John would just get irritated with him. Still, if he hadn't suggested the idea...

"Cheer up," John growled. "God works in mysterious ways, as Tuck was always telling us. We might still find the money to bribe some rich gentleman. After all, who would have believed a couple of outlaws would see and do everything that we have?"

It *had* been a strange time for the young outlaw leader. He'd been expecting to follow in his father's footsteps as a forester until that fateful Mayday in 1321 when his world had been turned arse-over-elbow and he'd found himself, lonely and frightened, in the forest with only a rudimentary knowledge of how to use his da's old sword and the longbow he'd spent years mastering but had never used in anger.

Now, here he was, on his way back from the most incredible city he'd ever seen or ever would see, after meeting the king himself!

John was right too – Edward did seem like a good sort. A man to drink with, indeed. Perhaps that was the trouble. Rather than spending evenings in village taverns with individual commoners like blacksmiths, as he notoriously had in Uxbridge, the monarch might have been better trying to do more for that whole underclass in general over the years by lowering taxes and holding back the marauding Scots as his father had.

"If he ever comes into our forest," Robin said, grinning, "we'll... *invite* him to dinner, as we did with Sir Richard."

The grin slowly left his face as he remembered their fallen comrade. The big Hospitaller knight had been a good friend to the outlaws but, like so many others in his life – not least his childhood friend Much – was now dead and, hopefully, buried, although it was probably more likely the knight's body had been left to rot on the gallows that stood so threateningly by the road outside Nottingham's walls.

Robin pictured his son, Arthur, and his spirits rose again. People lived and they died, it was the way of things.

All he could do was continue to do his best for those who depended on him – not only his little son, but the other outlaws who looked to him for leadership as they struggled just to survive and stay one step ahead of Sir Guy of Gisbourne and the foresters that scoured Barnsdale for poachers and rebels and other criminals like them.

He kicked his heels into his mount and drove it ahead of John's horse, gritting his teeth in determination. Aye, he'd make sure they all stayed out of Gisbourne's grasp and he would, somehow, see all his friends pardoned: free men.

But first, they had to get Allan-a-Dale out of Nottingham's jail, and, despite their letter from the king, it wasn't going to be easy...

* * *

"What's that you've got there, Tuck? Is that a sword?" The youth hooted derisively and Marjorie felt her face flush in embarrassment as her tormentor's companions giggled along with their leader.

She'd been lost in thought as she made her way to another all-too-rare sparring session with Matilda. Sir Guy of Gisbourne's recent visit to Wakefield and his subsequent burning of Patrick Prudhomme's house had outraged the girl. All the people of the village just stood by while the so-called Raven came along, threatened them all, then set alight to their headman's own home. If she'd been strong enough she'd have stood up to the crooked lawmen she thought, and it had given her even more desire to build her strength and skills.

She hadn't noticed the three younger girls loitering near the outskirts of the village until one of them had shouted at her.

Marjorie's practice sword had been safely tucked inside her skirts as she walked through the village but, at the worst moment, had worked itself free of its restraint and fallen between her legs to land on the ground with a small thump.

Of course, Helen, one of the village bullies, had been standing with her companions just as Marjorie passed and she'd spotted the training weapon when it dropped onto the sun-baked road.

Helen's mother had died three years earlier, leaving her with only her labourer father to take care of her. He was a decent man who did his best for his daughter but his work meant he was away from home for long hours every day and Helen had started to become something of a problem child despite the fact that, at 13, she was almost an adult and was expected to look after the household now that her mother was gone.

Marjorie ignored the shouts from the girls who, although they were all four or five years younger than her, were somewhat bigger, physically. She bent to retrieve the dropped practice sword, trying to shove it back inside her clothing before anyone else saw it then continued on her way towards the clearing in the woods where Matilda waited to start their training session.

"Hey, Tuck, I'm talking to you, you fat bastard!"

Marjorie gritted her teeth at Helen's sarcastic taunt, clenching her fists and wishing with all her heart she had her big brother's muscular frame. But she was used to people commenting on her diminutive stature so she walked on, trying to remain calm as Matilda had taught her.

It was no good; she heard the sound of running footsteps behind her and turned to face them, right hand clasping the wooden practice sword that she still held concealed within her woollen tunic.

"Fuck off, you little arseholes," she growled, drawing her eyebrows down in the fiercest glare she could manage. "I'm busy."

Her pursuers stopped short at that, looking at each other in disbelief before bursting into laughter.

"'Little'?" Helen demanded. "Who are you calling 'little', Tuck? We're all bigger than you, you skinny bastard." The girl moved forward to take up a position directly in front of Marjorie who stood her ground despite being outnumbered. "Or maybe you were comparing us to 'Little' John?" She laughed and looked at her two friends. "Aye, that would make sense. I'm the giant wolf's head and you're the big, fat fucking priest that's good for nothing but eating and praying. Fatty." The girl poked her finger maliciously towards Marjorie's flat belly as she ground out the final insult.

A couple of months earlier Robin's sister would have felt the tip of that finger pressing against her stomach painfully, humiliatingly, and she'd have just accepted it. The big always bested the small and weak after all – it was the way of the world.

But Marjorie had been practising with the wooden sword for weeks now. She'd run for miles to build up her stamina, and she'd forced more food down her neck than she'd eaten the entire year before so, although she was still thin, her muscles had become a little bigger and more defined than they'd ever been and she knew how to take a blow thanks to the sparring with her sister-in-law Matilda.

"Fuck off, Helen, you craven bastard. And don't call me 'Tuck'. You look more like him than I do."

There was a moment of shocked silence then Helen's two friends burst into near-hysterical laughter. No-one ever spoke back to their leader like that. This promised to be a hugely entertaining morning.

Marjorie expected to be called more names. Expected the verbal onslaught to grow to a crescendo before anyone got angry enough to throw a punch, but she was wrong.

Helen's hand, balled into a fist like any experienced soldier's, came towards her face like a battering ram and Marjorie was only just able to avoid what would have been a thunderous and no-doubt incapacitating punch.

Without even thinking, Robin's sister lifted her right knee up to her waist and, leaning back for more leverage, hammered her foot into Helen's ribs, sending the bigger, older girl flying into the grass where she lay clutching her side.

Marjorie wasn't finished yet, though – her blood was up and she knew she had to teach her tormentors a lesson or they'd never stop hassling her.

She turned to face the biggest of the remaining two girls – a tall lass with near-flawless skin and high cheekbones – who stood open mouthed, gazing at the downed Helen.

"You want some too?"

The girls backed away although their pride made sure they looked angry rather than frightened by the show of naked aggression and their leader's defeat. The fact they moved away was enough to bolster Marjorie's confidence though, and she raised her left fist threateningly before remembering she had the practice sword tucked inside her belt under her dress.

"Come on then," she growled, pulling the wooden weapon out and brandishing it menacingly. "Let's see how hard you are now."

The pair glanced at each other then, without a word, ran off into the village, leaving their fallen comrade behind without a backward glance.

By now Helen had recovered and, grasping her side with an enraged expression on her round face, got to her feet and stared at Marjorie, eyes brimming with tears of rage and pain.

"You'll be sorry you did that. I'll get you for it you bitch, in God's name I will."

Marjorie slapped the girl on the side of the leg with the sword. Not hard enough to do any real damage but with enough venom that Helen squealed in agony, grasping her stinging limb with both hands, the tears now spilling freely down her cheeks as Marjorie stepped forward and looked down on her, the rounded tip of the sword pointing at her face.

"No you won't. If you try to hassle me again, I'll break your leg with my sword. And if any of your little lackeys cause me any trouble I'll have a word with my brother and ask him to pay your da a visit. How d'you think your da would like that? If Robin and Little John and Will Scarlet were to turn up at his door?"

Helen remained silent but it was obvious Marjorie's words had hit home, hard. Everyone in the village knew what Little John had done the last time someone had messed with Robin Hood's family. The giant wolf's head had turned up and beat the hell out of Henry Woolemonger before impaling the man on the end of his sword. The outlaws weren't men to cross.

Helen's face twisted and she turned away to hide it, gasping an apology at the same time.

Marjorie felt like a giant – never in her whole life had such a sense of power coursed through her veins. It was incredible.

Without another word she straightened and walked off towards the trees and the clearing where Matilda waited to begin their sparring session. She listened warily as she went, just in case Helen's anger and humiliation drove her to seek retribution for her defeat but the girl never moved and, eventually, Marjorie pushed her way into the trees and, with a small sigh of relief, lost herself within the dense foliage.

Eventually, a broad grin spread across her gaunt face and she chuckled to herself. She'd never been in a real fight in her life before but, in the name of God, she'd enjoyed it. Enjoyed the great feeling of strength and power that had filled her as she'd glared down upon her beaten tormentor and seen the fear in the girl's moist eyes.

As she pushed the leaves and branches aside, though, the feeling of excitement left her and, strangely, was replaced by shame.

Helen had lost her mother not that long ago; it must have been difficult for the girl to lose a parent and, on top of that grief, to have all the household responsibilities thrown upon her young shoulders. Was it any wonder she sought to strike out? To take her rage at life's injustice out upon anyone that happened to walk past?

Marjorie shook her head and sighed again. She'd been right to defend herself but perhaps she'd gone too far and the fact she'd felt so alive when she'd hit the younger girl made her feel disgusted at herself.

Aye, it had been good to teach Helen a lesson and now, hopefully, she'd be left alone. But, in future, Marjorie would need to watch her temper or she'd end up in trouble, just as her older brother had when he'd attacked that prior two years ago.

CHAPTER SIXTEEN

Osferth proved to be an entertaining travel companion. Full of nervous energy and always ready to burst into one of his favourite hymns, Tuck was glad to have him along on his return to Yorkshire. For some reason the man didn't seem to care that he'd left his life – and vows – behind in Lewes.

After he'd punched de Monte Martini Tuck had made his way out of the priory and met up with the waiting Osferth not far from the walls. When the friar had returned to Lewes he'd ostensibly turned over any valuables he carried to the priory's treasurer, but the wily former wrestler had hidden the gold and silver he'd earned while part of Robin Hood's gang. It was a lot of money and he had no intention of relinquishing it into the fat, grasping hands of the prior who would, doubtless, spend it on finery to adorn his already treasure laden private chamber.

They used some of the small coins in Cooksbridge to buy a pair of horses and pushed them close to their limits now. Not only did they have to escape any pursuers the prior might send after them, but Tuck also prayed they'd be in time to warn Robin and the rest of his friends that their location had been found out and passed to Sir Guy of Gisbourne. The man that sold them the mounts had asked where they were going and eyed their cassocks with interest but Tuck had batted the questions aside, only telling the merchant they were headed north on church business.

Osferth had a thatch of straw-coloured hair and was as skinny as one of the rakes they used in the priory to gather fallen autumn leaves. The man could probably have run all the way to Wakefield with a grin on his slightly simple-looking face, Tuck thought, but he himself had found it hard even just to match Osferth's pace on the way to Cooksbridge.

Tuck's days of wandering around the countryside were done. He wondered how he'd survive now that he was a wolf's head again, for surely Prior de Monte Martini would have the law after his blood harder than ever. It was a worry...

But it was a worry for another day – right now they had to make their way north as quickly as possible and warn Robin if it wasn't already too late.

That morning, as the sun was high in the sky and the morning haze had burned away the mist leaving the country for miles around visible they passed what looked like a merchant riding on his wagon full of goods accompanied by a pair of grizzled guards on foot at the side and Osferth, grinning and apparently full of the joy of God's gift of life, began to sing, loudly and surprisingly melodiously, "All Creatures of our God and King". The hymn, incongruous in such a setting, brought only bemused looks from the mercenaries who fingered their sword hilts, wondering if the crazed Benedictine monk might prove to be a threat.

"Hush, Osferth," Tuck growled once they'd left the suspicious travellers behind. "You're going to leave a trail for our pursuers to follow as if we'd left arrows scratched into the road behind us. We're trying to be as invisible as possible and your loud singing only serves to draw attention to us."

"Sorry." Osferth smiled sheepishly. He had a powerful voice that belied his spare frame and he enjoyed nothing more than filling his lungs and belting out his love of God's creation. "I'll try to be invisible – like a shadow in the dark." He pulled the hood on his cassock over his thatch of straw-coloured hair and Tuck shook his head ruefully.

Osferth didn't seem to be quite 'all there', and Tuck wondered how the man would survive on his own in the world, but at least their flight was proving to be a memorable one.

"What's your story?" the portly friar asked, turning to look at his companion. "How did you become a Benedictine?"

Osferth shrugged and smiled but remained silent as they rode on.

He was a good Benedictine. In fact, in the eyes of his superiors he was almost the perfect monk, being docile, slightly slow and ready to believe whatever he was told without asking awkward questions. Despite the fact he occasionally lit fires and acted like a petulant child he was much less trouble than some of the more intelligent monks who continually demanded answers and fomented trouble amongst their brothers. The odd room pile of junk being found in flames was much less hassle than tough questions about the council of Nicea.

Life as a Benedictine suited Osferth well, although he hadn't become a monk by choice. His father had been a magistrate from Brighton, a minor noble with a considerable fortune and large estates to his name. He'd become caught up in a lawsuit between two of Sussex's most notorious – and wealthy – smugglers though, and the losing party had taken his revenge on Osferth's father, killing him and appropriating his entire estate, apparently by legal means.

Osferth had only been a youngster at the time and the course of his life had changed drastically as a result of his father's murder. His mother, already a fragile, weak woman, had left, disappearing one night never to be seen by the confused boy ever again. His only surviving kin, an uncle, had been unwilling and financially unable to take Osferth in so he'd been sent to the priory in nearby Lewes to become a novice.

The lad might have been the son of a well-liked and successful magistrate but he hadn't inherited any of his father's razor-sharp intellect or charisma so, although he had no interest in religion he'd gone along with his uncle's wishes and joined the Benedictines.

He knew he wasn't smart anyway; knew he couldn't have survived very well on his own, so he'd been relieved when Prior de Monte Martini had accepted him into their brotherhood. He'd been grateful ever since, even if he was poorly treated as a result of his slowness.

At least he had a roof over his head and decent food in his belly; more than his dead father had for sure.

Sometimes he heard a little voice inside telling him to do things but he'd never spoken to anyone about it. God was talking directly to him, just as He had done with Moses on Mount Sinai, or Elijah, who had heard the voice of God and been taken up into the sky by His mighty whirlwind. One day Osferth knew he too would be taken up to Heaven by God in such a fashion.

The fires the voices told him to start always created chaos and consternation within the priory. Once he'd burnt down much of the east wing with many of his brothers lucky to escape the smoke and flames but he was only doing God's work. The monks had feasted on beer and fish that day and needed to be reminded of the fragility of their own existence, not to mention God's dominion over their gluttonous, fat bodies.

Osferth's fire had cleansed the priory and, he was sure, had shown his brothers the error of their ways. They'd not feasted for two weeks after the conflagration and every one of them – except the prior and his dean obviously – had been forced to help with the restoration work.

Fire was good. It cleansed sins both corporeal and spiritual but it was just a means to an end for Osferth. He didn't love the flames and the heady, aromatic smoke they produced for themselves; fire was simply a tool to do God's work. And that was what he had been put on Earth to do, using whatever was at hand.

Friar Tuck was a good man and a good friend to Osferth but he kept bad company.

Like the outlaws in Barnsdale.

They weren't part of God's plan. Something would have to be done about them, and Osferth was the monk to do it.

* * *

165

The tournament had gone well, Sir Henry de Faucumberg thought, smiling to himself as he watched another wrestling match. The audience – pleasingly large in number – cheered and roared in delight as the two combatants traded blows, grunted curses and threw each other around the grass, sweat dripping from their well-muscled torsos. Occasionally the bout spilled out of the roped-off area and into the crowd, but that only brought even louder shouts of encouragement, especially from the women.

Yes, it had been a successful tournament so far and the local traders would be doing brisk business; making money to bring in more taxes. Now all he needed was that letter from the king giving him permission to hang the wolf's head Allan-a-Dale and, more importantly, send the increasingly erratic Sir Guy of Gisbourne back to London with his new toady Matt Groves. Christ above, what a waste of skin that man was, de Faucumberg mused, glancing over to his right where Gisbourne stood watching the wrestling match with Groves at his side like an eager puppy.

"God's bollocks, sit down, Gisbourne, you're making me nervous standing there," the sheriff growled, waving a hand to the seat next to him but the bounty hunter ignored the gesture. Only The Raven would prefer to stand on such a warm day, his pitch black armour oiled to perfection and his hand resting menacingly on the pommel of his sword as if he feared a peasant uprising at any moment.

Sir Henry muttered an oath and turned back to the wrestlers irritably, helping himself to another cup of wine from the table before him.

"My lord!" A soldier clad in the blue livery of de Faucumberg's own garrison, rather than one of the men under Gisbourne's command, breathlessly pushed his way through the throng of people and, puffing hard, whispered into the sheriff's ear.

The messenger was rewarded with a grin that split Sir Henry's face from ear to ear and, as Sir Guy walked across to find out what was going on the sheriff hurriedly

166

whispered his instructions to the soldier and waved him off back to his post at the Hun Gate.

"You look inordinately pleased with yourself," Gisbourne said, finally sitting in the sturdy wooden chair next to de Faucumberg and gazing at the sheriff while Matt Groves moved over to stand protectively behind his captain.

"The king sends word. The friars I dispatched to London have returned."

Gisbourne nodded, a smile playing around his lips. "Good news, then. The tournament will really come to life with a good hanging on Gallows Hill. Matt!" He turned his head to the side and beckoned the former outlaw over. "Fetch the minstrel from the dungeon –"

"You'll do no such thing!" de Faucumberg shouted, glaring at Groves who returned the look impudently, as if he knew his master Sir Guy was untouchable to the sheriff. "I'll read what the king has to say first, and then *I* will decide when to hang the outlaw. This is my city, Gisbourne, and my soldiers are in charge of the prisoner so you," he looked again at Groves, his lip curled in disgust, "can crawl back under your stone, you horrible bastard."

Groves's face turned crimson with rage but Sir Guy simply grinned at the sheriff's outburst. "Stand down, Matt, we'll wait and see what the king has to say about it. We are merely guests here after all." He helped himself to a small piece of roasted venison from the platter on the table and, still smiling, turned his attention back to the tournament.

By now the wrestling heats had been completed, the winners had their arms raised and all the competitors bowed to the sheriff before dispersing. Servants hurried to clear away the ropes that had marked the grappling ring and yet more servants carried archery targets onto the grass.

"Looks like the next event is archery," Matt Groves said, much to the amusement of Sir Guy who laughed even more when he saw the venomous look on the sheriff's face.

"You don't say?" de Faucumberg growled sarcastically. "Look, I invited you to sit with me, Gisbourne, but we don't need... that, here as well. He should be swinging from the gallows beside the minstrel anyway, not standing here at my table. You!" he barked, glowering at the erstwhile wolf's head. "Fuck off."

Groves looked like he might lose his temper and actually attack the sheriff whose personal guardsmen stepped in close and hefted their halberds threateningly.

"Go, Matt," Gisbourne waved without turning to look at his second-in-command. "Take yourself off to one of the taverns before the archery begins. I'll see you later."

Groves nodded to his captain and shoved his way past de Faucumberg's men, snarling at them like a petulant child.

"I thought your old sergeant was a blood-thirsty bastard," de Faucumberg told the bounty hunter with a shake of his head. "But at least Barnwell was a good soldier and had a modicum of intelligence. That wolf's head is nothing but an angry fool."

Gisbourne helped himself to another piece of venison which was perfectly cooked – moist and tender – and shrugged disinterestedly. "He is. But he hates Robin Hood even more than I do and he knows how the wolf's heads work. He'll lead us to them eventually, I'm sure. And if he doesn't, well..." He winked his good eye at the sheriff who had to suppress a shudder. "You can hang him if you like then."

The targets were in place by now and the crowd, which had thinned during the intermission, started to return, ale-skins refilled and meat pies or other savoury delights in hand, their obvious pleasure in this taking away some of de Faucumberg's annoyance. He tried to be a good sheriff to the people of Yorkshire and Nottingham, he truly did, and keeping the people entertained and well-fed and watered was the best way to avoid civil unrest while keeping the traders and merchants that paid so much to his treasury in taxes happy.

168

As the first of the longbowmen began to show off their skills de Faucumberg waited, occasionally glancing over his shoulder. Gisbourne watched him from the corner of his eye. It was obvious there was more to the king's letter than simple authorization to hang the outlaw minstrel. Like there had even been any need to petition the king for permission in the first place.

Clearly something else was going on, and Gisbourne watched the sheriff's sly smile warily.

"Oh, very good! Well done that man!" de Faucumberg raised his cup in salute to one of the archers who'd managed to hit the centre of the target, before, again, his glance turned to his rear. This time, though, he sat up in his chair and Gisbourne also swung around to watch the arrival of the Franciscan friars who had been sent south to the capital and King Edward II.

"What the hell is this?" the bounty hunter muttered, hand grasping his sword as he looked to the sheriff for his reaction to the newcomers approaching the table. The archery contest continued; the participants, and the crowd, oblivious to what was going on above them. "Those are no friars."

The two men in grey cassocks came towards them, the hoods on the garments pulled up to hide their faces in shadow but the great size of both, and one in particular who towered over everyone nearby marked them as a potential threat and Sir Guy got to his feet, sword instantly appearing in his hand from its exquisitely crafted black wood and leather sheath.

The sheriff's own blue-liveried guards, jumpy and nervous as a result of Matt Groves's dressing down and now Gisbourne's reaction to the two friars, crowded around de Faucumberg defensively but the clergymen continued their slow approach until they stood before the table, heads still bowed and faces hidden by their hoods.

"You're the messengers from the king?" de Faucumberg asked, standing to meet them, and was rewarded by the hood on the smaller – yet still massive – man bobbing up and down. "You seem to have grown

169

since I last saw you," the sheriff noted drily. "Take those hoods off. Slowly, now."

The friars hesitated for a moment before first one, then the other, threw their head's back and their faces were revealed.

The sheriff took an involuntary step backwards, while Gisbourne whispered in shock: "You...!"

The guards now had their halberds pointed straight at Robin and Little John who watched the sheriff's eyes stray downwards to the parchment the notorious wolf's head held in his hands.

"We bring word from the king."

For long moments no one spoke, they simply stared in disbelief at the two infamous outlaws who had so brazenly walked into the city before Gisbourne finally broke the spell.

"Kill them!"

CHAPTER SEVENTEEN

"Hold!" The sheriff was a man well used to command and his voice reflected that fact as it rang out over the sounds of the crowd. He was pleased to note that none of his own men had followed Gisbourne's command to attack the two wolf's heads, but they had moved in even closer to make sure the big men wouldn't be a threat.

The king's bounty hunter found his path to Hood blocked by blue-liveried guardsmen and he spat in disgust at de Faucumberg's refusal to cut the hated outlaw down where he stood, apparently unarmed and completely in their power.

"You're Hood, and you're the big impudent bastard that made a joke about my mother the last time we met, yes?"

Robin shook his head but Little John couldn't stop a smile from appearing on his still cleanly-shaven face. "Aye, lord sheriff, that was me," he agreed. "Sorry about that." His cheeky grin marked the apology as insincere but the sheriff just grunted irritably.

"I assume there's a good reason you've walked into my city, and my presence, dressed as friars?"

"As I said, we bring word from King Edward." Robin held out the rolled up parchment, slowly so as not to provoke a nervous thrust from any of the halberd-wielding guards.

De Faucumberg nodded to one of the soldiers to bring him the scroll and, as he was given it he inspected the wax seal closely. It certainly appeared to be Edward's royal seal. "How did you come to be in possession of this? And what happened to the two real friars that I sent to London? Or do I not want to know the answer to that?"

Robin shrugged. "They decided the journey was too far and too dangerous. We went in their stead."

Gisbourne laughed in disbelief and the sheriff raised a questioning eyebrow himself at that idea before he broke the wax seal and, sitting back down on his great seat, unrolled the letter from the king and began to read.

"Are you taking this seriously?" Sir Guy demanded into the silence. "Why haven't you had these two criminals – dangerous criminals," he pointed to his ruined face furiously, "chained like the animals they are?"

The sheriff ignored him as he read but it was obvious whatever was in the king's letter did not please him. Robin and John knew de Faucumberg would be angry at Edward's refusal to recall his erratic bounty hunter but it was when the letter moved onto Allan-a-Dale that the seated nobleman jumped up and roared in disbelief.

"The king wants me to release the wolf's head? What is this nonsense?" He re-read the entire letter in a state of rising fury and shock before turning to glare at the two big outlaws. "This is your doing isn't it, you bastards? You spun Edward some tale and he believed it." He shook his head and sighed, throwing the letter onto the table in resignation. "You really do seem to be touched by God, Hood, I'll say that for you."

"What are you talking about de Faucumberg?" Gisbourne demanded, shoving his way past the guards to reach for the letter which the sheriff retrieved before the king's man could read it. Couldn't have him knowing the sheriff was trying to get rid of him, could they? That would make things even more unpleasant than they already were...

"It seems we've been outwitted by the wolf's head again," de Faucumberg replied, still glaring at the young outlaw who always seemed to be one step ahead of their efforts to capture or kill him. "I can only guess that these two – in their disguise as holy men – gave the king some fabricated story about the minstrel's innocence and, as a result, Edward has ordered me to release him."

Gisbourne snorted. "How can you be sure that letter's from the king? It must be a forgery."

The sheriff shook his head. "Oh it's genuine, no doubt about it – the seal was real and I recognise his scribe's handwriting."

"Fine, the minstrel can go free. He's nothing anyway. It's *that* young prick that we really want and I assume the king says nothing about us letting him go as well." He pointed his sword at Robin and smiled. "You probably thought you were doing the noble thing coming here to free your friend, but you're going to suffer for it now. I've waited a long time to repay you for taking my eye."

"I have one more letter from the king, my lord."

The wolf's head produced another scroll from within the grey friar's cassock and proffered it to the sheriff whose guard passed it to him.

Again, the seal was inspected before being broken and the parchment unrolled and slowly read by de Faucumberg who could only shake his head, a small smile of defeat twitching at the corners of his mouth. "Hood thought you'd say something like that, Sir Guy, and had the king – who appears to have taken rather a liking to our outlaws here – write another letter of protection. This time for the pair of them."

Now he did pass the scroll to Gisbourne who read it in silence, rage colouring his face as he realised all three of Hood's gang were simply going to walk right out of the city gates and back to their camp in Barnsdale and there was absolutely nothing he could do about it.

There was a grudging respect in the sheriff's eyes as he looked up at Robin and issued the command to one of his guards to bring Allan-a-Dale from his cell in the dungeon along with all his possessions. "It's a shame you're on the other side of the law," he told the young man. "I could find a use for someone like you in my garrison. Oh well," he shrugged again and settled back down into his chair, grasping his wine cup with a twinkle in his eye. "You've beaten us again this day and, no doubt, your minstrel friend will come up with some song all about it that will enhance your legendary status among the common people even more." He emptied the cup and refilled it from a large jug. "Make the most of your victory, wolf's head, because we *will* catch you one day. He'll make damn sure of it."

He raised a finger from his cup and pointed at Sir Guy who still stood, sword drawn, looking as if he might still at any moment attack the two outlaws, despite the king's order of protection.

"And, as for the king... when he finds out you deceived him, well, I doubt he'll be too pleased."

Robin wasn't so sure. "We'll see, lord sheriff. We'll see. Ned told us he'd be coming north again soon to see things were being run properly and said he hoped to meet us again. We got on well with him didn't we, John? He even asked if we'd like to join his rowing team."

Gisbourne growled at Robin's use of a diminutive nickname for their monarch. "Aye, well, the king always did enjoy spending time with the lower end of the social scale. I'm not surprised he liked your company."

"Shut it, Gisbourne, you ugly twat," John replied with a grin. "No one cares what you think."

De Faucumberg hid his smile behind his cup and was relieved to see his guard returning, at last, with the captured minstrel in tow. "Here he is," he said, waving towards them as they approached and everyone except the fuming Raven turned to watch.

Allan, face caked with dried blood and dirt, looked confused when he spotted his two friends shorn and dressed as friars but he held his peace, not wanting to upset whatever game it was they were playing with the sheriff and Gisbourne.

"You're free to go," de Faucumberg said, waving his hand to encompass all three of the outlaws. "My men will escort you to the city gates safely. Gisbourne, you will remain here so you don't do anything rash that'll bring the king's wrath down upon me for disobeying his orders."

"Disobeying his orders? You really think the king wants you to let Robin Hood and two of his men walk free, just like that, as a result of this deception they've perpetrated? Robin Hood, the man the king sent me here specifically to deal with?"

"No, quite possibly not," the sheriff agreed. "But I am the king's servant and, as such, I am expected to carry out his orders without question, unfortunately. His letters state very clearly that these three are to be sent on their way and so that is what will happen. We will just need to recapture them another day."

Although de Faucumberg was dismayed to be letting the three outlaws walk free, it cheered him and somewhat softened the blow to see the rage that filled Gisbourne. It felt very good to see the bounty hunter taken down a peg or two again, even if it was at the hands of the wolf's head.

Robin could also see the black rage that twisted Sir Guy's face and threatened to overwhelm the king's man, so he slowly began to move backwards, away from the sheriff's high table, gesturing John and Allan to follow his lead.

"You alright?" he asked the minstrel, eyeing him with concern.

"Aye," Allan grunted with a smile. "Nothing damaged other than my pride."

As they neared the competitors in the archery tournament Robin hissed a curse as he spotted the one man in the world that he hated even more than Gisbourne: "Matt Groves."

The young outlaw captain spat the name like the vilest oath when he saw Groves appearing through the crowd, half-a-dozen of Gisbourne's own men – all in the simple brown and green clothing of foresters – in tow. "That filthy piece of shit's brought men to kill us, no matter what the sheriff's commanded."

Gisbourne had noticed Robin's angry gaze and he turned to see his second-in-command nearing. His thoughts whirled as he debated whether to go against de Faucumberg's orders; it might mean fighting the sheriff's soldiers, if they decided to try and stop him.

But he did despise the lowly yeoman from Wakefield who had so painfully taken half his face the previous year. "Good work, Matt," the king's man shouted. "We're not letting those criminals just walk out of Nottingham. Cut them down!"

De Faucumberg was practically foaming at the mouth, enraged that Groves had returned after he'd been told in no uncertain terms to leave, and not only that, the sullen-faced prick had brought soldiers to defy him.

"Stop them," he roared at his own men who outnumbered Gisbourne's small Groves-led force, but the soldiers moved slowly, not really sure what the hell was going on and reluctant to get involved in whatever power-struggle was being played out by the two noblemen. The sheriff might be their commander, but it was a brave man who defied the Raven, especially recently, when he'd become even more erratic and volatile than ever.

The outlaws were unarmed, and they looked uncertainly at each other as Gisbourne's men came for them, swords drawn and obviously prepared to use lethal force – there would be no mercy from them, that much was clear, and the blue-liveried sheriff's men, although they were moving now to head-off the newcomers, wouldn't reach them in time.

All of this was going on unnoticed by most of the large crowd who stood engrossed in the archery competition. The longbowmen were also oblivious to what was happening at their backs but as Robin and his hastily retreating companions came close to them one stocky man with a shock of red hair turned, surprised to see two friars and a filthy-looking peasant about to be cut down by a group of foresters.

"May I?"

The archer stood, open-mouthed in confusion but handed over his great warbow and the broadhead arrow he had been ready to loose and Robin smiled his thanks.

"God bless you, my son," he grunted before nocking the arrow to the hemp string and rolling his enormous shoulders, smiling at the oncoming Groves. "Hold, Matt, or I'll take your fucking head right off."

Their pursuers stopped dead in their tracks and the former outlaw's face turned pale with the realisation Hood held his life in his hands.

"You've seen what an arrow like this can do to a man," Robin shouted although he hardly needed to as the cheering, chattering crowd that had been so absorbed in the tourney spotted the friar taking the longbow and now fell silent to watch the even more entertaining drama unfold in front of them. "The iron tip will penetrate right through that ugly face of yours and out the back of your skull," Robin continued, buying time until the sheriff's soldiers finally reached Gisbourne's men and blocked them off, ready to stop their progress should they try to move again. "Your head will explode like an old apple, and it'll make me happy to know I've avenged Much's death at your hands, you evil scum."

Robin raised the bow a fraction, ready to draw and aim it right at Matt but his gaze moved to the sheriff who stood watching the confrontation stony-faced. "I don't think Sir Henry would allow me to walk free if I was to kill you though. It'll have to be another day."

Knowing they were safe, Robin suddenly turned, drew the string taut, sighted instinctively and loosed his arrow towards one of the big straw targets.

The spectators held their breath for a moment longer as they looked to see where the shot had landed before a young boy, his eyesight sharper than most in the crowd, muttered in a high-pitched voice, "Holy mother of God!"

Little John and Allan-a-Dale both turned to fix their leader with shocked smiles and the noise of the people rose to a deafening clamour.

"A bullseye! He hit a bullseye!"

"Not just a bullseye – he's split it! He's split the other arrow right down the middle!"

"It's a miracle!"

"How the fuck did you do that?" Little John grabbed Robin's arm and stared at him in awed disbelief. "I've never seen anything like it in my life; I didn't even think it was possible to make a shot like that. And you did it without even setting yourself properly, you just turned and let fly. How?"

Robin just smiled enigmatically as if this had been his plan all along. "Allan, you know how to work a crowd. Get them to start a chant – we're going to get that silver arrow and win our pardons after all. John – lift me up, quick, onto your shoulders."

The spectators crowded in around them while Groves and Gisbourne's men were shepherded away by the sheriff's soldiers. De Faucumberg himself stood watching, wondering what to make of the day so far.

Yes, he'd lost the chance to execute one of Robin Hood's gang, and on top of that he'd been forced to let Hood himself, along with his giant right-hand man, walk free. But Gisbourne, and now his vile little toady Groves, had been sorely humiliated and that shot the young man had made... it was the stuff of legend. People would tell stories and sing songs about the sheriff's tournament for months once the minstrels got word of what had happened here...

De Faucumberg looked at Allan-a-Dale, wondering what song the man would concoct, and he noticed the minstrel was chanting something already, leading the people who had by now hoisted Hood onto their shoulders.

The crowd swelled even further as the news of what had happened spread throughout the city and the chant slowly grew in volume until the sheriff could pick out the words and, slowly, his mood turned black.

"Silver arrow... Silver arrow... Silver arrow..!"

It was Gisbourne's turn to grin, and the bounty hunter laughed at the sheriff's consternation. "Not so fucking cheerful now, are you?"

CHAPTER EIGHTEEN

"I promise you, you'll like Robin," Tuck smiled at Osferth, the affection he felt for the outlaw leader plain on his jowly face. "Everyone likes Robin. Well, apart from Gisbourne. And the sheriff. And Adam Bell. And Matt Groves..." His face broke into a wide grin and he waved his hands happily. "Everyone else likes him though."

Osferth had noticed a major transformation in the friar since they'd left Lewes behind them and headed farther north. While he'd always seemed confident and competent and hid his emotions fairly well, Tuck had been subdued and plainly unhappy when he was cooped up inside St Mary's. Now, though, it was as if the man had grown ten years younger physically, and thirty years had dropped from his mental age, so he grinned and hummed hymns like a spry novice. Clearly the thought of joining up with his outlaw friends was pleasing to the aging Tuck.

The journey wasn't as swift as it might have been – Osferth may have been somewhat touched but his devotion to Christ couldn't be questioned. He insisted on saying prayers eight times a day, from Lauds at five in the morning to Compline in the evening and everything in between – just as they'd have done had they still been in the priory. Tuck fidgeted irritably every time they dallied with the worship but he felt guilty to have drawn his younger companion into this adventure and, as a result, he bit his tongue and joined in with the Pater Nosters, Ave Maria and Credo.

In truth, Tuck was somewhat taken aback by just how devout Osferth really was. Someone like him should have been at home in St Mary's and yet, here he was, tagging along with the former-wrestler having been more than happy to give up his life as a clergyman. True, Prior de Martini had been hard on Osferth, but still, people like him often saw that as a trial sent by God, or penance for some unknown sin.

It certainly made the journey more pleasant, if rather slower, having the man along. Flight from the authorities could be a frightening, lonely experience and Tuck was glad to have Osferth with him to keep his mind from their potential troubles.

"I've never been this far north," Osferth said, looking about him, eyes wide as if the land thereabouts was somehow different to Sussex where he'd spent all of his thirty-odd years. "I feel like Joseph of Arimathea, travelling north to strange new lands, carrying the word of God and Christ to any who'd listen." He smiled and Tuck smiled back, happy to be with such a delightfully strange travelling companion.

"I have a feeling Prior de Martini doesn't see us in the same light."

"Maybe not, Robert, maybe not," Osferth shrugged. "But God works in mysterious ways. Who knows what the prior is thinking right now? We're all tools of the Almighty after all – even Prior de Martini."

"That bastard's a tool of Satan," Tuck grunted, touching a hand to the crucifix he wore around his neck to avert any evil that might be drawn to them by the Dark One's name. "I thought that was why you'd come with me."

"It is," Osferth agreed, nodding vigorously. "I couldn't stay in the priory any longer – De Martini isn't fit to be in charge of our brothers. So... tell me about the giant: Little John."

The abrupt change in the conversation threw Tuck, but he'd come to expect odd behaviour from his companion, whose thoughts seemed to flit from one place to another like a sparrow seeking a mouldy crust. And Osferth was just as innocent as one of the little birds, even if he did appear to have something of a dark streak hidden just beneath the surface. Tuck wondered what they would do with the strange, child-like monk when they finally reached Barnsdale and found the outlaws.

But they would cross that bridge when they came to it. For now, Osferth had asked about Little John and there was nothing Tuck liked better than telling tales about the exploits of his old friends.

"Huge he is. Massive! Biggest man you've ever seen in your life."

Osferth listened, eyes shining with interest as their mounts carried them north, and Tuck knew he'd chosen the right path. God was leading him home.

* * *

"I can't give him the arrow, in the name of Christ. It's worth a fortune. We had it made from solid silver, remember?"

"I don't think you've got much choice," the grinning Gisbourne said, nodding his head towards the huge crowd that had gathered and was continuing to swell as the chant increased in volume. "The people have decided Hood's the winner of your tourney."

"Silver arrow! Silver arrow!"

"Fuck the people," de Faucumberg shouted, eyes blazing and spittle flecking his neatly-trimmed grey beard. "We're to let three notorious outlaws walk free, taking my silver arrow with them? How will I pay the taxes to the king without the silver in that arrow? This is your fault, Gisbourne, you fucking oaf. You had the clever idea to offer a real silver arrow and now look where it's got us."

Sir Guy shrugged, the smirk ever-present on his ruined face now. "It was a quite remarkable shot, you must admit – certainly worthy of winning the arrow. And it *is,* as you noted yourself not long ago, King Edward's orders that the wolf's heads should be allowed to walk free."

As they spoke, de Faucumberg realised a new chant had begun and now vied with the first for dominance. The sheriff groaned as the cries of "Robin Hood! Robin Hood!" filled the air and Allan-a-Dale clapped his hands encouragingly with the people that stood closest to them.

This was a disaster; another little story at his expense to add to the burgeoning legend that surrounded this young outlaw from Wakefield and his gang.

"Silence!" de Faucumberg roared, holding his hands aloft and looking murderously at the noisy mob before him. "Silence!" He beckoned to one of his soldiers and whispered in his ear. "Go to the castle and bring reinforcements, enough to quell any rioting here."

The crowd had stopped their chants, eager to hear their sheriff's words. They had no idea the silver arrow had simply been a ruse designed to lure Robin Hood to Nottingham. No idea that any eventual winner was never supposed to be allowed to keep the magnificent, and insanely expensive, piece.

"Good people of Nottingham, and visitors to our fine city," the sheriff began, forcing a benevolent smile onto his face, "you are right: before us stands the famous outlaw, Robin Hood, with two of his friends."

"That's Little John that is," someone piped up from within the crowd, and his assertion was met with agreement from all around. "Aye, must be – look at the size of the bastard, he's huge!"

John smiled a little shyly, his face turning red from the attention, not to mention the not-inconsiderable weight of Robin atop his shoulders, but de Faucumberg carried on, drawing all eyes back to himself.

"Hood has made a remarkable shot using a borrowed longbow –"

"Miraculous!"

"Never seen anything like it!"

"Yes, an excellent shot," the sheriff nodded, smiling in agreement. "And, as a reward, I will allow Hood and his two friends to go free, although I *should* place them in chains and throw them into the castle jail to await justice."

The crowd began to grumble and mutter and the sheriff again raised his hands. "The tournament is not over yet; it would not be fair to award the silver arrow to someone that wasn't even a listed competitor and, as such, is not entitled to any prize."

The sheriff watched the crowd, as did Gisbourne beside him and it seemed the speech had done its work.

The words were reasonable and fair and the people seemed happy enough to accept it.

Then the two noblemen spotted Allan-a-Dale saying something to the red-haired archer that Hood had taken the longbow from. The man nodded thoughtfully at whatever the wolf's head was telling him then he looked up from beneath the flaming curls and shouted towards the raised table.

"None of us will ever beat that shot, my lord sheriff. It was a once-in-a-lifetime effort. I forfeit any claim to the silver arrow for I'll never best that man's skill, aye, even if I lived 'til I were a hundred years old!"

Some of the other archers nodded and shouted agreement, giving up any claim to the great prize and, again, the troublemaking minstrel started the chanting.

"Silver arrow! Silver arrow! Robin Hood! Robin Hood!"

"Worthless bastard," de Faucumerg muttered, looking murderously at the clapping minstrel. "I should have hanged him the first day we had him in custody. Silence!" Again, he raised his hands and waited on the noise to abate before he spoke once more into the calm.

"I will not turn over the prize to an outlaw. It is enough that he's being given his freedom this day although, mark this well, Hood: Sir Guy and his men, along with my own garrison, will still be doing everything in our power to put an end to you and your criminal gang."

"You can bet your life on it," Gisbourne spat, pointing the tip of his elegant sword at the outlaws. "I won't rest until you're dead, you scum."

"Give Hood the arrow you swindler," someone shouted from the safe anonymity of the mob and many others cried out in angry agreement.

"Give him it or we'll burn the city to the ground!"

There were cheers at that shout and de Faucumberg noticed Allan-a-Dale had disappeared into the crowd. No doubt it was the minstrel who was trying to stoke the ire of the people and, unfortunately, it seemed to be working, as cries of "burn it!" began to ring out from various sections of the gathering.

From far to the rear of the mob there was a crashing sound as one of the vendor's stalls was tipped over and smoke slowly curled upwards from it, forming a greasy smear in the afternoon sky.

"Burn it to the ground!"

Another stall crashed over and some of the people began to howl and laugh making the sheriff realise his extra soldiers, who were now jogging into view, were not going to be able to contain this without a great deal of bloodshed. De Faucumberg was not the type of sheriff to deal with civil unrest with displays of brutality and killing, but that arrow... it was worth a fortune! He'd have to make up the missing tax monies from his own purse if he handed it over to the damned wolf's head.

"Whatever you're planning," Gisbourne barked, interrupting the sheriff's whirling thoughts, "you better get on with it. Either give Hood the arrow or set your men to cracking heads. That lot are about to erupt."

True enough, more and more of the people were joining in with the chants now, not just for the arrow and the outlaw, but, as they visibly steeled themselves for the inevitable outpouring of rage and destruction that accompanied any riot, many of them were taking up the cries of, "burn it!"

"Oh for Christ's sake. Alright!" De Faucumberg turned and waved a hand angrily towards the heavily guarded table that displayed the wondrous arrow. "Bring it to me, man, now."

The soldier that had been addressed hurried to obey, not relishing the idea of wading in amongst his own townsfolk with the halberd he wielded, simply to save the sheriff some money. He lifted the arrow, which was surprisingly heavy thanks to the high quality of the silver that had been used to construct it, and brought it over to his lord and commander.

"Come and get it, wolf's head," the sheriff shouted, shaking the arrow in the air furiously as the people, who had been readying themselves to go on a rampage now switched their mood and began to cheer and hoot in delight at their apparent victory over the nobles.

"Let me down," Robin said and John slowly bent his knees so his passenger could slide onto the ground. "Here, cover me."

He handed the giant the longbow, noting with satisfaction that Allan had also managed to procure one of the weapons from somewhere, then, making his way through the grinning crowd, he walked up the small flight of steps to the high table.

Sheriff de Faucumberg dropped the heavy silver trophy into the outlaw's open palms and Robin turned, a wide grin forming on his honest face as he raised the arrow skywards and was rewarded with a deafening cheer.

"Thank you, my lord sheriff," the young wolf's head winked over his shoulder as he danced past the impotent guards, down the steps and back towards his friends. When he reached them he looked at John and gestured for the giant to hand the longbow back to its red-haired owner. "Now, give me a boost."

John cupped his hands and Robin stepped into them, rising in the air so the entire crowd could see him. "This is a fine prize, my friends," he shouted, "and worth a fortune!" The people cheered and clapped, assuring him he deserved it for his fine shot. "But my companions and I have no use for wealth and finery in the greenwood. All we need are arrows, and food and friendship, and ale!"

"Lots of ale!" Little John roared agreement and everyone cheered again, thoroughly enjoying themselves.

"We'll take the sheriff's silver prize back to Barnsdale and cut slivers from it which we'll distribute amongst those most needy in the towns and villages hereabouts. God bless you all!"

The people went crazy, chanting Robin's name and patting the three outlaws on the back as they headed towards the city gates and freedom.

Sir Henry and Gisbourne watched them go, faces tight with rage and defeat.

"Look at the smug bastard, he has them eating out of his hand," the bounty hunter spat.

"This is your fault," de Faucumberg repeated his earlier accusation, turning to include Matt Groves who had reappeared behind his captain, Sir Guy. "You and that vermin. Not only was it your idea to offer the silver arrow as a prize, but it was your lackey's attempt to kill Hood that made the outlaw grab the longbow. If you'd have just let him leave like I ordered, Hood would never have made that unbelievable shot and I wouldn't be hundreds of pounds out of pocket!"

Groves opened his mouth to say something but the sheriff rounded on him viciously, eyes flaring, enraged like Gisbourne had never seen him before. "Get out of my sight, you arsehole! In fact, get the fuck out of my city. If I ever see you again I'll repeal your pardon and see you on the gibbet. And as for you," de Faucumberg glared at Sir Guy. "You can go with him. I don't want to see your face in Nottingham until you've destroyed Hood and his gang and returned that silver arrow to me."

* * *

"So you were a sailor, eh?"

Matt Groves nodded and took a long pull of the cheap ale that had been served to them in Horbury. When the sheriff threw them out of Nottingham, Sir Guy had taken Matt and the rest of his men north to begin their hunt for Robin Hood and his gang anew. The soldiers erected makeshift shelters outside the village while Gisbourne and Groves had come into the small village to rent a room for the night. If the place had been big enough all the men could have paid for their own rooms but the little inn only boasted four guest rooms and all were cramped, or 'cosy' as the landlord described them.

Now, the bounty hunter and his second-in-command sat in the inn's common room by a blazing fire which crackled and spit every so often apparently in protestation at the poor quality damp wood that was being burned.

Still, it gave off enough warmth and light to make the room comfortable and the ale that Matt had heated with a poker was also helping him relax after their enforced journey. Gisbourne, a man who always liked to be in total control of himself, was drinking the weaker ale that the landlord gave to his children.

"Aye, I've been a sailor. Twice." Matt said. "It was my first real job when I was about fourteen, then when I left Hood's gang and the money you'd given me for betraying them ran out I took a berth on a ship sailing from Hull to Bergen, in Norway." He took another sip, relishing the warm feeling that was spreading quickly outwards from his belly, and grimaced at his captain. "I'm not much of a sailor to be honest. Or much of an outlaw either come to think of it. I hate being stuck in a small space with a load of other men."

Gisbourne hid a small smile behind his hand, imagining how unpleasant Matt's company would be if one were stuck aboard a ship with him for weeks on end.

"Well, at least now you're free to come and go as you please," the king's man said but Matt shook his head with a scowl.

"Not really. We'll need to kill that arsehole Hood. I don't want to be looking over my shoulder for the rest of my life, wondering when he'll come for revenge because I killed his mate."

Groves had led Robin and his childhood friend, Much, the son of the miller from Wakefield, into a trap set by Gisbourne the previous year. Much had been shot by the Raven then run through by Matt himself and both men knew Hood would never forget that day.

"We'll find him, never fear," Gisbourne promised. "We just need to put even more pressure on the villagers who give aid to the outlaws. Eventually someone will decide enough is enough and see us as a worse threat than Hood or his men. Once we know the location of their camp we'll get them."

"I wouldn't be so sure," Matt replied gloomily. "Lawmen have known where we were hiding in the past but we still always managed to escape. They'll have lookouts posted and, apart from that, they're all hardy fighters. As you know yourself..." His voice trailed off as Gisbourne reached up unconsciously to touch his ruined eye and glared at him.

"Once we find their location," the Raven promised, "I'll send word back to Nottingham and ask – no, demand – that de Faucumberg sends us enough of his soldiers to make certain we can surround the outlaws' camp and outnumber them more than three to one before we even begin any attack. Trust me – I've learned a few lessons since I've been sparring with Hood. He's no military genius, he's just some peasant that's had a lucky streak." He sipped the weak ale and wiped his mouth neatly. "Well, his luck won't hold forever. I can feel it; the end of my long chase is coming."

Matt smiled, strangely pleased by the crazed look that filled his captain's eyes. He knew why Hood and the rest of them had never been captured yet: it was because the people hunting them – Gisbourne and the previous bailiff Adam Gurdon before that – had played it safe. Neither of them had wanted to upset the commoners too much – Sheriff de Faucumberg had specifically warned both lawmen to tread lightly and not cause any unrest among the locals.

When Adam Gurdon had taken the law into his own hands and falsely arrested Hood's sweetheart Matilda there had been disastrous consequences for the bailiff and, ever since, the sheriff had made sure the villagers were mostly left alone.

It was a ridiculous policy, Groves thought. How could they be expected to catch the outlaws while the locals provided them with supplies and pretended not to know their whereabouts when the law turned up looking for answers? No, if Matt had been in charge, Hood would have been strung up a long time ago. Squeeze the villagers so hard that they'd be desperate to do anything that restored peace to their lives, even if that mean turning over the now-legendary wolf's head, Robin Hood.

Up until now Gisbourne's orders from the sheriff, and his own strange code of honour, had meant the people of Wakefield, Hathersage, Penyston, and all the other little towns and villages, had been allowed to live their lives unmolested by the men hunting Hood. But recently there had been a little spark of insanity in Sir Guy's eye and Matt had done his best to fan that spark into a raging balefire.

"The people around here were always happy to help us," Matt said, watching his leader's face. "They knew you and your men wouldn't harm them. They used to laugh about it. 'The Raven,' they'd say to us, 'not much of a fucking raven that can't use his beak or talons.'"

Gisbourne was no fool and he had an inkling Groves was also somewhat smarter – or at least more devious – than people assumed. He suspected his new second-in-command was goading him, pushing him to take more forceful action in their hunt for the accursed outlaw. But, in truth, Gisbourne needed little goading. Ever since Hood had humiliated him, and sliced off half his face, the Raven had been nursing a growing hatred for the young man which had only grown fiercer in recent weeks.

It was indeed time to use harsher measures to deal with Hood and his men once and for all. If that meant bringing violence to the villages that lay dotted around the forest of Barnsdale, so be it. Burning Patrick Prudhomme's house would just be the beginning.

"How did you end up a sailor then?" Sir Guy asked, changing the subject abruptly. "I thought you were born in Sheffield. That's not exactly a port town."

Matt sat back, mug resting on his paunch, and stretched his legs out towards the fire, chair creaking in protest as he settled his considerable bulk comfortably.

"Aye, I'm a Sheffield man originally but I left there when I was old enough to grow my first beard. My mother died of fever when I was a lad, so it was just me, my da, and my big brother Philip."

Matt's voice trailed off and he sat, gazing into the dancing flames for a long time, until Gisbourne thought the man must have fallen asleep. "Philip was more of a father to me than my da," he eventually muttered, eyes still fixed on the hearth. "He was four years older than me, and my best mate. We used to go fishing together all the time; Philip was a fine fisherman. We'd always come home with something for the pot. It was never good enough for da, though..."

Gisbourne sighed and shifted in his seat, beginning to regret asking to hear this story. It was not going to be a barrel of laughs...

"My father was a carpenter," Matt went on, oblivious. "It was a decent job and we never had a leaky roof or draughts coming in through holes in the door at night, no – my da was fine and handy. But Philip and I never really felt comfortable in the house." He looked up at Sir Guy and nodded towards the bounty-hunter's mug. "I admire you for sticking to that weak, watered-down ale, even if it does taste like piss. This stuff," he hefted his own mug of strong ale ruefully, "is the devil's own brew. It's the source of all evil in this world."

Ignoring his own platitude, Matt took a long drink, gasping with pleasure as he leaned forward and slammed the empty wooden mug onto the table. "More, inn-keep!"

As the landlord hurried to obey, Groves stuck a poker in the fire to warm before crossing his hands in his lap and continuing his tale.

"I like a drink, I have to be honest, I do. Nothing better in the world than a few mugs of ale and a nice pair of tits to get your hands on, eh?" He grinned at his captain but Gisbourne only nodded politely, thinking of lots of things he'd enjoy more than either of those.

"Well, my da liked a drink as well, even more than I do. It was all the bastard lived for." The smile fell from Matt's face and his usual sour expression returned. "You'd think he'd have wanted to spend time with us – his boys. See us growing up into men. But no, the useless sot would take himself straight to the local alehouse as soon as he finished work and had his pay in his purse. Then, when the place shut for the night, or he got himself thrown out, he'd come home and..."

Again his voice trailed off and the inn-keeper hurried over to hand him another mug brimming with ale. He lifted the hot poker from the fire and placed the bright tip into the liquid which hissed and steamed in protest.

"Philip got it the worst, probably because he was bigger, and he had more of a mouth on him than I did. I don't know why my da was always angry when he came home – maybe my mother's death had done something to his head. Or maybe the drink made him like that. Some people get happy when they have a few ales – they sing songs and dance about like idiots. My da always seemed to get pissed off when he had a few though..."

A small smile flickered on his face. "Aye, Philip would give as good as he got, with his words. But it would just make da even angrier, then he'd take off his belt, or use his bare hands. I must have been about six or seven when this was going on, so my brother would have been only ten or eleven. A boy, nothing more than a boy. My da was a big man too. I remember his hands were huge and always covered in hard, flaky skin that would crack and bleed in the winter. Served the bastard right."

Gisbourne had no idea any of this had happened in his new sergeant's past, but it didn't surprise him in the least. His head nodded and he forced himself to sit up straighter to avoid drifting off into a comfortable sleep as Matt went on.

"I took a beating a few times, aye... got a few black eyes and my ears..." He rubbed the side of his head and Gisbourne noticed for the first time that, underneath Matt's poker-straight dirty-blonde hair, his ears were huge; thick and puffy in a way that looked almost obscene to the king's man who suppressed a shudder and hid his distaste by sipping his weak drink.

"But Philip took the worst of it. He grew big and strong and eventually, one night when my da came home drunk and tried to use his fists, Philip was too fast."

Matt's eyes lit-up gleefully, remembering that night, re-living it as if it were only yesterday. "Smashed da's nose he did. Blood everywhere!" His voice dropped and he looked down at the floor. "I was terrified," he admitted. "I thought my da would kill him." There was another sigh and another long pause as Matt took a drink of the warm ale, letting the bitter liquid seep into his belly as he watched the flames flicker and dance in the hearth before them.

"So what happened?" Gisbourne demanded, interested in spite of himself. "Did your father kill him?"

Matt shrugged. "I don't know. I've never seen Philip since that night." He looked up and met his captain's eyes. "I ran away out the house and slept under a bush. Didn't come back until the next morning. When I got there my da was out at work as usual and there was no sign of my brother."

"Did you not ask your father what'd happened?"

"Aye, I did, once, when he'd not been paid and couldn't afford to spend the whole night in the alehouse." Matt shook his head in consternation. "He said he'd no idea where Philip had gone and I believe he spoke the truth. I think he was so damn drunk that night that whatever happened was wiped from his memory. Wouldn't be the first time that's happened to someone – God's bollocks, it's happened to me more than once." He grinned, as if proud of himself. "I've no idea whether Philip was killed by my da and dumped in the river or... maybe my big brother ran off same as me, only he never came back in the morning like I did..."

Gisbourne wasn't surprised to see tears in Matt's eyes. The man was quite drunk, which seemed rather ironic to the bounty-hunter given the gist of Matt's story.

"None of this explains how you ended up a sailor," the king's man said, waving towards the inn-keeper for a refill of his own. Although the ale he drank had been watered-down, it was still just enough to get a man like Gisbourne – who drank alcohol infrequently – comfortably numb.

Matt's head was nodding as sleep threatened to overtake him but his whole body seemed to jerk awake again at his captain's words and he looked blearily at Sir Guy, as if wondering who the man was.

Eventually, with another deep draught of ale, he continued the story, the landlord watching surreptitiously from behind the bar.

"I've never seen Philip since that night," he repeated morosely. "For the next few years my da took out his frustrations on me. I'd lie awake in bed dreading him coming home. I don't know... it seems like he beat the shit out of me near enough every night but it can't really have been that often. And he normally used his belt rather than his fists which hurt like hell but at least it didn't break bones. Still have the scars on my legs though; don't expect they'll ever go away."

A log cracked and split loudly, causing Matt to jump and take another sip of ale. "Anyway, I eventually grew big enough that I could look after myself. My da must have known he'd have a fight on his hands if he continued to beat me once I was full-grown and it stopped." He looked over at Sir Guy, his eyes surprisingly lucid for the moment. "I'd not forgotten what had happened with my big brother though; I missed him and I wondered how our lives might have turned out if we'd had a sober father instead of a sot. Anyway – the resentment built up inside me over the years... it wasn't a happy household ours, not by a long way."

"What happened?"

The flare of lucidity dimmed in Matt's eyes as he retreated back into himself again, the firelight casting a ruddy glow on his dour face. "My da came home one night, in a foul mood. He must have lost money at dice or something; whatever it was, he came in shouting and hauled me out the bed before trying to throttle me for not clearing away my dinner plate or some stupid thing." His voice became hard and his eyes blazed as he remembered that night.

"For the first time in my life, I defended myself. I wasn't a little boy any more, I was almost the same size as I am now. I hit him. And I hit him again, and again. When he fell on the floor, covering his head in his hands – just like I'd done as a child – it made me mad." He growled in satisfaction. "I beat him senseless – there was blood all over the room – then I took what money he had on him, or hidden in the strongbox under our bed, along with his dagger and what little food there was in the house. And I left. I've never been back."

Gisbourne was getting tired himself by now, his head beginning to slump onto his chest, but the story was obviously nearing its conclusion and he wanted to hear it.

"You found a job on some ship then?"

"Eventually," Matt agreed. "Although I had to scratch a living for a few months – stealing money and food just to survive. Sleeping rough in various towns, trying to avoid the guards... Then I came to Hull and, by luck or by chance, got caught trying to steal the purse from a sailor. Older man, from some freezing country away up to the north – Norway or that. He saw I was starving and desperate and was kind enough to get his captain to find a place on their ship for me. I sailed with them for nearly two years, learned my trade and then moved from ship to ship wherever the work took me... Got fed up with it eventually though, it was a hard life."

Gisbourne gestured impatiently for him to continue.

"Got into a fight in a tavern in Coatham one day. Arsehole tried to cheat me at dice and I stabbed him with my dagger. The same dagger I took from my da." His hand patted his hip, feeling the reassuring bulk of the weapon safely tucked away. "I had to escape from the law, so it was back to hiding and moving from town to town, making a living where I could. I did a lot of bad things then."

He shrugged as if he'd only done what was necessary.

"Wound up in Barnsdale and found Adam Bell and his gang. They took me in and looked after me. Had some good times with Adam until that whoreson Robin Hood turned up and took over the place." He tried to empty the remainder of his drink into his mouth but most of it spilled down his chin and into his tunic although he didn't seem to notice. Blearily, he got to his feet and shouted for the inn-keeper to show him to the room they'd paid for.

As the man half-led, half-carried Matt along the gloomy corridor the former-outlaw mumbled to himself. "Bastard Hood. I'll see him dead one day, I swear it!"

CHAPTER NINETEEN

"They're home!" Young Gareth ran into camp, eyes shining and a huge grin on his narrow face. "They're back!"

"Who's back?" Stephen, the former Hospitaller sergeant-at-arms demanded, buckling on his sword-belt which he'd grabbed from beside his pallet as soon as he heard the skinny youngster from Wrangbrook tearing through the slowly thickening spring foliage towards them. The rest of the men that were around the camp that day followed his lead, grabbing weapons and strapping on whatever armour they owned, ready for whatever danger approached.

"Robin and John," Gareth shouted, barely panting despite his mad dash from his lookout post high in a Scots pine. "Although they're dressed like friars," he reported, a puzzled look on his face. "Even got their heads shaved like friars. Never seen John without his beard."

Will Scarlet kicked earth over the camp-fire to extinguish it and placed a wooden board on top to disperse the tell-tale smoke over a wider area so it wouldn't give away their position so obviously. He ran forward to stare at Gareth, hope flaring within him.

"Friars? Have you been on the drink again?" he demanded. "Are you sure it's Robin and John and not someone else? Like Gisbourne?"

Gareth shook his head, angry at Will's suggestion he was too drunk to know what some of his best friends looked like. "It's them Scarlet, and I think Allan's with them. I've not drank any more than the rest of you this morning. You were pretty legless yourself last night too, so don't act as if you're better than me you sour-faced c–"

"Enough of this," Stephen growled, stepping between the two men before Scarlet could do anything. "Maybe it's them, and maybe it's not. The fact they're heading this way suggests they know where our camp is, so I'm inclined to believe it *is* them. It was Robin himself that suggested we come here to Selby after all. You," he nodded at Gareth. "Good work warning us of their approach, lad, whoever it turns out to be – at least we'll meet them with sword in hand rather than lying on our backs on the grass. Now get back to your post in case anyone else is behind them." He patted the young man on his shoulder encouragingly and was rewarded with a steely nod of gratitude before Gareth sprinted off into the trees again.

Will looked somewhat sheepish at the Hospitaller's command of the situation since he'd done nothing other than irritate the lookout. He nodded his thanks to Stephen then turned and addressed the men. "Archers, take your positions in the trees. The rest of you get behind me in a semi-circle with your weapons drawn. Whoever these men are, they'll not find us sitting on our arses – we'll be ready for whatever they're bringing us."

A nervous silence came over the men but no-one appeared. The birds continued to sing and forage amongst the previous year's fallen leaves, but as the men watched the trees in the direction Gareth had said the travellers were coming from there was no sign of anyone approaching.

Will, string fitted to his longbow, fingered the goose-feathers of his arrow and, as time dragged by he cursed to himself, wishing something would happen.

"Where are they?" The voice belonged to Arthur, the stocky young man with hardly any teeth left despite his tender years, but Will couldn't see him to offer an angry rebuke, resorting instead to a furious hiss he hoped would discourage any further lack of discipline from the men.

At last, just as the sun reached its highest point in the sky, casting a wan yellow glow on the greenery that surrounded them, voices filtered through the trees towards them and Will nocked the arrow to his bowstring, happy in the knowledge the rest of the men would also be preparing themselves for whatever happened next. Or *who*ever...

"God be praised, it *is* them," Edmond said as Little John's great booming voice echoed around the forest and Robin's unmistakeable laugh followed.

"Shut your fucking mouth and keep your weapon at the ready!" Scarlet commanded in a low voice, his face flushing crimson, and Edmond nodded guiltily.

Then, as if they hadn't a care in the world, Robin, John and Allan-a-Dale wandered, grinning, into the clearing and looked around at the vast array of weaponry that met them.

"Lads, is that any way to welcome us home?" Robin laughed, and Will, forgetting his own demand for discipline, ran forward to embrace his friends.

* * *

Surprisingly, Helen didn't come after Marjorie to avenge her humiliation at the older girl's hands. In fact, Helen and her friends gave Robin's sister a wide berth whenever their paths happened to cross.

Marjorie felt – perhaps stupidly – guilty about what she'd done to the girl. Yes, she might have deserved to be taken down a peg or two, but the pained look on her face when Marjorie had kicked her to the ground still played on her mind. She felt some empathy with the girl; harsh bereavement was a common factor in both their young lives and it affected people in different ways.

Before her mother died Helen had been quite a popular girl and, although she'd tossed the odd insult Marjorie's way, well, so had almost every other girl in the village – it was just what children did and, although it had been hurtful, Marjorie knew now that it had all helped make her who she was. It had all strengthened her and was now contributing to her drive to break out of the role of weakling that seemed to have been assigned to her by God and everyone in Wakefield. Even her parents who doted on her.

Eventually, she'd had enough of the sullen looks and crossed the dusty street one morning when she'd spotted Helen walking on her own, on some errand or other.

"Wait."

"What do you want? We've left you alone, just like you wanted." Helen's bottom lip thrust out and her fists clenched, as if preparing for another physical altercation and Marjorie spoke fast to reassure the girl.

"Look, I'm sorry I hit you. You were being horrible and when you got into my face I just wanted to defend myself and keep you away from me. Truly, I'm sorry. I should have just ignored you."

Helen looked at her warily, hands still balled into fists, not really sure how to react. She knew herself she'd deserved to be beaten; she'd been mean to the other girl for no reason. Yet here was the lass she'd been tormenting, apologising for standing up to her.

Marjorie smiled, apparently sincerely, and Helen looked ashamed. She was bigger than this girl, which was one reason why she'd picked on her. Smaller people were usually easy targets; didn't normally fight back.

"No, *I'm* sorry," she said. "Everyone knows why you're small. I was being a bitch and I got what I deserved. If someone spoke to me like that I'd have beaten them bloody and... well, you had that wooden sword so I was glad you let me go." Her eyes dropped to Marjorie's midriff, looking to see if the practice weapon was concealed again and this was all just the prelude to a thrashing.

"I've got it, aye," Marjorie smiled in reply to the unspoken question. "I carry it with me all the time now, so it becomes second nature."

Helen stiffened almost imperceptibly as the girl pulled out the weapon; short, with many nicks in the dull edge but sturdy and dangerous looking. Her eyes widened at the freshly oiled wood which Marjorie was obviously proud of.

"Could... could you teach me how to use one?"

Marjorie hesitated. Fighting was *her* thing. She didn't want to let another girl – especially one already bigger than her despite being four years her junior – share it with her. Then she remembered something Matilda had told

199

her, a piece of wisdom that apparently originated with Will Scaflock: "If you truly want to master something, teach it."

From then on, Marjorie had a new sparring partner for those times Matilda was busy with little Arthur or with her work in the fletcher's. She and Helen became friends, finding they had much in common other than the fact they'd both suffered painful losses. The younger girl came to look up to Marjorie, impressed by her natural skill with the wooden sword and her dedication to improve herself despite the limitations of her body. Soon, other local girls were joining in with the sparring and training sessions. None took it as seriously as Marjorie, but all seemed to enjoy it and all seemed happy to look to her for instruction.

Marjorie found herself happier than she'd ever been in all her fifteen years on God's earth. She was close to her parents and enjoyed spending time with Matilda and Arthur as the baby grew and learned to walk properly and speak a few words. The way he pronounced her name always made her smile: "Mahjy." Proud Auntie Mahjy. She also progressed with her training – helping Helen and the girls was really paying off for her. She'd never be able to stand up to someone as big, or as skilled as, for example, Little John or Allan-a-Dale, but most men weren't like that. None of the villagers were as big as her brother and his companions, or as deadly with sword and longbow – those men were exceptional because they *had* to be to survive as outlaws.

Marjorie felt, somewhat naively, that she could hold her own if some village boy – like the miller's son who'd been giving her lecherous looks for weeks – had tried to molest her.

She felt good when she woke in the mornings now, and walked with a straight-backed swagger that people had started to notice and comment upon.

John and Martha Hood, of course, had seen the change in their previously skinny, quiet daughter and had

200

pried the truth from Matilda. They'd agreed to turn a blind eye, despite the antinomian nature of Marjorie's new pursuit, since the change in her was so plainly for the better.

Matilda watched as her sister-in-law grew into a confident young woman and prayed to God her eager student would never need to put her fighting skills to use for real.

Behind her smile, though, Marjorie still felt like something was missing.

* * *

"Let's stop here for the night," Osferth suggested as a small village appeared on the horizon. "We've made good time today and it'll be dark soon. I don't know about you but I'd rather sleep in a bed than on the damp grass again. My neck still aches from last night's 'sleep'." He grimaced and bent his head from side to side as if to demonstrate his pain. "I'm not used to sleeping outdoors like you."

Tuck nodded. "Fair enough. We're nearly in Yorkshire anyway. Should reach Horbury by tomorrow if we're on the road early enough. I know some people there who might be able to tell us where Robin and the boys are camping. Hopefully the sheriff hasn't caught them yet."

They rode into the village – Bryneford according to the almost-illegible sign – which was little more than a handful of houses and a little wooden building that doubled as both church and the local priest's dwelling. There wasn't even an inn but one of the locals, a man named Philip, had a spare room in his house as a result of some disease that had visited the place a few weeks earlier and he allowed the two clergymen to stay with him in return for some small coins.

The villager had some ale which he shared with the clergymen and they made idle chatter to pass the time as night fell. Tuck seemed to grow drowsy very quickly although Osferth's eyes remained alert despite appearing to consume just as much of the drink as the older man.

"Come on, we'll get you into the bed," Osferth smiled, helping Tuck off the bench that ran along one side of the villager's house. "I'll stay up with Philip here for a while longer; I'm enjoying sampling all these local ales on our adventure. Makes a nice change from the same old piss-water we got back in the priory."

The villager gave them a candle which he'd lit from the big fire in the centre of the room and Osferth helped his friend into the little room with its pair of straw mattresses. Philip assured them he'd burned the old beds to get rid of any dangerous fluids or vapours since the previous occupants – Philip's teenage sons – had gone to their final resting place. Without his boys to help him on the small plot of land he farmed the villager had to find some other source of income so, with no inn in the little place, it seemed a decent idea to offer his spare room to any travellers in return for a few coins.

"I haven't had any 'guests' yet, other than you two," he'd told them when they first arrived. "So the mattresses will be nice and plump for you."

And indeed they were, heavy and comfortable, even if it seemed something of an intrusion to be sleeping in a bed that belonged to a dead boy not so long ago. Still, within a few moments Tuck was sound asleep and snoring loud enough to shake the rafters until Osferth rolled him onto his front, quieting the rumbling only marginally, and left the room with a somewhat nervous backward glance.

"Another?" Philip looked up as the monk returned, the big ale pot hovering above Osferth's empty mug.

"Not right now. May I borrow this candle?"

Philip looked puzzled but nodded agreement. "It's not windy so it should stay alight for a while but... where are you going at this time of the night?"

"I need to speak with the priest. Will he be at home?"

"Father Martin? Aye, he should be in the church. Young man he is, but he never really goes anywhere outside of the village. I suppose he might be visiting someone but..." He shrugged as if to say that was unlikely and Osferth thanked him before opening the front door.

"I won't be long. My companion will not awaken while I'm away."

"Eh? How d'you know that?" Philip wondered, but Osferth had already shut the door and was gone.

CHAPTER TWENTY

Tuck woke in the morning, surprised to have slept such a deep, dreamless sleep in the recently deceased villagers' bedroom. He couldn't remember waking at all during the night which was unusual for him as he often had to get up to empty his bladder in the small hours. And yet, despite his unbroken slumber, his head ached just behind his eyes and his mouth was dry.

"God above," he mumbled as he rose and stretched the kinks from his back. "How much of that ale did I drink last night?"

Osferth, who was already up and looking fresh, simply smiled and tossed a water-skin to his companion who pulled out the stopper and sucked down the cool liquid greedily.

"What time is it?"

"Sun's just coming up," Osferth replied, pointing to a small chest in the corner upon which lay a bowl of tepid water. "Philip must have left that there for us."

Tuck used the liquid to rinse the sleep from his eyes before drying himself off with his sleeve. "All right, we better get moving then. We want to get to Dodworth as soon as we can. The longer we tarry the more chance there is that my friends will be captured." He threw his pack over his shoulder and lifted his great quarterstaff. "We can break our fast on the road, come on."

Philip wasn't about and the travellers assumed he must have gone off to work, trusting them not to steal anything from the house. Tuck looked around and wondered what they could steal even if they were so inclined; there was little of any value in the small dwelling which seemed to exude an air of sadness still, or maybe that was just the friar's imagination.

"Let's go." He opened the door and moved outside. Their horses were in a small stable adjoining the church and, as Osferth got the mounts ready Tuck decided it would be polite to give God's greetings to the local priest before they left.

He knocked on the door but no-one answered and a villager shouted across to him. "Father Martin's not in. He was up before dawn and borrowed my horse to run some errand. I've no idea where he's gone though."

"No matter," Tuck smiled with a wave of thanks to the man. "It's not important. God give you good day."

They climbed onto their mounts and resumed the journey north, with dark glances at a sky that was filled with looming thunderheads.

"Come on, Horbury isn't far," Tuck shouted, kicking his heels into the old palfrey. "Let's reach it before we get a soaking."

* * *

James had tried, he really had, but there just wasn't any honest work available for him in Horbury. He wasn't an outlaw himself, for he hadn't been caught doing anything illegal, but the locals knew he kept company with thieves and wolf's heads and, as a result he couldn't even get a job labouring in the fields or on the site of the building works at the new brewery that was being built just outside the town.

How was he supposed to live an honest life if no-one would give him the chance to support himself?

His meeting with the portly friar just weeks earlier had truly had a profound effect on him and he'd vowed to stop his robbing ways before he was either declared an outlaw or killed by a forester's arrow. Christ, Sir Guy of Gisbourne and his men were staying in the town; the close proximity of the feared bounty hunter should have been enough reason for James to live within the law.

And yet, here he was, hiding under a bush, hood up as the rain had come on with a vengeance, flanked by two of the men the friar had bested so violently. The third member of their gang hadn't been so lucky – Tuck's blow had cracked his skull and he'd died the next day. Not that any of the rest cared much – none of them were close friends, simply acquaintances and the threat of violent death was an ever-present threat when you earned a living stealing from people.

Now they sat and watched the road for unwary travellers with coin to spare and little chance of fighting off the robbers.

James scowled. If people wouldn't trust him enough to employ him, what choice did he have but to live like this? He needed to put food on his table didn't he? It was just as well his wife had died young, before she could give him a child. He could barely even fill his own belly never mind anyone else's.

There was movement on the road and he sat up straighter, squinting through the torrential rain to try and make out who approached.

"Someone's coming," Mark, their short leader growled, his voice hopeful. "Perhaps this one'll have more about him than that last bastard."

They'd stopped a young merchant a short time before, travelling alone, and it soon became apparent why he hadn't felt the need to hire mercenaries to guard him on the dangerous northern road: he had little money on him and his 'wares' consisted of a pack filled with strange smelling ointments and liquids in glass bottles. The man had tried to explain to them what they were – some kind of medicines apparently – but Mark had silenced him with a brutal punch to the side of the face before taking his purse and sending the sobbing man on his way in disgust.

"Medicines for fuck sake. What good's that to us?"

James didn't reply, he was staring at the road as their potential targets approached at a fair pace, their mounts' hooves covering the distance to their position in good time.

Suddenly Mark gave a small, gleeful hoot and turned to his friends happily. "It's the friar, he's back."

"So it is." Ivo, the man whose teeth Tuck had broken muttered agreement, his hand pressing unconsciously on his lips, feeling the empty spaces left by the friar's cudgel.

206

"Good. This time we'll be prepared for him. We'll see how *he* likes losing a few teeth."

"And his balls too," Mark spat the words viciously, still furious to have been beaten – humiliated – by a man of the cloth. "James, get an arrow ready. You can let his mate in the black robe ride on, but take out the greyfriar's horse. Once the prick's on the ground me and Ivo will take care of the rest."

James hadn't told his cohorts what had happened between himself and the friar when they had tried to rob the man before. How could he? They were already angry that he hadn't skewered the bastard when he had the chance; there was no way he could tell them he'd had a nice, friendly chat with the clergyman. Instead, he'd claimed to have been hit in the guts by the cudgel which he said the friar had thrown at him. Once he'd been on the ground, gasping for breath, he said, the friar had retrieved the weapon and raced off on his horse.

It was a feeble story and his cohorts had given him suspicious looks as he told it, but they had no reason to suspect he was lying. Little did they know Friar Tuck had made a friend of James that day and now, here was Mark demanding the young archer shoot the clergyman's horse...

"No."

The robbers swivelled their heads to glare at James who returned their looks with eyes as steely as their own.

"Do you not realise who he is?"

"I don't give a fuck who he is," Ivo spat. "He's going to pay for what he did to us."

Mark pointed his dagger angrily at James. "Just you get an arrow ready, dickhead, or it'll be *your* balls I'll be slicing off with this."

"Are you stupid?" James retorted more confidently than he felt in the face of his violent companions' ire. "How many friars have you heard about around here that can fight as well as he does? That's Friar Tuck. Robin Hood's mate."

Mark and Ivo were too angry to back down and their hated target was nearing their position rapidly, the horses

207

close enough now that the spray thrown up from their hooves was visible.

"Shoot him now," Mark ordered, his eyes blazing in anger. Never before had James stood up to him or refused to do as he was told by the older, if smaller man. "Shoot him you arsehole, before he escapes or so help me God I'll cut your fucking eyes out."

James shrank back from his leader, knowing the man was just deranged enough to carry out his threat. He looked towards the road and realized he only had moments to take his shot before Tuck would be past and safely out of range.

"Shoot him!" Ivo shouted, the rain slicking the long black hair against his angry face.

James took a deep breath, his stomach contorting as if filled with a dozen live larks like one of the extravagant pies the wealthy supposedly ate, and raised his longbow with the arrow already nocked and ready to loose.

"Holy Mary, mother of God, protect me," he prayed and aimed along the shaft of the big missile, pointing the iron broadhead not at the mounted clergymen, but towards his own robber-companions.

Stepping backwards, slowly and carefully he held his aim steady as he distanced himself from the shocked – and utterly furious – Mark and Ivo who stared at him vengefully.

"I knew that story you told us about him throwing his cudgel at you was bollocks," Mark grated.

"I'm not shooting his horse just so you two can kill him. The man spared all of our lives the first time we tried to rob him, when he could just as easily have slit our throats. Hell, he'd have been given a *reward* for killing us; but still he let us go." He held his bow steady in his left hand while he quickly leaned down and grabbed his small pack of food with the right, throwing its strap across his shoulder before drawing the bowstring taut again and resuming his slow, backward movement. "Besides, he's a man of God for fuck sake. You don't kill a man of God!"

"I'll fucking kill *you,* you whoreson," Mark roared, his face scarlet, and Ivo screamed his own murderous oath.

"And on top of all that," James continued, shouting himself now, "he's one of Robin Hood's gang. If they found out we'd killed him they'd come hunting for us. You want Little John coming after you? 'Cause I don't."

He was a fair distance away from them now and, with a sigh of relief lowered the longbow, fitted the arrow back inside his belt and, curses filling the air behind him, broke into a loping run towards Horbury. Mark and Ivo were both well-known outlaws and wouldn't come into the town after him, especially not with Guy of Gisbourne lodging in the Swan as he was.

Aye, the Swan, James thought as his long stride carried him north. *That's the safest place to be just now. Mark will never dare to follow me there.*

He'd use his share of the money they'd stolen from the medicine-seller to pay for a room, then decide what to do next in the morning.

It had been a foolhardy move to cross the two outlaws but... by God it had felt good!

* * *

Tuck and Osferth made fine time but were not quite fast enough to outrun the oncoming clouds which overtook them and spilled their chilly contents on the travellers when they were still some distance from Horbury.

They cantered past the three robbers hiding in the undergrowth at the side of the road, oblivious to the danger that was so close and, by the time they reached the town and found sanctuary from the downpour in an inn, the clergymen were both drenched.

"In God's name, it's Tuck." The landlord smiled in surprise when he spotted the dripping friar who shook the water from his tonsured head like a great dog.

"Aye, Andrew, it's me – don't just stand there grinning like a lack-wit, man. Warmed ale for my companion and I!"

The inn-keep hurried to do as he was told, bustling over a moment later with two gently steaming mugs, the smile still on his face as he looked down at the seated clergymen.

"I heard you'd left Robin Hood's gang and gone back down south; didn't expect you'd be back here again, but it's good to see you, father."

Tuck sipped his ale and wiped the remaining dampness from his forehead with a big hand before returning the landlord's smile. "I did leave Robin and the rest of the lads," he said. "But I need to find them again, and quickly. Do you have any word of their whereabouts?"

It was before noon and, apart from the three of them, the place was empty at that time of day, but a loose tongue could be fatal and the man's eyes settled on Osferth.

Tuck waved a hand reassuringly. "Have no fear, this is my friend, one of the Benedictines from Lewes: you may talk freely in front of him."

Still, the inn-keeper seemed inordinately nervous, his eyes casting about his own inn to make sure no-one was hiding in the shadows and he leaned in close to address the friar in hushed tones.

"I haven't seen any of your companions around here in a long time, but word is Will Scarlet and some Hospitaller were in Selby buying supplies a few days back. Maybe they have a camp near there?" He shrugged but remained bent over beside them. "You'd know better than me."

Tuck looked thoughtful. Maybe Robin did have a hideout somewhere close to Selby but they'd never camped there when Tuck was with them. Still, the friar hadn't been with them as long as most of the others and it was possible there were camps the outlaws knew of but Tuck had never visited himself.

"One other thing, Brother," the landlord continued, his eyes again darting nervously around the shadows.

"For God's sake, Andrew, spit it out. There's no one here other than us – it's *your* inn, you must know that yourself!"

The man looked somewhat embarrassed and gave a nervous smile before continuing. "You're right, of course, but it does no harm to be careful when the likes of Sir Guy of Gisbourne are about. Aye," he nodded in response to Tuck's anxious expression. "The Raven has taken lodgings just up the road in the Swan. Apparently the sheriff ran him out of Nottingham when Robin took the silver arrow."

Tuck held up his hands to stop the inn-keeper's words, a baffled look on his round face. "Wait, hold on man. I've been down in Lewes remember, I have no idea what you're talking about. Fetch Osferth and I another ale – get one for yourself too – and join us. Tell us the whole story. In fact," he groped inside his cassock for a moment before pulling out a couple of small silver coins and placing them on the table. "If that bastard Gisbourne's about we'd better not be seen. We'll take a room – a decent one, mind. We'll head for Selby in the morning and hope the rumours you heard prove correct. In the meantime – where's that ale? Let's hear about Robin and the silver arrow."

With freshly-filled mugs before them, Andrew told Tuck and Osferth what had happened when Robin and Little John had gone to the city to rescue the minstrel Allan-a-Dale. The tale bore little relation to what had actually happened, having grown in the telling as it travelled from mouth to mouth on its way to Horbury via any number of storytellers, each of whom had embellished the events of that day.

When the landlord finished, a broad smile on his face at the sheriff's humbling by the bold outlaw hero, Tuck couldn't help but return a broad grin of his own. He knew the tale had been exaggerated, but at the core of the thing seemed to be the fact his young friend Robin had won a near-priceless silver arrow from Sir Henry de Faucumberg while he and Little John had saved Allan from a certain hanging.

It sounded like the sort of legendary feat that seemed to happen when Robin was around. No doubt the minstrels – Allan especially – would be expanding the tale even further until every man, woman and child in England knew what had happened in Nottingham.

It was late afternoon by now and the men of the town were starting to filter in through the doors, looking for warm ale to chase the damp from their aching joints so Andrew stood up, cheeks flushed from the four mugs of ale he'd downed while chatting with the two clergymen, and excused himself to deal with his new customers.

"I assume your wife is slaving away in the kitchen," Tuck called after him, sniffing the air as the pleasant aroma of meat and vegetables roasting wafted through from the back of the building. "Send us out a couple of bowls of whatever that is she's cooking up in there."

The meal – beef and ale stew with chunks of fresh bread – proved to be both tasty and filling and Tuck settled back happily in his chair to let the food digest.

"Maybe it's not such a good idea to sit around here all night," Osferth said, watching nervously as the front door swung open again and another pair of labourers came in looking for meat and drink. "If that bounty hunter's about, I mean. The Raven did the inn-keep call him? He knows you doesn't he? No point in getting caught before you have a chance to warn your friends is there?"

Tuck nodded ruefully. "Aye, you have a point. From the sounds of it the news of Robin's whereabouts haven't reached Gisbourne yet or he'd not be hanging around here. So we still have some time, praise be to Our Lord. Aye," he slapped the table decisively. "You're right, we should keep out of sight. Let me go for a piss then we'll retire to our room for the evening. We can get a good night's sleep and be up early on the morrow."

The burly friar got unsteadily to his feet and waved to Andrew who stood behind the wooden bar serving another patron. "Night! We'll be up at dawn – have some bread and cheese ready for us to take will you? Oh, and refill our drinks," he grinned, waving blearily towards a random pair of empty mugs. "We'll drink 'em in our room."

With a final wave the friars lifted the freshly refilled mugs and stumbled from the common room. Stopping only

212

to relieve themselves at the latrine they made their way back to the lodgings Andrew had allocated to them for the night and Tuck slipped the bolt across the door with a satisfied sigh.

Ah, he'd always enjoyed travelling. Couldn't beat a night in a comfortable, cosy inn, with plenty of food, drink and good company – it was one of life's greatest pleasures.

He lay down on the bed and sipped at the mug he'd carried along the darkened corridor from the common room, savouring the delicious taste. Funny how even the vilest local ale tasted like Heaven's own nectar after seven or eight mugs he thought.

Osferth watched, his own mug resting untouched on a chest of drawers – the only piece of furniture in the room other than the two narrow beds, as Tuck's eyelids drooped and, after a short time, the big tonsured head fell forward on to his chest. The mug fell from limp fingers onto the floor, spilling the watery brown liquid on the grimy floorboards and a snore erupted from the friar's open mouth.

Osferth was glad it didn't take much dwale to send his companion into a deep sleep. Too heavy a dose of the stuff could be fatal and the younger monk liked his portly companion. He'd mixed the strange concoction – made from a variety of ingredients including henbane, vinegar and lettuce – with Tuck's ale whenever he needed the friar to take a long, unbroken nap. Like now.

The snoring filled the little room and Osferth smiled down at the slumbering form affectionately as he opened the door just wide enough to slip out into the hallway.

"Sleep tight, brother," he whispered, before losing himself in the shadows. "I'll be back just as soon as I've met the Raven."

CHAPTER TWENTY-ONE

James was lucky – the landlord of the Swan had one room remaining, a tiny cramped affair which seemed more like a storeroom than a place to spend a night but there was a pallet on the floor in which the young man could lie down if he kept his legs bent.

It was good enough for James who simply wanted a place to keep out of the reach of his erstwhile, murderous colleagues and the Swan, with its resident Raven, was perfect. Mark and Ivo, outlaws both, would never dare to set foot in the place, even if they knew their hated quarry was staying there for the night.

He had the silver they'd taken from the merchant and he decided to use it to enjoy his evening so he found a seat in the large common room as close to the fire as he could manage, although the place was busy and the benches nearest to the hearth were prime locations for cold and weary patrons.

He bought a mug of ale from the bald, bearded landlord and sipped at it contentedly. The king's bounty hunter was in the corner with his sergeant, much nearer to the fire than James. The man stood out like a fox in a henhouse; confidence and an air of barely repressed violence emanated from his black-clad figure and James was glad he'd decided to give up robbing folk with Mark and Ivo. The thought of the tall, wiry Raven hunting him down made him shiver.

A number of locals, clearly friends, sat together at a long table singing songs and telling jokes and James watched from the corner of his eye, enjoying the silly banter and ribald verse that was being belted out.

The bounty-hunter didn't seem to mind the drunken revelry but his companion, a dour-faced middle-aged man occasionally threw the noisy group an irritated glare and James suspected that hard looking lawman was more likely to be the source of trouble than any of the cheerful locals.

Another song ended and James finished his ale, smacking his lips in satisfaction and feeling in his coin-purse to see if he had enough for many more. *Plenty yet*, he said to himself and made his way to the bar, asking the man seated next to him to save his seat for him.

"Another of these, please, inn-keep."

The landlord held up a hand distractedly and James noticed the man was talking to a clergyman of some kind; a thin man in a black robe or cassock With a start, James realised it was Friar Tuck's travelling companion who'd ridden past him and the other thieves that afternoon. James scanned the room, fearful that Tuck might be there too and recognize him; he'd been friendly enough but still, the friar might give him away to Sir Guy.

The landlord was pointing at the sinister-looking bounty-hunter and, as Osferth apologetically shoved his way through the crowd of drinkers towards the lawman's corner seat James shook his head. Of course Tuck wouldn't give him away to Sir Guy – quite the opposite in fact, since the friar was, or had been, a member of Robin Hood's gang. It was common knowledge that Gisbourne and Hood's men were mortal enemies, there were even songs about it.

As Osferth leaned down and spoke into Sir Guy's ear James knew something was amiss. The barman handed him a fresh ale, taking a little coin in return, and the young man surreptitiously pushed his way through the patrons towards the fire.

He was curious and wondered why a companion of Tuck's would be sneaking into the Swan to talk privately with the king's man. As he went, muttering apologies to those he was gently moving aside, he made a show of blowing on his hands as if the warm, cosy hearth was what drew him nearer.

Gisbourne's sergeant watched his captain converse with the monk, a crooked smile on his face and, unnoticed by the trio, James stood with his back to them, straining to catch what was being said.

"How will we know where you're going?" Gisbourne was saying. "If we follow too closely the fat friar might hear us and lead us off in the wrong direction. Or the outlaws' lookouts will spot us and raise the alarm before we can silence them."

"I'll leave a trail for you to follow," the monk replied, smiling. "I'll carve a small cross on a tree whenever I can – all you'll have to do is look out for them to know the way. Tuck seems to think the camp will be about a mile north-east of the village."

"And you're sure the friar doesn't suspect you?"

"Aye, he's no fool," Gisbourne's sergeant put in. "A fat, pious prick, sure, but no fool."

Osferth shook his head but looked angry at the crude epithet the man had given Tuck. "No, he doesn't suspect anything. Why would he? I'm not acting nervously or anything like that which could give me away. I'm doing God's work and saving his soul." He glared at Sir Guy's right-hand man. "Tuck is a good man, whatever you think of him. He trusts me."

The bounty-hunter waved a dismissive hand in Matt's direction. "Ignore him brother – he thinks everyone's a prick. Well, that's it settled then: in the morning you and the friar will head for Selby. Me and Matt here will follow and look out for your carvings on the tree trunks. All being well, we'll discover Hood's camp and can prepare an overwhelming assault which will wipe out the wolf's head and his gang once and for all."

"You won't hurt Tuck, though," the monk said, looking straight into Sir Guy's eyes. Clearly the Benedictine wasn't overawed or frightened of the big bounty-hunter which made James wonder if the man was all right in the head.

"Fear not for your friend," Gisbourne said, then his hand dropped and he clasped the monk's wrist painfully. "If you lead us right in this I'm sure your prior back in Lewes will reward you with a promotion or whatever it is you desire, but..." A dagger seemed to appear from nowhere, its flawless blade glinting in the firelight as

Gisbourne placed it under the monk's chin. "If you double-cross us or think to lead us into a trap, well, let's just say Christ and all the saints of heaven won't be able to stop the pain and suffering I'll inflict upon you."

The monk pulled his wrist back, looking annoyed rather than scared by the Raven's violent vow. "Just remember not to hurt Tuck."

The conversation obviously neared a conclusion so James slowly squeezed back through the milling drinkers and retook his bench with a smile of thanks to his neighbour who gave a small wave in recognition and returned to his own conversation with the local on his other side.

What did it mean? James's mind whirled as he watched the thin monk leave the inn. Was Tuck really going to lead soldiers to Robin Hood's camp? He should warn the friar, he thought, but... how could he? Why would the man even believe him, a common thief?

Where did they say Hood's camp was? Selby, wasn't it? James knew the way to that village. Suddenly it was clear to him what he had to do. He couldn't find a job in the town anyway and he'd burnt his bridges with Mark too so there was little reason to hang around here.

No, he'd head for Selby and warn Robin Hood himself. With any luck the tales of the wolf's head's fairness and generosity hadn't been exaggerated too much and he'd be grateful to James for saving them... might even be a nice fat reward in it since the outlaws were famously wealthy from robbing rich merchants and churchmen.

His mind made up, and feeling better about his prospects than he had in months, James downed the last dregs in his mug and followed the departed monk into the chill night.

* * *

He knew he was taking a chance, what with Gisbourne being after his blood even harder than before, but Robin missed his family and so he'd travelled to Wakefield with

217

Will Scarlet that morning, which was where he heard the news.

"The king is coming," Matilda said, rearranging her clothes after a hurried but satisfying session of love-making.

Robin stared up at the wooden rafters for a moment, wondering if he'd heard his wife correctly before he sat up and stared at her, admiring her lithe figure as she buttoned the front of her tunic. "What?"

"The king's coming," she repeated. "He's visiting places around here to check they're being run correctly or something. Checking the sheriffs and the like are sending him as much tax as they're supposed to I expect."

"And he's coming here? To Wakefield?"

Matilda shrugged and sat on the bed next to him, a contented smile on her lips. God she'd missed Robin, it had felt good to feel his muscular body next to hers again. "Well, maybe not to Wakefield, but to Yorkshire. Maybe he'll pass through here on his way to one of the bigger towns or cities, who knows?" She fixed him with a hard glare. "Don't you even *think* about trying to rob him."

The big outlaw laughed and leaned forward, pulling his wife back down on top of him. "I'm not insane," he grinned. "Even if Edward is a personal acquaintance of mine, I doubt his guards would stand back while me and the lads stole his money."

"Get off," Matilda laughed in reply, pushing Robin's grasping hands away and standing back up. "Come on, little Arthur will be wanting something to eat. I've got some cheese he likes – you can share it too if you like."

A shadow passed over his face as he wondered how sensible it was to hang around in the village for too long but he pushed his fears aside and nodded. "Aye, it'd be nice to have a meal with my family again. I hope there's some of your ma's ale too. She knows how to brew, Mary, I'll say that for her."

"Yes, there's ale, and cheese, and bread too. Might even be some salted pork. My ma's out working a lot of the time now, though – I've started brewing the ale since I'm about the house with Arthur all day."

Although Robin's extended family, which included his own parents and sister as well as Matilda's mother and father, were well off thanks to Robin's success as a robber, the women were still expected to do their fair share of the chores, be it brewing ale, washing or mending clothes or cooking hearty meals.

The wolf's head clasped his wife's hand and squeezed. "That's good to hear, you were already the best wife in the world and now... you're making me ale. A man couldn't ask for more."

Without thinking the girl muttered something about him not being an outlaw and living at home with them, and she regretted the words as soon as they tumbled from her mouth, but Robin chose to pretend he hadn't heard her and they walked into the main room of the house still holding hands.

"There you are, you were in there for ages. What were you doing?" Robin's younger sister Marjorie asked innocently, her eyes taking in the unkempt hair and clothes of her brother and sister-in-law.

Matilda flushed crimson but Robin just raised an eyebrow and pointedly ignored the question. At her age Marjorie knew fine well what had been going on in the bed room - she'd be getting married herself soon enough he thought, wondering again if his father had found a husband for her yet.

"How was he?" Matilda asked, scooping her infant son out of Marjorie's arms, grinning and touching her nose to the boy's who squealed in delight, bringing a smile to Robin's face too.

Marjorie spent much of her time at the Fletcher's now, helping Matilda with chores and taking care of Arthur if his mother needed to do something. The girl had looked after him for the short time Robin and Matilda had been... busy.

"He was fine. Sat on the floor and played with his little animals." Marjorie waved to the finely carved little wooden toys – cows, sheep and pigs – that Robin had bought for his son in Barnsley when the big market was on.

"Oh, he loves those," Matilda said. "He sits and plays with them all day."

Robin was inordinately pleased to know his gift had brought his little boy so much pleasure but his gaze turned to his sister and he hid the frown that threatened to appear as he took in her diminutive stature. Despite Robin making sure his family always had enough money to buy nutritious food, his little sister's drawn face always made his heart heavy.

"How have you been?" He sat at the table, facing her, and smiled in gratitude as Matilda placed a wooden platter with bread, cheese and meat down in front of them. "Here," he said, handing a large slice of cheese to his sister who took it gladly.

"Fine," she said, shrugging as if his question was unimportant. "Did you know the king's coming?"

Robin allowed the shift in conversation to pass, not wanting to upset his sister. He hardly got to see her these days and the last thing he wanted to do was make her unhappy. So he simply nodded and smiled although he had to admit, as he watched her from the corner of his eye, she appeared to finally be putting a little weight on, God be praised.

"Aye, Matilda told me. He asked me to join his rowing team, you know. Well, it was John he asked, but he meant me too, I'm sure."

Marjorie rolled her eyes theatrically. He'd already told her earlier that day all about his meeting with King Edward, and Matilda groaned in the background.

"Yes, you already told us you met the king," his wife laughed. "Lucky him, eh?"

Marjorie sniggered and Robin grinned despite their teasing. It felt so good to be home again, to spend even a little time with the people he loved. Most men took a meal with their family completely for granted but, for Robin, it was a time to be treasured. He finished his meal then plucked Arthur from Matilda's arms and sat the boy on the floor where the two of them played with the wooden animals for a long time. His son was a beautiful little boy, always smiling, with a mischievous glint in his big blue eyes and Robin had great fun making the small toys moo, baa and snort as Arthur giggled and clapped delightedly.

Eventually though, Robin sighed as the shadows lengthened and he realised he'd have to head back into the greenwood before it grew dark and too treacherous to travel through the hidden paths and byways he knew so well in the daylight.

With a final hug for Arthur and Matilda, who surreptitiously squeezed him between the legs when she thought Marjorie wasn't looking, the young outlaw said his goodbyes – exhorting his sister to make sure she ate lots of meat and vegetables – and hurried off along the street and into the trees.

He shouldn't complain – he had a lot of money and a wonderful family which was a lot more than some people. His childhood friend Much, for example, whose father was murdered by Adam Gurdon, the previous bailiff, before Matt Groves and Sir Guy of Gisbourne had killed him too. Poor Much. At least Robin was still alive.

With each new day in the forest, though, he grew ever more bitter at the life fate had given him, but at least now he had the silver arrow.

He hadn't told Matilda but he'd already urged his men to put the word out – if any nobleman wanted the immensely valuable arrow they could have it, as long as they'd sign pardons for Robin and all his friends in return.

If Thomas, the former Earl of Lancaster, hadn't been executed by the king the previous year Robin knew he and his men would already be free. Thomas had the power to do as he pleased, pretty much, and he had been a friend to the outlaws. He'd have gladly taken the arrow off their hands and enjoyed rubbing Sir Henry's nose in it too.

The man was dead though and Robin wasn't sure who else would be powerful enough to go against the Sheriff of Nottingham and Yorkshire. De Faucumberg must be desperate for the return of the arrow after all – if some local lord was to take it from Robin in exchange for pardons the sheriff would surely not let the matter pass without a fight.

Perhaps one of the Despenser's would take the bait? Someone like that had power enough that they wouldn't need to worry about de Faucumberg's ire.

If not though, Robin had decided he use the wealth he'd already amassed to take Matilda and Arthur somewhere far away – Scotland or France perhaps – where they could start a new, free, life together.

Whatever happened, he wouldn't see another winter living rough in Barnsdale,. *By God and the Magdalene*, he vowed, *I* will *be free!*

CHAPTER TWENTY-TWO

Although James travelled light, carrying nothing but his longbow and some arrows, he was still exhausted by the time the sun started to show its face above the horizon.

He had no horse, so to beat Friar Tuck and his turncoat companion to Robin Hood's camp he'd had to travel through the night which, thankfully had been clear, with a gibbous moon overhead to shed at least some light on the road. If it had been cloudy or moonless it would have been impossible for him to make it to Selby – a trek of some thirty miles – in the dark. He simply didn't know the area well enough.

It had been a lonely, eerie journey and he'd ended up leaving the string fitted to his longbow with an arrow ready to draw from his belt at a moment's notice. The nocturnal sounds of owls and other animals, and the sight of shadowed trees almost seeming to sway of their own accord in the windless air made the young man's nerves frayed and stretched close to breaking. Twice he'd halted, breathing silently despite his fear, and aimed his weapon towards the foliage that crowded close.

He'd not seen whatever had spooked him on those occasions – presumably a fox or an owl – but he was glad when it began to grow light. The sinister forest had sapped his mental strength while the fast pace he'd been forced to set had made his body utterly fatigued. He hadn't slept that night either, of course, which no doubt played a part in the anxiety that assailed him through all that hellish flight.

Finally, as the day dawned and the chilly morning dew began to evaporate into the spring air, James wondered what the hell he was doing. Although he'd been in Selby before, he had no knowledge whatsoever of the land outside the village. It all looked much the same to him – trees and bushes interlaced with well-worn hunters paths and little-known, hidden tracks that only the most knowledgeable of locals could even find never mind traverse with any speed.

He began to feel rather foolish as his eyes scanned the apparently unchanging foliage all around him. How in God's name was he going to find Hood and his companions before the treacherous monk led the king's man straight to them? Well, James had come this far, he couldn't just turn back now. He had nowhere else to go anyway – Mark would cut his balls off if he went back to Horbury any time soon.

Some time after dawn but before noon he heaved a sigh of relief as his eyes picked out the gently-spiralling smoke from a number of fires. Some of it grey, denoting simple domestic, wood-burning hearths, and some of it dark and greasy, suggesting industrial processes of some kind. A village then, with perhaps a blacksmith working the bellows in his forge for a day spent repairing broken cartwheels or hammering new horseshoes into shape.

At least he'd be able to make sure he'd followed the stars correctly and hadn't travelled thirty miles in completely the wrong direction. And, God willing, those fires came from his destination: Selby.

"About a mile north-east of the village, the monk had said," James muttered to himself, steeling himself for that final section of his journey. "The outlaws are bound to have lookouts. All I need to do is find the general area and make enough noise that they come to see what's going on." *Or shoot me...*

He wondered if he should bypass the village altogether, rather than risk attracting any attention. Sir Guy of Gisbourne was due along after all and it would be safer for James if no-one could pass on his description. But James wasn't an outlaw – he had no reason to hide from anyone and, as long as he didn't ask after Hood or the rest of the notorious gang there was no reason for anyone to connect him with them. Besides, the River Ouse wound through Selby and the easiest way to reach the opposite bank would undoubtedly be the main road with its bridge near the centre of the village.

And his legs did ache, as did his parched throat. It hadn't been the most sensible or well-thought-out plan he'd come up with back in the Swan. He really should have bought some bread and a skin of water or wine from the landlord but, in his haste to make it to Selby before Tuck and his friend, James simply hadn't thought.

"Hail, friend, where can I buy a mug of ale?"

The local – a carpenter judging by the hard, callused hands that carried a pile of wooden planks and the leather bag at his waist presumably containing iron nails – nodded a gruff, "God give you good day, stranger," and waved the young traveller towards one of the small houses. No comfortable tavern in Selby then, but that didn't matter as long as the inhabitants of the little single-storey dwelling had some cool ale to spare and a bench where he could rest for a short while.

Nervously, he glanced over his shoulder, eyes scanning the road behind for signs of the two mounted clergymen, but he could see no-one. This would have to be a short rest though, or his trip would have been for naught.

"Can I help you, son?"

James smiled at the older woman who addressed him as he knocked and pushed open the door. "Aye, lady, you may. An ale, please? And a chance to take the load off my feet for a short while."

The woman must have been tall in her youth but age had curved her back and she stooped now, although her eyes were still bright and sharp as she looked James up and down, taking in the broad shoulders and great longbow he carried.

"Sit down, then," she nodded and shoved a rough, filthy-looking old curtain aside as she went into a different room, returning momentarily with a brimming mug which she handed to the bowman. "Expecting trouble?"

Somewhat shiftily James glanced at the woman as he swallowed a long gulp of the pale liquid. "No. What makes you ask that?"

"String's still on your bow."

He smiled sheepishly, took another sip of the ale which had been spiced with cinnamon, no doubt to hide the fact it wasn't particularly fresh, then stood up. Placing his left leg through the string and using his right leg to brace the bow he pulled gently backwards on the top of the great weapon to release the tension and slipped the string off before folding it neatly into his pouch.

"That'll be a farthing for the ale," the woman nodded. "The bench is free. You want another drink, or is whoever's chasing you too close behind?"

James couldn't help spluttering into the mug and he regretted coming into the damn alehouse with its shrewd proprietor. "No-one's chasing me," he said, trying unsuccessfully not to look guilty.

The woman simply shrugged, irritated that her customer wasn't going to give her some interesting gossip to share with the other women but pleased to see, by the big young man's nervous reaction, that she'd read the situation right. "Please yourself. Don't get many people coming into the place on foot this early in the day, though. You must have travelled through the night and no-one does that without good reason. You want another ale then, or not? Or maybe something else?"

James looked at her blankly, not understanding what the woman meant and she laughed, her eyes sparkling at his innocence. "My man's out in the far cornfields and won't return until near dark." She undid the laces of her bodice to reveal the top of her breasts and gazed wantonly at him.

He stared back, shocked at her brazen attempt to seduce him and felt his cheeks burn red in embarrassment. "I'll have another ale, lady," he agreed, "but that's all, thank you."

"Suit yourself," she nodded, looking down at his trousers and he hastily covered the bulge that had unexpectedly – given the fact she was old enough to be his mother – appeared there.

Flustered, he lowered his eyes to stare into the ale mug and, with a gleeful cackle the woman went into the back and brought another drink for the bemused young man who was relieved to see she'd covered herself up again.

"Where are you heading for?" the woman asked seriously. "It's not safe to travel around these parts on your own."

Glad at the change in the conversation James shrugged. "I spoke the truth: no one is chasing me. Indeed, no-one even knows I'm here. And I'm no outlaw, despite what you may think." He drained the mug and wiped his lips. "But I am in a hurry. I carry news that... well, it's a matter of life and death that I deliver my message before..." He trailed off, unwilling to tell this stranger any more about his business and, in fact, surprised to have told her as much as he had.

"Well, God grant you luck, wherever you're going," she told him as he stood and made his way out the front door after handing her a couple of coins. "And if your travels bring you back this way, be sure and come to see me. I have no problem with outlaws – my own son's one, for his sins."

James turned back at that, his eyes wide at the muttered revelation. "Your son?"

For the first time the woman looked flustered herself and she stepped back into her house. "Aye, my son," she admitted. "But I have no idea where he is, if you're a lawman. Is that why you're in such a hurry?" Her previous confidence and mastery of the situation had evaporated now and James stared at her, wondering what he should say or do.

He turned to glance back over his shoulder at the main road again and his blood ran cold. Two small, mounted, figures could be seen in the distance and James knew it was the clergymen. Friar Tuck would be known in this village – someone would tell him how to find Hood's camp and that would be the end of it all.

"Your son," he repeated, turning back to the nervous woman. "Tell me truthfully: is he one of Robin Hood's men?" He shook his head to stop the denial before it could escape her lips. "Listen to me, I am no lawman! The law *is* behind me though – Sir Guy of Gisbourne himself is on his way to butcher Hood and his gang unless someone warns them. For your son's sake, you have to trust me."

The woman stared at James but she had no reason to believe what he said. She tried to close the front door but the big bowman pressed his foot inside and blocked it open. "Wait! I've travelled all through the night to warn your son and his friends of the danger they face and now those two horsemen on the road there are about to overtake me and lead the Raven right to them. You must tell me how to find the outlaws, please!"

The sincerity in his voice touched the ale-seller but still doubts assailed her. "What is it to you if my son dies? Or Robin Hood? You say you're not an outlaw yourself so why would you go to all this trouble to help men who *are* wolf's heads?"

James sighed, exasperated at the delay which brought Tuck and the other monk ever closer. "It's a long story but... one of Robin's men spared my life when he might have killed me – indeed, would have been justified in doing so. I feel like I owe it to him to help him and his friends." He shrugged and gazed directly into the woman's fearful eyes. "And, on top of that – I'm not an outlaw but I might as well be. No-one will give me a job and I have no prospects. I thought maybe Robin Hood could use another good longbowman..."

The whole tale sounded ridiculous even to his own ears but, finally, sensing the truth of his words, the woman opened her door wide again and gestured him hurriedly inside.

"Swear in the name of Christ and all his saints that you mean my son no harm," she demanded, then, when James did so she gave him directions – as best she could, having never actually visited the place herself – to the outlaws' camp in the forest. "My boy told me how to find him if I ever needed him, although those directions won't bring you right out in the middle of their camp-site. Robin Hood is no fool, that's why they've been able to stay one step ahead of the sheriff and the foresters and Gisbourne for so long. But, if you go where I told you one of the gang members will find you. It'll be up to you to convince them not to kill you after that."

She moved over to the door and peered out, muttering to herself as she saw how close the horsemen were now.

"Go," she hissed. "Go. They're nearly here and no doubt this will be the first place they head for, looking for something to wet their dry throats, just as you did."

James stood and looked out into the street, relieved to see no-one was watching their furtive conversation as the woman clutched his arm in a surprisingly painful grip, digging her nails in and glaring at him.

"You better have been telling me the truth, boy, or Robin will come looking for you. Now... go and save my Peter!"

* * *

Since returning to the greenwood after Gisbourne's men had chased them out of Wakefield Robin had insisted the members of his band get back into the habit of training, hard, almost every day. Archery, hand-to-hand combat, and sparring with wooden practice swords or quarterstaffs made the men fit both physically and mentally. The young outlaw captain was proud of them and knew most of them felt more like soldiers than they ever had before.

He watched, a pleased smile on his face, as Little John held the fish-lipped tanner, Edmond, at bay with his giant staff. Although John looked comfortable, Robin could tell that the giant wasn't having as easy a time of it as he had when Edmond had first joined them. Aye, the tanner had been a hardy enough fighter, but he'd lacked true skill or finesse and relied more on brute force and aggression, which was all well and good, but useless when you came up against someone like Sir Guy of Gisbourne.

The addition too of the outcast Hospitaller sergeant-at-arms, Stephen, had given the men some new techniques to learn. The bluff Yorkshireman had been trained by the very best – knights of the cross – and he was able to show even the likes of Will Scaflock and Robin, who were both absolutely lethal with a blade, a few new tricks.

Little John suddenly stepped back, a look of surprise on his face as Edmond feinted to the left before reversing his momentum and ramming the point of his quarterstaff forward, almost hammering the breath from John. The giant was just able evade the blow but he grinned appreciatively at the gurning tanner and Robin moved away, happy in the knowledge his men were ready for almost anything Gisbourne could throw at them.

"How are they getting on?" He stepped up to stand next to Stephen who watched dispassionately as Gareth wrestled with another recent recruit, Piers, a twenty-two year old clerk from Nottingham who'd been caught fiddling his master's accounts and escaped into Barnsdale where Allan-a-Dale found him before the law could.

Stephen muttered something Robin couldn't catch but he was sure it wasn't anything pleasant. There was an angry cry as Gareth was tripped by the newcomer, who pinned him until he conceded the bout and Piers jumped up, breathing hard but smiling broadly over at the Hospitaller and Stephen nodded encouragingly, despite his stony expression.

"Well done, lad," Stephen said to Gareth though. "You're learning. Keep up the hard work. It might not feel like it's worth it but trust me, even taking a beating can be worthwhile. Rest a little then get yourself a practice sword; I'll spar with you for a bit" He cracked a rare, if small, smile and waved the young man away to take some refreshment and catch his breath again.

"He'll never be a fighter," Stephen muttered to Robin, watching as Gareth shuffled off, holding his back like an old man. "He's just not made for it."

Robin remained silent for a while. The young man was a valued member of the gang but he wasn't really much use for anything other than as a lookout or a messenger. His youth – he was still only eighteen after all – and skinny frame, meant he was a good, fast runner over long distances but... with the amount of ale the lad had started drinking recently he'd begun to thicken around the midriff and simply wasn't as fit as he should be.

Although they couldn't afford passengers in their group, Gareth's place would always be safe – by rescuing Friar Tuck from the freezing waters of the Don the previous year, saving the clergyman's life in the process, Gareth would always be looked upon gratefully by the men who had all counted Tuck as a great friend.

And yet, Gareth had to watch as the likes of Edmond, and now Piers, joined the group and surpassed him easily when it came to fighting and hunting and general usefulness about the camp. Held back by a body that had never recovered completely from the effects of malnutrition in childhood, Gareth would never be as valued a member of the gang as someone like the old Hospitaller or even Arthur, the stocky, toothless young man from Bichill.

Robin was sure all of that explained Gareth's excessive drinking over the past few months but... it wasn't up to him what the man drank, or how much. As long as it didn't cause them any harm, or bring danger upon them, Gareth could do what he wanted, just like all of them.

"What about the rest of them?" Robin asked, looking around at the other men training. "How would they fare if, say, a similar number of Hospitaller sergeants were to attack us?"

Stephen took a deep breath and exhaled slowly, looking at each man and calculating their potential in such a confrontation. He nodded at last. "Aye, they'd do alright. I'm not saying they'd win," he qualified his optimistic assessment, "but they'd hold their own, I'm sure."

Robin grinned. "Good. There's not much chance we'll be attacked by such a force, but if we're strong enough for that, we should have little to fear from the likes of the sheriff's soldiers or even Gisbourne's better-trained men." He clapped the sergeant-at-arms on the back gratefully. "You've been a fine addition to our group, Stephen, I'm glad to have you here."

Stephen returned the smile, happy to be appreciated, but his eyes were hard as he contemplated the circumstances that had brought him there. Betrayed by his own Order after a life of faithful service... it still rankled and always would, he knew.

Suddenly there was a whistle from the undergrowth to the south-west and the two men shared a wide-eyed glance for just a moment before racing to collect their weapons. "To arms!" Robin roared, buckling on his sword-belt and bending his bow between his legs to fit the hemp string to it. "Get your weapons."

They all knew what such a whistle meant – one of the lookouts was approaching with news of possible danger. Judging from the direction the sound had come from, it was Allan-a-Dale who made his way hurriedly towards the camp and Robin wondered what was afoot. *Let it be Gisbourne*, he prayed, *with just a few men so we can take him out once and for all*.

It couldn't be the king's man, though, Robin knew that was just wishful thinking. The outlaws had a simple but effective system: one whistle meant someone unknown was nearby but not, from appearances, much of a threat. Still, it was always good to be prepared so Robin continued to berate the men in hushed tones for not moving fast enough while Little John and Will marshalled them all into pre-determined places hidden within the foliage or, in some cases, up in the branches of the trees which now wore their almost full summer greenery and – after some judicious pruning – afforded a decent place to conceal a few longbowmen.

Robin himself stood alone, in the centre of the camp waiting to hear from the lookout, but his bow was in his left hand, ready just in case, as Allan jogged into camp, his eyes looking about the small clearing, glad to find everyone in position thanks to his warning.

"What's up?"

"A single traveller, a man, ran into the trees just west of my position," the lookout reported. "He was blowing hard – looked fit to drop so someone must be after him.

He's got a longbow, and looks sturdy enough to be able to use it."

"Recognize him?"

Allan shook his head. "Never seen him before. He was looking about him though, even up into the trees, as if he knew I – or someone at least – was up there watching."

Robin raised his voice so the hidden men could hear him clearly. "Any ideas anyone? A single bowman coming from the direction of Selby? Possibly knows we're camped about here? Piers?"

The clerk from Nottingham had come to them in similar fashion, although it had been purely by accident Allan had found him that day and brought him back to Robin and the rest. Maybe this was someone looking to do the same?

"Nothing to do with me," Piers shouted back, his surprisingly deep voice carrying easily from where he crouched behind a holly bush. "I told my family I was going to hide in the forest but I didn't even know myself whereabouts. No-one could have followed my trail all this time later."

"I watched for signs of anyone following him," Allan said, before Robin could even ask. "Couldn't see anyone, but I'm sure he was fleeing from something."

"Or *to* something...." Robin mused. "Right," decisively, "Allan, swap places with Gareth. Gareth, you head back to the lookout post and watch for signs of this lad's pursuers; we don't want to find ourselves discovered by an army."

Gareth nodded and ran to collect his belongings – short sword, a hunk of bread and a skin of ale which he furtively concealed inside his cloak before hurrying off to take up his post.

"Stephen, Scarlet – you two want to come with me?" Robin asked.

It was essentially an order from the outlaw captain, but he held his friends in such high regard that he often framed his orders as questions rather than statements. Of

233

course, Will and the Hospitaller gladly came forward to go with him to find this interloper in their forest.

"Hold your positions," he told the rest of the men. "John, you know what to do."

There was a shouted, "Aye," from the big man who followed it with a, "good luck!" as the three outlaws headed into the trees stealthily, weapons at the ready, curious to see who this exhausted archer might be.

* * *

There was a knock at the door and it opened, letting in the orange glow of sunset.

"Matilda, nice to see you, lass." John Hood smiled and gestured at one of the empty chairs. "Come and join us," he said. "We're playing draughts."

Robin's wife shook her head, looking down at the checkered board to see Martha was beating John quite soundly. "I just came to see if you fancied going for a walk."

Marjorie looked up. "Nah. Don't really feel like it tonight." She slumped in her seat, staring at the game board as if she was planning her tactics to defeat the eventual winner.

"Go on," Martha muttered to her daughter although her eyes never left the little wooden game pieces. "It'll do you good to get some fresh air."

"I've already had a walk today," the girl said, meeting Matilda's eyes with a knowing look. "My legs are tired."

"Oh. Fair enough then. I'll get off home and get back to sorting those feathers. My da got another order from a merchant in another town," she explained to John who was listening intently. "Apparently our good work on the 'eagle' feather arrows has got around – we've got enough work to last us well into winter. Farewell then."

She turned to go but Martha finally looked up then, her eyes damp from the smoke and gloom inside the house. "Wait a moment," she said then turned to address her fifteen year-old daughter.

234

"What's wrong with you now?"

Marjorie shrugged and Martha wanted nothing more than to reach out and take the girl into her arms. It would be a mistake to do so she knew, so she remained seated and crossed her hands on the table before her.

"You've been brooding for days now. Are you with child?"

Marjorie looked up, shocked, and shook her head. "No, for sure I'm not. What d'you mean asking me that?"

"I'll just be off then," Matilda muttered, making a grab for the door latch, but Martha glared at her.

"You can just wait there. You're bound up in all this and it's time we had it out."

"Had what out?"

"We know you've been learning to fight," Martha replied. "Don't we?"

John nodded, the expression on his face making it clear he would like to be elsewhere right then.

"And we know you've been out hunting. Apparently you've been doing well, at the fighting at least. Isn't that right?"

Matilda nodded. "She's got the same natural skill as her brother. One of you two must have it in your blood."

"How do you know about it?" Marjorie demanded. "It was supposed to be a secret."

"We're not stupid, lass," her father smiled. "It was obvious you were doing something when you started eating more and putting some weight on. We're proud of you. Happy that you've found something worthwhile to do."

Marjorie returned the smile fondly but her face dropped.

"Spit it out then," Martha said. "What's wrong?"

The girl didn't reply for a while, as she gathered her thoughts and tried to make sense of her own emotions before even attempting to put things into words her parents would understand.

As if reading her mind Martha laid a hand on hers and nodded. "We'll understand, trust me. You're not the first young girl to wonder what her purpose in life is and you won't be the last."

Finally, she spoke.

"Aye, Matilda's been teaching me how to use a sword. I've even started showing the other girls the things I've learned. It's been fun."

"But?" John prodded, gently.

"But..." Marjorie met her father's gaze, disappointment etched in her eyes. "They're all stronger than me. I'm supposed to be their teacher, but the bigger girls could beat me easy, if they wanted to. None of them have – they're all being nice to me. But they could if they felt like it." She leaned back in her chair, letting her arms flop to her side. "As for hunting... pfft, don't even mention that. I couldn't catch a hare if it was lying dead on the grass. It'd somehow slip through my fingers and escape."

She sighed heavily. "I'm just not very good at anything. I've tried my best – I've put everything into sparring with Matilda but... I'm useless."

"You're *not* –"

Martha laid a hand on her husband's and squeezed, silencing him.

"You're not," he repeated, leaning back himself and looking sadly at his girl who was still little despite her years.

"Look, lass, what is it you think you're going to do with your life?" Martha refilled an empty mug from the jug of ale that sat on the table between them and passed it to her daughter, gesturing the still standing Matilda to help herself to some of the cool liquid. "You think you're going to join the lord's army and go to fight the Scots? No? Well, you plan on joining the foresters? Even though there's not a single woman amongst them? No? Well, what then?"

Marjorie sat in sullen silence, hating the eyes of her family upon her but hating it even more that she genuinely couldn't answer her mother's questions. She really didn't have any idea what she wanted to do with her life but she knew she would never be a soldier or a forester. Even if

236

she *had* been stronger and fitter – women simply didn't do these things!

"What are you saying?" she demanded, meeting Martha's stare angrily. "That I've been wasting my time these past few weeks and months? That I should just give up and go back to doing nothing? Being nothing?"

"No!" Martha growled, clenching her fist and bringing it down on the table, making everyone, even Matilda jump. "No. I'm saying you need to accept who you are: a girl. A woman. And there's nothing wrong with that. Is there?" She cocked an eyebrow at her husband who raised his hands defensively.

"No, nothing," he replied. "Nothing at all – women are great. I think I'll go and milk the cow." He got his feet and hastily made his way out the front door.

"See?"

Marjorie smiled at her mother's triumphant look. "Who milks cows at sunset?"

"He knows his place, just as we all do," Martha told her. "And he knows who's the real head of this household." She smiled again and grasped her daughter's hand, looking over at Matilda to include her in her words too.

"You've been trying to learn all these skills and that's good; you've learned a lot from it, I can see that. But, first and foremost, you're a young woman. Your place is here in the home, with me for now and, when you're older, with your own children in your own house."

She lifted her right hand to silence any objections. "There's no shame in being a woman, lass. Just the opposite. There'd be no men in this world if it wasn't for the likes of us, right Matilda?"

Robin's wife nodded happily. "That's true," she agreed.

Still, Marjorie looked unconvinced.

"Look, Robin and his mates might live an exciting life but where do you think they'd rather be? Every one of them? They'd rather be at home with their families – with their women. Not out there, being chased around the greenwood by the likes of the Raven and his men."

"I know she speaks truly," Matilda chipped in. "Robin's told me as much himself many times. It might look like an exciting life they lead but... it eats him up inside. All he wants is to be with Arthur and I..."

The three women sat in silence for a time before Marjorie eventually spoke.

"So you're saying I should just accept my lot and be a good wife and mother?"

"Is there anything more important – or as rewarding – in the whole damn world, lass?"

Matilda nodded, thinking of her own beautiful little son. "Your ma's right. I've lived as an outlaw – as a fighter. I'd rather be at home making arrows for my da and shouting at Arthur to get away from the cooking pot before he scalds himself."

"Truly," Martha fixed her daughter with a piercing stare. "Women make the world go round. And you're as fine a girl as there's ever been."

Marjorie looked at her sister-in-law then back to her mother and stood up to embrace Martha, her eyes moist.

She knew now why she'd been so unhappy recently – she'd been trying to live a life that wasn't hers.

Still, she'd be the woman *she* wanted to be, not what everyone expected her to be...

CHAPTER TWENTY-THREE

James felt like he was about to pass out. His legs, particularly his thighs, ached terribly and it was an effort to keep lifting his feet as he pushed his way through the brambles and irritatingly lush foliage of the greenwood, insects, and wind-borne dandelion seeds, and god-knew-what-else flying into his eyes and gasping mouth as he went.

It was a shock, then, to realise a hooded man – and a big one at that – was standing silently in front of him, watching. The apparition wore a sword at his side and held a longbow, although neither weapon was raised threateningly.

James stopped, and let his head drop, resting his hands on his legs as his chest heaved and he tried to regain his breath without much success. Finally he managed to gasp, "In the name of Christ, I hope you're one of Robin Hood's men."

In his peripheral vision James noticed just a flicker of movement, first on the left and then on the right and he saw two more men flanking him. One was a grim-looking soldier with unblinking green eyes, while the other wore chain mail covered by a red surcoat emblazoned with the cross of some religious order, although the young man had no idea which one.

"I can do you one better than that," the biggest of the three said, smiling and appearing as relaxed as if he'd just met an old friend.

James returned the smile somewhat ruefully – he was a big man himself and he had his longbow but in the state he was in he was hardly a threat to these hard-looking lads. "Are you Hood?"

"I am. This is Will Scarlet and our friendly Hospitaller, Stephen. Now that the introductions are out of the way, let's make this quick since you're obviously running away from someone and I don't want to find a force of soldiers appearing at your back. What's your story?"

"You're right, I am running from someone but..." He stopped, wondering how to explain himself without the whole thing sounding insane but it seemed to be impossible.

"Spit it out, man!" The one Hood had introduced as Will Scarlet growled impatiently and James hurried to tell his tale. He was here now, he'd found Hood – if the man didn't believe him after all these miles, well...

"I don't know how much time you have, but Sir Guy of Gisbourne is coming for you, and he's bringing enough men to wipe you all out."

He expected disbelieving laughs or some other reaction from the men but they just stood, watching and waiting for him to continue.

"Your friend Friar Tuck is on his way here right now. He can't be far behind me and he's got a friend with him – a monk. Tuck doesn't know it, but his companion is working with Sir Guy. I don't know why; I saw the pair meeting in the Swan back in Horbury and tried to overhear their words as best I could but I only managed to catch some of it."

The outlaw leader glanced at his two companions who looked unsure of James's story before he turned round and beckoned the man to follow. "Come, you can tell us the rest as we head back to our camp."

The other two outlaws fell in behind James, who sighed in relief and began to move, trying to pick out the near-invisible trail Robin was striding along.

"If this is some trick, you'll find my blade in your back, my lad," Will Scarlet growled into his ear but James didn't reply, trying to save what remained of his stamina for the journey to the outlaw camp and praying fervently that it wasn't far.

"How did you know where we were?" The grizzled Hospitaller asked.

"I heard Tuck's mate telling Sir Guy you were camped somewhere near Selby, so I travelled there and, when I stopped at the ale-house to rest, the woman there told me her son, Peter, was one of your gang. I told her my story and she gave me rough directions how to find you."

"Is that all she gave you?" Scarlet demanded, laughing suggestively and James flushed as red as the outlaw's name. Peter Ordevill's mother had tried it on with all of the outlaws at one time or another, much to her son's chagrin.

"Their plan is for Tuck to come along and be found by your men, just as I was," James continued, trying to ignore the burning in his cheeks. "The monk with him will leave a trail for Sir Guy to follow, straight to your camp. And then..."

"And then we die," Robin said, to a grunt of agreement from the young archer behind him.

They lapsed into silence then, and, shortly, the foliage gave way and they walked into a clearing.

"John!" Robin shouted, summoning his giant lieutenant from the undergrowth. "The rest of you, stay hidden for now. We're still not sure what we face yet." He turned to James and pointed towards the fire. "There's ale and meat there. Help yourself and rest while we discuss this. Even if Tuck's right behind you, Gisbourne can't be too close – he'll have to keep a safe distance so our lookouts don't spot him and ruin his plan."

"Tuck?" Little John asked, baffled. "Gisbourne? What the fuck's going on? If the Raven's nearby shouldn't we be getting the hell out of here? He must have –"

Robin held up a hand to stop the flow of words. "Listen, and I'll explain what's happening, then we can decide what to do."

* * *

"They must be nearby," Tuck said, in reply to Osferth's grumbling about his sore feet and how much longer until they found the outlaws. They'd been advised to leave their mounts in the village by the residents of Selby, since the outlaws' nearby camp-site was hidden in a thick section of forest and both men were now thoroughly fed up with their walk.

"In fact," Tuck smiled encouragingly, "their lookout's probably spotted us already and ran to warn Robin and the lads of our approach. I'm sure they'll be along to see us any time now."

"You're not wrong there, father." A voice, seeming to come from directly overhead, startled both of them, Osferth almost dropping to his knees in fright but Tuck chuckled, recognizing the voice as that of Allan-a-Dale.

When Gareth had taken up Allan's recently vacated lookout spot, he'd been pleasantly surprised to see their old friend and mentor Friar Tuck appear with some other monk in tow. He'd sprinted back to camp as fast as he could to give the men the good news, only to find they were expecting the friar. He and the minstrel had then headed back, again, towards the lookout spot, Allan explaining things to his companion as they went, before he climbed a tree about halfway along the only obvious path the approaching clergymen could take. Gareth continued on, taking a circuitous route through the undergrowth back to the his lookout post high in the great oak tree with orders to stay and watch for Sir Guy of Gisbourne's inevitable approach.

Now, not for from the outlaws' camp-site, the minstrel jumped down and Tuck grabbed him in a great bear-hug, the joy at seeing one of his friends evident on his ruddy face. Osferth nodded a greeting of his own which was returned by the burly outlaw before the man stood back and looked Tuck up and down.

"You look... well, just the same as when you left us, really," he said. "Maybe a bit thinner again. You're not quite the big, pot-bellied friar I remember from that first meeting."

"Aye, well, Prior de Monte Martini didn't feed me as well as I'd have liked, the bastard. Still, I'm sure you've got plenty of meat and bread – and ale – at your camp. So, are you planning on standing there, gaping like a trout all day, or are you going to lead my companion and I to

242

sustenance? It's almost dinner time. And this is Osferth, by the way; a friend of mine from Lewes. He didn't like the prior much either."

Allan glanced at Osferth and a look flashed across his handsome features but it passed almost instantly and Tuck was unable to read it.

"You'll never change will you?" The outlaw smiled, before turning to lead the two travellers into the undergrowth. "Can't do anything unless your stomach's filled. Come on then, stay close."

Allan glanced back to make sure he was being followed by the pair and, from the corner of his eye, he noticed Osferth, a small blade in his hand, marking the trunk of the tree nearest to him.

"Gareth saw you coming," the minstrel said, turning quickly to face the front again. "Edmond's got the pot bubbling away nicely you'll be pleased to hear. The men'll be glad to see you; we've missed you, old man."

Tuck smiled. "I missed all of you too, Allan. I had to go back to Lewes though, and I'm glad I did. God had a purpose for me, which is why I'm back around Barnsdale again. For good this time, I hope."

"Well, save your breath for now, you can tell us all about it when we get back. Come on," he began to quicken his pace. "It's not far, but I'm starving myself so let's hurry."

Tuck was glad when, soon enough, they came into the clearing where his outlaw friends were camped. The exercise had left him puffing hard and he had a painful stitch, but the sight of a grinning Robin, flanked by the bear-like figure of Little John and the stocky Will Scarlet made him forget his discomfort and he hardly slowed as he skipped past the fire with its attendant cooking pot and gripped arms with the outlaws.

"I've never been so happy to see a priest in all my life," Will joked, shoving himself away from Tuck's embrace, a broad smile on his face. "It's good to see you again, you old bastard."

The rest of the men seemed to materialize from the trees like ghosts, greeting Tuck happily, but he was surprised when the vast majority of the outlaws all faded back into the undergrowth after their hasty welcome. His feeling of unease only increased when he spotted a man – not one of the gang – sitting on a log beside the fire, nursing a mug of ale and watching him from wary eyes.

"You..." The friar racked his brain for a moment, trying to recall where he knew the young man from, before he nodded in recognition. "James, isn't it? The archer who spared my life when his friends would gladly have robbed and killed me."

"You spared their lives too," James replied, not mentioning the fact that one of the men had died later from the whack in the skull the friar had given him. No need to place that burden on the good friar's soul...

Tuck shrugged, as if to say the brigands had been nothing but a minor irritation, to be swatted aside like insects. "What brings you here?" He turned then to address Robin before James could reply. "What's going on anyway? Why are the men concealed, as if expecting something?"

"Ask your friend."

Tuck looked at Osferth, who still stood at the edge of the camp, in confusion. "What? What are you talking about, Robin? Will someone please tell me what in God's name is happening here?"

Osferth's eyes had widened and his hand had fallen inside his cassock as if grasping for a weapon.

"Your mate is working with Gisbourne. He's been marking the trees along the way here so the Raven can bring his soldiers and wipe every last one of us out, once and for all."

Tuck laughed and sat down beside James, helping himself to a slice of salted beef from the wooden trencher in the man's lap. "Osferth's been with me on the entire road here from Lewes, he hasn't left my side. How could he be helping Gisbourne? Why would he do that anyway?"

"It's true, father," James said quietly, looking at the forest floor sadly. "I'm sorry, but I was in Horbury at the same time as you were. Your companion came to the inn I was staying at – the Swan – and met Sir Guy there. I overheard their conversation." He looked up to meet Tuck's irritated gaze. "You helped me even though my companions and I had tried to rob you. That means a lot to a man like me so... when I knew that little rat bastard was going to betray you I came here to try and stop it happening."

Tuck tossed his half-eaten slice of meat back onto the plate and rose to his feet, watching Osferth, who stood silently and serenely, as if he was simply back at the priory listening to evening mass.

"Well? Is it true?"

Osferth nodded. "It is, but fear not: the soldiers will not harm you."

"What?" Tuck shouted in disbelief. "Fear not?"

"Sir Guy is coming to do God's work, just as I have done. These murderers – *sinners* – will know justice, and the world will be a better place for it, but Sir Guy knows not to harm either of us. Once this is all over we shall return to Lewes where Prior de Monte Martini will reward us."

Tuck stared in astonishment at the man he'd thought was slightly unbalanced but this... it was unbelievable. "Are you insane, Osferth?" he demanded. "I punched the prior in the face. I stole his precious relic. You set half the bloody priory on fire, man! If we go back to Lewes we'll be excommunicated and strung up. That's assuming we survive this nightmare you've brought down upon us." He strode across and grabbed Osferth by the scruff of the neck, almost lifting the slight monk from his feet. "The prior *hates* me. Why would he want Gisbourne to spare my life? Of all these men here I'm the one he'd like to see dead the most! Are you really so naïve?"

Osferth shook his head in denial of Tuck's words.

It was clear the Benedictine was lost in some fantasy where everything would turn out well for them, as God intended.

Friar Tuck released him with a shake of his head and turned to glare at Robin. "Well, what the hell are we still here for? If Gisbourne's coming shouldn't we be on our way?" He spoke again to Osferth, spitting the words out furiously through gritted teeth. "How many men does he have at his command?"

"I've no idea. At least enough to outnumber these evil-doers. I told him to send for reinforcements when I first sent word to him back in that little village... Bryneford, wasn't it? Where we slept in that local's house because they didn't even have an inn. I had the priest there ride to Nottingham to tell Sir Guy where we were heading and what our plans were."

"You've been in contact with him since away back then?" Tuck roared, again grabbing his turncoat companion by the front of his cassock. "How? You never left my sight the whole way here."

"Gwale. The prior gave me it before we left."

Tuck's face froze for a second as the full reality of the situation finally hit him. De Monte Martini had planned this whole thing. Osferth befriending him; the tale about the prior knowing the location of Robin's camp; everything... "That's why I slept like a babe those times, yet woke up feeling as if I'd drank an entire barrel of ale by myself. You little shit!" He released Osferth and hammered his fist into the man's mouth, hurling him backwards where he lay sprawled on the bark and moss, a look of shock and disbelief on his face.

"You're supposed to be my friend," the young monk said through split lips, his eyes filling with tears. "I've come here to save your soul. Why did you hit me?"

Tuck suddenly felt, unbelievably given the circumstances, like he'd just kicked a playful puppy, and he swung back to Robin, his face a mask of fury and confusion.

"Well? What are we waiting for? We all know the whole story now, all about how I was such a fool and led the Raven right to you. Shouldn't we be off before he gets here and kills us all?"

Robin nodded to Little John and Will who gave Tuck a last apologetic look, unhappy to have been witness to their portly friend's humiliation, before they too slipped into the trees and out of sight.

"What about you, friend?" Robin asked James who swallowed the last of the ale in his mug and stood up, grasping his longbow. "You better get off if you don't want to be part of what happens next. Here..." he fumbled inside his gambeson before pulling out a small purse and tossing it the young archer. "For your trouble. Thank you for coming to warn us. There's enough in there to see you right."

James nodded gratefully but didn't look inside the purse, just held it in his hand as he returned the outlaw captain's gaze. "Seems to me you could do with another longbowman at your side this day. If you'll have me."

Robin shrugged. Time was running out, Gisbourne would be upon them any time. He didn't know anything about James's life, or why he had come here and now offered to stand with them but it was true – another archer would certainly be useful.

"You're more than welcome to stay," he nodded. "Keep beside me so you don't get in the way. You must be exhausted after walking all through the night."

Tuck shook his head in consternation at Robin's words. "You're talking as if you're not planning on escaping. What madness has come over you all?"

In reply Robin hefted his longbow, bending it back to slip the string onto it. "We're done running, Tuck." He pulled an arrow from his belt and nocked it to the string, raising the weapon as he continued. "For the past two years I've been running. Moving camp every time Gisbourne, or Adam Bell, or the sheriff or whoever got too close. No more." He pulled back the string to his ear as

Tuck watched, eyes widening when he realised what Robin was about to do. "No more running."

He released the arrow and watched dispassionately as it thudded home in Osferth's heart.

"Now we fight."

* * *

Sir Guy of Gisbourne reined in his big warhorse and looked warily from side to side, turning his head to do so since his missing left eye hampered his vision on that side. "What about their lookouts?" He lifted his leg over the saddle and slid easily to the ground to gaze into the thick trees that lay about a mile before them. "If they spot us coming there's little point in this – they'll simply run off and we'll be back where we started."

Matt Groves nodded grimly. "Don't worry about that. Wait here, and look for my signal."

Gisbourne watched as his sergeant kicked his heels into his mount and galloped off, not along the main road but to the left, through the long grass on the heath that ran parallel to the forest in front of them.

Matt had looked at that forest and knew exactly where a lookout would hide – he'd been an outlaw himself for years hadn't he? He could read the land as well as any of Hood's gang. One tree in particular stood out, even at this distance, for its height and the fact that its branches didn't grow so densely together as those surrounding it. A man could sit comfortably in a tree like that, he knew, with a fine view of the surrounding terrain.

He had to be sure the lookout didn't spot him so he rode for a while until the contours of the land and the sparse foliage dotted around the heath would mask his approach, then he turned his mount and galloped straight forward, towards the forest.

When he reached the thick line of trees he slid to the ground and tied his horse to a sturdy branch, the animal's chest heaving from the exertion but happy to rest and crop the rich grass that grew there. "Wait here, boy," Matt

248

muttered, patting the horse affectionately. "This won't take long."

He moved along the edge of the forest quickly, back towards the tall Scots pine tree he'd marked as being the most likely lookout post, wondering as he went which of the outlaws might be concealed there.

"I hope it's that prick Hood himself," he muttered, although he knew that was unlikely. Robin didn't take many lookout duties since, being the leader, he was needed in the main camp in the event of any danger being sighted but still, there was a possibility he was in the branches of that big tree and if he was... Matt clasped the hilt of his dagger and gritted his teeth, praying to God it *would* be the enemy he so despised hidden in the foliage ahead.

At last the tree came into sight not far ahead, and Groves slowed his pace, stalking through the undergrowth almost silently, his eyes searching for any signs of movement in the branches overhead until, at last, he reached the gnarled, aged trunk and pressed himself against it, listening intently.

He nodded in satisfaction as he spotted the iron nails that had been hammered into the bark to form makeshift steps for someone to climb up. This *was* the tree the outlaws used as a lookout post, now all he had to do was deal with whoever was concealed above...

CHAPTER TWENTY-FOUR

"We ready to move then?" Sir Guy demanded as Matt Groves returned, his horse's chest heaving with exertion since its rider had pushed hard to make it back to his captain as fast as possible.

"Aye, we can move. The lookout won't be a problem, you can count on that."

He had a strange sardonic smile on his seamed face that Gisbourne found repulsive and he wondered what the man had done to the lookout. Probably tortured him before throwing him out of the tree or worse...

"I'll take your word for it," Gisbourne grunted and turned to face his men, thirty-five well-armed and highly-trained soldiers, addressing them in a low but authoritative voice. "Listen to me. This isn't your usual gang of outlaws – these men are not some undisciplined peasants carrying sickles and pitchforks. They are not old greybeards, or untested youngsters. Robin Hood was skilled enough to hold his own against me." Gisbourne could not accept he'd been defeated; it had been a freak accident that had been his downfall, he knew, not any greater skill on the part of the wolf's head. He touched his empty eye-socket thoughtfully before continuing. "His men train hard and many of them have experience in wars, either here or abroad. Although they don't expect us, they will react as soon as we attack – I know this for a fact, as do any of you who were with me when we attacked their camp near Wakefield not so very long ago. So be ready for them. Our victory is certain, but whether you personally live or die this day will count on you being prepared for whatever is thrown at you."

He stared around at them for a few heartbeats, measuring their resolve, before looking away, apparently satisfied at what he saw reflected in the soldiers' eyes. "Let's move. Be as silent as possible. And one more thing." As he pushed his mount into a gallop he shouted venomously over his shoulder. "Leave no-one alive. No-one!"

* * *

Tuck stood next to Robin and Little John, holding his quarterstaff tightly, lips pressed together grimly, still shocked by the day's events. Betrayed by his pious friend, who still lay, staring at him from dead eyes, under the beech where he'd been skewered by the outlaw leader's wicked broadhead arrow.

"I don't understand why you feel the need to take on Gisbourne and his men. They'll outnumber you – us," he corrected himself, realizing he was as much a part of this as any of them now, "probably two-to-one, and it won't be wet-behind-the-ears foresters this time; it'll be hard mercenaries."

"And they think they'll catch us completely by surprise," Robin replied, eyes still fixed on the hidden pathway he expected Gareth to appear along at any moment. "They'll get the shock of their lives. We've never had an opportunity like this before, Tuck. Never. We can wipe that bastard Raven off the face of the earth, along with his right-hand man, Groves." His voice trailed off as he pictured Matt's hated face, remembered how the turncoat had murdered their friend Much. "The king and the sheriff will hopefully give up persecuting us when they understand it's not worth the price they have to pay. The lives they'll lose if they continue to hunt us."

Tuck looked at him sceptically. It didn't seem very likely to him that the sheriff would just allow a gang of outlaws to live peacefully in his forest, especially if they were to kill out so many of his own men. Still, it was true that Gisbourne had been a terrible danger to them ever since he'd arrived in Yorkshire the previous year.

"He's grown even more brutal since you've been away in Lewes," Robin continued. "Taken to burning down peoples' homes and threatening them with worse unless the villagers start to inform on us. It won't be long before the

251

people reach breaking point and give us up." He took his eyes from the path momentarily to gaze earnestly at the friar. "We won't be able to survive if that happens. This is our chance to put an end to him. We're living our lives in fear – what's the point in that? If we're so frightened of death, we might as well be dead!" He shook his head and looked back into the foliage again, white knuckles betraying his tension at the continued lack of action. "Where the fuck is Gareth? Surely Gisbourne's on his way by now."

Suddenly there was a small crack from the trees to the side, as of a dried-out twig snapping beneath a person's foot and Robin felt his blood run cold.

"They're here!"

* * *

Matt Groves knew better than anyone how deadly some of the outlaws were. He'd spent years living and fighting beside the likes of Little John and Will Scarlet and even newcomers to the gang like the Hospitaller sergeant-at-arms were well-versed in the arts of war. Matt had seen that for himself when, together with the sergeant and his master Sir Richard-at-Lee, the outlaws had robbed the manor house of Lord John de Bray less than two years ago.

The element of surprise that Sir Guy's men expected to enjoy here today would, though, be enough, along with their greater numbers, to rout the outlaws, Matt was certain. So when Gisbourne signalled their attack and the combined force of Sheriff de Faucumberg's and the Raven's own men moved in to begin the attack the former wolf's head had been somewhat surprised to hear his erstwhile young leader shouting "they're here," as if he'd been expecting them.

As a result, Matt had held himself back when the rest of the soldiers charged wildly into the clearing behind their black-clad, one-eyed leader. He wanted nothing more than to feel his blade bite into the skull of that bastard Hood, but he sensed something was amiss and the attack might not go quite to plan.

The scale of the rout – the brutality of it – probably shouldn't have been a shock to him, given Hood's lucky escapes in the past, but Groves really hadn't expected this today. The arrows flew from the trees, enormous lengths of ash or poplar, fletched with swan or goose-feathers and tipped with vicious iron heads that could blast right through a man's face or ribcage and out the other side with ease. Now the Raven's soldiers – the men Matt had been living and working with for the past few weeks – were dying in front of him and he was too horrified to help them.

He knew the outlaws' lookout hadn't given away the approach of Gisbourne's men, so how...? Then he spotted the monk, lying cold and dead on the forest floor, an arrow embedded deep in his chest and he cursed, misreading the situation. "Friar Tuck must have known all along, the fat bastard. We weren't springing a trap at all – Hood was the one leading *us* into an ambuscade of his own devising!"

The soldiers' numbers had been drastically reduced as a result of the first few volleys of the outlaws' arrows. Men lay unmoving or screaming in agony on the ground until another missile flew from the undergrowth to silence the pitiful, hellish cries, and Gisbourne's remaining men raced for cover behind the nearest trees, cursing loudly, eyes flickering all around as they searched for leadership which didn't appear to be forthcoming.

"Where the fuck are you?" Matt breathed, crouching low and searching for the Raven. He couldn't see him, or hear his voice in the bedlam that had erupted inside the previously calm forest. "Those arseholes must have killed him. Shit!"

He stared out from behind his leafy hiding place, watching as the outlaws decided their longbows were now ineffective and so appeared from the undergrowth like diabolical wraiths, long-swords drawn and held expertly before them as they moved with terrible efficiency to engage what remained of Gisbourne's great force of men.

He watched as the men Gisbourne had asked him to lead were cut down in front of his eyes. Their numbers were down to only a dozen or so now, although about half of those were giving a good account of themselves as the outlaws engaged them.

Little John was, as ever, wielding his massive quarterstaff, taking on two of the sheriff's blue-liveried men by himself. The staff moved in a blur, knocking the soldiers' blades to the side before first one man collapsed from a horrendous blow to the face, then the second was winded by a thrust to the guts. John appeared to be lost in the battle-fever though, and Matt glared through the leaves as the giant brought his weapon hammering down into his two downed enemies repeatedly until, chests smashed to a bloody ruined mess, the huge wolf's head looked up, crazed eyes searching for someone else to kill.

It was a similar, if slightly less brutal, scene all around the clearing. The soldiers' morale had been crushed by the death of so many of their comrades in that first wicked hail of arrows, and Robin Hood's men had spent so many hours training together that they fought as if they had some strange connection to one another's thoughts.

Matt sucked in a breath hopefully as he saw one of Sir Guy's men raise his sword for a killing blow behind Hood himself who hadn't noticed the man as he stepped out from behind a tree. The soldier's eyes blazed with a black fury as he lunged to skewer the wolf's head's liver and Matt grinned, but the minstrel, Allan-a-Dale, somehow appeared from nowhere, his sword hammering down and sending Gisbourne's man flying forward almost comically onto his face. There was no laughter though, as Hood spun and rammed his own sword-point into the downed man's temple. Even Matt grimaced at the resultant mess.

He watched as Will Scarlet and the snarling Hospitaller, still clad in his Order's impressive armour, fought side-by-side, hacking their way through their enemies with terrible efficiency, long-swords tearing flesh as if it was no more than the leafy green foliage that surrounded them so tightly.

It was painfully obvious to Matt that he was on the losing side. His leader had disappeared within the roiling, violent maelstrom of the outlaws' camp, no doubt impaled by an aggressor's blade, while the rest of the men they'd brought into Barnsdale – trained soldiers every one – were being ruthlessly cut down in front of him. There was no reason for him to die too.

He let go of the yew branch he was hiding behind and turned, sword in hand and still in a crouching position, to make his way back towards the safety of the main road.

A gasp, loud enough to be heard even over the battle that was winding down behind him, stopped him in his tracks and he raised his well-worn blade to face whoever was nearby.

It was the minstrel.

Matt had got along well enough with Allan. The outgoing younger man was essentially a show-off who always wanted to be the centre of attention, but he was a fine swordsman and an even better archer. Matt didn't like the fact the minstrel had been so close to his hated enemy Hood, but he appreciated the man's martial skill and had many happy half-drunken memories of sing-alongs to Allan's campfire performances.

"You!"

The near-whisper was almost a curse, and Matt found himself transfixed by Allan's hateful, venomous glare.

The two men, former comrades-in-arms, watched one another warily, mutual respect holding them in check despite the killing that was still going on behind them.

"You betrayed us," Allan growled, his hate-filled yet somehow baffled gaze boring into Matt like a drill. "You were one of us! And after everything we went through... you still betrayed us." He shook his head in wonderment at Matt's duplicity and his mouth twisted in disgust.

That look was enough. Groves had been viewed with distrust and even hatred for most of his life and the sight of a former companion eyeing him with such venom was enough to send him over the edge.

His blade licked out, catching the stunned minstrel on the side of the neck and a bead of crimson appeared as straight as an arrow on Allan's pale complexion. The scarlet line slowly turned into a dripping, gaping wound and the minstrel swayed, staring open-mouthed at his former comrade before he dropped unsteadily onto one knee, eyes still fixed on Matt in shocked disbelief.

"You filthy old..." Allan's left hand came up, flapping weakly at the bloody abrasion in his neck and he squeezed the skin together as best he could with one hand while brandishing his long-sword desperately in the other. Fear showed in his eyes though, and he tried to raise his voice, to berate Matt, but it was clear he was trying to attract attention to his plight.

Groves wasn't the sort of man to miss an opportunity. His eyes flared and he raised his blade high overhead, looking around for signs of oncoming attack but none of the minstrel's outlaw companions appeared to be close-by so he gritted his teeth and brought his weapon down as hard as he could.

Allan screamed as he saw the blow approach.

It was a pitiful, horrid sound, that made the combatants nearby stare in fear, almost forgetting their own dire peril, and his wide young eyes turned in disbelief to stare at the horrific gaping wound that had severed his right arm almost completely from his torso.

"I always thought you were one of the better ones," Matt grunted sadly, but he knew his side was losing and he'd become lost in the battle-fever that affected even the best of men. The point of his sword speared forward, directly into Allan's windpipe, silencing the minstrel's voice forever and the former-outlaw dragged his blade free, tearing skin and flesh apart in a bloody spray.

"Over there," a voice shouted and Matt knew he had to get away before the victorious outlaws found him and saw what he'd done to their friend. He broke into a run, forcing his way through the undergrowth as fast as he could, not even sure which direction he was going, but understanding the need to put as much distance between himself and his pursuers as he could.

He knew how to travel quickly through the densely packed forest, having done it for many years in the not-so-distant past, and it was just as well, he thought, smiling wickedly to himself as a cry of pure grief filled the trees. He knew that voice; Robin Hood had found his brutalized, dead minstrel pal. The smile on Matt's seamed face turned into a grin. Maybe he had lost today, but at least that prick Hood hadn't had it all his own way. The wolf's head still had to find his mate Gareth too...

He burst into a small clearing and allowed himself to stop and catch his breath. He wasn't a young man any more and, although he was fairly fit, he'd not done much training since joining Gisbourne's crew other than the occasional spar with his one-eyed leader, and his flight had tired him more than he wanted to admit to himself. He rested his hands on his thighs and sucked in lungfuls of air, the heaving in his chest eventually subsiding until, at last, he raised his head, still smiling, and spat a great glob of green phlegm into the old brown leaves underfoot. He noted the position of the sun and, since he had a fair idea what time it was, could work out which direction it was to Nottingham.

The sheriff might hate his guts, but someone had to tell de Faucumberg what had happened to all the soldiers he'd sent to deal with the notorious outlaws. He glanced back over his shoulder but there were no sounds of pursuit, just an almost even more unnerving silence and he turned slightly to the left to forge a path through the forest in the direction of the city.

He wondered what he'd do now, with his comfortable position as the Raven's second-in-command apparently finished. He wouldn't go back to a sailor's life again and, although he was a free man he didn't have any money; he'd blown it all on drink and whores. But Sir Henry was now short a dozen men in his garrison, so perhaps he could find employment there, with the sheriff.

Despite the overwhelming defeat his side had suffered that day, Groves felt strangely optimistic as he jogged towards Nottingham. Hood's gang were still at large after all, and who better to lead the chase now than one of their ex-members with his detailed knowledge of their habits, routines and local suppliers? Yes, the sheriff didn't like him very much, but perhaps he could persuade the arrogant, stuck-up arsehole to let him lead the search for Hood from now on.

The self-satisfied smile never left his face all the long road back to the city.

* * *

Somewhere in the dark recesses of his mind Robin knew he should control himself; his men were watching him and they needed leadership not a display of raw, naked emotion. But at that moment, when he saw his friend Allan-a-Dale lying, cold and bloody and dead, on the soft spring grass the young outlaw captain sank to his knees and held his head in his hands.

A tortured cry tore from his throat and tears filled his eyes, grief and a terrible rage warring within him and even Little John stood back respectfully and wary of disturbing his leader, lost as he was in his emotions.

Robin remembered that night when he and Allan had performed in the manor house, singing for the lords and ladies to much applause, before saving Will's daughter from her own hellish life the next morning. He remembered all the times the outlaws had sat around the campfire on a freezing night, with nothing but ale, Allan's music and one another's company to chase away the gloom. And he remembered just a few weeks ago, when he and John had rescued the minstrel from Nottingham. It had all turned out so nicely that day, as if God himself had been watching over them, but now...

Finally, the reality of their situation brought Robin back to his senses and, still looking down at his fallen companion, he growled, "Did we get them all?"

Will Scarlet shook his head. He, along with a couple of the other men, had checked the dead and wounded. "For our part," he said, "we only lost..." he stared at Allan's lifeless form, unwilling to say his comrade's name. "As for the enemy; who can say? We don't know for sure how many of them were in their party. We didn't get all of them though – whoever did that to Allan must have escaped into the trees. And... he's not the only one that's escaped..."

Robin sat for a moment, still unable to think straight, then he looked up, understanding flaring in his eyes. "Gisbourne?"

"Aye."

"We've looked but his body's not here," Stephen muttered confirmation.

Robin got to his feet slowly, his mind whirling. If they hadn't managed to kill the Raven, all this had been for naught. Gisbourne would simply return to Nottingham for reinforcements – perhaps the garrison would be too stretched and he'd need to wait on the king sending him more men, but, eventually they would come and then their hated enemy would return in a fury, again and again, until every last one of the outlaws lay rotting in the ground like Much and Harry Half-Hand and Wilfred and Sir Richard-at-Lee and...

"Allan died for nothing then. All of these men here today died for nothing."

"It gets worse." Little John hunched his great shoulders unconsciously, as he often did when talking to someone so he could look them in the eyes without appearing intimidating. "There's no sign of that arsehole Matt either."

Robin just stared in silence at the giant.

"We should deal with the survivors," the Hospitaller sergeant growled, breaking the spell that seemed to hold the entire forest in its grip and the men nodded, the agonized grunts and cries of badly injured men finally filtering through their shock at Allan's brutal demise.

"Stephen's right," Robin admitted, making a conscious effort to pull himself together, at least until all this was dealt with. "And we should try and find out where the fuck Gareth got to. That little prick should have warned us of Gisbourne's approach; if he's got drunk and fallen asleep while on watch I'll tear off his balls and feed them to him."

"I'll go," the newcomer, Piers, offered. "I know where the lookout post is and I'm a fast runner." In truth, the fight had appalled him – he'd never in his whole life witnessed so much blood and death, and the pitiful sounds coming from their maimed enemies were playing on his already frayed nerves. Even going off alone into the forest seemed better than staying around the camp right then.

Robin nodded, seeing the shock in their new recruit's face and knowing it would do the young man good to spend a little time alone. The memory of his own first battle as an outlaw was still fresh in Robin's mind – it seemed a lifetime ago, so much had happened since, and he'd become battle-hardened in the intervening time, but it was only... Christ above, it was only two years ago.

Piers hastened off through the undergrowth, trying to appear stoic and offering his captain a wave of salute as he went, while Robin moved back towards their camp to see who was still alive and what could, or should, be done with them.

Although Gisbourne's men were enemies, they were simply soldiers following their orders. The wolf's head felt no malice towards them for their actions, just a bitter sadness that so many men had to die to serve the purposes of their 'betters'. With the escape of Matt Groves and Sir Guy of Gisbourne Robin's battle-fury had left him and a gaping, maudlin hole remained.

Friar Tuck was already moving amongst the wounded, trying to help those most grievously harmed first. Stephen too had a decent knowledge of rudimentary healing skills and he tended to those Tuck couldn't get to quickly enough.

Of Gisbourne's force of approximately thirty-five men, twenty-two lay dead, sprawled on the ground or even slumped awkwardly over logs or lying cradled within the branches of some bush or other. Six were wounded, at least three of them mortally despite Tuck and Stephen's efforts. The rest of the soldiers were unaccounted for – presumably they'd decided to leave their comrades to their fate and had escaped into the trees along with their black-attired, one-eyed leader and his second-in-command, Groves.

Robin didn't know whether to curse the escapees for abandoning their companions or to be glad that at least some men would be able to return home to their families that night. It was all so damn senseless.

"What do we do now?" Little John asked, spreading his arms wide like some enormous bird-of-prey. "They know where we are."

"Aye, we should move camp again," Arthur agreed running a hand through his thick brown hair. "This place isn't safe any more."

Robin shook his head and filled a mug with ale from a cask on the wagon close to the fire before dropping onto one of the big logs they'd been using as seats for the past few weeks. "They won't return tonight. Or tomorrow for that matter. We have time yet." He felt weary. Drained. And not just from his part in the fight. Being the leader might seem glamorous to some but it placed a huge amount of stress on his shoulders and, although he was getting better at dealing with it all, times like this still took their toll on him.

John nodded, happy to accept Robin's decision and, along with a couple of the men who, like him, didn't feel like resting, moved off to find a spot to dig a grave for Allan-a-Dale.

What they would do with the near two-dozen enemy corpses John didn't know and, right then, didn't care. Robin wasn't the only one bone-weary and struggling to deal with the aftermath of the battle. Will and Stephen might have seen dead bodies piled up and blood saturating the ground when they'd fought in great armies overseas, but most of the men had never been a part of so much death.

261

Would the mood in the camp be different if Groves and Gisbourne had been killed? Would the men be celebrating, rather than moving silently around the place almost gingerly, as if they half-expected the sky to fall on them at any moment? The atmosphere was beyond eerie and only made worse by the fact one of the mortally wounded soldiers had begun to scream as the pain became unbearable. The tanner, Edmond, eyes wide and hands shaking, crammed a strip of linen into the man's mouth to muffle the horrible sound.

No-one even tried to stop him.

CHAPTER TWENTY-FIVE

Piers reached the lookout post in a short time, his youthful legs and loping stride carrying him through the undergrowth at a relentless pace as he tried to forget what he'd witnessed back at the camp. He'd seen death before, of course – who hadn't? But it had been *normal* death: his grandmother limp and ashen-faced in her bed one morning; his pet dog, murdered by a drunken sailor during the night; a vagrant, frozen to death the previous winter in one of Nottingham's side-streets when Piers had been making his way to work in the clerk's offices.

But to be attacked by so many soldiers, and to watch them being brutally cut down like chaff under a labourer's sickle... He shuddered and took a deep breath, glancing around himself, eyes searching the thick new-season foliage for hidden dangers but he saw nothing and looked up, spotting the cleverly concealed wooden platform the outlaws had built into the tree near the very top.

"Gareth," he hissed, trying again when there was no sign of movement from above, or even a sound of recognition. Perhaps the youngster *had* allowed himself to get drunk and fallen asleep as Robin suggested. Piers whacked the trunk of the tree – a venerable old Scots Pine – and tried shouting on Gareth again, louder this time.

Still no response from above.

A sense of foreboding came over him and he knew he'd have to climb the tree. He supposed if Gisbourne's men had somehow found the lookout post there would be blood or other signs of a struggle – Gareth wasn't much of a fighter but he had spirit and wouldn't just sit there while someone killed him. As he began the ascent, using the handily placed iron nails, Piers glanced down into the surrounding foliage, hoping desperately not to see Gareth's corpse there, thrown by some assailant.

A slight movement from beneath a juniper bush caught his eye but it was just a blackbird, foraging for worms, and he continued his ascent, trying to move as silently as possible, fearing what he might find on the rapidly nearing platform although he told himself it was more than likely empty.

Gareth must have decided he'd had enough of this life and buggered off, Piers surmised, finally grasping the platform and hauling himself up onto it.

He shrank back involuntarily, almost falling out of the tree, a horrified gasp escaping from his lips. "No!"

Gareth hadn't buggered off, he was still there. But the suggestion that he'd taken alcohol to his post appeared to be correct for an empty wine-skin lay by his side, flat and clearly drained. Rather like the empty shell that used to be Gareth's young body.

There wasn't a scratch on him but Gareth lay on his back, as if he'd fallen asleep after consuming all his wine. Dried vomit coated the man's mouth and neck though, suggesting he'd puked but been so drunk he hadn't even woken up. Piers wondered inanely whether Gareth had died from suffocation or drowning, as if the distinction somehow mattered.

The newcomer to the outlaw gang sat for a long time, just staring at his dead comrade, hoping to see some signs of life but it was futile and eventually the shock passed and allowed Piers to climb unsteadily back down to the ground, taking his time as his limbs were shaky and his head seemed to spin. When he finally reached the forest floor he made the sign of the cross, feeling somewhat silly and self-conscious but knowing he should offer some sign of respect for poor Gareth's departed soul, then without a backward glance, loped off into the trees to tell the rest of the men the bad news. As he ran his mind whirled; after a relatively pleasant few weeks as an outlaw living in the trees of Barnsdale things didn't seem quite so straightforward.

Holy Mary, mother of God! What have I let myself in for?

* * *

Twenty-three dead men in their camp. Their *home*! Robin sipped his ale, staring into the fire numbly. This wasn't his home, how could it be when his wife and little son were miles away in –

"Wakefield."

The voice carried to Robin through the still air and his eyes flicked up to see who had spoken. He didn't recognize the strangely accented voice and he knew it hadn't come from one of his own men. He jumped to his feet, and hurried across to the wounded prisoners that Tuck was still tending to.

"Who said that?" he demanded, glaring at the men.

One of them raised a hand weakly and Robin knelt beside him, offering him the ale cup he'd carried over without even realising it. "Here, lad, drink."

The soldier, probably not even out of his teens from the look of his unlined and beardless face, gratefully accepted the cup and gulped down its contents greedily.

"What about Wakefield?" Robin asked softly. He'd noted the great gaping hole in the man's side where the chain mail had been penetrated by a sword thrust and knew it wouldn't be too long before he expired.

The soldier gritted his teeth as a wave of nausea flooded through him and Robin watched impatiently, a sense of foreboding beginning to creep over him.

"Sir Guy... I heard him, just before he slipped into the trees and left us to die, the bastard." He sobbed, his hand fluttering weakly about the bloody gash in his side as the pain began to worsen.

"Rest easy, soldier." Robin forced a reassuring smile onto his face and held a comforting hand gently on the man's arm. "You're going to be all right. The good friar here will see to it."

The man shook his head, fear and resignation plain in his eyes as he met the wolf's head's gaze. "I'll be dead within the hour. Before that. But I can't go to my grave with more deaths on my conscience."

"Speak." Robin nodded, feeling guilt and sorrow for the man's agony but needing to know what the hell Gisbourne had said.

"Promise me you'll perform the last rites for me, brother," he gasped, before sighing in relief at Tuck's nod then gritting his teeth again. "When Sir Guy saw your lot's arrows coming out of the trees like some hellish rain he must have known he'd lost the battle before we'd even aimed a blow of our own. I heard him cursing to himself before he –"

Robin hissed at him as the light began to fade from his eyes and his fingers gripped hard on the soldier's wrist. "He what?"

"He said... if he couldn't kill you he was going to Wakefield. To kill your family instead."

Robin felt as if his blood had turned to ice but, before he had time to react, another voice burst in.

"He's dead too! Gareth's dead!"

There was an angry chorus from the stunned outlaws who crowded back into the centre of the camp to shoot questions at the overwhelmed Piers. Little John did his best to hold the men back so the young clerk could tell them what had happened, while Robin just stood, unable to move, mind reeling.

"Did Gisbourne's men get him too?" John demanded once he'd silenced the men and Piers had managed to get his breath back after the run.

"No. You were right," he glanced over at Robin who simply stared back uncomprehendingly. "He'd drank at least one full skin of wine then... he must have passed out and threw up while flat on his back." Piers shrugged, his face twisted in anguish. "He's dead," he finished simply.

No-one knew what to say. To rant about Gareth's stupidity seemed crass and disrespectful at a time like this, even if it was the first thing that came into most of the outlaws' minds.

"Fuck!" Little John finally broke the silence, his single shouted oath enough to sum up the feelings of every man in the camp.

"Looks like we'll have to dig another grave beside Allan's," Stephen muttered, collapsing wearily onto a log and picking at the skin on his fingers.

The men stood, or sat, for a long time in silence. It was a bad day and, mentally, if not physically, they were just about broken.

Suddenly Robin shook his head, and wide-eyed, he ran over to Little John, pointing at Will as he went. Their day wasn't over yet.

"That bastard Gisbourne's gone to Wakefield to kill Matilda and my son. I have to go after him, and he's got a head start. Will you two come with me?"

His two lieutenants nodded in unison.

"Of course we will," John rumbled.

"But we'll never be able to catch up with him now," Will fretted. "As you say, he's ages ahead of us."

Robin pointed at the wounded soldiers who were watching the outlaws with interest, despite their own predicament. "Those men came here on horseback. We need to find their mounts. It'll mean starting off in the wrong direction but it's the only way we'll be able to reach Wakefield in time." He knelt by the captured men. "Where are your horses?"

The soldiers, although wounded and even dying, were pleased to have been treated with respect by Hood's men since they'd been defeated.

"You've treated us fairly," one of them mumbled. "While our own leader pissed off and left us to die." He spat, a mixture of saliva and blood which he looked at balefully before continuing. "The horses are a little way to the west of your lookout post. Just follow the line of trees, you can't miss them. Poor beasts, they've been tied up there all day."

Robin, John and Will still wore their weapons and armour and Robin only tarried to grab his longbow and an ale-skin before giving his orders to the rest of the men.

"Stephen, you're in charge. As I say, I doubt there's much chance of any more attackers coming here within the next few days but be on your guard. Some of the soldiers we chased off might still be lurking nearby."

The Hospitaller nodded grimly. "Don't worry about us, lad, be on your way. God go with you."

Despite their exhaustion the three friends broke into a run and headed off into the trees to find the horses.

"Pray for us," Robin shouted over his shoulder.

* * *

A huge stretch of Ermine St, the main road connecting York and London amongst other places, was currently occupied by the great entourage that accompanied King Edward II on his travels around the country. He had spent much of the year visiting many of the towns and cities under his dominion, and planned to continue on until at least winter.

Travelling with him were an enormous number of people. From clerks and chaplains to cooks and bakers, and following behind them all came a goodly number of prostitutes and other undesirables who saw to the... *needs*, of the royal household which also included Edward's own personal bodyguard of twenty-odd archers and even more sergeants-at-arms.

It was late afternoon and they'd come from York with their destination being Castleford just a short distance south-east of Leeds, where they'd stop for the night. The king mostly enjoyed these journeys, often whipping his horse into a gallop and laughing at the freedom he felt as the great beast carried him off, away from the hangers-on and toadies that followed him everywhere.

Of course, his guards would keep him in sight at all times so he was never in any real danger – it would be an utterly insane criminal that tried to hold-up a royal party of such a size – but to Edward it was a wonderful release from the tedium of everyday politics, in-fighting and manoeuvering that seemed to occupy most of his time.

It had been a while since the king had treated himself and his mount to a mad dash into a field or along a minor road and he was beginning to get restless. The sun would remain high overhead for a while yet and it was swelteringly hot as a result, which was the only reason he'd held himself in check as his aides continually tried to engage him in trivia and matters of court which he really couldn't be bothered with.

"Boy!" Edward turned his head to look over his shoulder and gestured to one of the servants that remained near to him at all times. The lad's mount was laden with a wine-skin which he emptied into a silver, beautifully decorated chalice as he rode up to take his place respectfully behind the monarch. The wine, an extortionately expensive Malmsey from Italy, was warm, which rather spoiled the delicate taste, but it was refreshing nevertheless and Edward swallowed it quickly, wiping his handsome face with a big hand before tossing the near-priceless cup back to the boy whose eyes opened wide, terrified in case he should fumble the catch and damage it.

Edward looked back to the road, unaware of the terror he'd instilled in the poor page and gazed along the road into the distance, taking in the lush green, rolling hills, colourful fields with their various crops growing, blue, near-cloudless sky and watched as the heat made ripples on the horizon. Ah, it was terribly hot, but by God, England – *his* England – was a glorious land!

His eyesight was good and since he'd taken up position right at the very front of the great procession he was able to see for miles around. He caught a slight movement in his peripheral vision and turned to the left to get a better look, squinting against the sun's glare.

"Horsemen."

The captain of his guard kicked his horse forward to trot by the king's side, watching for himself as the shapes in the distance came closer, resolving eventually into three distinct figures, brown cloaks billowing behind them as they galloped towards the main road across a field.

The captain gestured to his men to draw their weapons and move into defensive positions all around the lengthy procession while he stayed by his master's side, hand ready on the pommel of his sword. The horsemen didn't appear to be coming in their direction – indeed they seemed oblivious to the king's presence on the road – but they had the look of soldiers about them and the captain wanted to be ready should they prove to herald a much larger force of possibly hostile men.

It wasn't that long since the Lancastrian revolt after all, and up here in the north the commoners saw the Earl of Lancaster as some sort of fallen hero. It made sense to prepare for attack, even if it was rather unlikely.

They continued to move forward, plodding at the interminable pace that irked the king but that such a large number of people necessitated and the three riders became ever clearer. Their paths wouldn't cross, not quite, but it would be close.

Behind the king, Sheriff de Faucumberg – who'd been ordered to travel from Nottingham and accompany the royal party for a week or so – watched the riders with a growing sense of unease. Something about them seemed familiar and he unconsciously moved his own mount forward, close to the king, to try and get a better view.

At last, one of the riders, the one at the head of the small triangle, became aware of the presence of the long procession of people and carts on the road to the north of them and he turned to look, just as they reached the small drystone wall that kept the sheep from straying out of the field.

The king screwed his face up even further, staring at the rider before them, who just returned the stare blankly, almost as if the man still hadn't registered their presence or perhaps didn't care.

"I know those men."

"Robin Hood!"

Recognition flared at the same time for both king and sheriff and, as Edward heard de Faucumberg muttering the name of the notorious outlaw he turned with a quizzical expression.

"Robin Hood? With the two friars?"

The sheriff looked baffled momentarily, until he remembered the whole blasted episode with the silver arrow and understood what his king was talking about.

"No, my liege, those are no friars. They passed themselves off as such to you, but they are, in actual fact, Hood himself, with his two companions, John Little and, I believe, Will Scaflock, popularly known as Scarlet."

The galloping riders slowed as they reached the small stone wall, betraying their inexperience on horseback as they tentatively coaxed the big palfreys across the minor impediment. Without another glance in the king's direction they rode into the trees on the other side of the road and disappeared from sight.

The king watched them go, an unreadable expression on his face, before he turned back to the sheriff.

"Clearly they're in a hurry. Too much of a hurry to use the road. What town lies yonder?"

De Faucumberg gazed into the trees, picturing the local area in his mind's-eye before replying. "Castleford," he shrugged. "Where we're headed ourselves."

"Anything else?"

Again, the sheriff thought for a moment, trying to access a mental map of the whole region before he nodded thoughtfully.

"Wakefield is basically on the same line from here as Castleford, sire. Wakefield is Hood's home, or was, before he became a wolf's head."

"Interesting." Edward continued to lead his people forward for a few moments, still staring into the undergrowth that had swallowed up the outlaws. Finally he turned to his captain.

"Bring half-a-dozen men and follow us," he swung back to de Faucumberg. "Sheriff – lead the way to Wakefield." He touched the hilt of his own great long-sword, grinning as he felt its reassuring bulk. "I'd very much like to see what's got my friar friends in such a state that they barely even register the presence of the royal household on the road next to them. Lead on, man, lead on!"

271

Sir Henry de Faucumberg, stunned as he was, knew better than to argue with a command from the king and he kicked his heels into his mount, urging it into a gallop and through the small gap in the trees which had recently claimed Hood and his companions.

King Edward II, monarch of all England, whooped like an excited child and followed, politics and all the other tedious nonsense he was forced to endure completely forgotten.

CHAPTER TWENTY-SIX

Sir Guy of Gisbourne wasn't in his right mind; he hadn't been for a long time now. Ever since that piece of filth Robin Hood had carved open his face. That was when it had begun. The defeat had done more than just wound him physically – his pride had suffered and he'd found himself having dark thoughts the like of which he'd never had before.

Self-doubt had begun to gnaw at him like a rat on a corpse.

Every time he thought of the wolf's head living on, enjoying a reputation not only as some legendary outlaw but, now, as the man who'd bested *him*, the king's own bounty hunter...

When Matt Groves had joined his group things had become much worse. Gisbourne might have known his new second-in-command was purposefully trying to stoke Gisbourne's hatred but it didn't matter – the black emotion had grown and grown until it became all-encompassing. When Hood and his giant mate had managed to free the minstrel from Nottingham it had felt like a physical blow to the king's man. After the sheriff had driven him out of the city and he'd managed to get some time alone, away from his men, he had actually vomited. The stress and fury inside him at Hood's charmed existence – while he himself was being made to seem like a bumbling oaf – had overcome him and it had been shocking to a man who prided himself on his rigid self-control.

He glanced up at the sky to check the sun's position overhead and make sure he was heading in the right direction. He'd have run all through the night if he could but exhaustion finally swamped him and it was probably just as well as travelling in the darkness was a sure way to suffer an injury by running into a tree branch or planting a foot in a dip in the ground and breaking an ankle or worse. So he'd found a small clearing and built a fire to keep inquisitive animals away, although it was cold and dead by the time he woke up before sunrise the following morning and his body ached terribly from the few hours sleep he'd had.

Some part of him knew he was acting irrationally and was planning to do something that went totally against his character, but he pushed his conscience to one side and upped his pace. He no longer cared about morals, honour, or appearances; all he wanted to do was bring pain down on Robin Hood, just as the despised wolf's head had done to him.

Life hadn't been good to him, he reflected. He'd never wanted to be a bounty-hunter, or even a soldier, but his wife, who he loved dearly, had cheated on him numerous times, prompting him to leave his home. Even then, under that sort of strain and knowing he was the talk of the village, he'd still never hit his wife. Striking a woman was something weak men did; men with little moral fibre and no self-control. It was a coward's response to a situation.

And yet here he was, on his way to murder not only a woman, but a child too. The thought didn't shock him or prompt any sort of emotional reaction at all – he felt numb and as if he was no longer in charge of his own body. Killing Hood's family was the only option open to Gisbourne now that the wolf's head had destroyed his soldiers again.

He wasn't going to Wakefield to indulge some sadistic fantasy – it was merely something he had to do to punish the outlaw leader. Gisbourne knew he wasn't half the swordsman he'd been before Hood had taken his eye, so there would be no wasting time once he reached the town.

He knew where to go; knew where the Fletcher's house was and once he'd completed his task, he'd head back to Nottingham. Or maybe London. Or France?

His mind seemed to spin frantically with ideas and emotions yet, paradoxically, he found himself in a serene sort of trance-like state as his soft black leather boots covered the miles and drew him ever closer to Wakefield.

Eventually, the smoke that rose from the hearths in the little town became visible over the tree-tops and

Gisbourne's hand dropped to his sword hilt. He still carried the deadly little crossbow with its hazel stock and steel bow that he'd had custom made in Italy but he didn't even carry ammunition for it these days – his depth perception had been ruined when he'd lost his eye and he simply couldn't hit the target with the projectile weapon no matter how much he practised with it. Still, it *looked* lethal, and impressed the peasants, which was why he still bore it.

No, he wouldn't be using the soft option when it came time to despatch Matilda Hood and her offspring. He would look them in the eye as he told them why they had to die and then he'd send them into God's arms on the end of his treasured longsword.

As Wakefield came nearer Gisbourne concealed himself in the trees that fringed the southern end of the village. The house that Matilda Hood shared with her parents was located quite close to the edge of town and it would be easier for the king's man to find his prey if he avoided walking through the streets for as long as possible.

He moved quietly, although he was no woodsman like Hood or one of his gang, and if anyone had been nearby they would surely have heard his approach. But the townsfolk were busy going about their daily work and no one suspected the danger that lurked so close-by. The air was filled with the sounds of that work – a hammer ringing brightly on an anvil; peasants singing as they tended the fields not too far off; women laughing and gossiping as they washed clothes in one of the streams that fed into the Calder...

It was a pleasant, sunny day like any other and Gisbourne felt a pang of jealousy at the simple, uncomplicated lives these commoners led. They were born, lived unremarkable little lives no-one outside of the town cared about, and then they died, forgotten and lost in the mists of time. And yet... they were happy, or at least they seemed to be happy enough as the king's bounty hunter watched from his hiding place.

Perhaps those peasants would never know what it felt like to be blessed with a rare and remarkable talent like

Gisbourne's skill with a blade but they had their families and their inexorable routines, and he watched, wishing he had a life like that, and he hated them for it.

Finally he reached a spot near the street that the Fletchers' house was on but he stopped, wondering how to proceed.

He couldn't simply walk into the town without people noticing him, and perhaps attempting to impede what he'd come to do. Although his reputation would likely be enough to stop anyone from accosting him unprovoked, without any of his guards to back him up the locals might become violent when he found Hood's wife and drew his sword.

Then, as he knelt on the soft, damp grass, pondering his next move, he offered a silent prayer of thanks to God as he spotted two girls and a small, toddling figure coming out of a house and turning to walk in his direction, broad smiles on their faces.

Hood's wife and infant son.

God was clearly on his side.

This would be easier than he'd hoped.

* * *

"Was that the fucking king?" Will Scarlet shouted in disbelief as their horses ploughed into the undergrowth, picking their way through the trees with an uncanny grace that Little John, who'd hardly ever ridden, found astonishing.

"Aye," the giant replied, also raising his voice to be heard over the drumming of hooves, jingling of harnesses and wind in their ears. "The king, and the sheriff too from the looks of it. Christ only knows what they made of us three riding across their path without so much as a 'Your Highness'."

"What if they follow us?" Will shouted, more to himself than John or Robin. "If de Faucumberg recognised us, and tells the king who we are... the royal guards will come looking for us."

John remained silent and Robin wasn't even listening to his companions, being too focused on making it to Wakefield as quickly as possible. They too had been forced to rest when the sun set and the night had almost sent the young wolf's head over the edge with worry before they were able to continue their pursuit.

He'd met King Edward's eyes as they passed the royal party, just for a fleeting moment, before they managed to coax their mounts over the low stone wall and into the undergrowth, but he felt sure there'd been a spark of recognition in the monarch's eyes.

Ultimately, it made no difference whether the king and his soldiers came after them; Robin had to stop Gisbourne before he could harm Matilda or Arthur, and his two friends were willing to put their own lives on the line to support their young leader. Even if it meant fighting the King of England himself.

Wakefield came into sight as they burst out of the foliage and found themselves racing through a field of barley which was being tended by a number of peasants. The farmers fell back instinctively at the sight of the heavily armed and armoured grim-faced horsemen charging towards the town.

One man, braver than the rest, shouted what was possibly a greeting at them and Little John waved a big hand, nodding reassuringly towards the farmer who took in the size of the rider before his eyes travelled across Will and Robin pulling away at the front of the equine triangle.

The man grinned, glad to see the outlaws who always brought food or money to the people of Wakefield but his expression wavered as the riders charged past without slowing, silent and grim, and clearly engaged on some errand that promised to end only in violence and death.

The man hefted his sickle and ran towards the village himself, shouting for his fellow workers to come too. Robin Hood and his men were friends – whatever they were doing, they would have support of the people of Wakefield.

277

The outlaws thundered into the village's main street, eyes scanning the area for either Matilda or Gisbourne, but all they could see were bemused locals who stared back, wondering what in God's name was happening.

"We'll split up," Robin said, rounding on his companions. "Gisbourne is still dangerous but with one eye missing he can't possibly be the swordsman he was; any one of us should be able to handle him alone if need be, and we'll cover much more ground if we go in separate directions. John, you head for the well in the centre of the village. Scarlet, you find Patrick, the headman, tell him to gather the tithing – the more men we have searching for Gisbourne the better."

Will opened his mouth to argue – to say he was heading for the Fletchers' himself, since his own daughter Beth lived there too, but he knew Robin's plan made sense. There was no point in the two of them going to the same place when Gisbourne could be anywhere in or around the village. Besides, there had been no threat made towards Beth – Scarlet doubted the king's man even knew about the girl. The danger was all centred on his captain's family, so Will simply nodded in grim agreement.

Robin looked around, eyes darting from shadow to shadow trying to find his hated enemy. "I'll head for the Fletchers' and pray to the Magdalene that Matilda and Arthur are safe there. Go! And take care – he might not be England's greatest swordsman any more, but he's still deadly."

He kicked his heels into his palfrey's sides and held on desperately, cursing his inexperience as the horse almost threw him back into the road, but he managed to hold on and soon spotted the simple two-storey house that belonged to Henry Fletcher and was also home to Matilda and Arthur, as well as Will's daughter.

As he reached the building he looked further along the road and his heart leapt in his chest as he spotted the familiar gait of his wife, accompanied by a smaller girl he recognised her as his sister Marjorie. They were walking away from him, following the tiny figure of Arthur, his son.

Praise be to God, they were safe!

Still warily scanning the houses on either side of the street he dismounted and began to walk towards his family, hand resting on the pommel of his sword. Before he could shout on them to wait, though, a black-armoured figure appeared from the dense foliage at the end of the street and ran forward, long-sword in hand, the naked blade glinting wickedly in the sunshine.

A cry of despair tore from Robin's throat and he broke into a sprint, dragging his own blade free from its leather scabbard, but he was much too far away to reach Arthur before the Raven would.

His long legs ate up the distance between them, and Robin watched in amazement as his skinny, malnourished little sister Marjorie, obviously spotting the approaching danger, began to move herself. She shouted in alarm at the toddler ahead of her who turned, eyes wide in surprise, soft face twisted in a grimace of fear and confusion at the terror in Marjorie's voice.

Behind him, though, the one-eyed bounty hunter came on, black as night and just as inexorable, and Robin screamed a challenge at him, to fight one-on-one, man-to-man, as they'd done before on the outskirts of Dalton not so many months ago.

The Raven looked up from the small figure in the road in front of him, seeing Hood coming towards them but too far away yet to be a threat and he roared in triumph, completely lost in the madness that had overcome his life-long iron discipline.

Gisbourne raised his exquisite oiled blade and, single eye blazing, targeted the child standing in the dusty road before him.

Matilda screamed, as did her husband who charged along the road towards their son knowing deep down that he had no chance of reaching Arthur in time to save him.

But Marjorie – skinny, withered Marjorie – had also run forward when she'd seen the danger approaching. The toddler stood, bewildered and terrified, in the centre of the road as his aunt pumped her legs harder than she'd ever done in her entire life, then a cry tore from Arthur's lips as the girl knocked him sideways, hard, away from the oncoming sword of Sir Guy of Gisbourne.

The infant was sent crashing to the ground at the side of Gisbourne's feet, howling, and again, Robin was astonished as Marjorie pulled a short wooden practice sword from beneath her skirts and used it to desperately batter the Raven's sword hand away to the side.

It was enough to buy Robin time to finally reach Marjorie and, as he did so he lunged at Gisbourne, trying to skewer his son's would-be murderer, but the king's man dodged to the side and the wolf's head's thrust missed its target.

Knowing he couldn't survive a fight with the burly outlaw Gisbourne reached out and grasped the arm of the young girl who had thwarted his mission. He was much too strong for her, although she tried desperately to break free, even sinking her teeth into the Raven's hand but he simply slapped her, hard across the head and she went limp in his arms.

"Stand down, Hood."

Robin froze, staring in horror at the crazed, one-eyed madman that held his sister's life in his hands. Matilda came up behind him, shouting on Arthur as he got to his feet unsteadily and, tears streaming down his face, toddled hurriedly towards his mother who lifted him with a sob of her own and cuddled him in protectively.

Gisbourne glared at the despised wolf's head, both of them breathing heavily as they eyed one another with murderous loathing. The king's man had no idea who this girl he held hostage was – if he'd known she was Hood's sister he'd have surely killed her right then. As it was, she'd be a useful bargaining tool that might see him escape from what had become a hopeless situation.

"Drop your sword, Hood, or I kill this little bitch. Her life's in your hands." He squeezed his arm around

Marjorie's throat until she started to turn blue and her attempts to break free stopped as she went limp.

Robin's mind whirled madly as he tried to take control of the situation but he could see no way out.

Suddenly the sound of pounding hooves came towards them and Gisbourne's wild eye widened in disbelief as he saw the newcomers behind Hood, although he never let go of Marjorie who appeared to be unconscious now.

"Robin!" From the street to the side even more voices approached and the outlaw captain saw Little John and Will Scarlet approaching in his peripheral vision.

"You men, drop your weapons."

Robin heard the voice and recognized it: King Edward II. He'd managed to follow them here after all. But the wolf's head ignored the king – he wasn't about to let the Raven murder his sister.

"Gisbourne!" Sheriff Henry de Faucumberg's furious voice filled the street now as he slid off the back of his mount with practised ease and walked imperiously towards the man he'd been saddled with for more than a year. "You heard your king. Let the girl go and drop your weapon."

Gisbourne remained silent, as if in shock at the sight of his liege-lord appearing so unexpectedly in this backwater village so far from London.

"I said drop the sword, you lunatic!"

De Faucumberg reached out, a look of disgust on his face, and grabbed Sir Guy's wrist.

Little John and Will hurried over to stand close to Robin, and Matilda turned to hand the frightened Arthur to the giant outlaw. The child went readily enough, despite the stressful situation, recognising the two men and knowing they'd keep him safe.

The king watched everything, bemused, wondering what the hell was going on and why his own bounty hunter was threatening a skinny local girl.

A crowd began to gather, eyes flicking in turn from the bizarre sight of a heavily guarded nobleman they assumed must be their king, here, in *their* village, and the

281

crazed Raven whose face twisted now in a fury as the sheriff's fingers wrapped around his arm.

Gisbourne had never liked the sheriff and now he saw an opportunity to teach the bastard a lesson. He let go of Marjorie who slumped forward onto the road and lay still as her erstwhile captor turned his attention to Sir Henry de Faucumberg.

The sheriff cried out and desperately tried to jump backwards as Gisbourne's long-sword licked out. It was a solid strike but de Faucumberg's chain mail was in good repair and stopped the wicked blade from slicing completely through his ribs although he stumbled as he dodged, and fell over to land on his back on the road, blood oozing from his wound.

"Hold!" King Edward's voice held an unmistakeable note of command that everyone in the crowd recognised. Apart from Gisbourne.

He ignored his master's command and, with a feral growl, pulled his blade back to deliver a killing blow to the fallen sheriff.

Robin wasn't near enough to block the strike and he wasn't even sure if he wanted to. It was the Sheriff of Nottingham and Yorkshire – the man who'd been trying to hunt him and the rest of the outlaws down like animals these past two years and more.

"No!" De Faucumberg was no coward. He'd fought in battles against the Scots, and for the king against the Contrariants. He'd faced death before, but the sight of the insane Gisbourne's sleek oiled blade coming towards him brought the involuntary, instinctive cry from his lips and he looked up helplessly as his doom approached.

A sharp crack came from behind Robin and there was a collective gasp from the gathered crowd, King Edward II included, as an arrow tore through the air and hit Gisbourne in the shoulder, halting his forward momentum and dropping him to one knee.

All eyes turned to see Matilda, hunting bow in hand which she'd snatched from one of the watching villagers, already hurrying to nock another arrow to its string so she could stop the scarred bounty hunter that had come to kill her and her infant son.

The missile had pierced his black leather breastplate and Gisbourne knew he was done. Even if he survived this, the king would never trust him again – he'd be out of a job and outcast, while Hood and his family were still alive. Ignoring the arrow, with its beautiful white goose-feather fletchings, that was embedded in his shoulder, he stared at the sheriff who still lay on his back on the ground, watching him fearfully.

Matilda was nervous and dropped her next arrow, losing vital moments as Gisbourne once more moved to skewer the prone sheriff.

Again, though, he was thwarted.

Marjorie had gone limp and apparently passed out when the Raven had begun to choke her, but she'd been been aware of what was happening when he dropped her on the road, and she'd played dead, catching her breath and watching events unfold from hooded eyes.

Now the girl gritted her teeth, furious at this bastard Gisbourne, and, from her position in the road, spun sideways and slammed the point of her wooden sword into the Raven's leg, directly behind his right knee.

It was a good strike, if lacking somewhat in power, and was just enough to make Gisbourne stumble. He reflexively dug the point of his own sword into the ground and used the weapon to steady himself so he didn't fall again, but Robin had spotted his sister as she began to move and guessed what she would do.

The big wolf's head was ready, and attacked just as Gisbourne regained his feet and lunged at the sheriff.

Their swords met with a ringing crack that filled the air and de Faucumberg tried to crawl away on his hands and knees as Hood batted his opponent's blade to the side then leaned in close to headbutt Gisbourne.

The king's man screamed in rage and despair as his cheekbone broke and he fell back, flailing his arms, trying desperately to keep his footing so he could defend himself but, again, there was a snap and another arrow flew through the air to hammer into Gisbourne's breastplate, just a finger's-width away from the other one.

"Hush, lad, look at your ma go." Little John grinned at Matilda in appreciation, and cuddled the still-whimpering Arthur against him as the bounty-hunter finally went down.

It was over.

"Stand down! Stand down I say!" King Edward's voice rang out again, filling the air with its authority and everyone stood still, the audience holding their breath and the combatants breathing heavily, as every eye turned to see what their ruler would do.

"No!"

Gisbourne's time was up and he knew it. Ignoring the king's command he pushed himself back to his feet and charged again at the nearest target: Robin.

The Raven came at him, eyes blazing in an insane fury and Robin found himself moving impossibly fast, his own elegant long-sword snaking out to deflect Gisbourne's desperate thrust then, dancing to the side and reversing his blade faster than the eye could follow, he slammed it into the Raven's spine with sickening force.

Gisbourne, crying out pitifully, was thrown forward to land face-down in the road, sword clattering onto the ground, his body sprawled awkwardly on top of the whimpering sheriff who was by now too weak to even try and move the weight that had landed on top of him.

Gisbourne still wasn't done, though, despite the two arrows in his shoulder and the obvious agony that blazed from his remaining eye. He looked a hellish sight, crazed and blood-caked, teeth gritted as he tried desperately to raise his fist for one final, desperate, hopeless punch at the sheriff.

Robin kicked the bounty-hunter in the side of the head, rolling him off the fallen de Faucumberg and placed the point of his sword on Gisbourne's throat before standing over him to gaze down into his eye.

"You killed my best friend," the wolf's head growled, before he pressed down, placing his whole considerable weight onto the blade which tore right through Gisbourne's neck and stuck fast in the ground underneath, the dry earth quickly becoming saturated with blood.

Robin let go of the weapon and it stood in the air, like a steel grave marker. "That was for Much."

Everyone in the village was silent then, even the king. All that could be heard was Arthur's gentle sobs and de Faucumberg's rattling, laboured breath.

"Someone help the sheriff, for God's sake," the king ordered, eyes casting about for a surgeon or barber. "Come on, where's your headman? Who's in charge here?"

Patrick Prudhomme stepped forward, eyes fearful to be in such close proximity to the king himself, especially after what had just happened.

"That's me, my lord... liege. Pardon my manners. I'll make sure the good sheriff is taken care of." He looked into the crowd and shouted at some of the bigger men to help him carry de Faucumberg to the nearest house where he could at least rest on a straw mattress instead of the hard-packed earth of the road. As they went he also shouted at one of the locals, a man who owned a horse, to ride for aid to Pontefract, which was the nearest town with a decent surgeon.

The king glanced around at the large crowd that had gathered to watch the afternoon's events. He thought about ordering them back to work then shrugged to himself. Let them enjoy the entertainment. He dismounted and waved at the captain of his guards.

"Take the wolf's heads into custody."

Will drew his sword and took up a defensive stance, while Little John handed Arthur back to Matilda and hefted his own great quarterstaff.

Robin, his sword still dripping blood, moved to stand beside his two friends and the three outlaws looked at each other grimly. They could hold their own against anyone, but the armoured men approaching them now were the king's own bodyguard – the very best swordsmen in the country, and they outnumbered the outlaws.

"No, please!" Matilda screamed, grabbing hold of Marjorie who made as if to run to her big brother's side. "Robin, don't fight them – there are too many." She turned to look at the king as Arthur started to sob again, rocking his little head back and forward, hitting it against her collarbone and slapping his ears with his hands in consternation. "Sire..."

"Peace." The king waved a hand imperiously, irritated now that the excitement was over. "Your husband is an outlaw – an enemy of the crown and he's just killed my own bounty hunter. But, he saved the life of my sheriff so... I'm arresting him, and his friends, for now. We'll see what's to be done with them later."

Robin sighed heavily and, not wanting his son to watch him die like a dog in the street, put up his hands in surrender and nodded at Will and John to throw down their weapons and submit.

John looked into the king's eyes and felt somewhat reassured by the amused glint he saw there. He dropped his staff into the road with a loud clatter and raised his own great arms.

Will looked furious, his face as red as his nickname and it was obvious he was wondering whether to stand and fight on his own, despite the overwhelming odds. In the end, reason triumphed over rage – his own daughter Beth was in the watching crowd after all – and he tossed his sword down, glaring at the king's guards, as if challenging them to try and best him even unarmed.

"Good," Edward nodded and clapped his hands in satisfaction before addressing the captain of his guards. "Bind them and have the headman gather the tithing to escort them to Nottingham. Assuming Sir Henry survives he can deal with them on his return home. Now..." he rubbed his stomach and smiled. "I'm hungry. Where's the nearest inn?"

CHAPTER TWENTY-SEVEN

It took almost a week for the sheriff to recover from Gisbourne's near-fatal strike. Six days that Robin, Will and Little John spent locked in a cell in Nottingham castle while de Faucumberg, who had been carried safely there by the men of Wakefield, lay in bed as his wound healed. They were held in a room on the ground floor rather than the dungeon, for which Robin was thankful, given his terrible ordeal there the previous year when Gisbourne had captured him and his spirit had almost been crushed. There was even a window to the outside, small and barred as it was, which at least let some sunlight and fresh air in and brought a small measure of cheer to the captives.

When the guards brought them sustenance – just watered-down ale and bread, with perhaps an occasional lump of hard cheese to share – the outlaws tried to get them to talk; to tell them what was happening with the king and the sheriff and Wakefield.

Most of the guards remained silent, not from hatred, but because it didn't do to get close to prisoners. They might be hanged the next day after all, or, worse, be set free and use the jailer's words against him somehow as had been known to happen in the past.

Finally, on their sixth morning in captivity the soldier that brought them a grubby wooden platter with two loaves and an ale-skin on it, replied to their questions.

"The king's gone; moved on to Faxfleet from what I hear." The guard was a short middle-aged man, with a large belly and a red nose, but he had laughter-lines by his eyes and a pleasant demeanour. "One of your friends is in the dungeon though; lad called Matt Groves?"

The outlaws shared a glance and Robin felt his heart race at the despised name but he kept his face calm. Groves wasn't important right now.

"What about the sheriff? Does he live?"

"Aye, he lives, although he's grumpier than I've ever known him. He'll be wanting to see you later on from what

I've been told. Reminds me of Sir Guy after you slashed his face apart." The man grinned as if he was talking about the fine weather lately. "Of course, the sheriff's all right, whereas Sir Guy was a fucking arsehole. Enjoy your lunch boys."

"Wait," Robin made to grasp the guard's arm but stopped himself, realising the man might see it as disrespectful. "What about our friends? Have you heard anything about them?"

"You mean your gang?" The guard turned back to look at the wolf's head but simply shrugged. "Not heard a thing I'm afraid, lad." All of a sudden his eyes narrowed and he glared at Will and John who returned the look with puzzled expressions. The guard's hand fell to his waist, apparently searching for the reassuring presence of his sword-hilt but, of course, he didn't have the weapon with him. Guards didn't carry swords into cells in case the prisoners managed to take it off them and went on a rampage.

"You expecting them to come for you again, like they did the last time you were imprisoned here?" The man shuffled backwards to the door, his expression grim, the pleasant smile gone. "Don't even think about it." He stepped out through the door and the guard waiting outside slammed it shut and slid the heavy bolts into place. "Don't even think about it you bastards!"

The guards' footsteps faded away along the corridor and Robin looked at his two companions in astonishment before all three burst into laughter at the soldier's sudden change in demeanour.

"They haven't forgotten you coming up the latrine wall to rescue me," Robin smiled at Will who grimaced, remembering the shit and filth he'd had to climb through to get inside the castle and free his young leader.

John stuffed a piece of bread the size of Robin's fist into his gaping mouth and mumbled as he chewed. "Shame no-one's going to come over the wall and get us out this time."

Their thoughts turned inevitably to Allan and the mood became maudlin as they remembered him, cold and dead, back in Barnsdale. The meagre meal was finished in silence after that and then the companions settled down on the wooden floor to await the sheriff's visit. Perhaps now that de Faucumberg was back on his feet they'd learn the date of their execution...

"What d'you think's going to happen to us?" Robin asked, eyes downcast, voice low.

John shrugged, stoic and apparently not worried about their situation. "He'll probably hang me for that joke about the men shagging his mum when we first met him," he said, smiling at the memory. "We *are* notorious outlaws after all – we always knew it might come to this one day. But you, Robin – you saved the sheriff's life. Gisbourne would have killed the bastard if it wasn't for you and Matilda."

"Aye, and Marjorie too, the girl did well," Scarlet agreed. "The sheriff owes you and your family."

"Maybe," Robin nodded. "But it might not be up to him. The king may have already told him what he was to do with us."

"No point worrying about it." John spread his palms wide and sat down to lean against the wall, his long legs drawn up against his chest. "We'll find out soon enough."

The shadows moved around their little cell as the sun wheeled in the sky overhead and it was close to midday when finally they heard more footsteps approaching, and the heavy bolts on the door were drawn back. It was a different guard who walked into the room this time, a tall man, competent and hard-looking, accompanied by half-a-dozen other soldiers.

"Follow me." The leader looked at them dispassionately, no trace of any emotion showing in his green eyes. The outlaws shuffled after him, the manacles that had been placed on their hands and feet when they'd first been placed in the cell not allowing them to move faster than a slow walk.

289

They were led along the corridor, through a great oak-panelled door that looked as if it could withstand a battering ram, and into another corridor, this one sumptuously decorated, with large windows that let in the afternoon sunshine. At last, their legs sore from walking in such an unusual manner, the outlaws stopped outside another sturdy door and the guardsman rapped on it with a gauntleted fist.

It opened from the inside, swinging inwards with just the merest hint of a sound, and Robin and his friends were ushered into the room which was apparently the castle's great hall. Sir Henry de Faucumberg, High Sheriff of Nottingham and Yorkshire sat on a high-backed, exquisitely carved, wooden chair which itself sat on a raised platform with more chairs on either side and a long table in front.

Only the sheriff sat at the table though, his skin pale and wan. He had a comfortable, expensive-looking robe on, which covered any trace of the wound Gisbourne had inflicted, and the heavy gold chain of office was around his neck. To the side, an elderly clerk sat at a desk with paper and pen.

Robin felt a knot of fear in his stomach. It was clear the sheriff had called them here to make their fate official. The sound of the big door closing behind them made him even more uncomfortable but he kept it from showing on his face. He glanced sideways to his comrades and felt a surge of pride at their apparent lack of fear or nervousness; both men gazed unblinkingly at the sheriff who looked back but didn't hold their eyes for long before he spoke.

"I'll make this quick. My wound is healing well enough but it requires constant cleaning and I have many other duties to attend to." He took a deep breath and lifted the goblet of wine on the table for a sip before continuing.

"You men are wolf's heads. For at least the past two years my men have been attempting to arrest the members of your gang with little success. You have robbed travellers on the road, including high-ranking members of the clergy. You have killed many of my own soldiers. You

290

even joined the Earl of Lancaster in his ill-fated rebellion against the king. And the three of you, from what I understand, are the leaders of your little gang. In short, gentlemen, you are probably the most wanted men in my entire jurisdiction. The king himself sent that bastard Gisbourne here to try and bring you to justice." He shook his head in disgust and muttered to himself more than anyone else. "That didn't turn out so well, did it?"

The clerk in the corner stopped writing at that part and the sheriff gave him a small smile before he went on.

"The punishment for just one of those many heinous crimes is death by hanging. Your friend Sir Richard-at-Lee has already received justice in such a fashion." He gave a small groan and took another pull of his wine, this time almost draining the cup, perhaps hoping the effects of the alcohol would dull the pain from his wound. "What am I to do with you?"

The outlaws watched the sheriff in silence. He had a reputation for being a fair man; they could only hope he would deal with them mercifully now.

"You found the king in a particularly good mood," the sheriff went on. "He was bored and the little episode in Wakefield – and the chase to find you – pleased him." He shrugged in exasperation. "The king values physical prowess highly and he enjoyed the... fight with Gisbourne. When he ate lunch in Wakefield he had some of the locals, including the headman, dine with him – they informed him of Gisbourne's recent excesses; burning down houses and whatnot so, although Sir Guy was the king's own man, our highness thought justice had been served by his death. He also remembered the pair of you," he nodded to Robin and Little John, "from your visit to London. Anyone else would be angered by your deception but again, the king found it all most amusing. So," he waved a hand, "he told me to deal with you as I saw fit but to be merciful."

"What does that mean?" Will growled. "A life sentence in your dungeon rather than a public hanging?"

De Faucumberg smiled. "Perhaps," he began, but Robin cut in before the man could say any more.

291

"We have your silver arrow."

The sheriff looked at him, mouth open since he'd been just about to speak again. He closed it, lips pressed together in a thin line. "I remember. How could I forget?"

"We have no need of it," Robin said. "I'll bring it back to you this very day." He held up a hand as the sheriff leaned forward in his chair eagerly, the thought of his missing wealth being returned to his near-bare coffers making his eyes sparkle.

"In return I want a pardon."

De Faucumberg nodded impatiently, but again Robin broke in before the nobleman could speak.

"For *all of us*."

There was silence then, a silence that seemed to last for a long, long time as the sheriff gazed at the wolf's head and his troublesome companions.

Robin glanced sidelong at Will, noting the man's aggressive stance. Even without a weapon the volatile Scarlet was ready to attack the blue-liveried soldiers.

Little John's face was unreadable.

Even the sheriff's guards looked unsure how this would play out; Robin could see more than one of them fidgeting nervously and he picked one to go for first should De Faucumberg order an attack.

"Fine. You win." The sheriff glared at his clerk. "Write pardons for these two," he waved a hand irritably at Will and John. "Scaflock and Little, I believe, yes? Yes." The clerk quickly but neatly filled in two small pieces of parchment then took them to de Faucumberg who lifted his own pen and signed the bottom of each.

"Here," he growled, holding them out towards the outlaws.

"What about Robin?" Will demanded, not moving towards the proffered document. "Where's his pardon? He saved your life."

"Your loyalty is, truly, a pleasure to see," de Faucumberg smiled, apparently sincerely. "But I have other business to attend to with him so... if you would so kind as to take these bloody pardons from me and stop

292

asking questions you can be on your way back to your homes."

John and Will looked at Robin and he grinned encouragingly. "Go on, what are you waiting for? This is what we've wanted – freedom! Don't worry about me, I'll see you soon. We still have his silver arrow don't we?"

The two outlaws walked forward and, still unsure of themselves, gingerly took the parchments from the sheriff, who nodded and ordered his guards to show them out.

"Our weapons?" Will wondered.

"Yes, yes, return their weapons to them," the sheriff grunted in exasperation. "Now get out will you? I wanted to get this over with quickly."

They followed the guard from the room, the door was closed over again, and Robin felt another pang of fear. Yes, de Faucumberg had proved himself to be – mostly – an honourable man, who'd tried to rein in the increasingly violent tendencies of the Raven, but Robin hadn't forgotten the time when the sheriff had double-crossed them. Only the timely intervention of Sir Richard-at-Lee and the Earl of Lancaster's soldiers had saved Robin and his friends that day, or the sheriff would have cut them down like animals.

So, although Sir Henry de Faucumberg appeared to be rather more honourable than many of his noble peers, the wolf's head didn't quite believe he could trust the man unquestioningly. After all, capturing Robin Hood and hanging him was always what the sheriff had wanted – it was the perfect way to send a message to any other would-be thieves and outlaws.

De Faucumberg beckoned him forward, to stand right in front of the table, and Robin wished he had his sword with him.

"You've led my men and I – not to mention Gisbourne – a merry dance these past couple of years, Hood. You appear to lead a charmed life or, perhaps I do you a disservice and you're really as skilled a leader as you are an archer. I suspect the truth lies somewhere in the middle and that makes you a formidable enemy."

Robin remained silent but he felt beads of sweat trickle down uncomfortably from under his armpits as the sheriff stared at him.

"But you saved my life and I am grateful so... I would like to offer you a position within my own household."

The wolf's head simply gazed up at de Faucumberg, knowing he must have imagined the man's words.

"As I say, you have proven your leadership abilities. I don't think any of my men have anything but respect for you in that regard, whatever they may feel for you personally. You and your fellows have killed rather a lot of them after all."

"Only in self-defence – what choice did we have –"

Sir Henry raised a hand. "There's no need to go into that right now. Perhaps once I'm fully healed we can discuss that sort of thing in more depth but for now... as I say I have other duties to carry out and the dressing of my wound takes up much of my time so...? What say you, Hood? I believe you have no official experience commanding men – you don't know the way things work in a castle garrison and that sort of thing, so I can't offer you the position of my personal captain just like that. However, I will find you a job that suits your exceptional capabilities. Who knows, I might even be able to find a place for others of your group. I lost a few men in that last, ill-fated, assault Gisbourne led on your camp, although I believe some of them still live, thanks to you."

That brought Robin back to Earth. *Others of your group*. Where were Stephen and Edmond and the rest of the men?

"What about the pardons for the other members of my gang?"

The clerk in the corner of the room rummaged amongst another pile of papers and lifted some in the air, showing them to the wolf's head.

"Those are blank." The sheriff said. "Once I have their names I can fill them in and your men will be pardoned. All of them." He raised a finger and looked seriously at Robin. "I only demand my silver arrow in return. Fair enough?"

The reality finally hit him and Robin crouched down, weeping in disbelief and happiness and sadness for all his friends who'd died before they could see this day. He didn't care what the sheriff or the clerk or the guardsmen thought of him, he was overcome by emotion and for long moments he simply stared at the stone floor, tears streaming down his face.

They'd done it. At last, they had finally earned their pardons, they would be free!

"Thank you, my lord." He rose, drawing himself up to his full impressive height and looked at the sheriff without bothering to wipe his tear-streaked face. "I would like to speak with my wife before I accept the offer of a position in your household. Before that, though, I have one more boon to ask..."

* * *

Matt Groves wished he'd never come back to Nottingham. He should have known how it would turn out. The fact the sheriff hated him didn't seem to matter though; he'd hoped de Faucumberg would have been so desperate for able-bodied, hard fighting men that he'd see Matt as a decent addition to his garrison.

But it hadn't turned out like that. When he'd made it back to the city from Selby the sheriff had been away with the king, so he'd made himself at home in one of the local taverns until the sheriff returned, spending what little coin he had left in his purse on a room and board for a few nights, hoping de Faucumberg wouldn't be gone too long.

When word had got around that the sheriff was back in the castle – and grievously wounded – Matt had made his way there to offer his good-wishes and support to the stricken nobleman.

Unfortunately for him, de Faucumberg had been well enough to recognise him and, in a near-delirious fury, had ordered his guards to imprison Matt until he was well enough to deal with Gisbourne's pet outlaw.

He'd languished in this shit-encrusted, vermin-infested cell for days now, with only black mouldy bread and tepid water for sustenance and he was thoroughly sick of it.

There was a noise from the end of the corridor which Matt recognised as the main entrance to the block of cells being opened and he held his breath, listening as footsteps approached. They stopped outside his cell and he got to his feet, stretching his muscles and plastering a smile on his face as the door swung open, hoping to see the sheriff or one of his lackeys come to free him at last.

One of the castle guards held a torch which burned brightly, blinding Groves momentarily as he squinted into the gloom at the two figures there, and then he found himself lying on the cold stone floor, amongst the shit and piss, his head spinning and his face aching.

"Get up you fucking arsehole." A low, gravelly voice came to him and he raised his hands defensively but they were batted aside and someone grabbed his short hair, pulling hard until he scrambled to his feet.

When he reached an upright position again fury rose in him and he swept his right arm out in an arc, trying to land a blow on the shadowy figure that now held him by the throat.

His attempt was weak though, and he fell backwards again, his teeth rattling as another blow landed on his face. He heard a crack as the punch landed and a searing pain blurred his vision. He fell backwards into the wall, knowing his cheek had been broken. He felt weak from his captivity over the past few days but, outraged at being struck, he roared, raising his arms and running forward towards the shadowman that tormented him.

Again, a closed fist hit him, this time in the solar-plexus, and he collapsed, retching onto the already filthy cell floor. He brought up the water and slimy half-digested bread that he'd eaten earlier on, burning tears streaming from his eyes, but he forced himself to stand up once more and raised his fists to block any more attacks.

"Do you know who I am?" he found himself shouting desperately. "I'm one of Robin Hood's men. Have you never heard how he looks after his men? He'll come for you when he hears about this, you bastard!"

His attacker halted his advance and Matt took heart. "Aye, that's right, dickhead. We look after each other in Robin Hood's gang."

He saw the next blow coming but was, again, too slow to dodge or even block it and a thunderous right hook landed on his face with a crunch of bone and cartilage and he fell backwards into the wall, blood pooling from his ruined nose.

"You look after each other?" The voice was low and filled with pure hate. "Then why did you betray Much?"

In the near-darkness Matt saw his attacker's foot coming towards him but before he could raise a hand he felt the crushing blow and he dropped, dazed and winded, onto the ground again. He didn't try to get up now; finally, he'd recognised that voice.

Robin Hood leaned down and glared into his eyes, the cowl he wore making him look distinctly sinister and wicked in the wan torchlight. "Get up and fight me like a man you old cunt. I've waited a long time for this; since I first joined the outlaws in fact. Remember? You almost broke my fingers the first time we sparred and then you knocked me into the river. Let's see how hard you are then, Groves. Let's see you break my fucking fingers now."

He heard Hood's ragged breathing as the big wolf's head glared down at him.

"We found Allan's body after the battle. Did you kill him too?"

For a moment Groves thought about denying it, but he knew he was done for anyway. At least this would be one final barb to throw at his former leader.

"Aye, I did. He just stood there, gaping at me like a fish. It was so easy for me to skewer the stupid-looking dullard. He cried like a girl when he sank onto the grass at my feet."

His words had the desired effect – Robin rocked back, eyes wet and filled with loathing for the man before him.

"Finish it then," Matt growled through split, bloody lips, unnerved by his attacker's glaring silence. "Or are you still too much of a fucking woman?"

He expected Hood to rain more blows down on him but none came and he lay on his back, sucking in lungfuls of air, his entire body numb.

For a long time nothing happened. The torch the guard outside in the corridor held cast flickering orange light on the walls and Hood's breath continued to come in laboured gasps while Matt just lay on the ground, almost passing out more than once.

Then, when he'd regained his breath, the wolf's head bent down and looked directly into Matt's eyes.

"I don't need to finish it, Matt. Justice will be served, have no fear. Your master Gisbourne is dead – aye, killed by me, my wife and my little sister – and your crimes will not go unpunished. I'm the sheriff's man now... and soon enough I'll see you on gallows hill, swinging by the neck for what you did to my friends."

CHAPTER TWENTY-EIGHT

It was a rather different Robin that returned to the outlaws' camp near Selby a day later, accompanied by Will and Little John. The smile was back on his handsome face and, apart from severe bruising around his knuckles he appeared to be in good health.

Of course, the lookouts had spotted the men approaching and sent word to the main camp where Stephen had gathered the men and ordered them to battle-readiness. It might have been their leader and his two lieutenants heading towards them but who knew what came at their back? It could very well be a trick of the sheriff's devising. So the former Hospitaller, careful as ever, had the men armed and ready for anything when he heard of Hood's return.

"Not the friendliest welcome I've ever had." Robin grinned at the sergeant-at-arms who met him, grim-faced, as he strode into the camp. "But it's good to see you have the men at the ready." He clasped Stephen's arm, grinning broadly and the man relaxed visibly, although he didn't return the grin; that wasn't his way.

"Are we safe?"

"Aye," Robin nodded, laughing as Little John came up behind him and barged past, grabbing the shocked Stephen in a massive bear-hug that he struggled vainly to break free from.

When he was back on his feet and before he had the time to berate the giant, Will Scarlet grabbed also him and pulled him into a friendly embrace, slapping him on the back and laughing loudly. "Well met, Hospitaller. Well met."

Robin could tell Stephen was inwardly pleased at the show of friendship, but the sergeant shoved Will away and glared at the three of them. "I take it we're not in any immediate danger? The sheriff's men aren't on their way to rout us?"

"No, they're not," Robin shook his head, still smiling and raising his voice so the rest of the men, still hidden in the foliage, could hear. "You can come out – we have news!"

They feasted that night, after freeing the sheriff's captured soldiers to return to their homes. Little John and Will had brought fresh black loaves and a pig from the kitchen in Nottingham Castle and, with that and the late spring vegetables stored in the outlaws' larder, Tuck made a wonderful thick stew which the men washed down with large amounts of ale and even some wine the sheriff's bottler had gifted to them before they'd left to return to their friends.

When Robin produced the papers that confirmed every man's pardon there had been disbelief and then deafening cheers that split the night like thunder and the young outlaw captain had cheered as loud as any of them. It was a momentous occasion. Even Stephen managed a grin, although things would be more complicated for him, since some of the Hospitallers had tried to kill him and, as far as he knew he was still outcast from the Order.

The rest of the men though, they were – at long last – free. Their young leader had often promised to win them freedom somehow and, well, now it seemed he had. It was incredible.

And yet the celebrations were tinged with more than a hint of sadness.

They wanted to return to their families, of course, but every man there now realised they'd possibly never see their companions again. They'd go back to their homes and, hopefully, take back the lives that had been stolen from them when they'd become wolf's heads, but most of them lived in different villages. Sure, they might pay one another the odd visit when they could but... it wouldn't be the same as spending long nights under the stars, with a roaring campfire, bread and meat and beer and brotherhood and music.

Music.

300

Robin had taken more than his own fill of ale and, although he felt a great joy in his heart to have finally – finally! – won a pardon, the lack of singing in the camp was obvious and it made him think of Allan-a-Dale.

The rest of the men didn't seem to share his melancholy, Robin noted thankfully. They ate and drank and told stories and talked about what they'd do when they returned home as rich men; the outlaws had lots of stolen gold and silver in the communal chest after all and it would make life very comfortable for each of them now.

"Cheer up – you're a free man. They all are!"

Robin looked up at the voice and smiled as he saw Friar Tuck.

"Aye, free at last," he agreed, patting the log beside him and sipping his ale as the friar sat down. "But at what cost...?"

They watched the other men for a while, drunk already, most of them. They had no need for lookouts any more, being free men, so the celebration of liberty was in full swing. Even the Hospitaller was half-pissed and deep in animated, but still friendly – so far – conversation with young Edmond the tanner.

Tuck, although he loved to eat and drink, never allowed himself to take so much that he lost control of his senses – Osferth's slipping dwale into his ale excepted. He'd learned his lesson when he was younger and now, although he still enjoyed a skinful, always stopped before he became too drunk to walk in a straight line.

Robin generally did the same – a good trait in a leader, Tuck thought.

Sometimes, though, it didn't hurt to let yourself go...

"Here." The friar handed a wine-skin to his captain. "Drink. Lose yourself for a while."

Robin took the drink but simply held it, unopened, in his lap as they watched the rest of the men. They'd finally begun to strike up a song or two, although they sorely lacked direction and a sweet, skilled, *tuneful* voice to lead them.

He pulled out the stopper and took a long pull, the wine burning in his chest pleasantly and he lifted the skin again, swallowing almost half the contents in one draught.

"You've lost a lot in the past couple of years," Tuck stated, his voice soft yet still audible over the carousing and Robin barely nodded in reply.

"Perhaps more than any of us," the friar continued. "The men that have died: Wilfred, Sir Richard, Allan... they were all our friends but... you also lost your childhood friend Much. It hurts, doesn't it?"

Robin nodded and took another drink from the wine-skin. "Harry Half-Hand died because of me," he muttered, remembering an event from when he'd first become an outlaw and, inexperienced, hadn't followed orders. "But all those who've died since are on my conscience too, since I was supposed to be their leader. I was supposed to keep them safe but I didn't. All dead. They should be celebrating their freedom like the rest of us tonight."

Tuck said nothing for a while, knowing Robin – despite his silence – wasn't finished yet.

"They're going to hang Matt."

"And you'll be there to see it," the friar replied.

"Aye, I'll be there," Robin growled. "I want to see that bastard die in agony, pissing and shitting himself as he goes."

Tuck nodded. "I understand. I too want to see justice for Much and Allan. But..."

Robin glanced at the friar. "But what?"

"Look at them," Tuck said, smiling and waving a hand at the happy former outlaws before them.

Robin shrugged, the wine already making his head foggy. "What about them?"

"They're happy. They are finally free." The clergyman grasped Robin's arm in a powerful grip. "You should be happy. You can watch Arthur grow up and be with Matilda."

"Are you saying I should forget Matt Groves?" Robin demanded. "Even if I could – the rest of the men won't.

They all want to come to Nottingham with me to see the bastard hang. And so they should, after what he's done."

Tuck shook his head, the flushed cheeks of his young friend betraying an unusual level of inebriation and he knew he had to step lightly.

"No, I'm not suggesting you forget – or forgive – Matt. I think we should *all* go to his hanging."

Robin eyed the friar suspiciously. The expected sermon wasn't going quite as he'd expected.

"It would be wrong to celebrate his death," Tuck said. "But... I see no harm in celebrating a new beginning."

Although he was becoming bleary-eyed from both lack of sleep and strong wine Robin understood the friar's point. It made perfect sense – a celebration of life in death... After all, hadn't this whole journey started in the same way, in that Mayday celebration of two years earlier?

"You're a genius, Tuck," the young man grinned. "But, in all the joy at our freedom we've forgotten you, haven't we? The sheriff's pardons are secular and no doubt won't be honoured by Prior de Monte Martini, the little red-faced prick. Where will you go now?" He stood up, shaking his head somewhat blearily and held out a hand to his portly friend who grasped it to lever himself up from the fallen log.

"Don't worry about me," Tuck smiled. "Just enjoy the night. You're free!"

Robin gripped him by the shoulder and they walked towards the centre of camp where the other men had started a raucous sing-along. "So are you," he said. "And I think I know where you can hide from Prior de Martini, at least for a while. You said you brought the relic back from Lewes didn't you..?"

For the first time ever the group celebrated long and loud and without fear of imprisonment or death, their joyful voices splitting the night air and carrying on the wind across the Ouse even to Selby, where the villagers looked fearfully across the fields and wondered what demons were abroad that night.

They were *free!*

The next day those who wished it travelled to Nottingham with Robin. They passed through Wakefield again, where Robin spoke to Patrick and told him Much's killer was going to be hanged should any of the villagers wish to come with them to see justice done.

Of course, the vast majority of the local people couldn't just take days off work and Much's family were all dead so, in the end, only Patrick travelled with them, along with Will Scarlet's daughter, Beth and, of course, Marjorie.

Robin's sister's dream of owning a crossbow had finally come true – she carried the sleek black Italian-made weapon that had belonged to Gisbourne although, when he asked her how she'd managed to steal it from the Raven's corpse she just shrugged and smiled. The girls she'd been training had all been hugely impressed by her part in the fight with the infamous bounty hunter, as, indeed had all of the adults in Wakefield. Robin too was extremely proud of his sister, grown into a strong, vibrant young woman.

"You fought well," he told her as they walked.

"Aye," she nodded, pleased at the praise, and at her new-found status in the village. "Just goes to show – women aren't only good for cooking and mending clothes."

"Oh, I already knew that," Robin laughed. "The wife never lets me forget it."

For a time they walked together in silence, then Marjorie grinned up at him.

"You know, for a while I wanted to be like you. But now... I'm happy just to be me."

Robin returned her smile although he had no idea of her long journey over the past few months. Still, he could see by the way she carried herself that she'd truly come of age and was at peace with the world.

That was all anyone could ask for in life.

Matilda also came on their journey south, of course, and brought little Arthur with her. She wasn't sure about the idea of the boy seeing someone die on the gallows, Robin knew, but he felt that it was something their son should witness. Life was hard, and it often had a way of repaying in kind those who treated others badly.

Arthur should see Much's murderer pay for his crimes.

Will brought Beth simply because he'd missed her terribly all throughout his years as a wolf's head and wanted to spend as much time with her as possible now he was a free man.

Not all of the outlaws had decided to go to Nottingham for the hanging though; some of them still couldn't believe the sheriff had granted them their freedom and didn't want to take a chance walking into the city where de Faucumberg could imprison or kill them if he decided to double-cross them. Others were so overjoyed at their pardons that they couldn't wait to see their families again and restart their lives with the welcome fortune they'd managed to gather as part of Robin's gang.

The likes of Edmond and Stephen had no warm welcome or loving family awaiting them in their home-towns so they went along with the others because there was nothing better to do, although neither man had any particular, personal hatred for Matt, having joined the outlaws after the dour man had left and gone to join the Raven.

It was a merry party, then, that made their way along the main road to the big city. They'd brought plenty of fresh meat, eggs, fish, cheese, bread and, of course, ale for the trip, all bought that day in Wakefield because they understood they'd have to spend more than one night camping out as they were all on foot. It wasn't an issue though – Robin knew the sheriff didn't plan on hanging Groves for a couple of days and it would be fun to spend time with friends and family, out in the open for once, without having to skulk in the trees as wolf's heads, fearful of discovery and capture or death.

That journey was the happiest time of Robin's entire life.

The weather wasn't great, raining quite heavily for much of the trip, but that gave Robin a chance to lift his little son who was still not two years-old and carry him in his strong arms, snuggled in under a waterproof sheep-skin that kept the worst of the weather off the pair of them.

Beth ran on ahead, laughing and skipping in the rain, splashing in the puddles that collected in the divots and pot-holes that liberally dotted the ancient Roman road, while Will, half-heartedly, demanded that she keep dry or catch a chill.

Everyone was, understandably, in high spirits and, when the thunder-heads passed and night began to fall they were glad to stop and set up camp in a clearing not far from the main road, surrounded by beech, yew and oak trees which felt just like home to the men who'd spent most of the recent years of their lives in just such a place.

Once a fire had been kindled and the smells of meat and fish cooking on spits above it filled the air, everyone felt truly blessed by God. And that was before they'd even broached the cask of newly-brewed ale portly Aexander Gilbert, landlord of Wakefield's tavern, had given them for the trip south.

It was the best meal Robin had ever eaten. Matilda sat on the grass beside him, laughing and cuddling into him as the travellers told ghost stories and bickered good-naturedly among themselves while Arthur sat on his knee, taking little pieces of cooked meat from his plate and chewing it contentedly, laughing in a wonderfully endearing way whenever he thought someone was being silly.

The young archer looked around at his friends and lifted his ale mug in silent thanks to the Magdalene who he'd prayed to ever since he'd become an outlaw. She too had been seen as an outcast, looked down on by the authorities, and so she'd seemed like the ideal patron for a wolf's head. He grinned as Will aimed a ferocious verbal barb at Little John whose mouth dropped open in dismay, the expression looking hilarious on the giant's face which bore a thick brown beard again.

He truly was blessed to have friends like these – the Magdalene had watched over him well these past two years.

"It's getting late." His wife's words broke into his comfortable reverie and he glanced at her, eyes sparkling in the orange firelight. "Let's bed down for the night. Arthur is about ready to go over anyway..."

She smiled, flicking her tongue over her teeth impishly and Robin felt a small thrill run through him.

"Good idea," he replied, standing up, cradling the dozing toddler in his left arm and using his other hand to help Matilda up.

There were ribald comments shouted after them – which they pointedly ignored – as they found a spot to sleep in for the night that was just far enough from the fire to hide them from watching eyes yet close enough to offer protection against any hungry animals, although wolves hadn't been seen in northern England for decades.

Arthur was soon asleep and, as they made love under the stars Robin allowed himself to become lost in the moment. They climaxed at the same time, holding each other tightly and stifling their joyful gasps as the happy feast carried on behind them.

After all the heartache and betrayal and death of the past two years, Robin was finally at peace.

It felt good to be alive.

CHAPTER TWENTY-NINE

"Time to die."

Robin stood in the cell that held Matt Groves, wearing the blue livery of Sheriff de Faucumberg although he retained his own weapons and leather gambeson – the same one with the patched up hole that he'd been given when he'd first joined the outlaws.

Although he wasn't due to become one of the sheriff's staff for another week – he'd specifically asked for that time so he could spend it with his family back in Wakefield – he wanted to be here for this, so, with de Faucumberg's blessing, he'd borrowed one of the guard's uniforms and, along with a couple of burly soldiers almost as big as he was, he walked into Matt's cell to take him to the gallows that stood outside the city walls.

The sight of hanged criminals on the road into Nottingham was supposed to scare potential law-breakers onto the straight and narrow path of the lawful but Robin didn't think it really worked. Certainly, it had never stopped him from robbing rich clergymen. Still, it was as good a place for justice as any other.

"Get up, Groves." He looked down dispassionately at his former gang-member who returned his gaze from wide, frightened eyes. Matt didn't want to die.

Robin shrugged and turned to the soldiers behind him. "Lift him."

The guardsmen moved to drag Matt up from the floor. He struggled but the bigger of the two soldiers punched him full in the mouth with a gauntleted fist and it was enough to make the prisoner more pliable. One of them squeezed his cheeks and the other poured a bitter, acrid liquid into his mouth. Unwatered wine, to stop the prisoner from causing trouble on the way to their destination.

They led him – half walking and half dragging – out of the grim, dank cell and along the corridor behind their new superior officer.

When they reached the courtyard there was a wagon with a wooden cage and the guards dragged the wild-eyed Groves up a ramp and threw him into it, their hard, threatening stares enough to stop him trying to escape or even protest at the humiliating captivity.

Penned like an animal on its way to the Shambles for slaughter.

Robin mounted a warhorse which wore simple barding in the same blue with red piping livery as he wore himself and nodded at the cart driver. "Move on – to Gallows Hill."

The wagon rumbled out of the castle grounds and into the city, heading north-east towards the carter gate. The cobbled streets weren't lined with cheering people as they would have been for a high profile hanging – most of them had never heard of Matt Groves – but there were still plenty of citizens around, either with nothing better to do than watch the prisoner's last, lonely journey or simply because they wanted to see a criminal meeting well-deserved justice.

Life was cheap for the lower-classes in Nottingham; the locals were just glad it was someone else being taken off to hang while they and their families lived another day.

Robin rode at the side of the slow-moving wagon. He was still no great horseman but was starting to become more comfortable when mounted; he no longer felt his thighs burning after a short distance and didn't expect his horse to turn and bite him whenever he offered it direction.

Matt tried to talk to him; to plead with him for his freedom, or at least for a lesser sentence than the death penalty. It was out of Robin's hands – the sheriff was the law in Nottingham, even if he had granted Robin more than one favour lately – but he had no desire to help the sour-faced, hateful old bastard Groves anyway. So he ignored the man, now desperately trying to recall times when he and Robin had shared moments of friendship back in Barnsdale.

Those moments were almost non-existent though. The only time Robin had felt like Matt was becoming close to him had been an act; a ruse to draw him and Much into the forests where, ultimately, Sir Guy and his men had ambushed them. Much had died that day, with the Raven's crossbow bolt in his chest and Matt's sword in his stomach.

Robin held his peace grimly as the wagon trundled on through the streets and out the Carter Gate into the open countryside where Gallows Hill could be seen in the near-distance.

He felt calm and almost emotionless. Even the memories of Much or Allan's bloodied bodies weren't enough to shake him on that sombre journey.

It didn't take very long to reach the place of execution. The gallows stood on the summit of Mansfield Road, close to a rickety old windmill. When the horses were reined in and the cart drew to a halt Matt became silent at the sight of the sinister wooden structure that stood a short distance away.

The gallows had been built with huge, thick timbers and its simple design spoke of cold, merciless efficiency. Matt had seen many such constructions in his life; indeed he'd witnessed them being put to use on a number of occasions. He'd always enjoyed the sight of a man being hanged, especially when the executioner wasn't very good at his job and had to swing on the victim's legs or even climb onto their shoulders to finish the job.

His arms and legs tingled with pins-and-needles and he couldn't stand when the pair of burly guardsmen dismounted and came to take him up the stairs to the platform. They knew their jobs though, and had seen this reaction before when men became so terrified that their limbs wouldn't work, so they unlocked the cage door and simply dragged him, feet-first, out of the cart, hauling him upright before his head cracked off the road below.

Robin watched dispassionately as his despised enemy stood shakily, eyes fixed on the gallows. The guards gave him a moment to regain his equilibrium then, grasping an arm each, hauled Groves up the stairs and onto the platform which was badly discoloured despite the cleaning it received after every execution. Some stains could never be washed off, no matter how much water and lye soap was used.

Looking out over the crowd that had gathered for the day's grisly entertainment Robin spotted Matilda with Marjorie, John, Will and the rest of their friends clustered around, watching in silence as the prisoner was made to stand, head bowed to hide his fear, beneath the crossbar of the gallows, just in front of the noose which swayed almost imperceptibly in the warm westerly breeze.

Robin almost wished he hadn't asked the sheriff if he could preside over this now that he saw the size of the audience; of course he had become accustomed to addressing the men in his gang, but those were his friends and weren't that great in number. There must have been at least a hundred people – strangers – gathered there that day though. People with no personal axe to grind with Groves but also with no work to go to for whatever reason, so they'd used their free time to come along and watch another criminal get his comeuppance.

Still, Robin had never been particularly shy, except around Matilda when they'd been younger, so he dismounted, handing the reins of his horse to a nearby guard with orders to return the beast to the castle stables. Then he climbed the steps up to the gallows and stood at the front of the raised platform where he gazed out at the crowd silently. Eventually, the people noticed the blue-liveried soldier and realised the show was about to begin. The clamour of happy, excited voices dropped until, at last, there was silence. Some unfortunate gossips failed to notice the quiet and were shouted down, red-faced and abashed at the dozens of angry eyes boring into them.

Robin took a deep breath, cleared his throat and, with a small smile towards his wife who returned the look encouragingly, addressed the gathering.

"This is Matthew Groves of Sheffield: convicted thief, murderer and rebel. By the authority of our King Edward, second of that name, and his representative Sir Henry de Faucumberg the High Sheriff of Nottingham and

Yorkshire, the criminal is sentenced to be hanged by the neck until death doth ensue."

Robin watched as the wide-eyed prisoner was readied for his doom then turned back momentarily to look at his friends and family. Will glared up at Groves as if he wanted to kill the man with his bare hands; Little John's steely eyes glistened and Robin wondered what was going through the giant's head; Friar Tuck made the sign of the cross and his lips moved in sad, silent prayer.

Matilda's expression was the one that hit him the hardest though – she was watching Matt almost as murderously as Will and Robin nodded to her in understanding. Much had grown up with her in Wakefield too after all.

He was glad little Arthur was nowhere to be seen. Aye, he'd wanted his son to be there to see justice done but now the time was upon them... it didn't seem right to make such a small child watch a man die. He wondered where the boy was, then recognised the back of his sister Marjorie's head moving away through the crowd, his son's small blonde head by her shoulder and another diminutive figure – Beth Scaflock – by their side.

The young-folk had no desire to see the execution.

Robin gazed around at the excited mob, cheerfully awaiting the sight of a man they didn't even know suffering a humiliating, painful death and he sighed heavily.

Such was the nature of man. It was why they were here today, after all.

He turned to look at his former outlaw companion whose glassy eyes focused on him, lip curling into a sneer of sheer hatred as Robin stood directly in front of him, hand raised.

"I'll see you in hell, Groves," he growled. "Say hello to Gisbourne and Adam Gurdon for me. I'll be along eventually with my sword and longbow to make eternity fucking miserable for you all."

His hand dropped and the hangman kicked the stool out from under Matt's feet.

Robin let out a long breath that he hadn't even realised he'd been holding in.

It was over.

Adam Gurdon/Bell. Sir Guy of Gisbourne. Matt Groves. All dead now. Only the bastard Prior John de Monte Martini still lived but he was an old, old man and would be dead within a year or two if Tuck's judgement was right, while Robin and his men and their families were free and had, God willing, many long happy years ahead of them.

Leaving Groves's corpse to swing Robin jumped down from the gallows and pushed his way through the cheering, hooting crowd to take Matilda in his great arms.

"I made you a promise," he told her. "To win a pardon, one way or another, so we could be a proper family. Well – now we can be a proper family."

They embraced, tears of both joy and sadness in their eyes and then, without a backward glance, the big yeoman led his wife away to find Arthur and Marjorie and all their friends.

For now, their adventure was over. They were free at last.

It was time to live.

TO BE CONTINUED...

Author's Note

I had to make some tough decisions when writing this, the penultimate book in my Forest Lord series. Allan-a-Dale being killed off was probably the hardest, being a character I really enjoyed writing, but outlaw life was dangerous and even the good die young...

The final scenes were also hard. In my original draft Matt Groves suffered a long, drawn-out and quite gruesome hanging. One of my first beta-readers suggested it was too much so I toned it down. Even at that my editor said it was too much. I felt it had to be in there in some way, though. Matt's been a big part of the series after all, so... hopefully I managed to strike a decent balance.

The first three books in this series have covered a period of only two years. The next, and final, book in this cycle will, necessarily cover a much longer time period. I always wanted to stick closely to the original Robin Hood ballads while throwing in little twists and ideas of my own and I plan to continue in that vein for the last Forest Lord novel. He's not an outlaw any more, but will he and his companions finally find the peace they've desired for so long?

I don't know, honestly, I haven't even begun to plan out the story! You'll just have to wait and see...

In the meantime I'm working on another novella, similar to Knight of the Cross. This one will star Friar Tuck, takes place in Christmas 1323 not long after the events in *Rise of the Wolf,* and will be published in December 2015.

After that... who knows?

Thank you all for joining me on this amazing journey. I never in my wildest dreams imagined so many of you would read and enjoy my books.

You rule!

If you enjoyed *Rise of the Wolf* please leave a review wherever you can. Good reviews are the lifeblood of self-published authors, so please take a few moments to let others know what you thought of the book.
Thank you!

If you would like a FREE short story take a moment to sign up for my mailing list. VIP subscribers will get exclusive access to giveaways, competitions, info on new releases and other freebies.
Just click the link below to sign up. As a thank you, you will be able to download my brand new short story "The Escape", starring Little John.

https://stevenamckay.wordpress.com/mailing-

list/

Otherwise, to find out what's happening with the author and any forthcoming books, point your browser to:

www.facebook.com/RobinHoodNovel

http://stevenamckay.wordpress.com/